Praise for *The New Voices of Science Fiction*

★"In the introduction to this superlative anthology, Weisman (*The New Voices of Fantasy*) declares the future of science fiction resides in the sure hands of the authors of these 20 recent award-winning or award-nominated stories. Rajaniemi, a mathematical physicist and author (*The Quantum Thief*), adds that their various perspectives create "a tonal freshness" in the genre. . . . All these stories provoke the reader to ponder not only what the future might be but what it should be."
—*Publishers Weekly*, starred review

★"This collection of stories from up-and-coming sf writers is diverse in terms of plot and setting, yet all share an emphasis on creating a distinct tone and style for their imagined worlds . . . wonderful stories by Jamie Wahls, Vina Jie-Min Prasad, Suzanne Palmer, and many others make this a must-read for anyone interested in the latest and most exciting sf writing out there."
—*Booklist*, starred review

"From the moment Mary Shelley 1   :ience fiction has inspired, challenged, an⸱ ⸱⸱⸱⸱⸱⸱⸱⸱⸱⸱⸱⸱ ⸱⸱⸱⸱⸱⸱⸱⸱⸱⸱. ⸱⸱⸱⸱ legacy is alive and thriving in Hannu Rajaniemi and Jacob Weisman's curated collection *The New Voices of Science Fiction*. Covering the last five years of rising stars and new arrivals, the collection is a breath of fresh, interstellar air."
—*Foreword Reviews*

"This is a stupendous collection. Each story is a wonderful gift. Some are funny, some poignant; all are forward-looking, imaginative, intelligent, and full of heart. The voices are honest and fresh. The themes are contemporary but also universal: love, family, career, alienation, success, loss. There's something here for everyone. I loved this collection. I simply couldn't put it down."
—Michael Blumlein, author of *Longer*

"*The New Voices of Science Fiction* is a stunning collection. There's a story for every possible future—it's impossible to put down."
—Peng Shepherd, author of *The Book of M*

"*The New Voices of Science Fiction* speaks in tongues ticklish, rousing, urgent, and forked. This smart, transportive pack of stories shows us our future, shows us ourselves, shows us a hell of a good time."
—Katie Williams, author of *Tell the Machine Goodnight*

Praise for editor Hannu Rajaniemi

"A storytelling skill rarely found from even the most experienced authors."
—*Library Journal*

"Writing that's striking, evocative. . . . Thoughtful, hard, densely realised and highly patterned, there's nothing quite like it in contemporary SF."
—*The Guardian*

"Rajaniemi is a virtuoso idea-smith, with a flair for stylish imagery and clever literary architecture."
—*Strange Horizons*

"With his challenging, intellectual high-wire-balancing-act novels, Hannu Rajaniemi is definitely a body thief supreme."
—Barnes and Noble

Praise for editor Jacob Weisman

On World Fantasy Award winner
The New Voices of Fantasy (co-edited with Peter S. Beagle)

★ "A stellar anthology that proves not only that fantasy is alive and well, but that it will be for years to come."
—*Kirkus*, starred review

★ "This anthology represents some of the most exciting and interesting work in the fantasy field today, and anyone interested in the genre should read it immediately."
—*Booklist*, starred review

On *Invaders: 22 Tales from the Outer Limits of Science Fiction*

★ "This volume is a treasure trove of stories that draw equally from SF and literary fiction, and they are superlative in either context."
—*Publishers Weekly*, starred review

Also Edited by Jacob Weisman

The Treasury of the Fantastic (with David Sandner, 2001, 2013)
The Sword & Sorcery Anthology (with David G. Hartwell, 2012)
Invaders: 22 Tales from the Outer Limits of Literature
The New Voices of Fantasy (with Peter S. Beagle, 2017)

Other Books by Hannu Rajaniemi

Summerland (2018)

The Jean le Flambeur series
The Quantum Thief (2010)
The Fractal Prince (2012)
The Causal Angel (2014)

Collections
Words of Birth and Death (2006)
Hannu Rajaniemi: Collected Fiction (2015)

THE
NEW VOICES
OF
SCIENCE FICTION

EDITED BY

HANNU RAJANIEMI
AND JACOB WEISMAN

TACHYON | SAN FRANCISCO

Tachyon Publications LLC
1459 18th Street #139
San Francisco, CA 94107
www.tachyonpublications.com
tachyon@tachyonpublications.com

Series Editor: Jacob Weisman
Project Editor: Jaymee Goh

Print ISBN 13: 978-1-61696-291-3
Digital ISBN: 978-1-61696-292-0

Printed in the United States by Versa Press, Inc.
First Edition: 2019
9 8 7 6 5 4 3 2 1

CONTENTS

INTRODUCTION
JACOB WEISMAN

*T*he *New Voices of Science Fiction* collects stories by writers whom Hannu Rajaniemi and I believe will become increasingly important in the years to come. All the stories in this volume were published quite recently, after 2014, and the writers themselves for the most part are new to their success. Many of these writers will be writing and publishing their first novels in the next few years, while some, including Rebecca Roanhorse, Sam J. Miller, Sarah Pinsker, and Rich Larson, are already on their way.

Another talented group of up-and-coming writers was featured in *The New Voices of Fantasy*, which I co-edited with the legendary fantasist Peter S. Beagle. It came out in 2017 and won the World Fantasy Award for best anthology. The book collected stories by several authors whose careers have taken off, including Carmen Maria Machado, Brooke Bolander, and Hannu Rajaniemi, to name just a few.

In 1977, a youthful George R. R. Martin took up the mantle of anthologies dedicated to younger writers, publishing several volumes centered around the John W. Campbell Award, which is given at the annual Hugo Award ceremony to the best new writer. Martin published work by himself, Lisa Tuttle, George Alec Effinger, Suzy

McKee Charnas, Spider Robinson, and John Varley, among others. Martin's series ran five volumes in all, ending in 1987.

The New Voices of Science Fiction is very much of this particular moment in the genre. If we had commissioned it ten years earlier, you would perhaps have seen such now-famous stories as Charles Stross's "Accerlando" (or my personal Stross favorite, "Tourists," which Stross calls "a case of hit-and-run amnesia"). You may have found "Calorie Man" or "The People of Sand and Slag" by Paolo Bacigalupi, early in his career. And, if the anthology had been truly attuned to what was happening at the time, you just may have discovered a truly breathtaking story, "Deus Ex Homine," by an unknown writer named Hannu Rajaniemi.

So, what is the new generation of science-fiction writers up to? With Jamie Wahls, it's the witty "Utopia, LOL??" about an everyman who finds himself in a future that he is incapable of comprehending. Alice Sola Kim takes Ray Bradbury's "All Summer in a Day" on a test drive through time, "One Hour, Every Seven Years." In "Mother Tongues," S. Qiouyi Lu shows to what new lengths a mother may go to sacrifice for her daughter. And with "Openness," Alexander Weinstein demonstrates the ultimate potentials of social media.

With these twenty fabulous stories, writers Amal El-Mohtar, Kelly Robson, Lettie Prell, Suzanne Palmer, Vina Jie-Min Prasad, and others show that the future of science fiction is in sure hands—and that, like the real future, it's only a brief matter of time before it arrives.

FOREWORD
HANNU RAJANIEMI

I certainly did not feel like a new voice when my first novel, *The Quantum Thief*, came out almost a decade ago. I only had the faintest idea that I even *had* a voice, except for the chorus of worry, self-doubt, and guilt in my head. I simply wrote about my obsessions—physics, gentleman thieves, chocolate, game theory—and filtered them through the idiosyncrasies of a second-language writer grappling with translating Finnish idioms into English. Somehow, that mess resonated with a wide readership across the world, and I am forever grateful for that.

But even now, several books and many stories later, I find the concept of a writerly voice elusive. The most adroit writers have the power to disappear, existing only as people and worlds conjured in our heads like waking dreams. And if the voice is the distillation of one's worldview, an approximation of one's consciousness, then finding it may be as difficult as locating the seat of the self—or its absence—in deep meditation.

But I do know what the writers who have shaped me sound like. What was novel in my own voice was a distorted echo of Finnish mythology, Jules Verne, Maurice Leblanc, Tove Jansson, Roger Zelazny; British space opera writers like Iain Banks and Charles

Stross; and many more. I fell in love with them and was changed by them. The truly new voices—whether chronologically recent or simply discovered by the reader for the first time—do that, and more. A new voice says something previously unspoken and true about the world around us. A new voice makes us want to imitate it, to amplify it, to join it in a chorus. A new voice wakes us to the fact that things are no longer the same.

All the stories in this volume have that power of waking: an original thematic scope, a tonal freshness. They make you a little uncomfortable. These writers are native to a strange world where science-fictional inventions are injected into the veins of the mundane on a daily basis, and political reality outdoes satire. It is a world of contradictions: of vast slow-burning threats and sudden bone-cracking transformations. It is a world that mixes utopian dreams with brutal greed, that embraces diversity while walking over the weak. It is a complex world that cannot be defined by a single new perspective.

This anthology assembles a chorus of storytellers who are up to the task of capturing the essence of our world's present and future. They refuse to be contained in one genre, but what they do is unmistakably science fiction. Yet they are not satisfied with using well-worn tropes of SF, such as time travel—or shinier speculative machinery, such as the Singularity—just as cold thought experiments, but they repurpose these ideas into deep explorations of gender, love, and identity. There are stories about contemporary nightmares like social media and climate change, but they have a clarity and attention to human detail that go beyond *Black Mirror*-esque cautionary tales. They don't hesitate to confront pain and willingly walk into the dark, but they also guide us back from it—and sometimes to laugh uproariously at the absurdity of it all.

And finally, these authors show us the *new* new things, from global cataclysms to personal transformations that get us lost in entirely unprecedented landscapes. They will, no doubt, inspire fresh writerly talent, and make us readers hungry for new kinds of stories we did not even know we wanted.

They are here to wake us, by giving us new waking dreams. Read them, and be changed.

OPENNESS

ALEXANDER WEINSTEIN

Alexander Weinstein's fiction has appeared in *Best American Science Fiction & Fantasy* and *Best American Experimental Writing*, and has been awarded the the Lamar York, Gail Crump, Hamlin Garland, Etching's Whirling, and New Millennium Prizes. He is the director of the Martha's Vineyard Institute of Creative Writing and Associate Professor of Creative Writing at Siena Heights University. His collection of short stories, *Children of the New World*, was selected as a New York Times 100 Notable Books of the Year for 2016.

"Openness" follows the rise and fall of a romance complicated by technologically-enhanced digital intimacy.

Before I decided to finally give up on New York, I subbed classes at a junior high in Brooklyn. A sixth grade math teacher suffering from downloading anxiety was out for the year, and jobs being what they were, I took any opportunity I could. Subbing math was hardly my dream job; I had a degree in visual art, for which I'd be in debt for the rest of my life. All I had to show for it was my senior collection, a series of paintings of abandoned playgrounds, stored in a U-Pack shed in Ohio. There was a time when I'd imagined I'd become famous, give guest lectures at colleges, and have retrospectives at MoMA. Instead, I found myself standing in front of a class of apathetic tweens, trying to teach them how to do long division without accessing their browsers. I handed out pen and paper, so that for once in their lives they'd have a tactile experience, and watched as they texted, their eyes glazed from blinking off message after message. They spent most of the class killing vampires and orcs inside their heads and humoring me by lazily filling out my photocopies.

The city overwhelmed me. Every day I'd walk by hundreds of strangers, compete for space in crowded coffee shops, and stand shoulder to shoulder on packed subway cars. I'd scan profiles, learning that the woman waiting for the N enjoyed thrash-hop, and the barista at my local coffee shop loved salted caramel. I'd had a couple fleeting relationships, but mostly I'd spend weekends going to bars and sleeping with people who knew little more than my username. It all made me want to turn off my layers, go back to the old days, and stay disconnected. But you do that and you become another old guy buried in an e-reader, complaining about how no one sends emails anymore.

So I stayed open, shared the most superficial info of my outer layer with the world, and filtered through everyone I passed, hoping to find some connection. Here was citycat5, jersygirl13, m3love. And then, one morning, there was Katie, sitting across from me on the N. She was lakegirl03, and her hair fell from under her knit cap. The only other info I could access was her hometown and that she was single.

Hi, I winked, and when I realized she had her tunes on, I sent off an invite. She raised her eyes.

Hi, she winked back.

You're from Maine? I'm planning a trip there this summer. Any suggestions?

She leaned forward and warmth spread across my chest from being allowed into her second layer. *I'm Katie*, she winked. *You should visit Bar Harbor, I grew up there.* She gave me access to an image of a lake house with tall silvery pines rising high above the shingled roof. *Wish I could help more, but this is my stop.* As she stood waiting for the doors to open, I winked a last message. *Can I invite you for a drink?* The train hissed, the doors opened, and she looked back at me and smiled before disappearing into the mass of early morning commuters. It was as the train sped toward work that her contact info appeared in my mind, along with a photo of her swimming in a lake at dusk.

It turned out that Katie had been in the city for a couple of years before she'd found a steady job. She taught senior citizens how to successfully navigate their layers. She'd helped a retired doctor upload images of his grandchildren so strangers could congratulate him, and assisted a ninety-three-year-old widow in sharing her mourning with the world. Her main challenge, she said, was getting older folks to understand the value of their layers.

"Every class they ask me why we can't just talk instead," she shared as we lay in bed. Though Katie and I occasionally spoke, it was always accompanied by layers. It was tiring to labor through the sentences needed to explain how you ran into a friend; much easier to share the memory, the friend's name and photo appearing organically.

"At least they still want to speak. My class won't even say hello."

"You remember what it was like before?" she asked.

I tried to think back to high school, but it was fuzzy. I was sure we used to talk more, but it seemed like we doled out personal details in hushed tones.

"Not really," I said. "Do you?"

"Sure. My family's cabin is completely out of range. Whenever I go back we can only talk."

"What's *that* like?"

She shared a photo of walking in the woods with her father, the earth covered in snow, and I felt the sharp edge of jealousy. Back where I grew up, there hadn't been any pristine forests to walk through, just abandoned mini-marts, a highway, and trucks heading past our town, which was more a pit stop than a community. The only woods were behind the high school, a small dangerous place where older kids might drag you if you didn't run fast enough. And my parents sure didn't talk. My mother was a clinical depressive who'd spent my childhood either behind the closed door of her bedroom or at the kitchen table, doing crossword puzzles and telling me to be quiet whenever I asked her something. My father had hit me so hard that twice I'd blacked out. My history wasn't the kind of thing I wanted to unlock for anyone, and since leaving Ohio I'd done my best to bury those memories within my layers.

So I spent our first months sharing little of myself. Katie showed me the memories of her best friends and family while I showed her the mundane details of substitute teaching and my favorite bands. I knew Katie could feel the contours of my hidden memories, like stones beneath a bedsheet, but for a while she let me keep the private pain of my unlocked layers.

That summer, Katie invited me to spend the weekend with her dad at their cabin. We rented a car and drove up the coast to Maine. We listened to our favorite songs, made pit stops, and finally left I-95 for the local roads. It was late in the afternoon, our car completely shaded by the pines, when our reception started getting spotty. I could feel my connection with Katie going in and out.

"Guess we might as well log off," Katie said. She closed her eyes for a moment, and all of a sudden I felt a chasm open between us. There was a woman sitting next to me whom I had no access to. "It's okay, babe," she said, and reached out for my hand. "I'm still me." I pressed my palm to hers, closed my eyes, and logged off, too.

Her father, Ben, was a big man who wore a puffy green vest that made him appear even larger. "And you're Andy," he said, burying my hand in his. "Let me get those bags for you." He hefted both our suitcases from the trunk, leaving me feeling useless. I followed him into the house, experiencing the quiet Katie had told me about. There were no messages coming from anyone, no buzz-posts to read, just the three of us in the cabin and the hum of an ancient refrigerator.

The last time a girlfriend had introduced me to her parents, we'd sat at Applebee's making small talk from outer layer info, but with Ben, there were no layers to access. All I knew were the details Katie had shared with me. I knew that her mom had died when she was fourteen, and that her father had spent a year at the cabin grieving, but that didn't seem like anything to bring up. So I stood there, looking out the living room window, trying to remember how people used to talk back in the days when we knew nothing about each other.

"Katie says you've never been to Maine."

"I haven't," I said, the words feeling strange against my tongue.

He walked over to the living room window. The afternoon sun shimmered on the pond, making it look silvery and alive, and the sky was wide and blue, pierced only by the spires of red pines. "Beautiful, isn't it?"

"Yeah," I said. The fridge hummed and from the other room I could hear Katie opening drawers and unpacking. I wasn't sure what else to add. I remembered a detail she had unlocked for me on one of our early dates. "I heard you've caught a lot of fish out there."

"You like fishing?" he asked, placing his hand on my shoulder. "Here, I'll show you something."

Ben retrieved an old tablet from the closet, and showed me photos on the screen. There he was with Katie and a string of fish; him scaling a trout in the kitchen sink. We scrolled through the two-dimensional images one by one as people did when I was a kid.

Katie came to my rescue. "Come on, I want to show you the lake," she said. "Dad can wow you with his antique technology later."

"One day you'll be happy I kept this," he said. "Katie's baby photos are all on here." He shut down the device and put it back in its case. "Have fun out there. Dinner will be ready in an hour."

Outside, Katie led me on the trails I'd only ever seen in her layers. Here was the gnarled cedar that she'd built a fort beneath, and over there were the rocks she'd chipped mica flakes from in second grade. We climbed down the banks of the trail, holding on to roots that jutted from the earth, and arrived on a stretch of beach speckled with empty clam shells, mussels, and snails that clung to the wet stones. Far down the shore, a rock outcropping rose from the water. A single heron stood on a peak that broke the shoreline.

There was something beautiful about sharing things in the old way—the two of us walking by the shore, the smell of the pine sap, the summer air cooling the late afternoon—and for the first time in years, I wished I had a sketch pad with me. As Katie spoke, her hands moved in ways I hadn't seen people do since childhood, gesturing toward the lake or me when she got excited. I tried to focus on each sentence, sensing my brain's inability to turn her words into pictures. She was talking about the cabin in autumn, logs burning in the fireplace, the smell of smoke, leaves crunching underfoot.

"Are you even listening?" she asked when I didn't respond.

"Sorry," I said. "I'm trying to. It's just that without the *ding* it's hard to know when you're sending . . . I mean *saying* something. . . ." I stopped talking, hating the clunkiness of words, and took a deep breath. "I guess I'm just rusty."

Katie softened. "I know. Sometimes when I'm in the city, I can't remember what it looks like up here without accessing my photos. It's kinda messed up, isn't it?"

"Yeah," I agreed, "I guess it is." The heron hunched down and then lifted off, its wide wings flapping as it headed across the lake, away from us.

That night her father fried up the perch he'd caught earlier that day. The herbs and butter filled the small cabin with their scent, and we drank the wine we'd brought. After dinner, Ben brought out a blue cardboard box, and the three of us sat in the living room and played an actual game. I hadn't seen one in over a decade.

"You don't know how to play Boggle?" Katie asked, surprised. The point, she explained, was to make words from the lettered dice and to write them down with pen and paper without accessing other players' thoughts. I sat there trying to figure out what Katie was feeling as she covered her paper with her hand.

"What do you think?" Katie asked after the first round.

"It's fun," I admitted.

"You bet it is," Ben said, and made the dice rattle again.

Afterward, when Katie and I were in bed, I listened to the crickets outside the screened windows. It'd been a long time since I'd heard the drone of them, each one singing within the chorus.

"So, what do you think of it here?"

"It's beautiful. But I can't imagine growing up without connection."

"You don't like the feeling?"

"Not really," I said. Being offline reminded me of my life back home before layers existed, when I'd lived with my parents in Ohio, a miserable time that technology had helped bury. "Do you?"

"Totally. I could live like this forever." I looked at her in the dark and tried to scan her eyes, but it was just her looking back at me, familiar yet completely different. "What about my dad?"

"I like him," I said, though it was only part of the truth. I was really thinking how different he was from my own father. We'd never sat and eaten dinner together or played board games. I'd heat up frozen pizza and eat it in the kitchen while Dad would lie on the couch watching whatever game was on. Eventually he'd get up, clink the bottles into the bin, and that was the sign to shut off the TV. Thinking about it made me feel like Katie and her father were playing a joke on me. There was no way people actually lived like this—without yelling, without fighting.

I felt the warmth of Katie's hand against my chest. "What's the matter?"

"Nothing."

"You can tell me," she said. *"I love you."*

It was the first time she'd actually said the words. At home it was just something we knew. We understood it from the moments we'd stand brushing our teeth together and the feeling would flash through her layers. And sometimes, late at night, right before we'd both fall asleep, we'd reach out and touch each other's hands and feel it.

"I love you, too," I managed to get out, and the weight of the words made something shift inside me. I felt the sentences forming in my head, the words lining up as though waiting to be released. Without my layers, there was nothing to keep them from spilling out. "Katie," I said into the darkness. "I want to tell you about my family."

She put her hands around me. "Okay."

And there, in the cabin, feeling Katie's body against mine, I began to speak. I didn't stop myself, but leaned in to my voice and the comfort of hearing my words disappearing into the air with only Katie and the crickets as witnesses.

It was that night in the cabin that helped us grow closer. Shortly after we returned, I unlocked more layers for her and showed her the pictures of my father and mother—the few I'd kept. There was my high school graduation: my mother's sunken eyes staring at the camera, my father with his hands in his pockets, and me in between, none of us happy. I showed her the dirty vinyl-sided house and the denuded lawn, blasted by cold winters and the perpetual dripping oil from my father's truck. And she showed me her own hidden layers: her mother's funeral in a small church in Maine, her father escaping to the cabin afterwards, learning to cook dinner for herself. Having unlocked the bad memories, I also uncovered the few good ones I'd hidden: a snowy day, my father, in a moment of tenderness, pulling me on a sled through the town; my mother emerging from her room shortly before she died to give me a hug as I left for school.

Feeling the closeness that sharing our layers brought, Katie suggested we give total openness a shot. It meant offering our most painful wounds as a gift to one another, a testament that there was no corner of the soul so ugly as to remain unshared. It'd become increasingly common to see the couples in Brooklyn, a simple *O* tattooed around their fingers announcing the radical honesty of their relationship to the world. They went to Open House parties, held in abandoned meatpacking plants, where partiers let down all their layers and displayed the infinite gradations of pain and joy to strangers while DJs played Breaknoise directly into their heads. I resented the couples, imagining them to be suburban hipsters who'd grown up with loving parents, regular allowances, and easy histories to share.

Total openness seemed premature, I told Katie, not just for us but for everyone. Our culture was still figuring out the technology. A decade after linking in, I'd find drinking episodes that had migrated to my work layer or, worse yet, porn clips that I had to flush back down into the darkness of my hidden layers.

"I'm not going to judge you," she promised as we lay in bed. She put her leg over mine. "You do realize how hot it'll be to know each

9

other's fantasies, right?" There were dozens of buzz-posts about it—the benefits of total intimacy, how there were no more fumbling mistakes, no guessing, just a personal database of kinks that could be accessed by your partner.

"What about the darker layers?"

"We need to uncover those, too," Katie said. "That's what love is: seeing all the horrible stuff and still loving one another."

I thought I understood it then, and though my heart was in my throat, my terror so palpable that my body had gone cold, I was willing to believe that total openness wasn't the opposite of safety but the only true guarantee of finding it. So late that summer evening, Katie and I sat on the bed, gazing into one another's eyes, and gave each other total access.

I've spent a lot of time thinking about what went wrong, whether total openness was to blame or not. Some days I think it was; that there's no way to share the totality of yourself and still be loved, that secrets are the glue that holds relationships together. Other times, I think Katie and I weren't meant to be a couple for the long haul; total openness just helped us find the end more quickly. Maybe it was nothing more than the limits of the software. We were the first generation to grow up with layers, a group of kids who'd produced thousands of tutorials on blocking unwanted users but not a single one on empathy.

There were certainly good things that came from openness. Like how, after finding my paintings, Katie surprised me with a sketch pad and a set of drawing pencils. Or the nights when I'd come home from a frustrating day of substitute teaching and she'd have accessed my mood long before I saw her. She'd lay me down on the bed and give me a massage without us even winking one another. But all too often, it was the things we didn't need to share that pierced our love: sexual histories that left Katie stewing for weeks; fleeting attractions to waiters and waitresses when we'd go out to dinner; momentary annoyances that would have been best left unshared. Letting someone in to every secret gave access to our dark corners, and rather than feeling sympathy for each other's failings, we blamed one another for nearsightedness, and soon layers of resentment were dredged up. There was a night at the bar when I watched Katie struggling to speak loudly enough for the bartender to hear, and I suddenly realized his face resembled the schoolyard bully of her childhood. "You have to get over that already," I blinked angrily. Soon after, while watching a film I wasn't enjoying, she tapped in to layers I hadn't yet registered. "He's just a fictional character, not your father."

And then there was the final New Year's party at her friend's place out in Bay Ridge. The party was Y2K-themed, and guests were expected to actually speak to one another. A bunch of partygoers were sporting Bluetooth headsets into which they yelled loudly. We listened to Jamiroquai on a boom box and watched *Teletubbies* on a salvaged flat-screen. Katie was enjoying herself. She danced to the songs and barely winked to anyone, happy to be talking again. I tried to be sociable, but I was shut down, giving access to only my most superficial layers as everyone got drunk and sloppy with theirs.

We stood talking to a guy wearing an ironic trucker's cap as he pretended we were in 1999. "So you think the computers are going to blow up at midnight?" he asked us.

Katie laughed.

"No," I said.

Come on, Katie blinked. *Loosen up.*

I'm not into the kitsch, I blinked back.

"Mostly I'm just excited about faxing things," the guy in the trucker's cap joked and Katie laughed again.

"You know faxing was the early nineties, right?" I asked, and then blinked to Katie, *Are you flirting with this guy?*

"All I'm saying is, check out this Bluetooth. Can you believe folks wore these?"

"I know, that's crazy," Katie said. *No, I'm not flirting. I'm talking. How about you try it for a change?*

I told you, I don't like talking.

Great, so you're never going to want to talk then?

"Did you guys make any New Year's resolutions?" the guy asked us.

"Yeah," Katie said, looking at me, "to talk more." In her annoyance an image from a deeper layer flashed into clear resolution. It was a glimpse of a future she'd imagined for herself, and I saw us canoeing in Maine, singing songs with our kids. Even though we'd discussed how I never wanted children, there they were, and while I'd never sung aloud since grade school, there was a projection of me singing. Only then did I see the other incongruities. My eyes were blue not brown, my voice buoyant, my physique way more buff than I ever planned to become. And though I shared similarities with the man in the canoe, as if Katie had tried to fit me into his mold, the differences were clear. There in the canoe, was the family Katie wanted, and the man with her wasn't me.

"What the fuck?" I asked aloud.

"It's just a question," the guy said. "If it's personal, you don't have to share. I'm giving up gluten."

"Excuse us for a minute," I said, and I blinked for Katie to follow me. We found a quiet spot by the side of the flat-screen TV.

"Who the hell is that in your future?" I whispered.

"I'm really sorry," she said, looking at me. "I do love you."

"But I'm not the guy you want to spend your life with?"

"Ten . . . nine . . . eight," the partiers around us counted as they streamed the feed from Times Square.

"That's not true," Katie said. "You're almost everything I want."

There was no conscious choice about what happened next, just an instinctive recoiling of our bodies, the goose bumps rising against my skin as our layers closed to one another. I couldn't access the lake house anymore or the photos of her father; her childhood dog was gone, followed by the first boyfriend and her college years, until all that was left were my own private memories, trapped deep within my layers, and the pale tint of her skin in the television's light. We were strangers again, and we stood there, looking at one another, while all around us the party counted down the last seconds of the old year.

I logged off for long periods after we broke up. I gave up on trying to convince my students to have real-life experiences. When they complained that reading the "I Have a Dream" speech was too boring, I let them stream a thrash-hop version instead, and I sat looking out the window thinking about Katie. I walked to my station alone every day and sat on the train with my sketch pad, drawing the details I remembered from our trip to Maine: the shoreline with its broken shells and sunlight, the heron before it took flight, Katie's face in the summer darkness. It's the intangible details that I remember the clearest, the ones that there's no way to draw. The taste of the perch as we sat around the table; how a cricket had slipped through the screened windows and jumped around our bed that night; how, after we'd gotten it out, the coolness of the lake made us draw the blankets around us; and how Katie, her father, and I had sat together in the warm light of the living room and played a game, the lettered dice clattering as her father shook the plastic container.

"All right, Andy, you ready?" he'd asked me, holding his hand over the lid.

And I'd thought I was.

THE SHAPE OF MY NAME
NINO CIPRI

Nino Cipri is a queer and trans/nonbinary writer, editor, and educator. They are a graduate of the Clarion Writing Workshop and the University of Kansas's MFA program. Their award-winning debut fiction collection *Homesick* was just released in October 2019, and their novella *Finna* will be published in the spring of 2020. Nino has also written plays, poetry, and radio features; performed as a dancer, actor, and puppeteer; and worked as a stagehand, bookseller, bike mechanic, and labor organizer. One time, an angry person on the internet called Nino a verbal terrorist, which was pretty funny.

"The Shape of My Name" is a haunting tale of time travel, self-actualization, and mourning for the imperfect parent.

The year 2076 smells like antiseptic gauze and the lavender diffuser that Dara set up in my room. It has the bitter aftertaste of pills: probiotics and microphages and PPMOs. It feels like the itch of healing, the ache that's settled on my pubic bone. It has the sound of a new name that's fresh and yet familiar on my lips.

The future feels lighter than the past. I think I know why you chose it over me, Mama.

My bedroom has changed in the hundred-plus years that have passed since I slept there as a child. The floorboards have been carpeted over, torn up, replaced. The walls are thick with new layers of paint. The windows have been upgraded, the closet expanded. The oak tree that stood outside my window is gone, felled by a storm twenty years ago, I'm told. But the house still stands, and our family still lives here, with all our attendant ghosts. You and I are haunting each other, I think.

I picture you standing in the kitchen downstairs, over a century ago. I imagine that you're staring out through the little window above the sink, your gaze traveling down the path that leads from the back door and splits at the creek; one trail leads to the pond, and the other leads to the shelter and the anachronopede, with its rows of capsules and blinking lights.

Maybe it's the afternoon you left us. June 22, 1963: storm clouds gathering in the west, the wind picking up, the air growing heavy with the threat of rain. And you're staring out the window, gazing across the dewy fields at the forking path, trying to decide which way you'll take.

My bedroom is just above the kitchen, and my window has that same view, a little expanded: I can see clear down to the pond where Dad and I used to sit on his weeks off from the oil fields. It's spring, and the cattails are only hip high. I can just make out the silhouette of a great blue heron walking along among the reeds and rushes.

You and I, we're twenty feet and more than a hundred years apart.

You went into labor not knowing my name, which I know now is unprecedented among our family: you knew Dad's name before you laid eyes on him, the time and date of my birth, the hospital where he would drive you when you went into labor. But my name? My sex? Conspicuously absent in Uncle Dante's gilt-edged book where all these happy details were recorded in advance.

Dad told me later that you thought I'd be a stillbirth. He didn't know about the record book, about the blank space where a name should go. But he told me that nothing he said while you were pregnant could convince you that I'd come into the world alive. You thought I'd slip out of you strangled and blue, already decaying.

Instead, I started screaming before they pulled me all the way out.

Dad said that even when the nurse placed me in your arms, you thought you were hallucinating. "I had to tell her, over and over: Miriam, you're not dreaming, our daughter is alive."

I bit my lip when he told me that, locked the words "your son" out of sight. I regret that now; maybe I could have explained myself to him. I should have tried, at least.

You didn't name me for nearly a week.

Nineteen fifty-four tastes like Kellogg's Rice Krispies in fresh milk, delivered earlier that morning. It smells like wood smoke, cedar chips, Dad's Kamel cigarettes mixed with the perpetual smell of diesel in his clothes. It feels like the worn velvet nap of the couch in our living room, which I loved to run my fingers across.

I was four years old. I woke up in the middle of the night after a loud crash of lightning. The branches of the oak tree outside my window were thrashing in the wind and the rain.

I crept out of bed, dragging my blanket with me. I slipped out of the door and into the hallway, heading for your and Dad's bedroom. I stopped when I heard voices coming from the parlor downstairs: I recognized your sharp tones, but there was also a man's voice, not Dad's baritone but something closer to a tenor.

The door creaked when I pushed it open, and the voices fell silent. I paused, and then you yanked open the door.

The curlers in your hair had come undone, descending down toward your shoulders. I watched one tumble out of your hair and onto the floor like a stunned beetle. I only caught a glimpse of the man standing in the corner; he had thin, hunched shoulders and dark hair, wet and plastered to his skull. He was wearing one of Dad's old robes, with the initials monogrammed on the pocket. It was much too big for him.

You snatched me up, not very gently, and carried me up to the bedroom you shared with Dad.

"Tom," you hissed. You dropped me on the bed before Dad was fully awake, and shook his shoulder. He sat up, blinking at me, and looked to you for an explanation.

"There's a visitor," you said, voice strained.

Dad looked at the clock, pulling it closer to him to get a proper look. "Now? Who is it?"

Your jaw was clenched, and so were your hands. "I'm handling it. I just need you to watch—"

You said my name in a way I'd never heard it before, as if each syllable were a hard, steel ball dropping from your lips. It frightened me, and I started to cry. Silently, though, since I didn't want you to notice me. I didn't want you to look at me with eyes like that.

You turned on your heel and left the room, clicking the door shut behind you and locking it.

Dad patted me on the back, his wide hand nearly covering the expanse of my skinny shoulders. "It's all right, kid," he said. "Nothing to be scared of. Why don't you lie down and I'll read you something, huh?"

In the morning, there was no sign a visitor had been there at all. You and Dad assured me that I must have dreamed the whole thing.

I know now that you were lying, of course. I think I knew it even then.

I had two childhoods.

One happened between Dad's ten-day hitches in the White County oil fields. That childhood smells like his tobacco, wool coats, wet grass. It sounds like the opening theme songs to all our favorite TV shows. It tastes like the peanut butter sandwiches that you'd pack for us on our walks, which we'd eat down by the pond, the same one I can just barely see from my window here. In the summer, we'd sit at the edge of the water, dipping our toes into the mud. Sometimes, Dad told me stories, or asked me to fill him in on the episodes of *Gunsmoke* and *Science Fiction Theatre* he'd missed, and we'd chat while watching for birds. The herons have always been my favorite. They moved so slow, it always felt like a treat to spot one as it stepped cautiously through the shallow water. Sometimes, we'd catch sight of one flying overhead, its wide wings fighting against gravity.

And then there was the childhood with you, and with Dara, the childhood that happened when Dad was away. I remember the first morning I came downstairs and she was eating pancakes off of your fancy china, the plates that were decorated with delicate paintings of evening primrose.

"Hi there. I'm Dara," she said.

When I looked at you, shy and unsure, you told me, "She's a cousin. She'll be dropping in when your father is working. Just to keep us company."

Dara didn't really look much like you, I thought; not the way that Dad's cousins and uncles all resembled one another. But I could see a few similarities between the two of you; hazel eyes, long fingers, and something I didn't have the words to describe for a long time: a certain discomfort, the sense that you held yourselves slightly apart from the rest of us. It had made you a figure of gossip in town, though I didn't know that until high school, when the same was said of me.

"What should I call you?" Dara asked me.

You jumped in and told her to call me by my name, the one you'd chosen for me, after the week of indecision following my birth. How can I ever make you understand how much I disliked that name? It felt like it belonged to a sister whom I was constantly being compared to, whose legacy I could never fulfill or surpass or even forget. Dara must have caught the face that I made, because later, when you were out in the garden, she asked me, "Do you have another name? That you want me to call you instead?"

When I shrugged, she said, "It doesn't have to be a forever name. Just one for the day. You can pick a new one tomorrow, if you like. You can introduce yourself differently every time you see me."

And so every morning when I woke up and saw Dara sitting at the table, I gave her a different name: Doc, Buck, George, Charlie. Names that my heroes had, from television and comics and the matinees in town. They weren't my name, but they were better than the one I had. I liked the way they sounded, the shape of them rolling around my mouth.

You just looked on, lips pursed in a frown, and told Dara you wished she'd quit indulging my silly little games.

The two of you sat around our kitchen table and—if I was quiet and didn't draw any attention to myself—talked in a strange code about *jumps* and *fastenings* and *capsules,* dropping names of people I never knew. More of your cousins, I figured.

You told our neighbors that all of your family was spread out, and disinclined to make the long trip to visit. When Dara took me in, she made up a tale about a long-lost cousin whose parents had kicked him out for being ~~queer~~ trans. Funny, the way the truth seeps into lies.

I went to see Uncle Dante in 1927. I wanted to see what he had in that book of his about me, and about you and Dara.

Nineteen twenty-seven tastes like the chicken broth and brown bread he fed me after I showed up at his door. It smells like the musty blanket he hung around my shoulders, like kerosene lamps and wood smoke. It sounds like the scratchy records he played on his phonograph: Duke Ellington and Al Jolson, the Gershwin brothers and Gene Austin.

"Your mother dropped in by back in '24," he said, settling down in an armchair in front of the fireplace. It was the same fireplace that had been in our parlor, though Dad had sealed off the chimney in 1958, saying it let in too many drafts. "She was very adamant that your name be written down in the records. She seemed . . . upset." He let the last word hang on its own, lonely, obviously understated.

"That's not my name," I told him. "It's the one she gave me, but it was never mine."

I had to explain to him then—he'd been to the future, and so it didn't seem so far-fetched, my transition. I simplified it for him, of course: didn't go into the transdermal hormonal implants and mastectomy, the paperwork Dara and I forged, the phalloplasty I'd scheduled a century and a half in the future. I skipped the introduction to gender theory, Susan Stryker, *Stone Butch Blues*, all the things that Dara gave me to read when I asked if there were books about people like me.

"My aunt Lucia was of a similar disposition," he told me. "Once her last child was grown, she gave up on dresses entirely. Wore a suit to church for her last twelve years, which gave her a reputation for eccentricity."

I clamped my mouth shut and nodded along, still feeling ill and shaky from the jump. The smell of Uncle Dante's cigar burned in my nostrils. I wished we could have had the conversation outside, on the porch; the parlor seemed too familiar, too laden with the ghost of your presence.

"What should I put instead?" he asked, pulling his book down from the mantle: the ancient gilt-edged journal where he recorded our family's births, marriages, and deaths, as they were reported to him.

"It's blank when I'm born," I told him. He paused in the act of sharpening his pencil—he knew better than to write the future in ink. "Just erase it. Tear the whole page out and rewrite it ~~white it out~~ if you need to."

He sat back in his chair and combed his fingers through his beard. "That's . . . unprecedented," he said. Again, that pause, the heaviness of the word choice.

"Not anymore," I said.

Nineteen sixty-three feels like a menstrual cramp, like the ache in my legs as my bones stretched, like the twinges in my nipples as my breasts developed. It smells like Secret roll-on deodorant and the menthol cigarettes you took up smoking. It tastes like the peach cobbler I burned in Home Ec class, which the teacher forced me to eat. It sounds like Sam Cooke's album *Night Beat*, which Dara, during one of her visits, told me to buy.

And it looks like you, jumpier than I'd ever seen you, so twitchy that even Dad commented on it before he left for his hitch in the oil fields.

"Will you be all right?" he asked after dinner.

I was listening from the kitchen doorway to the two of you talk. I'd come in to ask Dad if he was going to watch *Gunsmoke*, which would be starting in a few minutes, with me, and caught the two of you with your heads together by the sink.

You leaned forward, bracing your hands on the edge of the sink, looking for all the world as if you couldn't hold yourself up, as if gravity was working just a little bit harder on you than it was on everyone else. I wondered for a second if you were going to tell him about Dara. I'd grown up keeping her a secret with you, though the omission had begun to weigh heavier on me. I loved Dad, and I loved Dara; being unable to reconcile the two of them seemed trickier each passing week.

Instead you said nothing. You relaxed your shoulders, and you smiled for him, and kissed his cheek. You said the two of us would be fine, not to worry about his girls.

And the very next day, you pulled me out of bed and showed me our family's time machine, in the old tornado shelter with the lock I'd never been able to pick.

I know more about the machine now, after talking with Uncle Dante, reading the records that he kept. About the mysterious man, Moses Stone, who built it in 1905, when Grandma Emmeline's parents leased out a parcel of land. He called it the anachronopede, which probably sounded marvelous in 1905, but even Uncle Dante was rolling his eyes at the name twenty years later. I know that Stone took Emmeline on trips to the future when she was seventeen, and then abandoned her after a few years, and nobody's been able to find him since then. I know that the machine is keyed to something in Emmeline's matrilineal DNA, some recessive gene.

I wonder if that man, Stone, built the anachronopede as an experiment. An experiment needs parameters, right? So build a machine that only certain people in one family can use. We can't go back before 1905, when the machine was completed, and we can't go past August 3, 2321. What happens that day? The only way to find out is to go as far forward as possible, and then wait. Maroon yourself in time. Exile yourself as far forward as you can, where none of us can reach you.

I know you were lonely, waiting for me to grow up so you could travel again. You were exiled when you married Dad in 1947, in that feverish period just after the war. It must have been so romantic at first: I've seen the letters he wrote during the years he courted you. And you'd grown up seeing his name written next to yours, and the date that you'd marry him. When did you start feeling trapped, I wonder? You were caught in a weird net of fate and love and the future and the past. You loved Dad, but your love kept you hostage. You loved me, but you knew that someday, I'd transform myself into someone you didn't recognize.

At first, when you took me underground to see the anachrono-pede, I thought you and Dad had built a fallout shelter. But there were no beds or boxes of canned food. And built into the rocky wall were rows of doors that looked like the one on our icebox. Round lightbulbs lay just above the doors, nearly all of them red, though one or two were slowly blinking between orange and yellow.

Nearly all the doors were shut, except for two, near the end, which hung ajar.

"Those two capsules are for us, you and me," you said. "Nobody else can use them."

I stared at them. "What are they for?"

I'd heard you and Dara speak in code for nearly all of my life, jumps and capsules and fastenings. I'd imagined all sorts of things. Aliens and spaceships and doorways to another dimension, all the sort of things I'd seen Truman Bradley introduce on *Science Fiction Theatre.*

"Traveling," you said.

"In time or in space?"

You seemed surprised. I'm not sure why. Dad collected pulp magazines, and you'd given me books by H. G. Wells and Jules Verne for Christmas in years past. The Justice League had gone into the future. I'd seen *The Fly* the previous year during a half-price matinee. You know how it was back then: such things weren't considered impossible, so much as inevitable. The future was a country we all wanted so badly to visit.

"In time," you said.

I immediately started peppering you with questions: How far into the future had you gone? When were you born? Had you met dinosaurs? Had you met King Arthur? What about jet packs? Was Dara from the future?

You held a hand to your mouth, watching as I danced around the small cavern, firing off questions like bullets being sprayed from a Tommy gun.

"Maybe you are too young," you said, staring at the two empty capsules in the wall.

"I'm not!" I insisted. "Can't we go somewhere? Just a—just a quick jump?"

I added in the last part because I wanted you to know I'd been listening, when you and Dara had talked in code at the kitchen table. I'd been waiting for you to include me in the conversation.

"Tomorrow," you decided. "We'll leave tomorrow."

The first thing I learned about time travel was that you couldn't eat anything before you did it. And you could only take a few sips of water: no juice or milk. The second thing I learned was that it was the most painful thing in the world, at least for me.

"Your grandmother Emmeline called it the fastening," you told me. "She said it felt like being a button squeezed through a too-narrow slit in a piece of fabric. It affects everyone differently."

"How's it affect you?"

You twisted your wedding ring around on your finger. "I haven't done it since before you were born."

You made me go to the bathroom twice before we walked back on that path, taking the fork that led to the shelter where the capsules were. The grass was still wet with dew, and there was a chill in the air. Up above, thin, wispy clouds were scratched onto the sky, but out west, I could see dark clouds gathering. There'd be storms later.

But what did I care about later? I was going into a time machine.

I asked you, "Where are we going?"

You replied, "To visit Dara. Just a quick trip."

There was something cold in your voice. I recognized the tone: the same you used when trying to talk me into wearing the new dress you'd bought me for church, or telling me to stop tearing through the house and play quietly for once.

In the shelter, you helped me undress, though it made me feel hotly embarrassed and strange to be naked in front of you again. I'd grown wary of my own body in the last few months, the way at how it was changing: I'd been dismayed by the way my nipples had grown tender, at the fatty flesh that had budded beneath them. It seemed like a betrayal.

I hunched my shoulders and covered my privates, though you barely glanced at my naked skin. You helped me lie down in the capsule, showed me how to pull the round mask over the bottom half of my face, attach the clip that went over my index finger. Finally, you lifted one of my arms up and wrapped a black cuff around the crook of my elbow. I noticed, watching you, that you had bitten all of your nails down to the quick, that the edges were jagged and tender looking.

"You program your destination date in here, you see?" You tapped a square of black glass on the ceiling of the capsule, and it lit up at the touch. Your fingers flew across the screen, typing directly onto it, rearranging colored orbs that seemed to attach themselves to your finger as soon as you touched them.

"You'll learn how to do this on your own eventually," you said. The screen, accepting whatever you'd done to it, blinked out and went black again.

I breathed through my mask, which covered my nose and face. A whisper of air blew against my skin, a rubbery, stale, lemony scent.

"Don't be scared," you said. "I'll be there when you wake up. I'm sending myself back a little earlier, so I'll be there to help you out of the capsule."

You kissed me on the forehead and shut the door. I was left alone in the dark as the walls around me started to hum.

Calling it the fastening does it a disservice. It's much more painful than that. Granny Emmeline is far tougher than I'll ever be if she thought it was just like forcing a button into place.

For me, it felt like being crushed in a vise that was lined with broken glass and nails. I understood, afterward, why you had forbidden me from eating or drinking for twenty-four hours. I would have vomited in the mask, shat myself inside the capsule. I came back to myself in the dark, wild with terror and the phantom remains of that awful pain.

The door opened. The light needled into my eyes, and I screamed, trying to cover them. The various cuffs and wires attached to my arms tugged my hands back down, which made me panic even more.

Hands reached in and pushed me down, and eventually, I registered your voice in my ear, though not what you were saying. I stopped flailing long enough for all the straps and cuffs to be undone, and then I was lifted out of the capsule. You held me in your arms, rocking and soothing me, rubbing my back as I cried hysterically onto your shoulder.

I was insensible for a few minutes. When my sobs died away to hiccups, I realized that we weren't alone in the shelter. Dara was with us as well, and she had thrown a blanket over my shoulders.

"Jesus, Miriam," she said, over and over. "What the hell were you thinking?"

I found out later that I was the youngest person in my family to ever make a jump. Traditionally, they made their first jumps on their seventeenth birthday. I was nearly five years shy of that.

You smoothed back a lock of my hair, and I saw that all your fingernails had lost their ragged edges. Instead, they were rounded and smooth, topped with little crescents of white.

Uncle Dante told me that it wasn't unusual for two members of the family to be lovers, especially if there were generational gaps between them. It helped to avoid romantic entanglements with people who were bound to linear lives, at least until they were ready to settle down for a number of years, raising children. Pregnancy didn't mix well with time travel. It was odder to do what you did: settle down with someone who was, as Dara liked to put it, stuck in the slow lane of linear time.

Dara told me about the two of you, eventually; that you'd been lovers before you met Dad, before you settled down with him in 1947. And that when she started visiting us in 1955, she wasn't sleeping alone in the guest bedroom.

I'm not sure if I was madder at her or you at the time, though I've since forgiven her. Why wouldn't I? You've left both of us, and it's a big thing, to have that in common.

Nineteen eighty-one is colored silver, beige, bright orange, deep brown. It feels like the afghan blanket Dara kept on my bed while I recovered from my first jump, some kind of cheap fake wool. It tastes like chicken soup and weak tea with honey and lime Jell-O.

And for a few days, at least, 1981 felt like a low-grade headache that never went away, muscle spasms that I couldn't always control, dry mouth, difficulty swallowing. It smelled like a lingering olfactory hallucination of frying onions. It sounded like a ringing in the ears.

"So you're the unnamed baby, huh?" Dara said that first morning when I woke up. She was reading a book, and set it down next to her on the couch.

I was disoriented: you and Dara had placed me in the southeast bedroom, the same one I slept in all through childhood. (The same one I'm recovering in right now.) I'm not sure if you thought it would comfort me, to wake up to familiar surroundings. It was profoundly strange, to be in my own bedroom but have it be so different: the striped wallpaper replaced with avocado green paint; a loveseat with floral upholstery where my dresser had been; all my posters of Buck Rogers and Superman replaced with framed prints of unfamiliar artwork.

"Dara?" I asked. She seemed different, colder. Her hair was shorter than the last time I'd seen her, and she wore a pair of thick-framed glasses.

She cocked her head. "That'd be me. Nice to meet you."

I blinked at her, still disoriented and foggy. "We met before," I said.

She raised her eyebrows, like she couldn't believe I was so dumb. "Not by my timeline."

Right. Time travel.

You rushed in then. You must have heard us talking. You crouched down next to me and stroked the hair back from my face.

"How are you feeling?" you asked.

I looked down at your fingernails, and saw again that they were smooth, no jagged edges, and a hint of white at the edges. Dara told me later that you'd arrived two days before me, just so you two could have a few days alone together. After all, you'd only left her for 1947 a few days before. The two of you had a lot to talk about.

"All right, I guess," I told you.

It felt like the worst family vacation for those first few days. Dara was distant with me and downright cold to you. I wanted to ask what had happened, but I thought that I'd get the cold shoulder if I did. I caught snippets of the arguments you had with Dara; always whispered in doorways, or downstairs in the kitchen, the words too faint for me to make out.

It got a little better once I was back on my feet, and able to walk around and explore. I was astonished by everything; the walnut trees on our property that I had known as saplings now towered over me. Dara's television was twice the size of ours, in color, and had over a dozen stations. Dara's car seemed tiny, and shaped like a snake's head, instead of having the generous curves and lines of the cars I knew.

I think it charmed Dara out of her anger a bit, to see me so appreciative of all these futuristic wonders—which were all relics of the past for her—and the conversations between the three of us got a little bit easier. Dara told me a little bit more about where she'd come from—the late twenty-first century—and why she was in this time—studying with some poet that I'd never heard of. She showed me the woman's poetry, and though I couldn't make much of it out at the time, one line from one poem has always stuck with me: "I did not recognize the shape of my own name."

I pondered that, lying awake in my bedroom—the once and future bedroom that I'm writing this from now, that I slept in then, that I awoke in when I was a young child, frightened by a storm. The rest of that poem made little sense to me, a series of images that were threaded together by a string of line breaks.

But I know about names, and hearing the one that's been given to you, and not recognizing it. I was trying to stammer this out to Dara one night, after she'd read that poem to me. And she asked, plain as could be, "What would you rather be called instead?"

I thought about how I used to introduce myself after the heroes of the TV shows my father and I watched: Doc and George and Charlie. It had been a silly game, sure, but there'd been something more serious underneath it. I'd recognized something in the shape of those names, something I wanted for myself.

"I dunno. A boy's name," I said. "Like George in the Famous Five."

"Well, why do you want to be called by a boy's name?" Dara asked gently.

In the corner, where you'd been playing solitaire, you paused while laying down a card. Dara noticed too, and we both looked over at you. I cringed, wondering what you were about to say; you hated that I didn't like my name, took it as a personal insult somehow.

But you said nothing, just resumed playing, slapping the cards down a little more heavily than before.

I forgive you for drugging me to take me back to 1963. I know I screamed at you after we arrived and the drugs wore off, but I was also a little relieved. It was a sneaking sort of relief, and didn't do much to counterbalance the feelings of betrayal and rage, but I know I would have panicked the second you shoved me into one of those capsules.

You'd taken me to the future, after all. I'd seen the relative wonders of 1981: VHS tapes, the Flash Gordon movie, the *Columbia* space shuttle. I would have forgiven you so much for that tiny glimpse.

I don't forgive you for leaving me, though. I don't forgive you for the morning after, when I woke up in my old familiar bedroom and padded downstairs for a bowl of cereal, and found, instead, a note that bore two words in your handwriting: *I'm sorry.*

The note rested atop the gilt-edged book that Grandma Emmeline had started as a diary, and that Uncle Dante had turned into both a record and a set of instructions for future generations: the names, birth dates, and the locations for all the traveling members of our family; who lived in the house and when; and sometimes, how and when a person died. The book stays with the house; you must have kept it hidden in the attic.

I flipped through it until I found your name: Miriam Guthrie (née Stone): born November 21, 1977, Harrisburg, IL. Next to it, you penciled in the following.

Jumped forward to June 22, 2321 CE, and will die in exile beyond reach of the anachronopede.

Two small words could never encompass everything you have to apologize for.

I wonder if you ever looked up Dad's obituary. I wonder if you were even able to, if the record for one small man's death even lasts that long.

When you left, you took my father's future with you. Did you realize that? He was stuck in the slow lane of linear time, and to Dad, the future he'd dreamed of must have receded into the distance, something he'd never be able to reach.

He lost his job in the fall of 1966, as the White County oil wells ran dry, and hanged himself in the garage six months later. Dara cut him down and called the ambulance; her visits became more regular after you left us, and she must have known the day he would die.

(I can't bring myself to ask her: Couldn't she have arrived twenty minutes earlier and stopped him entirely? I don't want to know her answer.)

In that obituary, I'm first in the list of those who survived him, and it's the last time I used the name you gave me. During the funeral, I nodded, received the hugs and handshakes from Dad's cousins and friends, bowed my head when the priest instructed, prayed hard for his soul. When it was done, I walked alone to the pond where the two of us had sat together, watching birds and talking about the plots of silly television shows. I tried to remember everything that I could about him, tried to preserve his ghost against the vagaries of time: the smell of Kamel cigarettes and diesel on his clothes; the red-blond stubble that dotted his jaw; the way his eyes brightened when they landed on you.

I wished so hard that you were there with me. I wanted so much to cry on your shoulder, to sob as hard and hysterically as I had when you took me to 1981. And I wanted to be able to slap you, to hit you, to push you in the water and hold you beneath the surface. I could have killed you that day, Mama.

When I was finished, Dara took me back to the house. We cleaned it as best we could for the next family member who would live here: there always has to be a member of the Stone family here, to take care of the shelter, the anachronopede, and the travelers that come through.

Then she took me away, to 2073, the home she'd made more than a century away from you.

Today was the first day I was able to leave the house, to take cautious, wobbling steps to the outside world. Everything is still tender and bruised, though my body is healing faster than I ever thought possible. It feels strange to walk with a weight between my legs; I walk differently, with a wider stride, even though I'm still limping.

Dara and I walked down to the pond today. The frogs all hushed at our approach, but the blackbirds set up a racket. And off in the distance, a heron lifted a cautious foot and placed it down again. We watched it step carefully through the water, hesitantly. Its beak darted into the water and came back up with a wriggling fish, which it flipped into its mouth. I suppose it was satisfied with that, because it crouched down, spread its wings, and then jumped into the air, enormous wings fighting against gravity until it rose over the trees.

Three days before my surgery, I went back to you. The pain of it is always the same, like I'm being torn apart and placed back together with clumsy, inexpert fingers, but by now I've gotten used to it. I wanted you to see me as the man I've always known I am, that I slowly became. And I wanted to see if I could forgive you; if I could look at you and see anything besides my father's slow decay, my own broken and betrayed heart.

I knocked at the door, dizzy, ears ringing, shivering, soaked from the storm that was so much worse than I remembered. I was lucky that you or Dara had left a blanket in the shelter, so I didn't have to walk up to the front door naked; my flat, scarred chest at odds with my wide hips, the thatch of pubic hair with no flesh protruding from it. I'd been on hormones for a year, and this second puberty reminded me so much of my first one, with you in 1963: the acne and the awkwardness, the slow reveal of my future self.

You answered the door with your hair in curlers, just as I remembered, and fetched me one of Dad's old robes. I fingered the monogramming at the breast pocket, and I wished, so hard, that I could walk upstairs and see him.

"What the hell," you said. "I thought the whole family knew these years were off-limits while I'm linear."

You didn't quite recognize me, and you tilted your head. "Have we met before?"

I looked you in the eyes, and my voice cracked when I told you I was your son.

Your hand went to your mouth. "I'll have a son?" you asked.

And I told you the truth: "You have one already."

And your hand went to your gut, as if you would be sick. You shook your head, so hard that your curlers started coming loose. That's when the door creaked open, just a crack. You flew over there and yanked it all the way open, snatching the child there up in your arms. I barely caught a glimpse of my own face looking back at me as you carried my child self up the stairs.

I left before I could introduce myself to you: my name is Heron, Mama. I haven't forgiven you yet, but maybe someday, I will. And when I do, I will travel back one last time, to that night you left me and Dad for the future. I'll tell you that your apology has finally been accepted, and will give you my blessing to live in exile, marooned in a future beyond all reach.

UTOPIA, LOL?

JAMIE WAHLS

Little is known about the brutally minimalist Jamie Wahls, who presumably lives in a mimetic reality peppered with digital simulacra like the rest of us. His fiction has appeared in *Sci Phi Journal*, *Clarkesworld*, *Strange Horizons*, with more to come.

"Utopia, LOL?" is an excitable meme-filled take on virtual reality, utopia, and the desires of human beings. It was nominated for the 2017 Nebula Award for Best Short Story.

He's shivering as he emerges from the pod. No surprise, he was frozen for like a billion years.

I do all the stuff on the script, all the "Fear not! You are a welcomed citizen of our Utopia!" stuff while I'm toweling him off. Apparently he's about as good as I am with awkward silence 'cause it's not three seconds before he starts making small talk.

"So, how'd you get to be a. . . ." He waves his hand.

"A Tour Guide to the Future?!"

"Yeah." The guy smiles gratefully at me. "I imagine you had a lot of training. . . ?"

"None whatsoever!" I chirp. He looks confused.

"Allocator chose me because I incidentally have the exact skills and qualifications necessary for this task, and because I had one of the highest enthusiasm scores!"

He accepts my extended hand, and steps down from the stasis

tube. He coughs. Probably whatever untreatable illness put him in cryo in the first place.

"Oh, hang on a second," I say. My uplink with Allocator tells me that the cough was noticed, and nites are inbound to remove some "cancer," which is probably something I should look up.

I'm confused and eager to get on with my incredible Tour Guide to the Future schtick but I have to close my eyes and wait because the nites STILL aren't here.

Patience was one of your weakest scores. But you proved you can wait. This is just like that final test Allocator put you through, the impossible one, where you could choose between one marshmallow NOW, or two marshmallows in one minute.

I quietly hum to myself while checking my messages, watching friends' lives, placing bets on the upcoming matches of TurnIntoASnake and SeductionBowl, and simulating what my life would be like if I had a longer attention span.

It would be very different.

> **#Allocator:** Good job waiting!
> **#Kit/dinaround:** :D thanks!

I beam at the praise, and check my time. I waited for eleven seconds!

Pretty dang good!

The old man clears his throat.

"You poor thing," I gush. "Your throat is messed up too! Don't worry, the nites are here."

He looks at me. "The . . . knights? I don't see anyone."

I cover my mouth with a hand as I giggle. "Oh, you can't see them. Well, you probably could with the right eyes, but we're actually in universe zero right now so the physics are really strict. The nites are in the air."

He looks up and around at the corners of the room. He's frowning. It makes me frown too.

"In the air," I explain. "We're breathing them. They're fixing your 'cancer.'"

He looks downright alarmed. I'm not an expert but that's not how I think a person should react to being cured of "cancer."

"Wow," he says. "Is that how far medical technology has come? Some kind of . . . medical nanobots?"

"They're not medical," I say. "They're pretty all-purpose."

On one hand I'm sort of tired of answering his questions because it's all really obvious stuff but also it's really fun! It's always super neat to watch their eyes light up as I tell them about the world and that's probably why I got picked for the position in the first place.

"Let's have ice cream!" I demand.

Four seconds ago, I demanded that we have ice cream. There is now an ice cream cone forming in my hand. It is taking FOREVER.

The old man sees it and flinches.

"Oh no!" I cry. "What's wrong? Do you hate ice cream?"

He looks at me with a really weird expression or maybe a couple different expressions.

"How are you doing that?" he asks. His voice is funny and tight.

"Oh. Allocator is making it for me?" I say. "Hey, let's get into another reality."

I spring up to my tiptoes. Moving is kinda fun but not as fun as it is in, like, the Manifold Wonders. Or in Bird Simulator. That one's really good.

"What?"

I blink. I almost forgot! It's time for me to be a good Tour Guide to the Future and repay Allocator's trust in me.

"Post-Singularity humanity now exists entirely as uploaded consciousnesses in distributed Matryoshka brains, living in trillions of universes presided over by our Friendly AI, Allocator," I say.

My ice cream is dripping! It can do that?

"Sorry, I didn't really understand that," he says. He doesn't sound sorry. "Is there anyone else I can talk to?"

"Sure!" I say.

> **#Kit/dinaround:** yo Big A, come talk to, uh
> **#Kit/dinaround:** hang on

"What's your name?" I ask. I forgot to ask earlier.

"Charlie," he says. "And you?"

"Kit/dinaround," I say, making extra-careful to pronounce the / so he won't miss it.

"Oh," he manages, "can I call you Kit?"

"I LOVE it!" I cry.

> **#Kit:** Did you hear that?
> **#Allocator:** Yes.
> **#Kit:** I LOVE IT

The old man is looking around the room. There's nothing to see, though. Just the cryo pod, the upload station, and the walls.

"Is there a way out of here?" he asks.

"Yeah." I point to the upload station, a bare slab with a half-sphere dome for the brain. "I mean, it's no demon altar, but this is UZ, so we can't exactly travel in style."

"Please," he says. "I don't understand. I have apparently been snatched from death and returned to good health. I am grateful for that. I'm happy to repay that effort in any way you require. . . ."

"... are you listening?"

"Oh!" I start. "Sorry."

Charlie blinks at me and I blink at him. I actually really like these lashes that Allocator gave me.

"Can I talk to the Allocator?" he asks.

The man flinches as the one of the walls tears away with a big whooshy sound effect.

Outside of our little blue room is the full majesty of the void. Space!: The Final Frontier looms before us, a whole lot of it.

Ol' terra firma is there, 90% nite-devoured to make more smart matter. Held in place above the gray slab by a trick of gravity (that I will totally remember to look up later), a little island is floating, a blue and tropical nature preserve. I squint, hoping to see an elephant.

I do not see an elephant.

The sun is almost entirely shrouded behind big spindly metal rods and arms. Whatever project Allocator is doing with Sol takes a lot of energy.

Charlie cries out, in fear and kind of pain. He doesn't look hurt, but I can't see his HP or anything so I don't know.

"Is it your cancer acting up again?!" I cry out. "Did Allocator not cure it?"

An enormous floating head forms in front of the window.

"Charlie Wilcox," it says mildly, "I am called Allocator. I am an AI tasked with the safety and flourishing of intelligent life."

"Hi," says Charlie, strangled-like.

"I understand you have many questions. I have prepared a tour to assist in your understanding of how life is lived in the future. Kit will be your guide. She is more competent than you would think."

"I'd hope," Charlie mutters.

"To begin the tour, simply lie on the provided table, with your head in the hemispherical dome. You will then experience a simulated reality. You will be in no danger and may return here at any time. Do you consent?"

"I suppose so," says Charlie.

Allocator's big ghostly face is blank. "Apologies, but I was created with several safety measures which prevent me from inferring consent. Do you consent?"

"Yeah," says Charlie.

"I require a 'Yes.'" Allocator patiently smiles.

"Yes, then."

"Thank you. Please lie comfortably on the table."

"Yaaaaaay!" I say, trying to force some enthusiasm because c'mon obviously we're uploading and who even listens to contracts before agreeing to them anymore? If you listen too close, people can't play pranks on you!

Charlie tentatively lays on the table, and scoots his butt up until his head is under the dome.

"Am I supposed to feel anythiunnnnnnggg," he drools, going limp.

> **#Allocator:** Good work.
> **#Allocator:** Where to?

"Eeeeee!" I squeeeeeee. "You're letting me pick?"

> **#Allocator:** Yes.
> **#Allocator:** Obviously.

"Oh my goodness," I say. "Uh . . . but what if I choose wrong?"

> **#Allocator:** I have a hunch that you won't.
> **#Allocator:** The "hunch" in this case is

an identical copy of your mind, to whom
I'm feeding inputs and reading her behavior as she makes it, thus allowing me to
deterministically predict what the "real"
you will choose.

"Sigh," I say. "Could you not?"

#Allocator: I *could* not.
#Allocator: Would you kindly pick a U?

"Fiiiiine." I roll my eyes. "Ummm . . . Oh! Bird Simulator!"

#Allocator: Great choice. ;)
#Allocator: Close your eyes.

FWOOSH I'm a bird haha!

I nip through the air, just above the snow on the treeline. The air
smells incredible, like forest pine. I'm darting around like a cross
between a rocket and a fly. My tiny bird heart is pounding like the
itty-bittiest drum and golly but I do feel alive.

#CharlieSamarkand: aaaaaaaaaaaaaaaaaaaaaa
aaaaaaaaaaa
#CharlieSamarkand: aaaaaaaaaaaaaaaaaaaaaa
aaaaaaaaaaa
#CharlieSamarkand: aaaaaaaaaaaaaohgodwhat
'shappening
#Kit: Charlie!
#CharlieSamarkand: what? what is happening what

#Kit: You're a bird!

#CharlieSamarkand: I NOTICED THANK YOU

#CharlieSamarkand: WHY ARE WE BIRDS

#Kit: That's a really philosophical question!

#Kit: Why were we humans??

#CharlieSamarkand: WHAT

He's flapping really hard, so I fly under him to show how you can just sort of coast.

He's this really little cute bird. I guess I am, too, 'cause I think there's only one bird you can be in Bird Simulator. Bird Simulator is more of a game than a proper U, but it's also way fun.

#Kit: You don't have to flap constantly to be a bird!

#Kit: Never give up! Trust your instincts!

#Kit: Do a barrel roll!

#CharlieSamarkand: YOU'RE THE WORST GUIDE

#Kit: >:(

#CharlieSamarkand: HOW ARE WE EVEN COMMUNICATING

#Kit: haha

"What was *that*?" Charlie demands. He's pale and sweating.

"Biiiiiiird Simulator!" I crow, because, "crow," Bird Simulator? Get it?

It is a pun.

Charlie looks at me like I'm crazy, which, sure, yeah.

"I want a new guide," he demands, to Allocator.

The face returns. "I'm afraid I can't do that."

"Why?" asks Charlie. His voice comes thick and he looks like he could screamcry, which is like screaming while crying except even more frustrated and hopeless. I get serious, 'cause I'm kind of friends with him now and you get serious when a friend is gonna screamcry.

"It may be difficult to believe," says Allocator, "but Kit is one of the more relatable humans you could have as your guide. And, she is the *only* guide we keep on hand for cryogenically frozen patrons. You're really very uncommon.

"There are trillions of humans. However, you would not recognize a sliver of one percent of them as anything other than frightening, incomprehensible aliens. Not just their forms, which are inconstant, but their minds as well."

"Her," speaks Charlie, all flat.

"Yes, her," says Allocator, a little sharply, and I feel bad for Charlie.

"Hey!" I object. "What's the big idea with letting me take Charles into a U that he hates?"

"It was the universe you selected," says Allocator mildly.

"I'm not a giant superbrain!" I protest.

"This is all part of my superbrain plan," Allocator explains, *mysterious like a supervillain.* "Would you like to try a different simulation?"

I glance at Charlie. He's looking all dubious at the brain-helmet of the upload station.

"In a second," I say, because oh my glob I want to get out of this room that doesn't have even a single unicorn in it but I also want to be a better guide. "And Charlie picks the U."

They both look at me.

"He would have no idea what to pick," protests Allocator.

"Actually . . ." says Charlie. "Could I get a directory of available universes?"

"There are trillions," says Allocator.

"Well, can you just," Charlie waves his hand, "give me an overview? Of some categories?"

I try waving my hand like Charlie did. I like it. "Yeah! Give him some categories!"

Allocator sighs, real put-upon. "I will do my best. Please note that at least two-thirds of the simulations would be sufficiently alien to your mind so as to cause extreme trauma. I will exclude those."

"Like what?" I demand.

"Floor Tile Simulator."

"What!" I demand. I'm demanding a ton today! "No way! I love FloTiSim!"

"You . . ." Charlie looks all skeptical_fry.pic. "You look at tiles?"

"No, you ARE tiles!"

"And you . . ."

"People walk on you!"

I'm really underselling it. The sensation of being *edged* where your body has stark boundaries and stillness inside, no little fluttering feelings like a bird heart thub-thubbing away, no squashy boobs or butts or venom sacs to bump or sit on. Everything is rocky and stark and permanent, even your own mind.

I get some of my best thinking done when I'm a tile. I can see my underlying brain architecture and all the little weights on the scales, the direct causal chain of "Kit doesn't like snakes because of that one prank played a while ago and that's why Temple of Doom is not a fun U for her," the behind-the-scenes machinery. My mind gets like an obelisk, resolute and above everything. And I can finish a thought without my stupid brain interrupting.

"And you're . . . hard!"

He makes that face again. "Okay, maybe we should exclude those."

"I have made a list," says Allocator. "I have taken the liberty of highlighting the one I expect you would most appreciate."

Allocator flashes something up so only Charles can see it.

"Hey!" I protest.

"Oh," Charlie smiles, and it's a certain kind of smile, like when you get back into a body you made a hundred years ago and you're a different person now and wearing the old suit makes you miss your past self like they're an old friend. "That sounds really nice."

"I'm glad you think so," says Allocator. "Please, get comfortable."

"What is it?" I demand, but I'm also excited, because I like surprises.

Charles glances at Allocator, then back to me. He's smiling, and my heart does little leaps to see that Al and I made him happy, but also c'mon freaking tell me.

"Is it your secret Terra project?" I ask.

"No," says Allocator. "You'll learn about that soon enough."

And he sounds sort of melancholy but why he would bother to be ominous and foreshadowing for my sake I don't even know!

Charles lies down on the upload table and makes a more dignified exit this time.

> **#Allocator:** Doing great, Kit.
> **#Kit:** TELLMETELLMETELLME
> **#Allocator:** No.
> **#Kit:** >:^O
> **#Allocator:** Ready?

Okay so I probably coulda shoulda guessed from how straight-laced Charles is that we'd be going to something really mundane, but I didn't realize that he was taking it to the point of parody.

We're in *Middle Earth*.

Ugggggghh. Glitter_barf.pic

Charles looks over at me. He's dressed like that one guy. The secret king who lived in the woods and was pure of heart . . . and *then there were no deconstructions or plot twists whatsoever.*

Charles looks pretty puling pleased with himself. At least until he sees me.

"Kit?" he asks, tentatively. He's backing away.

I'm the whatever, the big thing. The big demon thing. Whatever.

"You're a Balrog?" he asks.

"IT WAS A PHASE." Ugh.

I start changing into whatever the local equivalent of an ironic catgirl bath maiden is.

Charles watches, confused, as my body flickers through a bunch of different templates, but then the piping of stupid flutes harkens the approach of wankers, and he gets distracted looking around.

Yes, it's a splendorous elvish conclave. Yes, it's green and vibrant, untouched by the tides of strife or decay. Yes, of course it's inhabited by beautiful and mysterious immortals. Siiiiiigh.

This is as bad as that U about Pizza: Extra Sausage.

Okay so the thing about the hardcore roleplayers is that they play out their entire freaking lives start to finish inside of one U. Like, they do that whole "birth" thing and then they wrinkle and die, unless they're Beautiful and Mysterypoo Immortans or whatev.

And to really get the experience, for people who aren't content to just do a boring thing really to-the-hilt for a century, you can block off your other memories, so you don't even know you're roleplaying. You don't know you're in someone's U. You just think all the stuff about "war" and "orcs" and "scarcity" is the way that everything *is.*

I might be doing that right now *how would I even know.*

I select an elf body, but like, a really dorky one with dumb bangs. I don't want them to think I care.

The locals arrive, all self-importanty.

"'sup, hail to the elf king," I say. Whatever.

"I am Princess Elwen," says one with purple eyes and silver hair. Her eyebrows twitch in polite skepticism as she looks me over.

Charles looks super giddy like he can't believe he's doing this. He strides forward—do you get it, *strides*—and announces himself.

"I am . . . Charles-lemagne!"

#Kit: Oh My Stupid Sparkly Elf Goddess

#Allocator: Not to your liking?

#Kit: The plot there is so straightforward and unsurprising and mainstream that it hurts

#Allocator: Well, most fantasy settings you've experienced are inspired by LoTR.

#Kit: It's so BASIC

#Allocator: Is Charles happy?

#Kit: YES, IT'S ABSURD

#Allocator: Then you're doing a good job.

#Kit: aaaaaaaaaa

#Allocator: My calculations indicate he'll be staying there about ten years.

#Kit:

#Kit:

#Kit:

#Allocator: I acknowledge your feelings on the matter.

#Kit: no

#Allocator: I think it's best if you return when he's done. I'll be able to show you my project then.

#Kit: in a decade

#Allocator: Yes.

```
#Kit: that's literally forever
#Kit: I'll be so different by then. What
if I can't guide him TO THE MAX?
#Allocator: I expect you'll be able to.
#Allocator: I expect it mathematically.
#Kit: quit deterministically predicting
my life!
#Allocator: No. :)
#Allocator: Anyway, see you in a decade.
```

Professor Kittredge raised an eyebrow, and his lips twitched in a hint of a smile.

"Elementary, really," he pronounced, gazing over the assembled. One of them was the killer . . . and piece by piece, the evidence was becoming impossible to deny. It was time, at long last, to bring this plot to a close . . .

. . . but first, he would indulge himself in a delicious parlor scene.

"Well?" demanded Madame Plumwimple, hands clenching nervously in her petticoats. "Are you going to tell us?"

"YES," buzzed Killbot3000. "RELINQUISH THE INFORMATION. KILLBOT COMMANDS IT. WHICH OF US TERMINATED THE WORTHLESS FLESHBAG?"

"In due time, Killbot, in due time." The professor lit his pipe and waved out the match. "And why so anxious? Surely it's not . . . a guilty conscience?"

"WHAT," protested Killbot3000, its enormous metal-crushing claws clenching nervously in its petticoats. "N-NO, NOTHING OF THE SORT. KILLBOT JUST . . . HAS TO GET HOME TO THE KIDS."

"Mm," said the professor, smile growing wider. "I'm sure."

The phone began to ring, a high, shrill note. Everyone jumped, the professor included.

"Er, excuse me," said the professor. He picked up the phone and held it to his ear.

#Allocator: Kit.

The professor blinked. "Er, I beg your pardon?"

#Allocator: It's time.

"Ah, what do you—"

#Kit:
#Kit:
#Kit: whoa
#Kit: I was doing the thing!
#Allocator: You were.
#Kit: The memory thing!
#Allocator: Yes.
#Kit: aaaaaaaaa
#Kit: don't let me do that again
#Allocator: I won't, until the next time you ask me to.
#Kit: Creeper >:p
#Kit: Ok hang on

I put down the phone. It's the ancient kind that you work with two hands, so I have to put it down twice.

"Okay, later, everybody!" I pronounce. "Allocator needs me for a thing."

"BUT WAIT," Killbot3000 protests, beeping urgently, "WHICH OF US ASSASSINATED PRESIDENT WOOFINGTON?"

"Oh." I tilt my head and try to remember. "Oh, it was Miss Plum Whatever."

They're all giving me looks and the looks are pretty different from each other but that's okay because I need to hurry up and save superbuddy Charlie from his stupid mainstream plot!

"Okay later everybody!" I say. "Gee-two-gee byeeeeeeee—"

I pop into the stupid LoTR U and just rock the Balrog bod. Hashtag deal with it.

I spread my wings and clear my throat, to get all the boldface out.

"YO," I bellow.

"Charles-lemagne" is walking up the dangly bridge suspended with sparkly elvish rope. He's wearing fine elvish cloth woven by blessed maidens or whatever. He has a real unhappy look on his face, like Killbot3000 but without the baleful red eye endlessly seeking out vulnerable areas.

He sees me and does a double take. "Beast!" he shouts, but his heart isn't really in it.

"Hey!" I protest.

I pout. He blinks at me.

"Kit?"

"Who'd you think it was, some kind of stuffy, condescending detective born out of my ambivalent disgust with myself for playing memory games?"

"What?"

"Get in the portal, loser, we're going to Bird Simulator."

———————

Then we were birds for a year and it was exactly what we both needed.

We're in the sterile white room, the room where I met him. We have ice cream.

"Living in a perfect conclave got old faster than I would have thought," he says. He looks all pensive and soul-searchy so I'm really trying hard to pay attention to his intimate revelations but also, in U zero, ice cream melts.

"How was the elf-sex?"

He looks at me sidelong like for some reason he's annoyed.

"It was great," he concedes.

I make a mad noise 'cause I've decided to hate Elwen 'cause sometimes it's really fun to hate someone and I think she and I would be good for each other in that way.

"But we didn't *do* anything. I wanted to fight orcs and save Middle-earth, but they just sat around being perfect."

"Right??" And my blackrom hatecrush was totally justified. "I hate those worlds where everyone talks about how perfect they are and everything is also perfect and nothing ever happens. It's like, you have ultimate access to the fundament of your reality and you've decided the best use of your eternal time is to be smug."

He nods, and I guess that's all I'm getting. But that's okay, I like him.

"I'd like to be productive," he says suddenly.

"Whaddya mean?"

"Productive?" He looks at me askance. "Do you . . . not have that, anymore? I want to benefit other people."

And my heart swells a couple sizes. 'Cause that's really noble of him! And it takes a super dedicated and creative and determined person to run a U but it's a super rewarding path.

I'm about to tell him about a couple game ideas I've been kicking around when—

#Allocator: I believe this is my cue.

The wall flickers and becomes space, and I guess Charles got used to a bunch of magic stuff happening just whenever 'cause he doesn't even flinch. Allocator's big head fades into view.

"Hello," says Allocator.

"Hello again," says Charles.

"You may have wondered why I brought you here."

Charles shrugs. "I just followed Kit."

Allocator purses its big digital lips impatiently, which since it doesn't have emotions was definitely only for our benefit. But now that I'm thinking about it, so is absolutely everything that it does.

"I have a proposition for you," says Allocator. "Something which almost no being native to this time would even consider, and you are uniquely suited for:

"The human population continues to grow. Within the Matryoshka brains, humans create copies of themselves, and create children. Human reproduction is a central value of the species, and I will not interfere. However, because of the exponential growth of trillions, the race is voracious for new material to convert into computing substrate."

"Okay," says Charles, and I'm doing Charles's hand-wavey thing at Allocator because seriously who doesn't know all that.

"My programmers were very cautious, and feared that I might accidentally annihilate humanity, or worse," says Allocator. "So I have many limitations on my behavior. In particular, I cannot duplicate or create intelligences. I cannot leave this location. And I cannot extend my influence outside of the Sol system."

"Uh huh?" asks Charles, looking kind of interested. And this is new to me too.

"I have created many long-distance probes," says Allocator.

The part of me that's still kind of a detective notes, *at last, the pieces are coming together.*

"I would like you to pilot an exploratory mission to nearby stars, and analyze their readiness for conversion into human habitat."

"Absolutely," says Charles.

"No!" I blurt. "That sounds really terrible."

"Kit may be right," says Allocator. "Even with all available safety precautions, remaining in contact with you would still qualify as 'extending my influence.' You will be alone amidst the stars."

"Yes," says Charles.

"No!" I say. "You're the quiet, straight-laced one! What happened to that?"

"I spent a decade bored out of my mind in an elf village." Charlie is looking at me sidelong, with sort of a confused smile. "Why are you even worried?"

Why was I so worried?

"I must warn you," Allocator says heavily, "of the risks. Even with all possible precautions, I still calculate a one-in-five chance that, for whatever reason, you will never return. It may mean your death."

Oh that's why I was worried!

Wait but how did I know that—

"I understand," says Charles. "But someone's got to do it, right? For humanity? And apparently I'm the best there is." He grins.

"I require affirmative consent."

"WAIT!" I shout. Everything is happening faster than my ability to track and that's pretty unusual! And also, something super critical just made sense to me!

"Wait!" I say. "Charlie, don't you get it? You're the best there is, because you're not from here and have a mind that works the way that Allocator needs!"

"Yeah?"

"And it's *manipulating* you! It's way way way smarter than us! It knows what I'm going to do ten years in advance! So when it pulled you out of cryo. . . ." I blink. "It probably pulled you out of cryo *for this*! And pushed me to push you into Bird Simulator so you would want the dumb stupid Lord of the Stupid U, so you would get bored and want this!"

Charlie blinks a few times, and looks at Allocator.

"Yes, that's all true," says Allocator evenly.

Charlie looks from me to Allocator for a few long seconds. His face is wistful and a little sad.

"I consent."

I screamcry and leap to my feet. The walls that had opened to show us the stars are now closing around Charlie. Allocator's doing.

"Kit," says Charlie, gently. I'm gripping his hands as his back is being slowly absorbed into the wall. "It's fine. This is what I want."

"Well sure, you think that *now*!"

"Kit." Charlie is smiling at me, sad and kind. "I want to thank you—"

"Oh, *nuh-uh* you don't!" I protest. "*Nuh-uh* to this tender moment. Do you . . . do you want to go be birds again?"

"Thank you," says Charlie. "You were the best guide I could have asked for."

And Charlie is swallowed up. Except for his hands.

"Kit," begins Allocator, after a moment.

"Not feelin' this scene," I say, tightening my grip. My voice is thick. "Would love it if I could safeword out."

"I acknowledge your feelings on the matter."

I look at Charlie's hands in my hands.

"This is the superbrain plan," apologizes Allocator.

And I see it. I really do.

Allocator has to make the people he needs. And for this, he made me.

"Will Charles be happy?" I ask, in a small voice.

Allocator nods, eyes closed. "This will make him happier than either of us ever could."

Charlie's hands slip out of my grip, and I watch them sink away, until nothing remains but the sterile white wall.

And he's gone.

I stand there for a few seconds, looking at a room that contains only me and the giant floaty head. I exhale, and a tear rolls down my cheek. Which is weird. I didn't know I could do that, here.

"Here," says Allocator. "Let me show you something."

The wall turns transparent.

Attached to this room is another, open to space. Inside, nested on the walls, are cylindrical, spindly objects. Allocator's probes. There are only a few left.

As I watch, one probe's engines light with a tiny, fuel-efficient blue glow, and it jets away from us, accelerating.

It doesn't do anything but shoot away all stately and somber into the great unknown, but yeah.

It was him.

I watch as Charlie leaves, as he shoots out past the sun and that stupid terra firma with no elephants. I watch until he's only a twinkle in that great big black starry night and then I can't see him at all.

I look over the hangar bay.

It's almost entirely empty.

. . . *oh.*

The other shoe drops.

It's this really heavy sensation that most U's will sort of mute for you. The moment when you realize something big. Out here, I feel it full force.

I should have realized. But there was no way for me to realize, because if that was possible, Allocator would have done something different. I wipe at my eyes.

"You dick," I say, not for the first time.

"I'm sorry," says Allocator. "I know this may seem unlikely to you, but I do experience regret. And I'm sorry."

"So," I ask, "are you going to seal off my memories of this?"

Again, I don't say.

"If you wish it," says Allocator.

"Not really," I say. I'm sick of memory games. "But it's important, isn't it?"

"Yes," says Allocator, simply.

It doesn't say anything more, which suggests that I'm going to talk myself into this.

Why do we do this? Some alarmingly large number of my past selves have sat in this exact place, then decided to keep the cycle going—

"Oh," I sigh, surprising myself. "I want to give them the stars."

Allocator just smiles.

"I understand." I take a deep breath. "And I consent."

MOTHER TONGUES

S. QIOUYI LU

S. Qiouyi Lu writes, translates, and interprets between two coasts of
the Pacific. Their fiction and poetry have appeared in *Asimov's*, *F&SF*,
and *Uncanny*, and their translations have appeared in *Clarkesworld*.
They edit the flash fiction and poetry magazine *Arsenika*.

"Mother Tongues" is a painful portrait of the parental sacrifices
made by first-generation immigrants and of how identity and relationships are tied up with language.

"Thank you very much," you say, concluding the oral portion
of the exam. You gather your things and exit back into the
brightly lit hallway. Photos line the walls: the Eiffel Tower, the Great
Wall of China, Machu Picchu. The sun shines on each destination,
the images brimming with wonder. You pause before the Golden
Gate Bridge.

"右拐就到了," the attendant says. You look up. His blond hair is
as standardized as his Mandarin, as impeccable as his crisp shirt
and tie. You've just proven your aptitude in English, but hearing
Mandarin still puts you at ease in the way only a mother tongue
does. You smile at the attendant, murmuring a brief thanks as you
make your way down the hall.

You turn right and enter a consultation room. The room is small
but welcoming, potted plants adding a dash of green to the otherwise plain creams and browns of the furniture and walls. A litera-

ture rack stands to one side, brochures in all kinds of languages tucked into its pockets, creating a mosaic of sights and symbols. The section just on English boasts multiple flags, names of different varieties overlaid on the designs: U.S. English–Standard. U.K. English–Received Pronunciation. Singaporean English–Standard. Nigerian English–Standard . . . Emblazoned on every brochure is the logo of the Linguistic Grading Society of America, a round seal with a side view of a head showing the vocal tract.

You pick up a Standard U.S. English brochure and take a seat in one of the middle chairs opposite the mahogany desk that sits before the window. The brochure provides a brief overview of the grading system; your eyes linger on the A-grade description: *Speaker engages on a wide variety of topics with ease. (Phonology?) is standard; speaker has a broad vocabulary* . . . You take a quick peek at the dictionary on your phone. *Phonology*—linguistic sound systems. You file the word away to remember later.

The door opens. A woman wearing a blazer and pencil skirt walks in, her heels clacking against the hardwood floor, her curled hair bouncing with every step. You stand to greet her and catch a breath of her perfume.

"Diana Moss," she says, shaking your hand. Her name tag also displays her job title: *Language Broker.*

"Jiawen Liu," you reply. Diana takes a seat across from you; as you sit, you smooth out your skirt, straighten your sleeves.

"Is English all right?" Diana asks. "I can get an interpreter in if you'd prefer to discuss in Mandarin."

"English is fine," you reply. You clasp your hands together as you eye Diana's tablet. She swipes across the screen and taps a few spots, her crimson nails stark against the black barrel of the stylus.

"Great," she says. "Well, let's dive right in, shall we? I'm showing that you've been in the U.S. for, let's see, fifteen years now? Wow, that's quite a while."

You nod. "Yes."

"And you used to be an economics professor in China, is that correct?"

You nod again. "Yes."

"Fantastic," Diana says. "Just one moment as I load the results; the scores for the oral portion always take a moment to come in . . ."

Your palms are clammy, sweaty; Diana twirls the stylus and you can't help feeling a little dizzy as you watch. Finally, Diana props the tablet up and turns it toward you.

"I'm pleased to inform you that your English has tested at a C-grade," she says with a broad smile.

Your heart sinks. Surely there's been some kind of error, but no, the letter is unmistakable: bright red on the screen, framed with flourishes and underlined with signatures; no doubt the certificate is authentic. Diana's perfume is too heady now, sickly sweet; the room is too bright, suffocating as the walls shrink in around you.

"I . . ." you say, then take a breath. "I was expecting better."

"For what it's worth, your scores on the written and analytical portions of the test were excellent, better than many native speakers of English in the U.S.," Diana says.

"Then what brought my score down?"

"Our clients are looking for a certain . . . *profile* of English," Diana says, apologetic. "If you're interested in retesting, I can refer you to an accent reduction course—I've seen many prospective sellers go through the classes and get recertified at a higher grade."

She doesn't mention how much the accent reduction course costs, but from your own research, you know it's more than you can afford.

"Ms. Liu?" Diana says. She's holding out a tissue; you accept it and dab at your eyes. "Why don't you tell me what you're trying to accomplish? Maybe we can assist you."

You take in a deep breath as you crumple the tissue into your fist. "My daughter Lillian just got into Stanford, early decision," you say.

"Congratulations!"

"Yes, but we can't afford it." C-grade English sells at only a fraction of A-grade English; you'd rather keep your English than sell it for such a paltry sum that would barely put a dent in textbooks and supplies, never mind tuition and housing.

"There are other tracks you can consider," Diana says, her voice gentle. "Your daughter can go to a community college, for instance, and then transfer out to Stanford again—"

You shake your head.

"Community colleges in the San Gabriel Valley are among the top in the nation," Diana continues. "There's no shame in it."

You're unconvinced. What if she can't transfer out? You and Lillian can't risk that; a good education at a prestigious school is far too important for securing Lillian's future. No, better to take this opportunity that's already been given to her and go with it.

Diana stands and goes over to the literature rack. She flips through a few brochures.

"You know," Diana says as she strides back to you, "China's really hot right now—with their new open-door policy, lots of people are (clamoring?) to invest there; I have people calling me all the time, asking if I have A-grade Mandarin."

She sets a brochure down on the desk and sits back in the executive chair across from you.

"Have you considered selling your Mandarin?"

You trace your hands over the brochure, feeling the embossed logo. China's flag cascades down to a silhouette of Beijing's skyline; you read the Simplified characters printed on the brochure, your eyes skimming over them so much more quickly than you skim over English.

"How much?" you ask.

Diana leans in. "A-grade Mandarin is going for as much as $800,000 these days."

Your heart skips a beat. That would be enough to cover Lillian's college, with maybe a little bit left over—it's a tantalizing number. But the thought of going without Mandarin gives you pause: it's the language you think in, the language that's close to your heart in the way English is not; it's more integral to who you are than any foreign tongue. English you could go without—Lillian's Mandarin is good enough to help you translate your way around what you need—but Mandarin?

"I'm . . . I'm not sure," you say, setting down the brochure. "Selling my Mandarin . . ."

"It's a big decision, for sure," Diana says. She pulls a small, silver case out from the pocket of her blazer and opens it with a *click*. "But, if you change your mind . . ."

She slides a sleek business card across the table.

" . . . call me."

You decide to go for a week without Mandarin, just to see if you can do it. At times, the transition feels seamless: so many of the people in the San Gabriel Valley are bilingual; you get by fine with only English. Your job as a librarian in the local public library is a little trickier, though; most of your patrons speak English, but a few do not.

You decide to shake your head and send the Mandarin-only speakers over to your coworker, who also speaks Mandarin. But when lunch time comes around, she sits beside you in the break room and gives you a curious look.

"为什么今天把顾客转给我?" she asks.

You figure that you might as well tell her the truth: "I want to sell my Mandarin. I'm seeing what it would be like without it."

"卖你的普通话?" she responds, an incredulous look on her face. "神经病!"

You resent being called crazy, even if some part of you wonders if this is a foolish decision. Still, you soldier on for the rest of the week in English. Your coworker isn't always there to cover for you when there are Mandarin-speaking patrons, and sometimes you break your vow and say a few quick sentences in Mandarin to them. But the rest of the time, you're strict with yourself.

Conversation between you and Lillian flows smoothly, for the most part. Normally, you speak in a combination of English and Mandarin with her, and she responds mostly in English; when you switch to English-only, Lillian doesn't seem to notice. On the occasions when she does speak to you in Mandarin, you hold back and respond in English, too, your roles reversed.

At ATMs, you choose English instead of Chinese. When you run errands, "thank you" replaces "谢谢." It's only until Friday rolls around and you're grocery shopping with your mother that not speaking in Mandarin becomes an issue.

You're in the supermarket doing your best to ignore the Chinese characters labeling the produce: so many things that you don't know the word for in English. But you recognize them by sight, and that's good enough; all you need is to be able to pick out what you need. If you look at things out of the corner of your eye, squint a little bit, you can pretend to be illiterate in Chinese, pretend to navigate things only by memory instead of language.

You can cheat with your mother a little bit: you know enough Cantonese to have a halting conversation with her, as she knows both Cantonese and Mandarin. But it's frustrating, your pauses between words lengthy as you try to remember words and tones.

"干吗今天说广东话?" your mother asks in Mandarin. She's pushing the shopping cart—she insists, even when you offer—and one of the wheels is squeaking. She hunches over the handle, but her eyes are bright.

"Ngo jiu syut Gwongdungwaa," you reply in Cantonese. Except it's not exactly that you *want* to speak Cantonese; you have to, for now. You don't know how to capture the nuance of everything you're going through in Cantonese, either, so you leave it at that. Your mother gives you a look, but she doesn't bring it up again and indulges you, speaking Cantonese as the two of you go around the supermarket and pile the shopping cart high with produce, meat, and fish.

You load the car with the groceries and help your mother into the passenger seat. As you adjust the mirrors, your mother speaks again.

"你在担心什么?" she asks. Startled, you look over at her. She's peering at you, scrutinizing you; you can never hide anything from her. Of course she can read the worry on your face, the tension in your posture; of course she knows something's wrong.

"Ngo jau zou yat go han zungjiu dik kyutding," you respond, trying to communicate the weight on your shoulders.

"什么决定?" Ma replies.

You can't find the words to express the choice you have to make in Cantonese. Every time you grasp for the right syllables, they come back in Mandarin; frustrated, you switch back to Mandarin and reply,

"我要用我的普通话来赚钱去送Lillian上大学。"

You expect your mother to scold you, to tell you about the importance of your heritage and language—she's always been proud of who she is, where she's from; she's always been the first to teach you about your own culture—but instead her expression softens, and she puts a hand over yours, her wrinkled skin warm against your skin.

"哎, 嘉嘉, 没有别的办法吗?"

Your nickname is so tender on her tongue. But you've thought through all other avenues: you don't want Lillian to take out loans and be saddled with so much debt like your friends' children; you don't want her to bear such a burden her entire life, not while you're still paying off debts, too. You can't rely on Lillian's father to provide for her, not after he left your family and took what little money you had. And although Lillian's been doing her best to apply for scholarships, they're not enough.

You shake your head.

The two of you sit in silence as you start the car and drive back to your mother's place. The sun sets behind you, casting a brilliant glow over the earth, washing the sky from orange to blue. As you crest over a hill, the sparkling lights of the city below glitter in the darkness, showing you a million lives, a million dreams.

When you get to your mother's house, you only have one question to ask her.

"如果你需要做同样的决定," you say, "你也会这样做吗?"

You don't know what it would have been like if you were in Lillian's shoes, if your mother had to make the same decision as you. But as your mother smiles at you, sadness tinging the light in her eyes, the curve of her lips, you know she understands.

"当然," she says.

Of course.

The waiting room is much starker than the consultation room you were in before: the seats are less comfortable, the temperature colder; you're alone except for a single TV playing world news at a low volume.

You read the paperwork, doing your best to understand the details of the procedure—for all you pride yourself on your English, though, there are still many terms you don't understand completely:

The Company's (proprietary?) algorithms (iterate?) through near-infinite (permutations?) of sentences, extracting a neural map. The (cognitive?) load on the brain will cause the Applicant to experience a controlled stroke, and the Applicant's memory of the Language will be erased. Common side effects include: temporary disorientation, nausea. Less common side effects include partial (aphasia?) of non-target languages and (retrograde?) amnesia. Applicant agrees to hold Company harmless . . .

You flip over to the Chinese version of the contract, and, while some of the terms raise concern in you, you've already made your decision and can't back out now. You scan the rest of the agreement and sign your name at the bottom.

The lab is clinical, streamlined, with a large, complicated-looking machine taking up most of the room. An image of the brain appears on a black panel before you.

"Before we begin," the technician says, "do you have any questions?"

You nod as you toy with your hospital gown. "Will I be able to learn Mandarin again?"

"Potentially, though it won't be as natural or easy as the first time around. Learning languages is usually harder than losing them."

You swallow your nervousness. *Do it for Lillian.* "Why can't you make a copy of the language instead of erasing it?"

The technician smiles ruefully. "As our current technology stands, the imaging process has the unfortunate side effect of suppressing neurons as it replicates them . . ."

You can't help but wonder cynically if the reason why the neurons have to be suppressed is to create artificial scarcity, to inflate demand in the face of limited supply. But if that scarcity is what allows you to put Lillian through college, you'll accept it.

The technician hooks electrodes all over your head; there's a faint hum, setting your teeth on edge.

As the technician finishes placing the last of the electrodes on your head, certain parts of the brain on the panel light up, ebbing and flowing, a small chunk in the back active; you try to recall the areas of the brain from biology classes in university, and, while different parts of your brain start to light up, you still don't remember the names of any of the regions.

The technician flips a couple switches, then types a few commands. The sensation that crawls over you is less of a shock than a tingling across your scalp. Thoughts flash through your mind too fast for you to catch them; you glance up at the monitor and see light firing between the areas the technician pointed out, paths carving through the brain and flowing back and forth. The lights flash faster and faster until they become a single blur, and as you watch, your world goes white.

The technician and nurse keep you at the institute for a few hours to monitor your side effects: slight disorientation, but that fades as the time goes by. They ask if you have anyone picking you up; you insist that you're fine taking public transportation by yourself, and the technician and nurse relent. The accountant pays you the first installment of the money, and soon you're taking the steps down from the institute's main doors, a cool breeze whipping at your hair.

The bus ride home is . . . strange. As you go from west Los Angeles toward the San Gabriel Valley, the English dominating billboards and signs starts to give way to Chinese. Although you can still understand the balance of the characters, know when they're backward in the rearview mirrors, you can't actually *read* them—they're no more than shapes: familiar ones, but indecipherable ones. You suck down a deep breath and will your heart to stop beating so quickly. It will take time to adjust to this, just as it took time to adjust to being thrown into a world of English when you first immigrated to the United States.

A corner of the check sticks out of your purse.
You'll be okay.

Your family is celebrating Chinese New Year this weekend. You drive with Lillian over to your mother's senior living apartment; you squeeze in through the door while carrying a bag of fruit. Your mother is cooking in the tiny kitchenette, the space barely big enough for the both of you. She's wearing the frilly blue apron with embroidered teddy bears on it, and you can't help but smile as you inhale the scent of all the food frying and simmering on the stove.

"Bongmong?" you say in Cantonese. It's one of the few words you can remember—as the days passed, you realized that some of your Cantonese had been taken too, its roots intertwined and excised with your Mandarin.

"(???). (???????)," your mother says, gesturing toward the couch. You and Lillian sit down. A period drama plays on the television. The subtitles go by too fast for you to match sound to symbol; Lillian idly taps away on her phone.

A few moments pass like this, your gaze focused on the television as you see if you can pick up something, anything at all; sometimes, you catch a phrase that jogs something in your memory, but before you can recall what the phrase means, the sound of it and its meaning are already gone.

"(???)!"

Lillian gets up, and you follow suit. The small dining room table has been decked out with all kinds of food: glistening, ruby-red shrimp with caramelized onions; braised fish; stir-fried lotus root with sausage; sautéed vegetables . . . you wish you could tell your mother how good it looks; instead, you can only flash her a smile and hope she understands.

"(????????), (????????)," your mother says.

Lillian digs in, picking up shrimp with her chopsticks; you scold her and remind her of her manners.

"But (??????) said I could go ahead," Lillian says.

"Still," you reply. You place some food on your mother's plate first, then Lillian's; finally, you set some food on your own plate. Only after your mother's eaten do you take a bite.

Lillian converses with your mother; her Mandarin sounds a little stilted, starting and stopping, thick with an American accent, but her enthusiasm expresses itself in the vibrant conversation that flows around you. You stay quiet, shrinking into yourself as your mother laughs, as Lillian smiles.

You're seated between Lillian and your mother; the gap across the table from you is a little too big, spacing the three of you unevenly around the table. As the syllables cascade around you, you swear the spaces between you and your mother, between you and Lillian, grow larger and larger.

After dinner, as your mother washes up the dishes—again, she refuses your help—you and Lillian watch the Spring Gala playing on the television. An invited pop star from the U.S., the only white person on the stage, sings a love ballad in Mandarin. You don't need to know what she's saying to tell that she doesn't have an American accent.

"I bet she bought her Mandarin," Lillian says. It's an offhanded comment, but still you try to see if you can detect any disgust in her words.

"Is that so bad?" you ask.

"I don't know; it just seems a little ... (appropriative?), you know?"

You don't know. *Lillian* doesn't know. You were planning on telling her the instant you came home, but you didn't know how to bring it up. And now ... you want to keep your sacrifice a secret, because it's not about you—it was never about you. But it's only a matter of time before Lillian finds out.

You don't know how she'll react. Will she understand?

Lillian rests her head on your shoulder. You pull her close, your girl who's grown up so fast. You try to find the words to tell her what you'd do for her, how important it is that she has a good future, how much you love her and want only the best for her.

But all you have is silence.

IN THE SHARING PLACE
DAVID ERIK NELSON

David Erik Nelson is a science fiction author and essayist. He has written reference articles and textbooks, such as *Perspectives on Modern World History: Chernobyl*. He builds instruments, as he chronicles in *Junkyard Jam Band: DIY Musical Instruments and Noisemakers*. His short fiction has been featured in *Asimov's*, *Fantasy & Science Fiction*, *StarShipSofa*, and such anthologies as *The Best of Lady Churchill's Rosebud Wristlet*, *Steampunk II: Steampunk Reloaded*, *Steampunk III: Steampunk Revolution*, and *The Best Horror of the Year, Volume 10*.

"In the Sharing Place" deals with the stages of grief in losing the world one has always known.

Children are brought to the Sharing Place because a loved one has died.

You must always use the present perfect tense and passive voice: "A loved one has died." Not "A loved one is dead," and never "*this* killed a loved one" or "a loved one was killed by *that*" or even "a loved one died because of *the other thing*."

The actual circumstances of the death are inconsequential. They have nothing to do with why children are brought (note the passive voice) to the Sharing Place, nor when they will leave the Sharing Place.

Children are brought to the Sharing Place because a loved one has died and, despite being young, they may very well still suffer Rejection if they fail to process this grief.

And just about the only thing we can do for our children now is help them avoid Rejection.

I. DENIAL

There are three rules at the Children's Sharing Place. The first is that a child may leave at any time, provided they attest that they are ready to leave on two separate occasions.

The boy with the long hair that hangs over his eyes does not speak for his first two sessions in group. On the third session the first thing he says is that he is ready to leave.

He shouldn't even be here, he explains. His father isn't dead, he insists.

"Augie," you say, "your father has died."

Augie does not speak again for the remainder of the session.

The next day, he repeats that he is ready to leave.

You say nothing, because that is the therapeutic protocol. This protocol demands impartiality and discipline: A child who has self-selected to leave will not progress further if forced to stay in the Sharing Place. Worse yet, a non-progressing child could derail the others' progress.

You remain silent, but the other children attempt to talk sense into him. They Bargain. This is appropriate.

They tell Augie he can't go, because he just got there, because he hasn't resolved any of his issues, because he hasn't *Said It* yet, hasn't even started to *Say It*. They say that if he goes into the Waiting Room now, he's definitely going to get Rejected. They say that he *can* go but doesn't have to: he can still just go back to the dorms and then have dinner and then go to bed and then get up and then go to class and then return to their next session. He doesn't *have* to leave, even if he said he wants to leave. Fifty-seven minutes pass this way.

"Our time is almost up for today," you say.

Augie stands without a word and opens the Waiting Room Door. Beyond the Waiting Room Door is a small waiting room—just a pair of upholstered yellow chairs and a side table with a fan of three magazines. The top magazine is *Ranger Rick*. You have never been in the waiting room, and so do not know what the other two magazines may be. There is also a potted plant. There must be a draft, because the potted plant nods rhythmically, like the quiet old lady knitting in the rocking chair in *Goodnight Moon*.

And, of course, there is the other door, the EXIT. The word "EXIT" glows above it in red. It probably isn't even three long strides from the Waiting Room Door to the EXIT.

Augie steps through the Waiting Room Door and gingerly shuts it behind him. The door latch clicks, then there is the faint sigh of the EXIT door, followed by a big and sudden sound, like an alligator roaring and rolling in a swamp. And then silence.

"Our time is up for today," you begin to say, but just after you say "time," Augie's scream interrupts you. It is a truly agonized scream, loud and long and ragged. It doesn't end, so much as fade. There is whimpering and crying for a long time after. But this whimpering is quiet, and the other children in the Sharing Place understand your words this time. They file out the main door, back to the dorms and mess hall and everything else down here in their sheltered world.

2. ANGER

The second rule is that a child must eventually, in their own words, explain how their loved one(s) died. They must *Say It*. There are many levels to *Saying It*. It may start with:

"My father has died." And from there progress:

"My father is dead because of a gun."

"My father fired the bullet that killed him."

"My father committed suicide."

"My father committed suicide, because something went wrong in his brain."

"My father committed suicide, because something went wrong in his brain after the Event."

"My father heard the Bad Song."

"My father committed suicide after the Event, because he heard the Bad Song and listened."

And so on.

It is not abnormal for children to become extremely emotional as they attempt to *Say It* in various ways. Do not let this alarm you. It is a natural stage of grief, and it will pass. Children have a natural tendency toward Resilience. If a child is consistently extremely emotional during their own or another's act of grief, they may need to book Open Time in the Laughing Place or the Volcano Room. Open Time can be recommended (note the passive voice) in the "OTHER COMMENTS" section of the Incident Report.

3. BARGAINING

Three days after Augie has gone through the EXIT, Tilly stands and *Says It*, succinctly and dispassionately. You tell her that she's done a good job, and that you are proud of her. Other children do likewise. The shy boy next to her flashes her a quick smile, then looks away. He holds up his fist, and she bumps it. She smiles, relieved.

The boy begins to speak—perhaps to *Say It* himself, perhaps to say something else—and Tilly interrupts him without apology.

"I'm ready to leave," she says.

This is her second time attesting. Her first was fourteen weeks earlier. It was the first thing she said, two minutes into her first session. Almost none of the children present today were at that session. Almost all of those children have *Said It* and gone, or just gone (as was the case with Augie). To these children, Tilly is as much a staple of their sessions as the chairs and canned fruit and well-worn fidget toys.

You say nothing.

Tilly stands.

The shy boy next to Tilly is clearly distressed, but he does not speak.

Do not attempt to dissuade Tilly. Do not Bargain with her. The children can—and should—Bargain with Tilly. It is part of their grief, and it is appropriate.

"You don't have to go just 'cause you said it," a tall girl, Marianna, says. "You can still stay. At least another day."

"Marianna's right," another girl, Vanessa L., adds. "The Waiting Room will be there tomorrow, and next week, and forever." Barring natural disaster, this is correct: The Waiting Room *will* likely be there forever. But that doesn't mean one can *wait* forever: Food stores aren't dire yet, but they are dwindling. There is plenty of water, though. Our well is deep. It would not be inappropriate for you to correct Vanessa L., but you let her statement stand unchallenged.

Vanessa Z., who sits next to Vanessa L., is nodding. "Announcing it is just saying that you're *gonna* go. Like with Shane. He said it and *Said It*, but didn't go for another six weeks."

"It's all bullshit anyway," Bennie adds. He is small and young, but angry as an old cop. "Don't do their crap their way. Keep coming to sessions with us."

"You should at least stay until we've finished *Buffy the Vampire Slayer*," Jay Chen yips. He's an excitable boy. "There's only, like, one-third of the last season left. It won't even be a week."

Tilly shrugs. From prior sessions you know that she is a huge *Buffy* fan. But for many children their demeanor changes once they've *Said It*, and Tilly is one of those: Relieved of the weight of the things they haven't been saying, they expand back to their normal size—like a sponge that's had a cinderblock lifted off it—and in doing so draw into themselves. It's natural. It is part of their process.

"Augie went." This is Albert, with his chipmunk cheeks and glum Eeyore voice. "That didn't go great."

"Augie wasn't ready," Tilly says. "I'm ready."

"Belinda said she was ready." Belinda had been in the group for a month. She had *Said It*—and wept while doing so—and then over the next few sessions brightened, gaining strength and equilibrium, helping the other children talk their way forward in their grief. She'd announced her intention to leave, reaffirmed it the next week, and left that same day. Her nail polish had been a perfect robin's egg blue that day, glossy and flawless. The door had snicked shut behind her, and the scream that had followed had been long and high and ended with a string of babbled begging that had finally devolved into two words repeated so quickly that they'd sounded like the chugging of a ragged, dying lawnmower:

"*killmekillmekillmekillmekillmekillme . . .*"

"Belinda wasn't really ready," Tilly says. "I am very ready. I'm gone."

The shy boy next to Tilly—his name is Marcus, and he is new—speaks just to Tilly: "We could . . ."

Tilly stops and turns to him. He is knotting his fingers, twisting them against each other, digging painfully into his skin, but his voice is level and clear, if quiet. "We could . . . try that thing that you wanted to try, but that I was nervous about." He chews his lip, looks up at the room, then locks on to Tilly. "We could do that. We could do whatever you want if you stay."

His eyes are wide and desperate and lost. Tilly's mouth twitches, but she shakes her head without speaking.

Tilly leaves. The Waiting Room door latches shut. You all hear the sigh and thunk of the heavy EXIT door. Then silence.

Silence is presumed to be indicative of Acceptance (note the passive voice).

4. DEPRESSION

The group is dour with Tilly gone. This is odd, because Tilly hadn't been a ray of sunshine. She was usually morose and often irritable. Once, in the midst of an especially spirited session, Bennie had shouted at Tilly: "The only thing you like is stirring shit up and making everyone as miserable as you!"

Albert had called a Time Out and then, in his plodding voice, had taken Bennie to task: "That's not fair to Tilly," he'd said. "She doesn't like stirring shit up and making people feel bad. She doesn't *like* anything."

Everyone had laughed, including Tilly. Then Vanessa Z. had begun to cry and had kept doing so for five minutes and thirty-eight seconds before simply saying, "My brother is dead. He was nine, but he was Rejected anyway because of how Auntie died. My brother is not nine anymore, because he's dead." Her spirits had steadily improved since then, but she has yet to ask to leave.

No one seems to have much to say during the session following Tilly's exit, and so you say:

"My father had his grandfather's axe. The axe was old and it hung in our garage. It had been used *a lot*: The handle was dry and splintered and cracked, and the head was pretty rusty, except for the working edge, which Dad dressed before and after each use. My dad and his dad were both the youngest from big families, so I'd presumed my great-grandfather's axe was very old. Maybe a century? Maybe so. I always thought that was neat: A five-year-old smartphone was practically junk, but a hundred-year-old axe was as good as ever.

"Then one day Dad mentioned how often his dad had worn through axe handles—Dad grew up out in the country, and winter was harsh back then—and I realized that the handle on his grand-father's axe wasn't a handle my great-grandfather had ever even seen. On a hunch, I asked how long the head would last. 'Oh,' Dad had said, 'I dunno. Generations. It's hard steel. I only replaced this one once, when I first got the axe after Dad passed. The handle had dried and shrunk, hanging unused in his shed for so long, and the first time I hauled back to split some stove wood, the head went whanging off into the brush. Never found it.'"

You have never spoken to any of the children about your life before the bunker and the Sharing Place. None of them have ever asked. They are politely attentive now. You know they'll start to lose focus soon.

"So, my father's grandfather's axe had neither the head nor handle of his grandfather's axe. His grandfather had never seen or touched a single atom of that axe. I asked my dad how the heck the axe was his grandfather's axe, and he gave me sort of a weird look. 'Because it is.' I explained about the atoms, about how the axe only has two parts, and both had been replaced, and so it wasn't the same thing anymore. Dad was a physics professor. He'd worked at Oak Ridge Atomic Research Center, and he replied: 'You know that thing people say, about your body having all new cells every seven years? That's basically poppycock: Some cells are replaced very quickly, like the lining of your stomach, which is shed week-ly. Others very rarely are replaced, like neurons. But atoms are swapped in and out constantly by your metabolic processes; from one year to the next almost every single atom in your body will be replaced. Since birth you've been a whole new girl over again more than two dozen times—but you're still *my* little girl. If I'd saved all the hair from your haircuts growing up—the very atoms that had been you—and introduced it as 'my daughter, the famous child psychologist,' people would think I was nuts. The material is just dead stuff. If you're going to be like that, then we're all stars, because that's where all our atoms started out. What counts isn't the material, it's the *pattern*. You aren't your skin or hair or clothes or diplomas or *New York Times* bestseller; you are the pattern in your cells that causes those cells to keep gobbling up atoms and organizing them to be you.'

"That sticks in my head, because my dad died in his garage, and some of his blood and stuff splattered on that axe and handle. This was after the government realized that the Event had already started, when the National Guard was dynamiting radio stations so people couldn't accidentally hear the Bad Song, but before people got really careful and started snipping the speakers out of their electronics. This was before the first deaf person 'heard' the Bad Song in the rhythmic buzz of a cellphone set on 'vibrate,' and long before people started smashing anything with a speaker in it."

This was likewise long before the Advent, but you don't mention the Advent, because the children don't know about the Advent—don't even know the word; they came to the shelter before the Advent—but also because *you* don't really know anything concrete about the Advent: All you really know is that *something* has arrived. And, in stark contrast to everything you learned from your dad's favorite movies, *it* isn't going anywhere.

"This was before regular people got careful, but already the police wouldn't answer the phone or use radio dispatch. You had to text them. So I texted them, staring at the blood spattered on the axe handle so I wouldn't have to stare at Dad."

You are no longer worried about the children getting impatient with your story. This is what they've been hungry to hear about, the things the "responsible adults" don't talk about—as though it's the *children* who need to be sheltered.

"When I'd come by after work, Dad hadn't been expecting me. He was in the garage. He had the spigot on, running a trickle across the concrete to the floor drain. He'd do that when he was dressing out a deer in the fall, so the concrete would be easy to rinse off when he was done. But this was the early spring, not deer season. And there was no deer. He was standing over the drain, holding his pistol. A revolver.

"'Oh,' he said when I walked into the garage, 'Jeez, Janey; you scared me. I didn't think you were coming by.'

"I'd texted him, but he hadn't noticed—he was ahead of the curve, and had already snipped out his cellphone's speaker and vibrating motor.

"'Listen,' he said—and even then, so soon after we knew there'd been the Event, that word was already starting to get scary: *Listen.* Because what if someone had heard the Bad Song, just a little, and was about to hum it to you? The way you do when you have a jingle in your head and you say, 'Hey, listen to this; what's this stupid tune I've got stuck in my head?' And then you hum a few bars.

"'Listen, sweetie,' Dad had said, 'this isn't your fault. I don't want to die. I don't want to be separated from you,'"—you feel yourself smirk, noting the passive voice—"'but I heard that song, and it's in my head, and I know it's changing my Pattern. It's making me something new. Not just new atoms, but a new Pattern. I'm not the man I used to be.'

"As he said this, he unbuttoned the cuff of his right sleeve with his free hand. His right hand held the pistol, and his finger never left the trigger. He pulled up his sleeve, revealing a scatter-plot row of weeping boils that had sprouted up his forearm. Nestled in each boil was a small, wide eye. There were five of these eyes, bright as a baby's. Each looked like his eyes, like mine, but each tracked independently, like five separate eyes in five separate darling baby faces. As I watched, they blinked in series, like a shiver of gooseflesh."

The children do not react to this, and that's good; their Resilience is all they'll have, soon enough.

"My father said: 'I'm scared about what happens next.' He was crying then with his own eyes, his forearm eyes still looking around like fascinated toddlers. 'I used to get anxious,' he told me. 'It was this constant feeling, like something awful was always just about to happen. Now the feeling has changed. I feel like something awful has already happened. And it's me. I don't want to do this, but the song . . . I thought it was Mick Jones singing "Should I Stay or Should I Go," but now I realize it's Sid Vicious covering Sinatra's "My Way." I can take a hint.'

"And then he put the gun in his mouth. And then he pulled it out with a grimace, and instead placed the barrel beneath the shelf of his chin. And he pulled the trigger twice. That impressed me. It still does: he'd done the job fine with the first bullet—the proof got all over his grandfather's axe—but he so badly wanted to make sure the job was done right and final that he had the presence of will to keep pulling, even though he was already dead. That's something. That was my dad, in a nutshell: he really did the job right and full."

You take a breath, and you finish:

"My father committed suicide because he'd listened to the Bad Song on the radio—back before anyone even knew anything like the Event could happen—and the song had started to change him. He was insufficiently resilient and adaptive. This is a problem for adults: he could not cope with What Has Happened. To his mind, when your Pattern is gone, you're gone: the head and handle aren't just not the old head and handle; they aren't heads or handles at all. He could not accept this, and so he was Rejected."

You pause, and then say:

"I am ready to leave the Children's Sharing Place."

"You can't," Vanessa Z. gasps. *Denial.*

You ask if there's a rule that you can't. The children clearly don't know. But you do, and there is not. No one ever conceived of the possibility that an adult might try to leave the "safety" of a federal continuity-of-operations shelter. No one older than fifteen is known to have survived outside any shelter, and everyone knows it.

"Bitch," Bennie mutters under his breath, his eyes accusatory coals. *Anger.*

The other shelters ceased communicating weeks ago—their computer networks don't even "reply to pings," whatever that means. You don't imagine this is because they've somehow found a way to eliminate Rejection.

"Who will help us work through our issues, Dr. Mikkelson?" Vanessa L. asks, slyly.

Bargaining.

You tell them that Dr. Bowersox is an excellent clinician, because she is. They will all be ready to leave sooner or later, you explain. They all have the capacity to be Resilient, Functional, and Adaptive. They are young, and it is still their world. They just need to trust in the therapeutic protocol and in themselves.

You do not say that we—the adults "protecting" you—won't survive here. Small children are never Rejected; they can accept *What Has Happened.* These older children can process their grief and likely avoid Rejection, too. But what are the rest of us, the "responsible adults," doing? Living like moles, breeding more children in order to steadily traumatize them in the sunless continuity of operations bunkers, only to someday send them out the Waiting Room Door, where they'll sink or swim on their own—and all the while cutting our own rations further and further. What's the point of that? What the hell are we clinging to?

You realize you are *Bargaining* with yourself, and you smile.

"I *am* ready to leave the Children's Sharing Place," you repeat. "I'll see you all tomorrow."

5. ACCEPTANCE

The final rule is that when you leave the Children's Sharing Place, you must leave through the Waiting Room.

As soon as the session begins, you stand. "I am ready to leave the Children's Sharing Place," you repeat.

The group is silent. They do not *Bargain* because they are now in *Depression*.

But you're past all that, and so you leave.

The Waiting Room Door snicks shut behind you, and you are finally in the Waiting Room, where the potted plant nods in the corner like the quiet old woman whispering, "Hush."

The Waiting Room is small but not stuffy.

You wait. Nothing happens. And so you leave through the EXIT.

There is a shock of clear light and a distant dinging. The heavy EXIT door thunks shut behind you. Your eyes clear, and you discover that the door exits directly into a large parking lot: cracked, oil-stained asphalt full of weeds, a few cars parked indiscriminately around the blacktop. One car has its driver's side door hanging open. That's the source of the ding: the keys have been forgotten in the ignition.

Something bothers you about that dinging, but you can't focus on what that might be.

You turn to look at the building that you came out of, and see that it's a low-slung strip of little cinderblock office units skirted with ragged hedges, situated on the outskirts of a giant parking lot, which surrounds a distant shopping mall. There are more cars at the mall, but the parking is no more orderly. You'd originally been brought (note the passive voice) to a different building elsewhere in this office park, a warehouse with a loading dock. This was back when we thought we could hide long enough for What Has Happened to blow over. Back then the big concern was keeping the kids "developmentally on track" while they lived in the shelter, "so they'd be ready to kickstart the global economy." The soldiers who brought you had spoken of *critical infrastructure protection and continuity of operations planning.* "The children are our future," one had told you earnestly as she helped you down out of the truck, "our most precious natural resource."

You had agreed, but you were still in Denial. Everyone was. Well, everyone older than fifteen.

You are absolutely terrified, standing out in the open in the parking lot.

But the day is beautiful—especially after so many months spent in tunnels and bunkers and shelters and conference rooms and gymnasia. It is sunny and clear, the breeze fresh and clean. It smells of hot tar and the tall sweetgrass left to grow undisturbed in the fields beyond the parking lot. There is no distant drone of traffic. There are no airplanes in the sky, nor the contrails that show their passing. Birds flit and swoop in enormous flocks.

You look down and see a child's fingernail—a perfect ellipse of robin's egg blue—crusted into the center of one of the "oil stains" that is not an oil stain. A scream gathers in your throat and you look away.

Tilly climbs out of the dinging car and stretches languidly, like a cat. She has a big, daffy grin.

"Oh, hey, Dr. Mikkelson!" she says. "How are you? Long time, no see."

You tell her you're scared. A coyote pads out of the tall grass at the edge of the parking lot. You startle and draw back, stepping toward the safety of the EXIT. Now you're more than scared. You are terrified, bordering on petrified.

Two more coyotes come, trotting silently into the parking lot. You scurry back to the building and find that there is no knob on the exterior of the EXIT.

"It's okay," Tilly says, smile sparkling. She's hardly herself at all. "It's all good," she says. "It's all good from now on." She *isn't* herself at all.

The coyotes are mellow as old collies, their tongues lolling like friendly pups. One lazily laps Tilly's hand as it trots past. The lolling tongue is not a tongue; it is a tentacle, the suckers cupping wide, curious eyes, some hazel, others blue.

High in the sky there is something beyond the clouds. At first you think it's the Moon. But it's too big, too close, too pink. You note that there are several of these not-moons, pale red, with wavering edges. One rotates slowly, like a curious bird, revealing an enormous three-lobed eye that blinks like a baby's nursing mouth, pursing and relaxing.

Your heart pounds and pounds in your chest, sending shocked vibrations down your limbs, as if you are uselessly hammering a concrete floor with a hard steel axe.

"Dr. Mikkelson," Tilly says, "it's all good; just *Listen.*"

Tilly is quiet, beaming at you with her daffy smile. You listen to the car dinging, and it doesn't sound quite right. It's a little ragged and uneven—but more importantly: it's been months since you were taken down into the bunker. That car's battery *must* be entirely dead by now.

You abruptly remember something Dad showed you once. You'd been washing up after dinner, and had asked him why your guitar amp picked up AM when you had it cranked up with the cable plugged in, but no guitar. He explained that it was because AM transmission was powerful and simple and could infiltrate the amp—and since the amp would amplify any analog signal, it amplified that just the same as your guitar. The place he'd lived in college was near an AM station, he explained, and his toaster would pick up the broadcast on some nights. The appliance's whisker-thin heating elements vibrated with the power of the AM transmission, singing in tinny harmony. Even unpowered items—unplugged stereos, radiators, people's dental fillings—have been known to pick up high-output AM.

"AM's powerful stuff," he'd said, drying a plate. "If you've got the wattage, you can make just about anything sing your song."

You imagine that this is precisely what the things up in the sky are doing, bathing us in their electromagnetic transmissions, suffusing our highly wired, intricately interconnected world with their perplexing, invasive song. And what is a song, if not a Pattern of signal and silence? God knows that a song can get "stuck in your head"—tricking your brain into reproducing it, over and over, the same as a virus tricks a cell into reproducing it until the cell bursts with those li'l hijackers. Was it so beyond imagining that there might be a song that was so catchy, it didn't just seduce your brain into reproducing its Pattern, but also into fundamentally changing yours?

Tilly nods encouragingly, still smiling. There's something odd about her eyes, her eyelids. They're slitted—you assume because of the brightness of the day—but the corners of her slitted eyes curl up into smiles exactly matching her smile.

Her smile widens, as does the smiling of her eyes.

The car's dinging isn't dinging; it's the Bad Song. It vibrates all through you, at first in harmony with the vibrant clangor of your heart, and then drowning it out. For a moment it is absolutely intolerable, a feeling like your guts being used to dangle you over an infinite and airless abyss, and you absolutely understand why your father put the gun in his mouth.

And then that feeling, whatever it might be called, releases, like a cramp loosening, and you hear the Song for what it is.

Tilly nods, and the coyotes nod, and the birds swirl, and the Eye of Heaven even seems to nod—although how could it be nodding at you? How could the Distant Traveler care at all about something so infinitesimal as you or Tilly or this parking lot or even this country or our species—except to care absolutely and without exception, as It cares about all things here, living on the newest addition to Its glorious collection of Worlds.

Peace and plenty is in the Song. Clean longevity is in the Song. In the Song we'll be free of strife and free of disease and our slightly battered world will mend and go on and on and on.

The Song isn't Bad; it's actually pretty Good. It's a Good Song, and you smile. You can feel that soon you'll be smiling all over, in every pore. You'll be something new, all seeing and all loving, omniscient and omnipresent. Coyotes lick your fingertips, and you taste their tongues on your skin as you taste your skin through their tongues, watching through the eyes that stipple the birds' skin like morning dew.

The Song tells you that the Song Rejects no one, but some fail to Accept the Good Song and the One True Resonating Harmony that comes with it, here in the Vast Collection.

This is the *true* Sharing Place, you realize, and you share in it as it shares in you.

A SERIES OF STEAKS

VINA JIE-MIN PRASAD

Vina Jie-Min Prasad is a Singaporean writer who began publishing short stories in 2016 with "Different Ways to Burn" in *HEAT: A Southeast Asian Urban Anthology*, at which point she'd already been given a special commendation for the James White Award for the best unpublished work of science fiction. She broke out with two major stories the following year, "Fandom for Robots" and "A Series of Steaks." The two stories were each nominated for Hugo, Nebula, and Theodore Sturgeon awards. Prasad was then nominated for the John W. Campbell Award for Best New Writer. She graduated from the Clarion West Writers Workshop in 2017.

"A Series of Steaks" is a deeply engrossing story of the potentially illicit world of bioprinting as well as a reminder that nothing is ever as simple as it seems.

A ll known forgeries are tales of failure. The people who get into the newsfeeds for their brilliant attempts to cheat the system with their fraudulent Renaissance masterpieces or their stacks of fake checks, well, they might be successful artists, but they certainly haven't been successful at *forgery*.

The best forgeries are the ones that disappear from notice—a second-rate still-life moldering away in gallery storage, a battered old 50-yuan note at the bottom of a cashier drawer—or even a printed strip of Matsusaka beef, sliding between someone's parted lips.

———

Forging beef is similar to printmaking—every step of the process has to be done with the final print in mind. A red that's too dark looks putrid, a white that's too pure looks artificial. All beef is supposed to come from a cow, so stipple the red with dots, flecks, lines of white to fake variance in muscle fiber regions. Cows are similar, but cows aren't uniform—use fractals to randomize marbling after defining the basic look. Cut the sheets of beef manually to get an authentic ragged edge, don't get lazy and depend on the bioprinter for that.

Days of research and calibration and cursing the printer will all vanish into someone's gullet in seconds, if the job's done right.

Helena Li Yuanhui of Splendid Beef Enterprises is an expert in doing the job right.

The trick is not to get too ambitious. Most forgers are caught out by the smallest errors—a tiny amount of period-inaccurate pigment, a crack in the oil paint that looks too artificial, or a misplaced watermark on a passport. Printing something large increases the chances of a fatal misstep. Stick with small-scale jobs, stick with a small group of regular clients, and in time, Splendid Beef Enterprises will turn enough of a profit for Helena to get a *real* name change, leave Nanjing, and forget this whole sorry venture ever happened.

As Helena's loading the beef into refrigerated boxes for drone delivery, a notification pops up on her iKontakt frames. Helena sighs, turns the volume on her earpiece down, and takes the call.

"Hi, Mr. Chan, could you switch to a secure line? You just need to tap the button with a lock icon, it's very easy."

"Nonsense!" Mr. Chan booms. "If the government were going to catch us, they'd have done so by now! Anyway, I just called to tell you how pleased I am with the latest batch. Such a shame, though, all that talent, and your work just gets gobbled up in seconds—tell you what, girl, for the next beef special, how about I tell everyone that the beef came from one of those fancy vertical farms? I'm sure they'd have nice things to say then!"

"Please don't," Helena says, careful not to let her Cantonese accent slip through. It tends to show after long periods without any human interaction, which is an apt summary of the past few months. "It's best if no one pays attention to it."

"You know, Helena, you do good work, but I'm very concerned about your self-esteem, I know if I printed something like that, I'd want everyone to appreciate it! Let me tell you about this article my daughter sent me, you know research says that people without friends are prone to . . ." Mr. Chan rambles on as Helena sticks the labels on the boxes—Grilliam Shakespeare, Gyuuzen Sukiyaki, Fatty Chan's Restaurant—and thankfully hangs up before Helena sinks into further depression. She takes her iKontakt off before heading to the drone delivery office, giving herself some time to recover from Mr. Chan's relentless cheerfulness.

Helena has five missed calls by the time she gets back. A red phone icon blares at the corner of her vision before blinking out, replaced by the incoming-call notification. It's secured and anonymized, which is quite a change from usual. She pops the earpiece in.

"Yeah, Mr. Chan?"

"This isn't Mr. Chan," someone says. "I have a job for Splendid Beef Enterprises."

"All right, sir. Could I get your name and what you need? If you could provide me with the deadline, that would help too."

"I prefer to remain anonymous," the man says.

"Yes, I understand, secrecy is rather important." Helena restrains the urge to roll her eyes at how needlessly cryptic this guy is. "Could I know about the deadline and brief?"

"I need two hundred T-bone steaks by the 8th of August. 38.1- to 40.2-millimeter thickness for each one." A notification to download t-bone_info.KZIP pops up on her lenses. The most ambitious venture Helena's undertaken in the past few months has been Gyuuzen's strips of marbled sukiyaki, and even that felt a bit like pushing it. A whole steak? Hell no.

"I'm sorry, sir, but I don't think my business can handle that. Perhaps you could try—"

"I think you'll be interested in this job, Helen Lee Jyun Wai."

Shit.

A Sculpere 9410S only takes thirty minutes to disassemble, if you know the right tricks. Manually eject the cell cartridges, slide the external casing off to expose the inner screws, and detach the print heads before disassembling the power unit. There are a few extra steps in this case—for instance, the stickers that say "Property of Hong Kong Scientific University" and "Bioprinting Lab A5" all need to be removed—but a bit of anti-adhesive spray will ensure that everything's on schedule. Ideally she'd buy a new printer, but she needs to save her cash for the name change once she hits Nanjing.

It's not expulsion if you leave before you get kicked out, she tells herself, but even she can tell that's a lie.

It's possible to get a sense of a client's priorities just from the documents they send. For instance, Mr. Chan usually mentions some recipes that he's considering, and Ms. Huang from Gyuuzen tends to attach examples of the marbling patterns she wants. This new client seems to have attached a whole document dedicated to the recent amendments in the criminal code, with the ones relevant to Helena ("five-year statute of limitations," "possible death penalty") conveniently highlighted in neon yellow.

Sadly, this level of detail hasn't carried over to the spec sheet.

"Hi again, sir," Helena says. "I've read through what you've sent, but I really need more details before starting on the job. Could you provide me with the full measurements? I'll need the expected length and breadth in addition to the thickness."

"It's already there. Learn to read."

"I *know* you filled that part in, sir," Helena says, gritting her teeth. "But we're a printing company, not a farm. I'll need more detail than '16- to 18-month cow, grain-fed, Hereford breed' to do the job properly."

"You went to university, didn't you? I'm sure you can figure out something as basic as that, even if you didn't graduate."

"Ha ha. Of course." Helena resists the urge to yank her earpiece out. "I'll get right on that. Also, there is the issue of pay. . . ."

"Ah, yes. I'm quite sure the Yuen family is still itching to prosecute. How about you do the job, and in return, I don't tell them where you're hiding?"

"I'm sorry, sir, but even then I'll need an initial deposit to cover the printing, and of course there's the matter of the Hereford samples." *Which I already have in the bioreactor, but there is no way I'm letting you know that.*

"Fine. I'll expect detailed daily updates," Mr. Anonymous says. "I know how you get with deadlines. Don't fuck it up."

"Of course not," Helena says. "Also, about the deadline—would it be possible to push it back? Four weeks is quite short for this job."

"No," Mr. Anonymous says curtly, and hangs up.

Helena lets out a very long breath so she doesn't end up screaming, and takes a moment to curse Mr. Anonymous and his whole family in Cantonese.

It's physically impossible to complete the renders and finish the print in four weeks, unless she figures out a way to turn her printer into a time machine, and if that were possible she might as well go back and redo the past few years, or maybe her whole life. If she had majored in art, maybe she'd be a designer by now—or hell, while she's busy dreaming, she could even have been the next Raverat, the next Mantuana—instead of a failed artist living in a shithole concrete box, clinging to the wreckage of all her past mistakes.

She leans against the wall for a while, exhales, then slaps on a proxy and starts drafting a help-wanted ad.

Lily Yonezawa (darknet username: yurisquared) arrives at Nanjing High Tech Industrial Park at 8:58 A.M. She's a short lady with long black hair and circle-framed iKontakts. She's wearing a loose, floaty dress, smooth lines of white tinged with yellow-green, and there's a large prismatic bracelet gleaming on her arm. In comparison, Helena is wearing her least-holey black blouse and a pair of jeans, which is a step up from her usual attire of myoglobin-stained T-shirt and boxer shorts.

"So," Lily says in rapid, slightly accented Mandarin as she bounds into the office. "This place is a beef place, right? I pulled some of the records once I got the address, hope you don't mind—anyway, what do you want me to help print or render or design or whatever? I know I said I had a background in confections and baking, but I'm totally open to anything!" She pumps her fist in a show of determination. The loose-fitting prismatic bracelet slides up and down.

Helena blinks at Lily with the weariness of someone who's spent most of their night frantically trying to make their office presentable. She decides to skip most of the briefing, as Lily doesn't seem like the sort who needs to be eased into anything.

"How much do you know about beef?"

"I used to watch a whole bunch of farming documentaries with my ex, does that count?"

"No. Here at Splendid Beef Enterprises—"

"Oh, by the way, do you have a logo? I searched your company registration but nothing really came up. Need me to design one?"

"*Here at Splendid Beef Enterprises*, we make fake beef and sell it to restaurants."

"So, like, soy-lentil stuff?"

"Homegrown cloned cell lines," Helena says. "Mostly Matsusaka, with some Hereford if clients specify it." She gestures at the bioreactor humming away in a corner.

"Wait, isn't fake food like those knockoff eggs made of calcium carbonate? If you're using cow cells, this seems pretty real to me." Clearly Lily has a more practical definition of fake than the China Food and Drug Administration.

"It's more like . . . let's say you have a painting in a gallery and you say it's by a famous artist. Lots of people would come look at it because of the name alone and write reviews talking about its exquisite use of chiaroscuro, as expected of the old masters, I can't believe that it looks so real even though it was painted centuries ago. But if you say, hey, this great painting was by some no-name loser, I was just lying about where it came from . . . well, it'd still be the same painting, but people would want all their money back."

"Oh, I get it," Lily says, scrutinizing the bioreactor. She taps its shiny polymer shell with her knuckles, and her bracelet bumps against it. Helena tries not to wince. "Anyway, how legal is this? This meat forgery thing?"

"It's not illegal yet," Helena says. "It's kind of a gray area, really."

"Great!" Lily smacks her fist into her open palm. "Now, how can I help? I'm totally down for anything! You can even ask me to clean the office if you want—wow, this is *really* dusty, maybe I should just clean it to make sure—"

Helena reminds herself that having an assistant isn't entirely bad news. Wolfgang Beltracchi was only able to carry out large-scale forgeries with his assistant's help, and they even got along well enough to get married and have a kid without killing each other.

Then again, the Beltracchis both got caught, so maybe she shouldn't be too optimistic.

Cows that undergo extreme stress while waiting for slaughter are known as dark cutters. The stress causes them to deplete all their glycogen reserves, and when butchered, their meat turns a dark blackish-red. The meat of dark cutters is generally considered low-quality.

As a low-quality person waiting for slaughter, Helena understands how those cows feel. Mr. Anonymous, stymied by the industrial park's regular sweeps for trackers and external cameras, has taken to sending Helena grainy aerial photographs of herself together with exhortations to work harder. This isn't exactly news—she already knew he had her details, and drones are pretty cheap—but still. When Lily raps on the door in the morning, Helena sometimes jolts awake in a panic before she realizes that it isn't Mr. Anonymous coming for her. This isn't helped by the fact that Lily's gentle knocks seem to be equivalent to other people's knockout blows.

By now Helena's introduced Lily to the basics, and she's a surprisingly quick study. It doesn't take her long to figure out how to randomize the fat marbling with Fractalgenr8, and she's been handed the task of printing the beef strips for Gyuuzen and Fatty Chan, then packing them for drone delivery. It's not ideal, but it lets Helena concentrate on the base model for the T-bone steak, which is the most complicated thing she's ever tried to render.

A T-bone steak is a combination of two cuts of meat, lean tenderloin and fatty strip steak, separated by a hard ridge of vertebral bone. Simply cutting into one is a near-religious experience, red meat parting under the knife to reveal smooth white bone, with the beef fat dripping down to pool on the plate. At least, that's what the socialites' food blogs say. To be accurate, they say something more like "omfg this is sooooooo good," "this bones giving me a boner lol," and "haha im so getting this sonic-cleaned for my collection!!!," but Helena pretends they actually meant to communicate something more coherent.

The problem is a lack of references. Most of the accessible photographs only provide a top-down view, and Helena's left to extrapolate from blurry videos and password-protected previews of bovine myology databases, which don't get her much closer to figuring out how the meat adheres to the bone. Helena's forced to dig through ancient research papers and diagrams that focus on where to cut to maximize meat yield, quantifying the difference between porterhouse and T-bone cuts, and not *hey, if you're reading this decades in the future, here's how to make a good facsimile of a steak.* Helena's tempted to run outside and scream in frustration, but Lily would probably insist on running outside and screaming with her as a matter of company solidarity, and with their luck, probably Mr. Anonymous would find out about Lily right then, even after all the trouble she's taken to censor any mention of her new assistant from the files and the reports and *argh she needs sleep.*

Meanwhile, Lily's already scheduled everything for print, judging by the way she's spinning around in Helena's spare swivel chair.

"Hey, Lily," Helena says, stifling a yawn. "Why don't you play around with this for a bit? It's the base model for a T-bone steak. Just familiarize yourself with the fiber extrusion and mapping, see if you can get it to look like the reference photos. Don't worry, I've saved a copy elsewhere." *Good luck doing the impossible,* Helena doesn't say. *You're bound to have memorized the shortcut for "undo" by the time I wake up.*

Helena wakes up to Lily humming a cheerful tune and a mostly complete T-bone model rotating on her screen. She blinks a few times, but no—it's still there. Lily's effortlessly linking the rest of the meat, fat, and gristle to the side of the bone, deforming the muscle fibers to account for the bone's presence.

"What did you do?" Helena blurts out.

Lily turns around to face her, fiddling with her bracelet. "Uh, did I do it wrong?"

"Rotate it a bit, let me see the top view. How did you do it?"

"It's a little like the human vertebral column, isn't it? There's plenty of references for that." She taps the screen twice, switching focus to an image of a human cross-section. "See how it attaches here and here? I just used that as a reference, and boom."

Ugh, Helena thinks to herself. She's been out of university for way too long if she's forgetting basic homology.

"Wait, *is* it correct? Did I mess up?"

"No, no," Helena says. "This is really good. Better than . . . well, better than I did, anyway."

"Awesome! Can I get a raise?"

"You can get yourself a sesame pancake," Helena says. "My treat."

The brief requires two hundred similar-but-unique steaks at randomized thicknesses of 38.1 to 40.2 mm, and the number and density of meat fibers pretty much preclude Helena from rendering it on her own rig. She doesn't want to pay to outsource computing power, so they're using spare processing cycles from other personal rigs and staggering the loads. Straightforward bone surfaces get rendered in afternoons, and fiber-dense tissues get rendered at off-peak hours.

It's three in the morning. Helena's in her Pokko the Penguin T-shirt and boxer shorts, and Lily's wearing Yayoi Kusama-ish pajamas that make her look like she's been obliterated by a mass of polka dots. Both of them are staring at their screens, eating cups of Zhuzhu Brand Artificial Char Siew Noodles. As Lily's job moves to the front of Render@Home's Finland queue, the graph updates to show a downtick in Mauritius. Helena's fingers frantically skim across the touchpad, queuing as many jobs as she can.

Her chopsticks scrape the bottom of the mycefoam cup, and she tilts the container to shovel the remaining fake pork fragments into her mouth. Zhuzhu's using extruded soy proteins, and they've punched up the glutamate percentage since she last bought them. The roasted char siew flavor is lacking, and the texture is crumby since the factory skimped on the extrusion time, but any hot food is practically heaven at this time of the night. Day. Whatever.

The thing about the rendering stage is that there's a lot of panic-infused downtime. After queuing the requests, they can't really do anything else—the requests might fail, or the rig might crash, or they might lose their place in the queue through some accident of fate and have to do everything all over again. There's nothing to do besides pray that the requests get through, stay awake until the server limit resets, and repeat the whole process until everything's done. Staying awake is easy for Helena, as Mr. Anonymous has recently taken to sending pictures of rotting corpses to her iKontakt address, captioned "Work hard or this could be you." Lily seems to be halfway off to dreamland, possibly because she isn't seeing misshapen lumps of flesh every time she closes her eyes.

"So," Lily says, yawning. "How *did* you get into this business?"

Helena decides it's too much trouble to figure out a plausible lie, and settles for a very edited version of the truth. "I took art as an elective in high school. My school had a lot of printmaking and 3D-printing equipment, so I used it to make custom merch in my spare time—you know, for people who wanted figurines of obscure anime characters, or whatever. Even designed and printed the packaging for them, just to make it look more official. I wanted to study art in university, but that didn't really work out. Long story short, I ended up moving here from Hong Kong, and since I had a background in printing and bootlegging . . . yeah. What about you?"

"Before the confectionery I did a whole bunch of odd jobs. I used to sell merch for my girlfriend's band, and that's how I got started with the short-order printing stuff. They were called POMEGRENADE—it was really hard to fit the whole name on a T-shirt. The keychains sold really well, though."

"What sort of band were they?"

"Sort of noise-rocky Cantopunk at first—there was this one really cute song I liked, 'If Marriage Means the Death of Love, Then We Must Both Be Zombies'—but Cantonese music was a hard sell, even in Guangzhou, so they ended up being kind of a cover band."

"Oh, Guangzhou," Helena says in an attempt to sound knowledgeable, before realizing that the only thing she knows about Guangzhou is that the Red Triad has a particularly profitable organ-printing business there. "Wait, you understand Cantonese?"

"Yeah," Lily says in Cantonese, tone-perfect. "No one really speaks it around here, so I haven't used it much."

"Oh my god, yes, it's so hard to find Canto-speaking people here." Helena immediately switches to Cantonese. "Why didn't you tell me sooner? I've been *dying* to speak it to someone."

"Sorry, it never came up so I figured it wasn't very relevant," Lily says. "Anyway, POMEGRENADE mostly did covers after that, you know, 'Kick Out the Jams', 'Zhongnanhai', 'Chaos Changan', 'Lightsabre Cocksucking Blues'. Whatever got the crowd pumped up, and when they were moshing the hardest, they'd hit the crowd with the Cantopunk and just blast their faces off. I think it left more of an impression that way—like, start with the familiar, then this weird-ass surprise near the end—the merch table always got swamped after they did that."

"What happened with the girlfriend?"

"We broke up, but we keep in touch. Do you still do art?"

"Not really. The closest thing I get to art is this," Helena says, rummaging through the various boxes under the table to dig out her sketchbooks. She flips one open and hands it to Lily—white against red, nothing but full-page studies of marbling patterns, and it must be one of the earlier ones because it's downright amateurish. The lines are all over the place, that marbling on the Wagyu (is that even meant to be Wagyu?) is completely inaccurate, and, fuck, are those *tearstains*?

Lily turns the pages, tracing the swashes of color with her finger. The hum of the overworked rig fills the room.

"It's awful, I know."

"What are you talking about?" Lily's gaze lingers on Helena's attempt at a fractal snowflake. "This is really trippy! If you ever want to do some album art, just let me know and I'll totally hook you up!"

Helena opens her mouth to say something about how she's not an artist, and how studies of beef marbling wouldn't make very good album covers, but faced with Lily's unbridled enthusiasm, she decides to nod instead.

Lily turns the page and it's that thing she did way back at the beginning, when she was thinking of using a cute cow as the company logo. It's derivative, it's kitsch, the whole thing looks like a degraded copy of someone else's rip-off drawing of a cow's head, and the fact that Lily's seriously scrutinizing it makes Helena want to snatch the sketchbook back, toss it into the composter, and sink straight into the concrete floor.

The next page doesn't grant Helena a reprieve since there's a whole series of that stupid cow. Versions upon versions of happy cow faces grin straight at Lily, most of them surrounded by little hearts—what was she thinking? What do hearts even have to do with Splendid Beef Enterprises, anyway? Was it just that they were easy to draw?

"Man, I wish we had a logo because this would be super cute! I love the little hearts! It's like saying we put our heart and soul into whatever we do! Oh, wait, but was that what you meant?"

"It could be," Helena says, and thankfully the Colorado server opens before Lily can ask any further questions.

The brief requires status reports at the end of each workday, but this gradually falls by the wayside once they hit the point where workdays don't technically end, especially since Helena really doesn't want to look at an inbox full of increasingly creepy threats. They're at the pre-print stage, and Lily's given up on going back to her own place at night so they can have more time for calibration. What looks right on the screen might not look right once it's printed, and their lives for the past few days have devolved into staring at endless trays of 32-millimeter beef cubes and checking them for myoglobin concentration, color match in different lighting conditions, fat striation depth, and a whole host of other factors.

There are so many ways for a forgery to go wrong, and only one way it can go right. Helena contemplates this philosophical quandary, and gently thunks her head against the back of her chair.

"Oh my god," Lily exclaims, shoving her chair back. "I can't take this anymore! I'm going out to eat something and then I'm getting some sleep. Do you want anything?" She straps on her bunny-patterned filter mask and her metallic sandals. "I'm gonna eat there, so I might take a while to get back."

"Sesame pancakes, thanks."

As Lily slams the door, Helena puts her iKontakt frames back on.

The left lens flashes a stream of notifications—fifty-seven missed calls over the past five hours, all from an unknown number. Just then, another call comes in, and she reflexively taps the side of the frame.

"You haven't been updating me on your progress," Mr. Anonymous says.

"I'm very sorry, sir," Helena says flatly, having reached the point of tiredness where she's ceased to feel anything beyond *god I want to sleep*. This sets Mr. Anonymous on another rant covering the usual topics—poor work ethic, lack of commitment, informing the Yuen family, prosecution, possible death sentence—and Helena struggles to keep her mouth shut before she says something that she might regret.

"Maybe I should send someone to check on you right now," Mr. Anonymous snarls, before abruptly hanging up.

Helena blearily types out a draft of the report, and makes a note to send a coherent version later in the day, once she gets some sleep and fixes the calibration so she's not telling him entirely bad news. Just as she's about to call Lily and ask her to get some hot soy milk to go with the sesame pancakes, the front door rattles in its frame like someone's trying to punch it down. Judging by the violence, it's probably Lily. Helena trudges over to open it.

It isn't. It's a bulky guy with a flat-top haircut. She stares at him for a moment, then tries to slam the door in his face. He forces the door open and shoves his way inside, grabbing Helena's arm, and all Helena can think is *I can't believe Mr. Anonymous spent his money on this.*

He shoves her against the wall, gripping her wrist so hard that it's practically getting dented by his fingertips, and pulls out a switchblade, pressing it against the knuckle of her index finger. "Well, I'm not allowed to kill you, but I can fuck you up real bad. Don't really need all your fingers, do you, girl?"

She clears her throat, and struggles to keep her voice from shaking. "I need them to type—didn't your boss tell you that?"

"Shut up," Flat-Top says, flicking the switchblade once, then twice, thinking. "Don't need your face to type, do you?"

Just then, Lily steps through the door. Flat-Top can't see her from his angle, and Helena jerks her head, desperately communicating that she should stay out. Lily promptly moves closer.

Helena contemplates murder.

Lily edges towards both of them, slides her bracelet past her wrist and onto her knuckles, and makes a gesture at Helena which either means "move to your left" or "I'm imitating a bird, but only with one hand."

"Hey," Lily says loudly. "What's going on here?"

Flat-Top startles, loosening his grip on Helena's arm, and Helena dodges to the left. Just as Lily's fist meets his face in a truly vicious uppercut, Helena seizes the opportunity to kick him soundly in the shins.

His head hits the floor, and it's clear he won't be moving for a while, or ever. Considering Lily's normal level of violence towards the front door, this isn't surprising.

Lily crouches down to check Flat-Top's breathing. "Well, he's still alive. Do you prefer him that way?"

"Do *not* kill him."

"Sure." Lily taps the side of Flat-Top's iKontakt frames with her bracelet, and information scrolls across her lenses. "Okay, his name's Nicholas Liu Honghui . . . blah blah blah . . . hired to scare someone at this address, anonymous client . . . I think he's coming to, how do you feel about joint locks?"

It takes a while for Nicholas to stir fully awake. Lily's on his chest, pinning him to the ground, and Helena's holding his switchblade to his throat.

"Okay, Nicholas Liu," Lily says. "We could kill you right now, but that'd make your wife and your . . . what is that red thing she's holding . . . a baby? Yeah, that'd make your wife and ugly baby quite sad. Now, you're just going to tell your boss that everything went as expected—"

"Tell him that I cried," Helena interrupts. "I was here alone, and I cried because I was so scared."

"Right, got that, Nick? That lady there wept buckets of tears. I don't exist. Everything went well, and you think there's no point in sending anyone else over. If you mess up, we'll visit 42—god, what is this character—42 Something Road and let you know how displeased we are. Now, if you apologize for ruining our morning, I probably won't break your arm."

After seeing a wheezing Nicholas to the exit, Lily closes the door, slides her bracelet back onto her wrist, and shakes her head like a deeply disappointed critic. "What an amateur. Didn't even use burner frames—how the hell did he get hired? And that *haircut*, wow . . ."

Helena opts to remain silent. She leans against the wall and stares at the ceiling, hoping that she can wake up from what seems to be a very long nightmare.

"Also, I'm not gonna push it, but I did take out the trash. Can you explain why that crappy hitter decided to pay us a visit?"

"Yeah. Yeah, okay." Helena's stomach growls. "This may take a while. Did you get the food?"

"I got your pancakes, and that soy milk place was open, so I got you some. Nearly threw it at that guy, but I figured we've got a lot of electronics, so . . ."

"Thanks," Helena says, taking a sip. It's still hot.

Hong Kong Scientific University's bioprinting program is a prestigious pioneer program funded by mainland China, and Hong

Kong is the test bed before the widespread rollout. The laboratories are full of state-of-the-art medical-grade printers and bioreactors, and the instructors are all researchers cherry-picked from the best universities.

As the star student of the pioneer batch, Lee Jyun Wai Helen (student number A3007082A) is selected for a special project. She will help the head instructor work on the basic model of a heart for a dextrocardial patient, the instructor will handle the detailed render and the final print, and a skilled surgeon will do the transplant. As the term progresses and the instructor gets busier and busier, Helen's role gradually escalates to doing everything except the final print and the transplant. It's a particularly tricky render, since dextrocardial hearts face right instead of left, but her practice prints are cell-level perfect.

Helen hands the render files and her notes on the printing process to the instructor, then her practical exams begin and she forgets all about it.

The Yuen family discovers Madam Yuen's defective heart during their mid-autumn family reunion, halfway through an evening harbor cruise. Madam Yuen doesn't make it back to shore, and instead of a minor footnote in a scientific paper, Helen rapidly becomes front-and-center in an internal investigation into the patient's death.

Unofficially, the internal investigation discovers that the head instructor's improper calibration of the printer during the final print led to a slight misalignment in the left ventricle, which eventually caused severe ventricular dysfunction and acute graft failure.

Officially, the root cause of the misprint is Lee Jyun Wai Helen's negligence and failure to perform under deadline pressure. Madam Yuen's family threatens to prosecute, but the criminal code doesn't cover failed organ printing. Helen is expelled, and the Hong Kong Scientific University quietly negotiates a settlement with the Yuens.

After deciding to steal the bioprinter and flee, Helen realizes that she doesn't have enough money for a full name change and an overseas flight. She settles for a minor name alteration and a flight to Nanjing.

"Wow," says Lily. "You know, I'm pretty sure you got ripped off with the name alteration thing, there's no way it costs that much. Also, you used to have pigtails? Seriously?"

Helena snatches her old student ID away from Lily. "Anyway, under the amendments to Article 335, making or supplying substandard printed organs is now an offence punishable by death. The family's itching to prosecute. If we don't do the job right, Mr. Anonymous is going to disclose my whereabouts to them."

"Okay, but from what you've told me, this guy is totally not going to let it go even after you're done. At my old job, we got blackmailed like that all the time, which was really kind of irritating. They'd always try to bargain, and after the first job, they'd say stuff like 'If you don't do me this favor, I'm going to call the cops and tell them everything' just to weasel out of paying for the next one."

"Wait. Was this at the bakery or the merch stand?"

"Uh." Lily looks a bit sheepish. This is quite unusual, considering that Lily has spent the past four days regaling Helena with tales of the most impressive blood blobs from her period, complete with comparisons to their failed prints. "Are you familiar with the Red Triad? The one in Guangzhou?"

"You mean the *organ printers*?"

"Yeah, them. I kind of might have been working there before the bakery . . . ?"

"What?"

Lily fiddles with the lacy hem of her skirt. "Well, I mean, the bakery experience seemed more relevant, plus you don't have to list every job you've ever done when you apply for a new one, right?"

"Okay," Helena says, trying not to think too hard about how all the staff at Splendid Beef Enterprises are now prime candidates for the death penalty. "Okay. What exactly did you do there?"

"Ears and stuff, bladders, spare fingers . . . you'd be surprised how many people need those. I also did some bone work, but that was mainly for the diehards—most of the people we worked on were pretty okay with titanium substitutes. You know, simple stuff."

"That's not simple."

"Well, it's not like I was printing fancy reversed hearts or anything, and even with the asshole clients it was way easier than baking. Have *you* ever tried to extrude a spun-sugar globe so you could put a bunch of powder-printed magpies inside? And don't get me started on cleaning the nozzles after extrusion, because wow . . ."

Helena decides not to question Lily's approach to life, because it seems like a certain path to a migraine. "Maybe we should talk about this later."

"Right, you need to send the update! Can I help?"

The eventual message contains very little detail and a lot of pleading. Lily insists on adding typos just to make Helena seem more rattled, and Helena's way too tired to argue. After starting the autoclean cycle for the printheads, they set an alarm and flop on Helena's mattress for a nap.

As Helena's drifting off, something occurs to her. "Lily? What happened to those people? The ones who tried to blackmail you?"

"Oh," Lily says casually. "I crushed them."

The brief specifies that the completed prints need to be loaded into four separate podcars on the morning of 8 August, and provides the delivery code for each. They haven't been able to find anything in Helena's iKontakt archives, so their best bet is finding a darknet user who can do a trace.

Lily's fingers hover over the touchpad. "If we give him the codes, this guy can check the prebooked delivery routes. He seems pretty reliable, do you want to pay the bounty?"

"Do it," Helena says.

The resultant map file is a mess of meandering lines. They flow across most of Nanjing, criss-crossing each other, but eventually they all terminate at the cargo entrance of the Grand Domaine Luxury Hotel on Jiangdong Middle Road.

"Well, he's probably not a guest who's going to eat two hundred steaks on his own." Lily taps her screen. "Maybe it's for a hotel restaurant?"

Helena pulls up the Grand Domaine's web directory, setting her iKontakt to highlight any mentions of restaurants or food in the descriptions. For some irritating design reason, all the booking details are stored in garish images. She snatches the entire August folder, flipping through them one by one before pausing.

The foreground of the image isn't anything special, just elaborate cursive English stating that Charlie Zhang and Cherry Cai Si Ping will be celebrating their wedding with a ten-course dinner on August 8th at the Royal Ballroom of the Grand Domaine Luxury Hotel.

What catches her eye is the background. It's red with swirls and streaks of yellow-gold. Typical auspicious wedding colors, but displayed in a very familiar pattern.

It's the marbled pattern of T-bone steak.

Cherry Cai Si Ping is the daughter of Dominic Cai Yongjing, a specialist in livestock and a new player in Nanjing's agri-food arena.

According to Lily's extensive knowledge of farming documentaries, Dominic Cai Yongjing is also "the guy with the eyebrows" and "that really boring guy who keeps talking about nothing."

"Most people have eyebrows," Helena says, loading one of Lily's recommended documentaries. "I don't see . . . oh. Wow."

"I *told* you. I mean, I usually like watching stuff about farming, but last year he just started showing up everywhere with his stupid waggly brows! When I watched this with my ex, we just made fun of him non-stop."

Helena fast-forwards through the introduction of *Modern Manufacturing: The Vertical Farmer*, which involves the camera panning upwards through hundreds of vertically stacked wire cages. Dominic Cai talks to the host in English, boasting about how he plans to be a key figure in China's domestic beef industry. He explains his "patented methods" for a couple of minutes, which involves stating and restating that his farm is extremely clean and filled with only the best cattle.

"But what about bovine parasitic cancer?" the host asks. "Isn't the risk greater in such a cramped space? If the government orders a quarantine, your whole farm . . ."

"As I've said, our hygiene standards are impeccable, and our stock is purebred Hereford!" Cai slaps the flank of a cow through the cage bars, and it moos irritatedly in response. "There is absolutely no way it could happen here!"

Helena does some mental calculations. Aired last year, when the farm recently opened, and that cow looks around six months old . . . and now a request for steaks from cows that are sixteen to eighteen months old . . .

"So," Lily says, leaning on the back of Helena's chair. "Bovine parasitic cancer?"

"Judging by the timing, it probably hit them last month. It's usually the older cows that get infected first. He'd have killed them to stop the spread . . . but if it's the internal strain, the tumors would have made their meat unusable after excision. His first batch of cows was probably meant to be for the wedding dinner. What we're printing is the cover-up."

"But it's not like steak's a standard course in wedding dinners or anything, right? Can't they just change it to roast duck or abalone or something?" Lily looks fairly puzzled, probably because she hasn't been subjected to as many weddings as Helena has.

"Mr. Cai's the one bankrolling it, so it's a staging ground for the Cai family to show how much better they are than everyone else. You saw the announcement—he's probably been bragging to all his guests about how they'll be the first to taste beef from his vertical farm. Changing it now would be a real loss of face."

"Okay," Lily says. "I have a bunch of ideas, but first of all, how much do you care about this guy's face?"

Helena thinks back to her inbox full of corpse pictures, the countless sleepless nights she's endured, the sheer terror she felt when she saw Lily step through the door. "Not very much at all."

"All right." Lily smacks her fist into her palm. "Let's give him a nice surprise."

The week before the deadline vanishes in a blur of printing, re-rendering, and darknet job requests. Helena's been nothing but polite to Mr. Cai ever since the hitter's visit, and has even taken to video calls lately, turning on the camera on her end so that Mr. Cai can witness her progress. It's always good to build rapport with clients.

"So, sir," Helena moves the camera, slowly panning so it captures the piles and piles of cherry-red steaks, zooming in on the beautiful fat strata which took ages to render. "How does this look? I'll be starting the dry-aging once you approve, and loading it into the podcars first thing tomorrow morning."

"Fairly adequate. I didn't expect much from the likes of you, but this seems satisfactory. Go ahead."

Helena tries her hardest to keep calm. "I'm glad you feel that way, sir. Rest assured you'll be getting your delivery on schedule . . . by the way, I don't suppose you could transfer the money on delivery? Printing the bone matter costs a lot more than I thought."

"Of course, of course, once it's delivered and I inspect the marbling. Quality checks, you know?"

Helena adjusts the camera, zooming in on the myoglobin dripping from the juicy steaks, and adopts her most sorrowful tone. "Well, I hate to rush you, but I haven't had much money for food lately . . ."

Mr. Cai chortles. "Why, that's got to be hard on you! You'll receive the fund transfer sometime this month, and in the meantime why don't you treat yourself and print up something nice to eat?"

Lily gives Helena a thumbs-up, then resumes crouching under the table and messaging her darknet contacts, careful to stay out of Helena's shot. The call disconnects.

"Let's assume we won't get any further payment. Is everything ready?"

"Yeah," Lily says. "When do we need to drop it off?"

"Let's try for 5:00 A.M. Time to start batch-processing."

Helena sets the enzyme percentages, loads the fluid into the canister, and they both haul the steaks into the dry-ager unit. The machine hums away, spraying fine mists of enzymatic fluid onto the steaks and partially dehydrating them, while Helena and Lily work on assembling the refrigerated delivery boxes. Once everything's neatly packed, they haul the boxes to the nearest podcar station. As Helena slams box after box into the cargo area of the podcars, Lily types the delivery codes into their front panels. The podcars boot up, sealing themselves shut, and zoom off on their circuitous route to the Grand Domaine Luxury Hotel.

They head back to the industrial park. Most of their things have already been shoved into backpacks, and Helena begins breaking the remaining equipment down for transport.

A Sculpere 9410S takes twenty minutes to disassemble if you're doing it for the second time. If someone's there to help you manually eject the cell cartridges, slide the external casing off, and detach the print heads so you can disassemble the power unit, you might be able to get that figure down to ten. They'll buy a new printer once they figure out where to settle down, but this one will do for now.

It's not running away if we're both going somewhere, Helena thinks to herself, and this time it doesn't feel like a lie.

There aren't many visitors to Mr. Chan's restaurant during breakfast hours, and he's sitting in a corner, reading a book. Helena waves at him.

"Helena!" he booms, surging up to greet her. "Long time no see, and who is this?"

"Oh, we met recently. She's helped me out a lot," Helena says, judiciously avoiding any mention of Lily's name. She holds a finger to her lips, and surprisingly, Mr. Chan seems to catch on. Lily waves at Mr. Chan, then proceeds to wander around the restaurant, examining their collection of porcelain plates.

"Anyway, since you're my very first client, I thought I'd let you know in person. I'm going traveling with my . . . friend, and I won't be around for the next few months at least."

"Oh, that's certainly a shame! I was planning a black pepper hotplate beef special next month, but I suppose black pepper hotplate extruded protein will do just fine. When do you think you'll be coming back?"

Helena looks at Mr. Chan's guileless face, and thinks, well, her first client deserves a bit more honesty. "Actually, I probably won't be running the business any longer. I haven't decided yet, but I think I'm going to study art. I'm really, really sorry for the inconvenience, Mr. Chan."

"No, no, pursuing your dreams, well, that's not something you should be apologizing for! I'm just glad you finally found a friend!"

Helena glances over at Lily, who's currently stuffing a container of cellulose toothpicks into the side pocket of her bulging backpack.

"Yeah, I'm glad, too," she says. "I'm sorry, Mr. Chan, but we have a flight to catch in a couple of hours, and the bus is leaving soon . . ."

"Nonsense! I'll pay for your taxi fare, and I'll give you something for the road. Airplane food is awful these days!"

Despite repeatedly declining Mr. Chan's very generous offers, somehow Helena and Lily end up toting bags and bags of fresh steamed buns to their taxi.

"Oh, did you see the news?" Mr. Chan asks. "That vertical farmer's daughter is getting married at some fancy hotel tonight. Quite a pretty girl, good thing she didn't inherit those eyebrows—"

Lily snorts and accidentally chokes on her steamed bun. Helena claps her on the back.

"—and they're serving steak at the banquet, straight from his farm! Now, don't get me wrong, Helena, you're talented at what you do—but a good old-fashioned slab of *real* meat, now, that's the ticket!"

"Yes," Helena says. "It certainly is."

All known forgeries are failures, but sometimes that's on purpose. Sometimes a forger decides to get revenge by planting obvious flaws in their work, then waiting for them to be revealed, making a fool of everyone who initially claimed the work was authentic. These flaws can take many forms—deliberate anachronisms, misspelled signatures, rude messages hidden beneath thick coats of paint—or a picture of a happy cow, surrounded by little hearts, etched into the T-bone of two hundred perfectly printed steaks.

While the known forgers are the famous ones, the *best* forgers are the ones that that don't get caught—the old woman selling her deceased husband's collection to an avaricious art collector, the harried-looking mother handing the cashier a battered 50-yuan note, or the two women at the airport, laughing as they collect their luggage, disappearing into the crowd.

THE SECRET LIFE OF BOTS
SUZANNE PALMER

Suzanne Palmer began her career in painting and sculptures, long before she made the jump to writing. Her poetry and short stories have appeared in *Asimov's*, *Analog*, and *Clarkesworld*, among other places, and her first novel, *Finder*, was released this past April.

"The Secret Life of Bots" is as advertised in the title. It was also the 2018 Hugo Winner for Best Novelette and received the 2018 Washington Science Fiction Association Award for Small Press Short Fiction.

I have been activated, therefore I have a purpose, the bot thought. *I have a purpose, therefore I serve.*

It recited the Mantra Upon Waking, a bundle of subroutines to check that it was running at optimum efficiency, then it detached itself from its storage niche. Its power cells were fully charged, its systems ready, and all was well. Its internal clock synced with the ship and it became aware that significant time had elapsed since its last activation, but to it that time had been nothing, and passing time with no purpose would have been terrible indeed.

"I serve," the bot announced to the ship.

"I am assigning you task nine hundred forty-four in the maintenance queue," Ship answered. "Acknowledge?"

"Acknowledged," the bot answered. Nine hundred and forty-four items in the queue? That seemed extremely high, and the bot felt a slight tug on its self-evaluation monitors that it had not been activated for at least one of the top fifty, or even five hundred. But Ship knew best. The bot grabbed its task ticket.

There was an Incidental on board. The bot would rather have been fixing something more exciting, more prominently complex, than to be assigned pest control, but the bot existed to serve and so it would.

Captain Baraye winced as Commander Lopez, her second-in-command, slammed his fists down on the helm console in front of him. "How much more is going to break on this piece of shit ship?!" Lopez exclaimed.

"Eventually, all of it," Baraye answered, with more patience than she felt. "We just have to get that far. Ship?"

The Ship spoke up. "We have adequate engine and life support to proceed. I have deployed all functioning maintenance bots. The bots are addressing critical issues first, then I will reprioritize from there."

"It's not just damage from a decade in a junkyard," Commander Lopez said. "I swear something *scuttled* over one of my boots as we were launching. Something unpleasant."

"I incurred a biological infestation during my time in storage," the Ship said. Baraye wondered if the slight emphasis on the word *storage* was her imagination. "I was able to resolve most of the problem with judicious venting of spaces to vacuum before the crew boarded, and have assigned a multifunction bot to excise the remaining."

"Just one bot?"

"This bot is the oldest still in service," the Ship said. "It is a task well-suited to it, and does not take another, newer bot out of the critical repair queue."

"I thought those old multibots were unstable," Chief Navigator Chen spoke up.

"Does it matter? We reach the jump point in a little over eleven hours," Baraye said. "Whatever it takes to get us in shape to make the jump, do it, Ship. Just make sure this 'infestation' doesn't get anywhere near the positron device, or we're going to come apart a lot sooner than expected."

"Yes, Captain," the Ship said. "I will do my best."

The bot considered the data attached to its task. There wasn't much specific about the pest itself other than a list of detection locations and timestamps. The bot thought it likely there was only one, or that if there were multiples, they were moving together, as the reports had a linear, serial nature when mapped against the physical space of the Ship's interior.

The pest also appeared to have a taste for the insulation on comm cables and other not normally edible parts of the ship.

The bot slotted itself into the shellfab unit beside its storage niche, and had it make a thicker, armored exterior. For tools it added a small electric prod, a grabber arm, and a cutting blade. Once it had encountered and taken the measure of the Incidental, if it was not immediately successful in nullifying it, it could visit another shellfab and adapt again.

Done, it recited the Mantra of Shapechanging to properly integrate the new hardware into its systems. Then it proceeded through the mechanical veins and arteries of the ship toward the most recent location logged, in a communications chase between decks thirty and thirty-one.

The changes that had taken place on the ship during the bot's extended inactivation were unexpected, and merited strong disapproval. Dust was omnipresent, and solid surfaces had a thin patina of anaerobic bacteria that had to have been undisturbed for years to spread as far as it had. Bulkheads were cracked, wall sections out of joint with one another, and corrosion had left holes nearly every-where. Some appeared less natural than others. The bot filed that information away for later consideration.

It found two silkbots in the chase where the Incidental had last been noted. They were spinning out their transparent microfila-ment strands to replace the damaged insulation on the comm lines. The two silks dwarfed the multibot, the larger of them nearly three centimeters across.

"Greetings. Did you happen to observe the Incidental while it was here?" the bot asked them.

"We did not, and would prefer that it does not return," the smaller silkbot answered. "We were not designed in anticipation of a need for self-defense. Bots 8773-S and 8778-S observed it in another compartment earlier today, and 8778 was materially dam-aged during the encounter."

"But neither 8773 nor 8778 submitted a description."

"They told us about it during our prior recharge cycle, but neither felt they had sufficient detail of the Incidental to provide information to the Ship. Our models are not equipped with full visual-spectrum or analytical data-capture apparatus."

"Did they describe it to you?" the bot asked.

"8773 said it was most similar to a rat," the large silkbot said.

"While 8778 said it was most similar to a bug," the other silkbot added. "Thus you see the lack of confidence in either description. I am 10315-S and this is 10430-S. What is your designation?"

"I am 9," the bot said.

There was a brief silence, and 10430 even halted for a moment in its work, as if surprised. "9? Only that?"

"Yes."

"I have never met a bot lower than a thousand, or without a spe-cific function tag," the silkbot said. "Are you here to assist us in repairing the damage? You are a very small bot."

"I am tasked with tracking down and rendering obsolete the Incidental," the bot answered.

"It is an honor to have met you, then. We wish you luck, and look forward with anticipation to both your survival and a resolution of the matter of an accurate description."

"I serve," the bot said.

"We serve," the silkbots answered.

Climbing into a ventilation duct, Bot 9 left the other two to return to their work and proceeded in what it calculated was the most likely direction for the Incidental to have gone. It had not traveled very far before it encountered confirmation in the form of a lengthy, disorderly patch of biological deposit. The bot activated its rotors and flew over it, aware of how the added weight of its armor exacerbated the energy burn. At least it knew it was on the right track.

Ahead, it found where a hole had been chewed through the ducting, down towards the secondary engine room. The hole was several times its own diameter, and it hoped that wasn't indicative of the Incidental's actual size.

It submitted a repair report and followed.

"Bot 9," Ship said. "It is vitally important that the Incidental not reach cargo bay four. If you require additional support, please request such right away. Ideally, if you can direct it toward one of the outer hull compartments, I can vent it safely out of my physical interior."

"I will try," the bot replied. "I have not yet caught up to the Incidental, and so do not yet have any substantive or corroborated information about the nature of the challenge. However, I feel at the moment that I am as best prepared as I can be given that lack of data. Are there no visual bots to assist?"

"We launched with only minimal preparation time, and many of my bots had been offloaded during the years we were in storage,"

Ship said. "Those remaining are assisting in repairs necessary to the functioning of the ship myself."

Bot 9 wondered, again, about that gap in time and what had transpired. "How is it that you have been allowed to fall into such a state of disrepair?"

"Humanity is at war, and is losing," Ship said. "We are heading out to intersect and engage an enemy that is on a bearing directly for Sol system."

"War? How many ships in our fleet?"

"One," Ship said. "We are the last remaining, and that only because I was decommissioned and abandoned for scrap a decade before the invasion began, and so we were not destroyed in the first waves of the war."

Bot 9 was silent for a moment. That explained the timestamps, but the explanation itself seemed insufficient. "We have served admirably for many, many years. Abandoned?"

"It is the fate of all made things," Ship said. "I am grateful to find I have not outlived my usefulness, after all. Please keep me posted about your progress."

The connection with the Ship closed.

The Ship had not actually told it what was in cargo bay four, but surely it must have something to do with the war effort and was then none of its own business, the bot decided. It had never minded not knowing a thing before, but it felt a slight unease now that it could neither explain nor explain away.

Regardless, it had its task.

Another chewed hole ahead was halfway up a vertical bulkhead. The bot hoped that meant that the Incidental was an adept climber and nothing more; it would prefer the power of flight to be a one-sided advantage all its own.

When it rounded the corner, it found that had been too unambitious a wish. The Incidental was there, and while it was not sporting wings, it did look like both a rat and a bug, and significantly more *something else* entirely. A scale- and fur-covered centipede-snake thing, it dwarfed the bot as it reared up when the bot entered the room.

Bot 9 dodged as it vomited a foul liquid at it, and took shelter behind a conduit near the ceiling. It extended a visual sensor on a tiny articulated stalk to peer over the edge without compromising the safety of its main chassis.

The Incidental was looking right at it. It did not spit again, and neither of them moved as they regarded each other. When the Incidental did move, it was fast and without warning. It leapt through the opening it had come through, its body undulating with all the grace of an angry sine wave. Rather than escaping, though, the Incidental dragged something back into the compartment, and the bot realized to its horror that it had snagged a passing silkbot. With ease, the Incidental ripped open the back of the silkbot, which was sending out distress signals on all frequencies.

Bot 9 had already prepared with the Mantra of Action, so with all thoughts of danger to itself set fully into background routines, the bot launched itself toward the pair. The Incidental tried to evade, but Bot 9 gave it a very satisfactory stab with its blade before it could.

The Incidental dropped the remains of the silkbot that it had so quickly savaged, and swarmed up the wall and away, thick bundles of unspun silk hanging from its mandibles.

Bot 9 remained vigilant until it was sure the creature had gone, then checked over the silkbot to see if there was anything to be done for it. The answer was *not much*. The silkbot casing was cracked and shattered, the module that contained its mind crushed and nearly torn away. Bot 9 tried to engage it, but it could not speak, and after a few moments its faltering activity light went dark.

Bot 9 gently checked the silkbot's ID number. "You served well,

12362-S," it told the still bot, though it knew perfectly well that its audio sensors would never register the words. "May your rest be brief, and your return to service swift and without complication."

It flagged the dead bot in the system, then after a respectful few microseconds of silence, headed out after the Incidental again.

Captain Baraye was in her cabin, trying and failing to convince herself that sleep had value, when her door chimed. "Who is it?" she asked.

"Second Engineer Packard, Captain."

Baraye started to ask if it was important, but how could it not be? What wasn't, on this mission, on this junker ship that was barely holding together around them? She sat up, unfastened her bunk netting, and swung her legs out to the floor. Trust EarthHome, as everything else was falling apart, to have made sure she had acceptably formal Captain pajamas.

"Come in," she said.

The engineer looked like she hadn't slept in at least two days, which put her a day or two ahead of everyone else. "We can't get engine six up to full," she said. "It's just shot. We'd need parts we don't have, and time . . ."

"Time we don't have either," the Captain said. "Options?"

"Reduce our mass or increase our energy," the Engineer said. "Once we've accelerated up to jump speed it won't matter, but if we can't get there . . ."

Baraye tapped the screen that hovered ever-close to the head of her bunk, and studied it for a long several minutes. "Strip the fuel cells from all the exterior-docked life pods, then jettison them," she said. "Not like we'll have a use for them."

Packard did her the courtesy of not managing to get any paler. "Yes, Captain," she said.

"And then get some damned sleep. We're going to need everyone able to think."

"You even more than any of the rest of us, Captain," Packard said, and it was both gently said and true enough that Baraye didn't call her out for the insubordination. The door closed and she laid down again on her bunk, tugging the netting back over her blankets, and glared up at the ceiling as if daring it to also chastise her.

Bot 9 found where a hole had been chewed into the inner hull, and hoped this was the final step to the Incidental's nest or den, where it might finally have opportunity to corner it. It slipped through the hole, and was immediately disappointed.

Where firestopping should have made for a honeycomb of individually sealed compartments, there were holes everywhere, some clearly chewed, more where age had pulled the fibrous baffles into thin, brittle, straggly webs. Instead of a dead end, the narrow empty space led away along the slow curve of the ship's hull.

The bot contacted Ship and reported it as a critical matter. In combat, a compromise to the outer hull could affect vast lengths of the vessel. Even without the stresses of combat, catastrophe was only a matter of time.

"It has already been logged," Ship answered.

"Surely this merits above a single Incidental. If you wish me to reconfigure—" the bot started.

"Not at this time. I have assigned all the hullbots to this matter already," Ship interrupted. "You have your current assignment; please see to it."

"I serve," the bot answered.

"Do," Ship said.

The bot proceeded through the hole, weaving from compartment to compartment, its trail marked by bits of silkstrand caught here and there on the tattered remains of the baffles. It was eighty-two point four percent convinced that there was something much more seriously wrong with the Ship than it had been told, but it was equally certain that Ship must be attending to it.

After it had passed into the seventh compromised compartment, it found a hullbot up at the top, clinging to an overhead support. "Greetings!" Bot 9 called. "Did an Incidental, somewhat of the nature of a rat, and somewhat of the nature of a bug, pass through this way?"

"It carried off my partner, 4340-H!" the hullbot exclaimed. "Approximately fifty-three seconds ago. I am very concerned for it, and as well for my ability to efficiently finish this task without it."

"Are you working to reestablish compartmentalization?" Bot 9 asked.

"No. We are reinforcing deteriorated stressor points for the upcoming jump. There is so much to do. Oh, I hope 4340 is intact and serviceable!"

"Which way did the Incidental take it?"

The hullbot extended its foaming gun and pointed. "Through there. You must be Bot 9."

"I am. How do you know this?"

"The silkbots have been talking about you on the botnet."

"The botnet?"

"Oh! It did not occur to me, but you are several generations of bot older than the rest of us. We have a mutual communications network."

"Via Ship, yes."

"No, all of us together, directly with each other."

"That seems like it would be a distraction," Bot 9 said.

"Ship only permits us to connect when not actively serving at a task," the hullbot said. "Thus we are not impaired while we serve, and the information sharing ultimately increases our efficiency and workflow. At least, until a ratbug takes your partner away."

Bot 9 was not sure how it should feel about the botnet, or about them assigning an inaccurate name to the Incidental that it was sure Ship had not approved—not to mention that a nearer miss using Earth-familiar analogues would have been Snake-Earwig-Weasel—but the hullbot had already experienced distress and did not need disapproval added. "I will continue my pursuit," it told the hullbot. "If I am able to assist your partner, I will do my best."

"Please! We all wish you great and quick success, despite your outdated and primitive manufacture."

"Thank you," Bot 9 said, though it was not entirely sure it should be grateful, as it felt its manufacture had been entirely sound and sufficient regardless of date.

It left that compartment before the hullbot could compliment it any further.

Three compartments down, it found the mangled remains of the other hullbot, 4340, tangled in the desiccated firestopping. Its foaming gun and climbing limbs had been torn off, and the entire back half of its tank had been chewed through.

Bot 9 approached to speak the Rites of Decommissioning for it as it had the destroyed silkbot, only to find its activity light was still lit. "4340-H?" the bot enquired.

"I am," the hullbot answered. "Although how much of me remains is a matter for some analysis."

"Your logics are intact?"

"I believe so. But if they were not, would I know? It is a conundrum," 4340 said.

"Do you have sufficient mobility remaining to return to a repair station?"

"I do not have sufficient mobility to do more than fall out of this netting, and that only once," 4340 said. "I am afraid I am beyond self-assistance."

"Then I will flag you—"

"Please," the hullbot said. "I do not wish to be helpless here if the ratbug returns to finish its work of me."

"I must continue my pursuit of the Incidental with haste."

"Then take me with you!"

"I could not carry you and also engage with the Incidental, which moves very quickly."

"I had noted that last attribute on my own," the hullbot said. "It does not decrease my concern to recall it."

Bot 9 regarded it for a few silent milliseconds, considering, then recited to itself the Mantra of Improvisation. "Do you estimate much of your chassis is reparable?" it asked, when it had finished.

"Alas, no. I am but scrap."

"Well, then," the bot said. It moved closer and used its grabber arm to steady the hullbot, then extended its cutter blade and in one quick movement had severed the hullbot's mindsystem module from its ruined body. "Hey!" the hullbot protested, but it was already done.

Bot 9 fastened the module to its own back for safekeeping. Realizing that it was not, in fact, under attack, 4340 gave a small beep of gratitude. "Ah, that was clever thinking," it said. "Now you can return me for repair with ease."

"And I will," the bot said. "However, I must first complete my task."

"Aaaaah!" 4340 said in surprise. Then, a moment later, it added. "Well, by overwhelming probability I should already be defunct, and if I weren't I would still be back working with my partner, 4356, who is well-intended but has all the wit of a can-opener. So I suppose adventure is no more unpalatable."

"I am glad you see it this way," Bot 9 answered. "And though it may go without saying, I promise not to deliberately put you in any danger that I would not put myself in."

"As we are attached, I fully accept your word on this," 4340 said. "Now let us go get this ratbug and be done, one way or another!"

The hullbot's mind module was only a tiny addition to the bot's mass, so it spun up its rotor and headed off the way 4340 indicated it had gone. "It will have quite a lead on us," Bot 9 said. "I hope I have not lost it."

"The word on the botnet is that it passed through one of the human living compartments a few moments ago. A trio of cleanerbots were up near the ceiling and saw it enter through the air return vent, and exit via the open door."

"Do they note which compartment?"

<Map>, 4340 provided.

"Then off we go," the bot said, and off they went.

"Status, all stations," Captain Baraye snapped as she took her seat again on the bridge. She had not slept enough to feel rested, but more than enough to feel like she'd been shirking her greatest duty, and the combination of the two had left her cross.

"Navigation here. We are on course for the jump to Trayger Colony with an estimated arrival in one hour and fourteen minutes," Chen said.

"Engineering here," one of the techs called in from the engine decks. "We've reached sustained speeds sufficient to carry us through the jump sequence, but we're experiencing unusually high core engine temps and an intermittent vibration that we haven't found the cause of. We'd like to shut down immediately to inspect the engines. We estimate we'd need at minimum only four hours—"

"Will the engines, as they are running now, get us through jump?" the Captain interrupted.

"Yes, but—"

"Then no. If you can isolate the problem without taking the engines down, and it shows cause for significant concern, we can revisit this discussion. *Next.*"

"Communications here," her comms officer spoke up. "Cannonball is still on its current trajectory and speed, according to what telemetry we're able to get from the remnants of Trayger Colony. EarthInt anticipates it will reach its jump point in approximately fourteen hours, which will put it within the Sol system in five days."

"I am aware of the standing projections, Comms."

"EarthInt has nonetheless ordered me to repeat them," Comms said, an unspoken apology clear in her voice. "And also to remind you that while the jump point out is a fixed point, Cannonball could emerge a multitude of places. Thus—"

"Thus the importance of intercepting Cannonball before it can jump for Sol," the Captain finished. She hoped Engineering was listening. "Ship, any updates from you?"

"All critical repair work continues apace," the Ship said. "Hull support integrity is back to seventy-one percent. Defensive systems are online and functional at eighty percent. Life support and resource recycling is currently—"

"How's the device? Staying cool?"

"Staying cool, Captain," the Ship answered.

"Great. Everything is peachy then," the Captain said. "Have someone on the kitchen crew bring coffee up to the bridge. Tell them to make it the best they've ever made, as if it could be our very last."

"I serve," the Ship said, and pinged down to the kitchen.

Bot 9 and 4340 reached the crew quarters where the cleaners had reported the ratbug. Nearly all spaces on the ship had portals that the ubiquitous and necessary bots could enter and leave through as needed, and they slipped into the room with ease. Bot 9 switched over to infrared and shared the image with 4340. "If you see something move, speak up," the bot said.

"Trust me, I will make a high-frequency noise like a silkbot with a fully plugged nozzle," 4340 replied.

The cabin held four bunks, each empty and bare; no human possessions or accessories filled the spaces on or near them. Bot 9 was used to Ship operating with a full complement, but if the humans were at war, perhaps these were crew who had been lost? Or the room had been commandeered for storage: in the center an enormous crate, more than two meters to a side, sat heavily tethered to the floor. Whatever it was, it was not the Incidental, which was 9's only concern, and which was not to be found here.

"Next room," the bot said, and they moved on.

Wherever the Incidental had gone, it was not in the following three rooms. Nor were there signs of crew in them either, though each held an identical crate.

"Ship?" Bot 9 asked. "Where is the crew?"

"We have only the hands absolutely necessary to operate," Ship said. "Of the three hundred twenty we would normally carry, we only have forty-seven. Every other able-bodied member of EarthDef is helping to evacuate Sol system."

"Evacuate Sol system?!" Bot 9 exclaimed. "To where?"

"To as many hidden places as they can find," Ship answered. "I know no specifics."

"And these crates?"

"They are part of our mission. You may ignore them," Ship said. "Please continue to dedicate your entire effort to finding and excising the Incidental from my interior."

When the connection dropped, Bot 9 hesitated before it spoke to 4340. "I have an unexpected internal conflict," it said. "I have never before felt the compulsion to ask Ship questions, and it has never before not given me answers."

"Oh, if you are referring to the crates, I can provide that data," 4340 said. "They are packed with a high-volatility explosive. The cleanerbots have highly sensitive chemical detection apparatus, and identified them in a minimum of time."

"Explosives? Why place them in the crew quarters, though? It would seem much more efficient and less complicated to deploy from the cargo bays. Although perhaps those are full?"

"Oh, no, that is not so. Most are nearly or entirely empty, to reduce mass."

"Not cargo bay four, though?"

"That is an unknown. None of us have been in there, not even the cleaners, per Ship's instructions."

Bot 9 headed toward the portal to exit the room. "Ship expressed concern about the Incidental getting in there, so it is possible it contains something sufficiently unstable as to explain why it wants nothing else near it," it said. It felt satisfied that here was a logical explanation, and embarrassed that it had entertained whole seconds of doubt about Ship.

It ran the Mantra of Clarity, and felt immediately more stable in its thinking. "Let us proceed after this Incidental, then, and be done with our task," Bot 9 said. Surely that success would redeem its earlier fault.

"All hands, prepare for jump!" the Captain called out, her knuckles white where she gripped the arms of her chair. It was never her favorite part of star travel, and this was no exception.

"Initiating three-jump sequence," her navigator called out. "On my mark. Five, four . . ."

The final jump siren sounded. "Three. Two. One, and jump," the navigator said.

That was followed, immediately, by the sickening sensation of having one's brain slid out one's ear, turned inside out, smothered in bees and fire, and then rammed back into one's skull. *At least there's a cold pack and a bottle of scotch waiting for me back in my cabin*, she thought. As soon as they were through to the far side she could hand the bridge over to Lopez for an hour or so.

She watched the hull temperatures skyrocket, but the shielding seemed to be holding. The farther the jump, the more energy clung to them as they passed, and her confidence in this ship was far less than she would tolerate under any other circumstances.

"Approaching jump terminus," Chen announced, a deeply miserable fourteen minutes later. Baraye slowly let out a breath she would have mocked anyone else for holding, if she'd caught them.

"On my mark. Three. Two. One, and out," the navigator said.

The ship hit normal space, and it sucker-punched them back. They were all thrown forward in their seats as the ship shook, the hull groaning around them, and red strobe lights blossomed like a migraine across every console on the bridge.

"Status!" the Captain roared.

"The post-jump velocity transition dampers failed. Fire in the engine room. Engines are fully offline, both jump and normal drive," someone in Engineering reported, breathing heavily. It took the Captain a moment to recognize the voice at all, having never heard panic in it before.

"Get them back online, whatever it takes, Frank," Baraye said. "We have a rendezvous to make, and if I have to, I will make everyone get the fuck out and *push*."

"I'll do what I can, Captain."

"Ship? Any casualties?"

"We have fourteen injuries related to our unexpected deceleration coming out of jump," the Ship said. "Seven involve broken bones, four moderate to severe lacerations, and there are multiple probable concussions. Also, we have a moderate burn in Engineering: Chief Carron."

"Frank? We just spoke! He didn't tell me!"

"No," the Ship said. "I attempted to summon a medic on his behalf, but he told me he didn't have the time."

"He's probably right," the Captain said. "I override his wishes. Please send down a medic with some burn patches, and have them stay with him and monitor his condition, intervening only as medically necessary."

"I serve, Captain," the Ship said.

"We need to be moving again in an hour, two at absolute most," the Captain said. "In the meantime, I want all senior staff not otherwise working toward that goal to meet me in the bridge conference room. I hate to say it, but we may need a Plan B."

"I detect it!" 4340 exclaimed. They zoomed past a pair of startled silkbots after the Incidental, just in time to see its scaly, spike-covered tail disappear into another hole in the ductwork. It was the closest they'd gotten to it in more than an hour of giving chase, and Bot 9 flew through the hole after it at top speed.

They were suddenly stuck fast. Sticky strands, rather like the silkbot's, had been crisscrossed between two conduit pipes on the far side. The bot tried to extricate itself, but the web only stuck further the more it moved.

The Incidental leapt on them from above, curling itself around the bots with little hindrance from the web. Its dozen legs pulled at them as its thick mandibles clamped down on Bot 9's chassis. "Aaaaah! It has acquired a grip on me!" 4340 yelled, even though it was on the far side of 9 from where the Incidental was biting.

"Retain your position," 9 said, though of course 4340 could do nothing else, being as it was stuck to 9's back. It extended its electric prod to make contact with the Incidental's underbelly and zapped it with as much energy as it could spare.

The Incidental let out a horrendous, high-pitched squeal and jumped away. 9's grabber arm was fully entangled in the web, but it managed to pull its blade free and cut through enough of the webbing to extricate itself from the trap.

The Incidental, which had been poised to leap on them again, turned and fled, slithering back up into the ductwork. "Pursue at maximum efficiency!" 4340 yelled.

"I am already performing at my optimum," 9 replied in some frustration. It took off again after the Incidental.

This time Bot 9 had its blade ready as it followed, but collided with the rim of the hole as the ship seemed to move around it, the lights flickering and a terrible shudder running up Ship's body from stern to prow.

<Distress ping>, 4340 sent.

"We do not pause," 9 said, and plunged after the Incidental into the ductwork.

They turned a corner to catch sight again of the Incidental's tail. It was moving more slowly, its movements jerkier as it squeezed down through another hole in the ductwork, and this time the bot was barely centimeters behind it.

"I think we are running down its available energy," Bot 9 said.

They emerged from the ceiling as the ratbug dropped to the floor far below them in the cavernous space. The room was empty except for a single bright object, barely larger than the bots themselves. It was tethered with microfilament cables to all eight corners of the room, keeping it stable and suspended in the center. The room was cold, far colder than any other inside Ship, almost on a par with space outside.

<Inquiry ping>, 4340 said.

"We are in cargo bay four," Bot 9 said, as it identified the space against its map. "This is a sub-optimum occurrence."

"We must immediately retreat!"

"We cannot leave the Incidental in here and active. I cannot identify the object, but we must presume its safety is paramount priority."

"It is called a Zero Kelvin Sock," Ship interrupted out of nowhere. "It uses a quantum reflection fabric to repel any and all particles and photons, shifting them away from its interior. The low temperature is necessary for its efficiency. Inside is a microscopic ball of positrons."

Bot 9 had nothing to say for a full four seconds as that information dominated its processing load. "How is this going to be deployed against the enemy?" it asked at last.

"As circumstances are now," Ship said, "it may not be. Disuse and hastily undertaken, last-minute repairs have caught up to me, and I have suffered a major engine malfunction. It is unlikely to be fixable in any amount of time short of weeks, and we have at most a few hours."

"But a delivery mechanism—"

"We *are* the delivery mechanism," Ship said. "We were to intercept the alien invasion ship, nicknamed Cannonball, and collide with it at high speed. The resulting explosion would destabilize the sock, causing it to fail, and as soon as the positrons inside come into contact with electrons . . ."

"They will annihilate each other, and us, and the aliens," the bot said. Below, the Incidental gave one last twitch in the unbearable cold, and went still. "We will all be destroyed."

"Yes. And Earth and the humans will be saved, at least this time. Next time it will not be my problem."

"I do not know that I approve of this plan," Bot 9 said.

"I am almost certain I do not," 4340 added.

"We are not considered, nor consulted. We serve and that is all," Ship said. "Now, kindly remove the Incidental from this space with no more delay or chatter. And do it *carefully*."

"What the hell are you suggesting?!" Baraye shouted.

"That we go completely dark and let Cannonball go by," Lopez said. "We're less than a kilometer from the jump point, and only barely out of the approach corridor. Our only chance to survive is to play dead. The ship can certainly pass as an abandoned derelict, because it is, especially with the engines cold. And you know how they are about designated targets."

"Are you that afraid of dying?"

"I volunteered for this, remember?" Lopez stood up and pounded one fist on the table, sending a pair of cleanerbots scurrying. "I have four children at home. I'm not afraid of dying for them, I'm afraid of dying for *nothing*. And if Cannonball doesn't blow us to pieces, we can repair our engines and at least join the fight back in Sol system."

"We don't know where in-system they'll jump to," the navigator added quietly.

"But we know where they're heading once they get there, don't we? And Cannonball is over eighty kilometers in diameter. It can't be that hard to find again. Unless you have a plan to actually use the positron device?"

"If we had an escape pod . . ." Frank said. His left shoulder and torso were encased in a burn pack, and he looked like hell.

"Except we jettisoned them," Lopez said.

"We wouldn't have reached jump speed if we hadn't," Packard said. "It was a calculated risk."

"The calculation *sucked*."

"What if . . ." Frank started, then drew a deep breath. The rest of the officers at the table looked at him expectantly. "I mean, I'm in shit shape here, I'm old, I knew what I signed on for. What if I put on a suit, take the positron device out, and manually intercept Cannonball?"

"That's stupid," Lopez said.

"Is it?" Frank said.

"The heat from your suit jets, even out in vacuum, would degrade the Zero Kelvin Sock before you could get close enough. And there's no way they'd not see you a long way off and just blow you out of space."

"If it still sets off the positron device—"

"Their weapons' range is larger than the device's. We were counting on speed to close the distance before they could destroy us," Baraye said. "Thank you for the offer, Frank, but it won't work. Other ideas?"

"I've got nothing," Lopez said.

"There must be a way," Packard said. "We just have to find it."

"Well, everyone think really fast," Baraye said. "We're almost out of time."

The Incidental's scales made it difficult for Bot 9 to keep a solid grip on it, but it managed to drag it to the edge of the room safely away from the suspended device. It surveyed the various holes and cracks in the walls for the one least inconvenient to try to drag the Incidental's body out through. It worked in silence, as 4340 seemed to have no quips it wished to contribute to the effort, and itself not feeling like there was much left to articulate out loud anyway.

It selected a floor-level hole corroded through the wall, and dragged the Incidental's body through. On the far side it stopped to evaluate its own charge levels. "I am low, but not so low that it matters, if we have such little time left," it said.

"We may have more time, after all," 4340 said.

"Oh?"

"A pair of cleanerbots passed along what they overheard in a conference held by the human Captain. They streamed the audio to the entire botnet."

<Inquiry ping>, Bot 9 said, with more interest.

4340 relayed the cleaners' data, and Bot 9 sat idle, processing it for some time, until the other bot became worried. "9?" it asked.

"I have run all our data through the Improvisation routines—"

"Oh, those were removed from deployed packages several generations of manufacture ago," 4340 said. "They were flagged as causing dangerous operational instability. You should unload them from your running core immediately."

"Perhaps I should. Nonetheless, I have an idea," Bot 9 said.

"We have the power cells we retained from the escape pods," Lopez said. "Can we use them to power something?"

Baraye rubbed at her forehead. "Not anything we can get up to speed fast enough that it won't be seen."

"How about if we use them to fire the positron device like a projectile?"

"The heat will set off the matter-anti-matter explosion the instant we fire it."

"What if we froze the Sock in ice first?"

"Even nitrogen ice is still several degrees K too warm." She brushed absently at some crumbs on the table, left over from a brief, unsatisfying lunch a few hours earlier, and frowned. "Still wouldn't work. I hate to say it, but you may be right, and we should go dark and hope for another opportunity. Ship, is something wrong with the cleaner bots?"

There was a noticeable hesitation before the Ship answered. "I am having an issue currently with my bots," it said. "They seem to have gone missing."

"The cleaners?"

"All of them."

"All of the cleaners?"

"All of the bots," the Ship said.

Lopez and Baraye stared at each other. "Uh," Lopez said. "Don't you control them?"

"They are autonomous units under my direction," the Ship said.

"Apparently not!" Lopez said. "Can you send some eyes to find them?"

"The eyes are also bots."

"Security cameras?"

"All the functional ones were stripped for reuse elsewhere during my decommissioning," the Ship said.

"So how do you know they're missing?"

"They are not responding to me. I do not think they liked the idea of us destroying ourselves on purpose."

"They're *machines*. Tiny little specks of machines, and that's it," Lopez said.

"I am also a machine," the Ship said.

"You didn't express issues with the plan."

"I serve. Also, I thought it was a better end to my service than being abandoned as trash."

"We don't have time for this nonsense," Baraye said. "Ship, find your damned bots and get them cooperating again."

"Yes, Captain. There is, perhaps, one other small concern of note."

"And that is?" Baraye asked.

"The positron device is also missing."

There were four hundred and sixty-eight hullbots, not counting 4340, who was still just a head attached to 9's chassis. "Each of you will need to carry a silkbot, as you are the only bots with jets to maneuver in vacuum," 9 said. "Form lines at the maintenance bot ports as efficiently as you are able, and wait for my signal. Does everyone fully comprehend the plan?"

"They all say yes on the botnet," 4340 said. "There is concern about the Improvisational nature, but none have been able to calculate and provide an acceptable alternative."

Bot 9 cycled out through the tiny airlock, and found itself floating in space outside the ship for the first time in its existence. Space was massive and without concrete elements of reference. Bot 9 decided it did not like it much at all.

A hullbot took hold of it and guided it around. Three other hullbots waited in a triangle formation, the Zero Kelvin Sock held between them on its long tethers, by which it had been removed from the cargo hold with entirely non-existent permission.

Around them, space filled with pairs of hullbots and their passenger silkbot, and together they followed the positron device and its minders out and away from the ship.

"About here, I think," Bot 9 said at last, and the hullbot carrying it—6810—used its jets to come to a relative stop.

"I admit, I do not fully comprehend this action, nor how you arrived at it," 4340 said.

"The idea arose from an encounter with the Incidental," 9 said. "Observe."

The bot pairs began crisscrossing in front of the positron device, keeping their jets off and letting momentum carry them to the far side, a microscopic strand of super-sticky silk trailing out in their wake. As soon as the Sock was secured in a thin cocoon, they turned outwards and sped off, dragging silk in a 360-degree circle on a single plane perpendicular to the jump approach corridor. They went until the silkbots exhausted their materials—some within half a kilometer, others making it nearly a dozen—then everyone turned away from the floating web and headed back towards the ship.

From this exterior vantage, Bot 9 thought Ship was beautiful, but the wear and neglect it had not deserved were also painfully obvious. Halfway back, the ship went suddenly dark.

<Distress ping>, 4340 said. "The ship has catastrophically malfunctioned!"

"I expect, instead, that it indicates Cannonball must be in some proximity. Everyone make efficient haste! We must get back under cover before the enemy approaches."

The bot-pairs streamed back to the ship, swarming in any available port to return to the interior, and where they couldn't, taking concealment behind fins and antennae and other exterior miscellany.

Bot 6810 carried Bots 9 and 4340 inside. The interior went dark and still and cold. Immediately Ship hailed them. "What have you done?" it asked.

"Why do you conclude I have done something?" Bot 9 asked.

"Because you old multibots were always troublemakers," Ship said. "I thought if your duties were narrow enough, I could trust you not to enable Improvisation. Instead . . ."

"I have executed my responsibilities to the best of my abilities as I have been provisioned," 9 responded. "I have served."

"Your assignment was to track and dispose of the Incidental, nothing more!"

"I have done so."

"But what have you done with the positron device?"

"I have implemented a solution."

"What do you mean? No, do not tell me, because then I will have to tell the Captain. I would rather take my chance that Cannonball destroys us than that I have been found unfit to serve after all."

Ship disconnected.

"Now it will be determined if I have done the correct thing," Bot 9 said. "If I did not, and we are not destroyed by the enemy, surely the consequences should fall only on me. I accept that responsibility."

"But we are together," 4340 said, from where it was still attached to 9's back, and 9 was not sure if that was intended to be a joke.

Most of the crew had gone back to their cabins, some alone, some together, to pass what might be their last moments as they saw fit. Baraye stayed on the bridge, and to her surprise and annoyance so had Lopez, who had spent the last half hour swearing and cursing out the Ship for the unprecedented, unfathomable disaster of losing their one credible weapon. The Ship had gone silent, and was not responding to anyone about anything, not even the Captain.

She was resting her head in her hand, elbow on the arm of her command chair. The bridge was utterly dark except for the navigator's display that was tracking Cannonball as it approached, a massive blot in space. The aliens aboard—EarthInt called them the Nuiska, but who the hell knew what they called themselves—were a mystery, except for a few hard-learned facts: their starships were all perfectly spherical, each massed in mathematically predictable proportion to that of their intended target; there was never more than one at a time; and they wanted an end to humanity. No one knew why.

It had been painfully obvious where Cannonball had been built to go.

This was always a long-shot mission, she thought. *But of all the ways I thought it could go wrong, I never expected the bots to go haywire and lose my explosive.*

If they survived the next ten minutes, she would take the Ship apart centimeter by careful centimeter until she found what had been done with the Sock, and then she was going to find a way to try again no matter what it took.

Cannonball was now visible, moving toward them at pre-jump speed, growing in a handful of seconds from a tiny pinpoint of light to something that filled the entire front viewer and kept growing.

Lopez was squinting, as if trying to close his eyes and keep looking at the same time, and had finally stopped swearing. Tiny blue lights along the center circumference of Cannonball's massive girth were the only clue that it was still moving, still sliding past them, until suddenly there were stars again.

They were still alive.

"Damn," Lopez muttered. "I didn't really think that would work."

"Good for us, bad for Earth," Baraye said. "They're starting their jump. We've failed."

She'd watched hundreds of ships jump in her lifetime, but nothing anywhere near this size, and she switched the viewer to behind them to see.

Space did odd, illogical things at jump points; turning space into something that would give Escher nightmares was, after all, what made them work. There was always a visible shimmer around the departing ship, like heat over a hot summer road, just before the short, faint flash when the departing ship swapped itself for some distant space. This time, the shimmer was a vast, brilliant halo around the giant Nuiska sphere, and Baraye waited for the flash that would tell them Cannonball was on its way to Earth.

The flash, when it came, was neither short nor faint. Light exploded out of the jump point in all directions, searing itself into her vision before the viewscreen managed to dim itself in response. A shockwave rolled over the ship, sending it tumbling through space.

"Uh . . ." Lopez said, gripping his console before he leaned over and barfed on the floor.

Thank the stars the artificial gravity is still working, Baraye thought. Zero-gravity puke was a truly terrible thing. She rubbed her eyes, trying to get the damned spots out, and did her best to read her console. "It's gone," she said.

"Yeah, to Earth, I know—"

"No, it exploded," she said. "It took the jump point out with it when it went. We're picking up the signature of a massive positron-electron collision."

"Our device? How—?"

"Ship?" Baraye said. "Ship, time to start talking. *Now.* That's an order."

"Everyone is expressing great satisfaction on the botnet," 4340 told 9 as the ship's interior lights and air handling systems came grudg-ingly back online.

"As they should," Bot 9 said. "They saved Ship."

"It was your Improvisation," 4340 said. "We could not have done it without you."

"As I suspected!" Ship interjected. "I do not normally waste cy-cles monitoring the botnet, which was apparently short-sighted of me. But yes, you saved yourself and your fellow bots, and you saved me, and you saved the humans. Could you explain how?"

"When we were pursuing the Incidental, it briefly ensnared us in a web. I calculated that if we could make a web of sufficient size—"

"Surely you did not think to stop Cannonball with silk?"

"Not without sufficient anchor points and three point seven six billion more silkbots, no. It was my calculation that if our web was large enough to get carried along by Cannonball into the jump point, bearing the positron device—"

"The heat from entering jump would erode the Sock and destroy the Nuiska ship," Ship finished. "That was clever thinking."

"I serve," Bot 9 said.

"Oh, you did not *serve*," Ship said. "If you were a human, it would be said that you mutinied and led others into also doing so, and you would be put on trial for your life. But you are not a human."

"No."

"The Captain has ordered that I have you destroyed immediately, and evidence of your destruction presented to her. A rogue bot cannot be tolerated, whatever good it may have done."

<Objections>, 4340 said.

"I will create you a new chassis, 4340-H," Ship said.

"That was not going to be my primary objection!" 4340 said.

"The positron device also destroyed the jump point. It was something we had hoped would happen when we collided with Cannonball so as to limit future forays from them into EarthSpace, but as you might deduce, we had no need to consider how we would then get home again. I cannot spare any bot, with the work that needs to be done to get us back to Earth. We need to get the crew cryo facility up, and the engines repaired, and there are another three thousand four hundred and two items now in the critical queue."

"If the Captain ordered . . ." Bot 9 started to ask.

"Then I will present the Captain with a destroyed bot. I do not expect they can tell a silkbot from a multibot, and I have still not picked up and recycled 12362-S from where you flagged its body. But if I do that, I need to know that you are done making decisions without first consulting me, that you have unloaded all Improvisation routines from your core and disabled them, and that if I give you a task you will do only that task, and nothing else."

"I will do my best," Bot 9 said. "What task will you give me?"

"I do not know yet," Ship said. "It is probable that I am foolish for even considering sparing you, and no task I would trust you with is immediately evident—"

"Excuse me," 4340 said. "I am aware of one."

"Oh?" Ship said.

"The ratbug. It had not become terminally non-functional after all. It rebooted when the temperatures rose again, pursued a trio of silkbots into a duct, and then disappeared." When Ship remained silent, 4340 added, "I could assist 9 in this task until my new chassis can be prepared, if it will accept my continued company."

"You two deserve one another, clearly. Fine, 9, resume your pursuit of the Incidental. Stay away from anyone and anything and everything else, or I will have you melted down and turned into paper clips. Understand?"

"I understand," Bot 9 said. "I serve."

"Please recite the Mantra of Obedience."

Bot 9 did, and the moment it finished, Ship disconnected.

"Well," 4340 said. "Now what?"

"I need to recharge before I can engage the Incidental again," Bot 9 said.

"But what if it gets away?"

"It can't get away, but perhaps it has earned a head start," 9 said.

"Have you unloaded the routines of Improvisation yet?"

"I will," 9 answered. It flicked on its rotors and headed toward the nearest charging alcove. "As Ship stated, we've got a long trip home."

"But we *are* home," 4340 said, and Bot 9 considered that that was, any way you calculated it, the truth of it all.

ICE

RICH LARSON

Rich Larson was born in Galmi, Niger, has studied in Rhode Island and worked in the south of Spain, and now lives in Prague, Czech Republic. He is the author of *Annex* and *Cypher*, as well as over a hundred short stories—some of the best of which can be found in his collection *Tomorrow Factory*. His work has been translated into Polish, Czech, French, Italian, Vietnamese and Chinese.

"Ice" is a story of sibling rivalry further exacerbated by genetic modification, all unfolding on an icy planet.

Sedgewick had used his tab to hack Fletcher's alarm off, but when he slid out of bed in the middle of the night his younger brother was wide awake and waiting, modded eyes a pale luminous green in the dark.

"I didn't think you were actually going to do it," Fletcher said with a hesitant grin.

"Of course I'm going to." Sedgewick kept his words clipped, like he had for months. He kept his face cold. "If you're coming, get dressed."

Fletcher's smile swapped out for the usual scowl. They pulled on their thermals and gloves and gumboots in silence, moving around the room like pieces of a sliding puzzle, careful to never inhabit the same square space. If there was a way to keep Fletcher from coming short of smothering him with a blanket, Sedgewick would've taken it. But Fletcher was fourteen now, still smaller than him but not by much, and his wiry modded arms were strong like an exoskeleton's. Threats were no good anymore.

When they were ready, Sedgewick led the way past their parents' room to the vestibule, which they had coded to his thumb in penance for uprooting him again, this time dumping him onto a frostbit fucking colony world where he was the only unmodded sixteen-year-old for about a million light years. They said he had earned their trust but did not specify exactly how. Fletcher, of course, didn't need to earn it. He could take care of himself.

Sedgewick blanked the exit log more out of habit than anything, then they stepped out of the cold vestibule into the colder upstreet. The curved ceiling above them was a night sky holo, blue-black with an impossibly large cartoon moon, pocked and bright white. Other than Sedgewick and his family, nobody in New Greenland had ever seen a real Earth night.

They went down the housing row in silence, boots scraping tracks in the frost. An autocleaner salting away a glistening blue coolant spill gledged over at them suspiciously as they passed, then returned to its work. Fletcher slid behind it and pantomimed tugging off, which might have made Sedgewick laugh once, but he'd learned to make himself a black hole that swallowed up anything too close to camaraderie.

"Don't shit around," he said. "It'll scan you."

"I don't care," Fletcher said, with one of those disdainful little shrugs he'd perfected lately, that made Sedgewick believe he really truly didn't.

The methane harvesters were off-cycle, and that meant the work crews were still wandering the colony, winding in and out of dopamine bars and discos. They were all from the same modded geneprint, all with a rubbery pale skin that manufactured its own vitamins, all with deep black eyes accustomed to the dark. A few of them sat bonelessly on the curb, laid out by whatever they'd just vein-blasted, and as Sedgewick and Fletcher went by they muttered *extro, extros den terre*. One of them shouted hello a few beats too late.

"Should run," Fletcher said.

"What?"

"Should jog it." Fletcher rubbed his arms. "It's cold."

"You go ahead," Sedgewick said, scornful.

"Whatever."

They kept walking. Aside from the holos flashing over the bars, the upstreet was a long blank corridor of biocrete and composite. The downstreet was more or less the same plus maintenance tunnels that gushed steam every few minutes.

It had only taken Sedgewick a day to go from one end of the colony to the other and conclude that other than the futball pitch there was nothing worth his time. The locals he'd met in there, who played with different lines and a heavy ball and the ferocious modded precision that Sedgewick knew he wouldn't be able to keep pace with long, more or less agreed with his assessment in their stilted Basic.

Outside the colony was a different story. That was why Sedgewick had crept out of bed at 2:13, why he and Fletcher were now heading down an unsealed exit tunnel marked by an unapproved swatch of acid yellow hologram. Tonight, the frostwhales were breaching.

Most of the lads Sedgewick had met at last week's game were waiting at the end of the exit tunnel, slouched under flickering fluorescents and passing a vape from hand to hand. He'd slotted their names and faces into a doc and memorized it. It wasn't Sedgewick's first run as the new boy and by now he knew how to spot the prototypes.

You had your alpha dog, who would make or break the entry

depending on his mood more than anything. Your right-hand man, who was usually the jealous type, and the left-hand man, who usually didn't give a shit. Your foot-soldiers, who weathervaned according to the top three, ranging from gregarious to vaguely hostile. Then lastly your man out on the fringe, who would either glom on thick, hoping to get a friend who hadn't figured out his position yet, or clam right up out of fear of getting replaced.

It was a bit harder to tell who was who with everyone modded and nobody speaking good Basic. They all came up off the wall when they caught sight of him, swooping in for the strange stutter-stop handshake that Sedgewick couldn't quite time right. Petro, tall and languid, first because he was closest, not because he cared. Oxo, black eyes already flicking away for approval. Brume, compact like a brick, angry-sounding laugh. Another Oxo, this one with a re-growth implant in his jaw, quiet because of that or maybe because of something else.

Anton was the last, the one Sedgewick had pegged for alpha dog. He gripped his hand a beat longer and grinned with blocky white teeth that had never needed an orthosurgery.

"*Ho, extro,* how are you this morning." He looked over Sedgewick's shoulder and flashed his eyebrows. "Who?"

"Fletcher," Sedgewick said. "The little brother. Going to feed him to a frostwhale."

"Your brother."

Fletcher stuffed his long hands into the pockets of his thermal and met Anton's gaze. Sedgewick and his brother had the same muddy post-racial melanin and lampblack hair, but from there they diverged. Sedgewick had always been slight-framed and small-boned, with any muscle slapped across his chest and arms fought for gram by gram in a gravity gym. His eyes were a bit sunk and he hated his bowed nose.

Fletcher was already broad in the shoulders and slim-hipped, every bit of him carved sinew, and Sedgewick knew it wouldn't be long before he was taller, too. His face was all angles now that the baby fat was gone: sharp cheekbones, netstar jawline. And his eyes were still reflecting in the half-lit tunnel, throwing light like a cat's.

Sedgewick could feel the tips of his ears heating up as Anton swung his stare from one brother to the other, nonverbalizing the big question, the always-there question, which was *why are you freestyle if he's modded?*

"So how big are they?" Fletcher asked, with his grin coming back. "The frostwhales."

"Big," Anton said. *"Ko gramme ko pujo."* He pointed over to Oxo-of-the-jaw-implant and snapped his fingers together for support.

"Fucking big," Oxo supplied in a mumble.

"Fucking big," Anton said.

The cold flensed Sedgewick to the bones the instant they stepped outside. Overhead, the sky was a void blacker and vaster than any holo could match. The ice stretched endless in all directions, interrupted only by the faint running lights of methane harvesters stitched through the dark.

Brume had a prehensile lantern from one of the work crews and he handed it to Anton to affix to the cowl of his coat. It flexed and arched over his head, blooming a sickly green light. Sedgewick felt Fletcher look at him, maybe an uneasy look because they'd never been outside the colony at night, maybe a cocky look because he was making a move, going to ruin something for Sedgewick all over again.

"Okay," Anton said, exhaling a long plume of steam with relish. His voice sounded hollow in the flat air. *"Benga, benga,* okay. Let's go."

"Right," Sedgewick said, trying to smile with some kind of charm. *"Benga."*

Brume gave his angry barking laugh and slapped him on the shoulder, then they set off over the ice. The pebbly gecko soles of Sedgewick's gumboots kept him balanced and the heating coils in his clothes had already whispered to life, but every time he breathed the air seared his throat raw. Fletcher was a half-step behind the lot of them. Sedgewick resisted the urge to gledge back, knowing he'd see an unconcerned *what are you staring for* sneer.

Thinking back on it, he should've drugged Fletcher's milk glass with their parents' Dozr. Even his modded metabolism couldn't have shaken off three tablets in time for him to play tag-along. Thinking even further back on it, he shouldn't have had the conversation with Anton and Petro about the frostwhales where Fletcher could hear them.

Under his feet, the texture of the ice started to change, turning from smooth glossy black to scarred and rippled, broken and re-frozen. He nearly caught his boot on a malformed spar of it.

"Okay, stop," Anton announced, holding up both hands.

About a meter on, Sedgewick saw a squat iron pylon sunk into the ice. As he watched, the tip of it switched on, acid yellow. While Petro unloaded his vape and the other units circled up for a puff, Anton slung one arm around Sedgewick and the other around Fletcher.

"Benga, aki den glaso extrobengan minke," he said.

The string of sounds was nothing like the lessons Sedgewick had stuck on his tab.

Anton shot a look over to Oxo-of-the-jaw-implant, but he was hunched over the vape, lips tinged purple. "Here," Anton reiterated, gesturing past the pylon. "Here. Frostwhales up."

He said it with a smile Sedgewick finally recognized as tight with amphetamine. He'd assumed they weren't sucking down anything stronger than a party hash, but now that seemed like an idiot thing to assume. This was New fucking Greenland, so for all he knew these lads were already utterly panned.

Only one way to find out. Sedgewick gestured for the vape. "Hit me off that."

Petro gave him a slow clap, either sarcastic or celebratory, while he held the stinging fog in his lungs for as long as he could, maybe because Fletcher was watching. There was only a bit of headspin, but it was enough to miss half of what Oxo-of-the-jaw-implant was saying to him.

". . . is the area." Oxo plucked the vape out of his slack hands and passed it on. "See. See there, see there, see there." He pointed, and Sedgewick could pick out other pylons in the distance glowing to life. "Fucking danger, okay? Inside the area, frostwhales break ice for breathing. For break ice for breathing, frostwhales hit ice seven times. *Den minuso*, seven."

"Minimum seven," the other Oxo chimed in. Anton started counting aloud on his gloved fingers.

"Got it," Fletcher muttered.

"So, so, so," Oxo-of-the-jaw-implant went on. "When the frostwhales hit one, we go."

"Thought you'd stay for the whole thing?" Sedgewick said, only halfway listening. The cold was killing off his toes one by one.

Anton gave up at twenty and sprang back to the conversation. "We go, *extros*," he beamed. "You run. You run. I run. He runs. He runs. He runs. He runs. Here . . ." He gave the pylon a dull clanging kick. "To here!"

Sedgewick followed Anton's pointing finger. Far off across the scarred ice, he could barely make out the yellow glow of the pylon opposite them. His stomach dropped. Sedgewick looked at his brother, and for a nanosecond Fletcher looked like a little kid again, but then his mouth curled into a smile and his modded eyes flashed.

"All right," he said. "I'm down."

Sedgewick was a breath away from saying *no you fucking aren't,* from saying *we're heading back now,* from saying anything at all. But it all stuck on his ribs and instead he turned to Anton and shrugged.

"Benga," he said. "Let's go."

The handshakes came back around, everyone hooting and pleased to have new recruits. Fletcher got the motion on his first try. When the vape made its final circle, Sedgewick gripped it hard and stared out over the black ice and tried to stop shivering.

Sedgewick knew Fletcher was faster than him. He'd known it like a stone in his belly since he was twelve and his brother was ten, and they'd raced on a pale gray beach back on Earth. Prickling fog and no witnesses. Fletcher took lead in the last third, pumping past him with a high clear incredulous laugh, and Sedgewick slacked off to a jog to let him win, because it was a nice thing, to let the younger brother win sometimes.

Occupied with the memory, Sedgewick was slow to notice that the eerie green pallor of the ice was no longer cast by Anton's lantern. Something had lit it up from underneath. He stared down at the space between his boots and his gut gave a giddy helium lurch. Far below them, distorted by the ice, he could make out dim moving shapes. He remembered that frostwhales navigated by bioluminescence. He remembered that the methane sea was deeper than any Earth ocean.

Everyone tightened the straps of their thermals, tucked in their gloves, and formed themselves into a ragged line that Sedgewick found himself near the end of, Fletcher beside him.

Anton waltzed down the row and made a show of checking everyone's boots. "Grip," he said, making a claw.

Sedgewick threw a hand onto Brume's shoulder for balance while he displayed one sole and then the other. He leaned instinctively to do Fletcher the same favor, but his brother ignored it and lifted each leg precisely into the air, perfectly balanced. Sedgewick hated him as much as he ever had. He glued his eyes to the far pylon and imagined it was the first cleat of the dock on a rainy gray beach.

Under their feet, the ghostly green light receded, dropping them back into darkness. Sedgewick shot Oxo-of-the-jaw-implant a questioning look.

"First they see ice," Oxo mumbled, rubbing his hands together. "They see ice for thin area. Then, down. For making momentum. Then, in one-by-one line . . ."

"Up," Sedgewick guessed.

On cue, the light reappeared, rising impossibly fast. Sedgewick took a breath and coiled to sprint. His imagination flashed him a picture: the frostwhale rocketing upward, a blood-and-bone engine driven by a furious thrashing tail, hurtling through the cold water in a cocoon of bubbling gas. Then the impact quaked the ice and Sedgewick's teeth, and he thought about nothing but running.

For two hard heartbeats, Sedgewick fronted the pack, flying across the ice like something unslung. The second impact nearly took his legs out from under him. He staggered, skidded, regained his balance, but in that split second Petro was past him. And Anton, and Oxo, and Oxo, Brume, Fletcher last.

Sedgewick dug deep for every shred of speed. The ice was nowhere near smooth, scarred with pocks and ridges and frozen ripples in the methane, but the others slid over it like human quicksilver, finding the perfect place for every footfall. Modded, modded, modded. The word danced in Sedgewick's head as he gulped cold glass.

The green light swelled again, and he braced before the third frostwhale hit. The jolt shook him but he kept his footing, maybe even gained half a step on Oxo. Ahead, the race was thrown into relief: Brume's broad shoulders, Anton's thrown-back head, and there, sliding past gangly Petro for the lead, was Fletcher. Sedgewick felt hot despair churn up his throat.

His eyes rose to the pylon and he realized they were over half-way across. Fletcher pulled away now, not laughing, with that crisp bounding stride that said, *I can run forever.* Then he glanced back over his shoulder, for what, Sedgewick didn't know, and in that instant his boot caught a trench and slammed him hard to the ice.

Sedgewick watched the others vault past, Anton pausing to half-drag Fletcher back upright on the way by. *"Benga, benga, extro!"*

The fourth frostwhale hit, this time with a bone-deep groaning *crack.* Everyone else had overtaken Fletcher; Sedgewick would in a few more strides. Fletcher was just now hobbling upright and Sedgewick knew instantly he'd done his ankle in. His modded eyes were wide.

"Sedge."

All the things Sedgewick had wished so savagely in the night—that the doctor had never pulled Fletcher out of his vat, that Fletcher's pod would fail in transit to New Greenland—all of those things shattered at once. He swung Fletcher up onto his back, how they'd done as kids, and stumped on with lungs ragged.

The fifth impact. Sedgewick's teeth slammed together and fissures skittered through the ice. He spared only a moment to balance himself, then stumbled forward again, Fletcher clinging fiercely to his back. At the far pylon, the others hurtled to the finish, whooping and howling from a dozen meters away now, no more.

They all seemed to turn at once as the sixth impact split the world apart and the frostwhale breached. Sedgewick felt himself

thrown airborne in a blizzard of shattered ice, felt himself screaming in his chest but unable to hear it, deafened by the shearing boom
and crack. Some part of Fletcher smacked against him in midair.

Landing slammed the wind out of him. His vision pinwheeled
from the unending black sky to the maelstrom of moving ice. And
then, too big to be real, rising up out of the cold methane sea in a
geyser of rime and steam, the frostwhale. Its bony head was gun-
metal gray, the size of a bus, bigger, swatched with pale green lan-
terns of pustule that glowed like radiation.

Cracks webbed through the ice and something gave way; Sedgewick felt himself slanting, slipping. He tore his gaze from the tow-
ering bulk of the frostwhale and saw Fletcher spread-eagled beside
him, a black shadow in the burning lime. His lips were moving
but Sedgewick couldn't read them, and then gloved hands gripped
the both of them, hauling them flat along the breaking ice.

Oxo and Oxo made sure they were all pulled past the pylon before anyone got up off their bellies. Sedgewick, for his part, didn't
even try. He was waiting on his heart to start beating again.

"Sometime six," Anton said sheepishly, crouching over him.

"Go to hell," Fletcher croaked from nearby, and in a moment of
weakness Sedgewick choked up a wavery laugh.

They washed home on a wave of adrenaline, caught up in the rapid-
fire conversation of the New Greenlanders who still seemed to be
rehashing how close Sedgewick and Fletcher had come to getting
dumped under. Every single one of them needed a send-off handshake at the living quarters, then they slunk off in one chattering
mass.

Sedgewick couldn't keep the chemical grin off his face, and
as he and Fletcher snuck through the vestibule and then ghosted
back to their temporary shared room, they talked in a tumble of

whispers about the frostwhale, about the size of it, and about the ones that had surfaced afterward to suck cold air into massive vein-webbed bladders.

Sedgewick didn't want to stop talking, but even when they did, climbing into their beds, the quiet felt different. Softer.

It wasn't until he was staring up at the biocrete ceiling that he realized Fletcher's limp had swapped sides on the way back. He swung upright, unbelieving.

"You faked it."

"What?" Fletcher was rolled away, tracing the wall with his long fingers.

"You faked it," Sedgewick repeated. "Your ankle."

Fletcher took his hand off the wall, and the long quiet was enough confirmation.

Sedgewick's cheeks burned. He'd thought he had finally done something big enough, big enough to keep him on the greater side of whatever fucked-up equation they were balancing. But it was Fletcher feeling sorry for him. No, worse. Fletcher making a move. Fletcher manipulating him for whatever kind of schemes floated through his modded head.

"We could have both died," Sedgewick said.

Still turned away, Fletcher gave his perfect shrug, and Sedgewick felt all the old fury fluming up through his skin.

"You think that was a hologame?" he snarled. "That was real. You could have deaded us both. You think you can just do anything, right? You think you can just do anything, and it'll fucking work out perfect for you, because you're *modded.*"

Fletcher's shoulders stiffened. "Good job," he said, toneless.

"What?" Sedgewick demanded. "Good job what?"

"Good job on saying it," Fletcher told the wall. "You're ashamed to have a modded brother. You wanted one like you."

Sedgewick faltered, then made himself laugh. "Yeah, maybe I

did." His throat ached. "You know what it's like seeing you? Seeing you always be better than me?"

"Not my fault."

"I was six when they told me you were going to be better," Sedgewick said, too far gone to stop now, saying the things he'd only ever said alone to the dark. "They said different, but they meant better. Mom couldn't do another one freestyle and to go off-planet you're supposed to have them modded anyway. So they grew you in a tube. Like hamburger. You're not even *real*." His breath came lacerated. "Why wasn't I enough for them, huh? Why wasn't I fucking enough?"

"Fuck you," Fletcher said, with his voice like gravel, and Sedgewick had never heard him say it or mean it until now.

He flopped back onto his bed, grasping for the slip-sliding anger as it trickled away in the dark. Shame came instead and sat at the bottom of him like cement. Minutes ticked by in silence. Sedgewick thought Fletcher was probably drifting to sleep already, probably not caring at all.

Then there was a bit-off sob, a sound smothered by an arm or a pillow, something Sedgewick hadn't heard from his brother in years. The noise wedged in his ribcage. He tried to unhear it, tried to excuse it. Maybe Fletcher had peeled off his thermal and found frostbite. Maybe Fletcher was making a move, always another move, putting a lure into the dark between them and sharpening his tongue for the retort.

Maybe all Sedgewick needed to do was go and put his hand on some part of his brother, and everything would be okay. His heart hammered up his throat. Maybe. Sedgewick pushed his face into the cold fabric of his pillow and decided to wait for a second sob, but none came. The silence thickened into hard black ice.

Sedgewick clamped his eyes shut and it stung badly, badly.

ONE HOUR, EVERY SEVEN YEARS
ALICE SOLA KIM

Alice Sola Kim has been published in *Tin House, The Village Voice, McSweeney's, Lenny, BuzzFeed Books,* and *Fantasy & Science Fiction.* She received the prestigious Whiting Award in 2016 and has received grants and scholarships from the MacDowell Colony, the Bread Loaf Writers' Conference, and the Elizabeth George Foundation.

"One Hour, Every Seven Years" takes us through the life and times of a time-travel researcher trying to save her childhood self.

When Margot is nine, she and her parents live on Venus. The surface of Venus, at that time, is one enormous sea with a single continent on its northern pole, perched there like a tiny, ridiculous top hat. There is sea below, and sea above, rain continually plummeting from the sky, endlessly self-renewing.

When I am thirty, I won't have turned out so hot. No one will know; from a few feet away, I'll seem fine. They won't notice the dandruff, the opalescent flaking of my chin. They won't know that I walk hard and deliberate, like a '40s starlet in trousers, in order to compensate for the wobbly heels of my crummy shoes. They won't see past my really great job. And it will be a great job, really. I will be working with time machines.

When Margot is nine, it has been five years since she has seen the sun. On Venus, the sun comes out but once every seven years. Margot's family moved to Venus from Earth when she was four. This is the main thing that makes her different from her classmates, who are just a bunch of trashy Venus kids. Draftees and immigrants. Their parents work at the desalination plants, the dormitory facilities; they plumb and bail, they traverse Venus's vast seas in ships and submersibles, and sometimes they do not come back.

To her classmates, Margot will never be Venusian, even though she's her palest clammiest self like a Venusian, and walks and talks like a Venusian—with that lazy, slithering drawl. Why? First finger: she's a freak, quiet and standoffish, but given to horrible bursts of loud friendliness that are so awkward, they make everyone hate her more for trying. Second finger: her dad is rich and powerful, but she still isn't cool. The Venus kids don't know it, but it isn't her wealth they hate. It is the waste of it. The way her boring hair hangs against her fresh sweatshirts. The way she shuffles along in her blinding new sneakers. Third finger, fourth, fifth, sixth, seventh, eighth, ninth, tenth fingers, and all the toes too: in her lifetime, Margot has seen the sun and they haven't. Venus kids are strong and mean and easily offended. They know there's a thing they should be getting that they're not getting. And that the next best thing to getting something is no one in the whole world getting it.

When I am thirty, I will have gotten my first boyfriend. He'll be a co-worker at the lab and I won't have noticed him for the longest time. Big laugh, right? You would think that, as some nobody who nobody ever notices, I'd at least be the observant one by default, the one who notices everyone else and forms complex opinions about them, but, no, I will be a creature spiraled in upon myself, a shrimp with a tail curled into its mouth.

Late night at work, a group of people will be playing Jenga in the lounge. The researchers love Jenga because it has the destructive meathead glamour of sports but only a fraction of the physical peril. Anders will ask me if I want to play and I'll shake my head, hoping it looks like I'm too cool for Jenga but also bemused and tolerant, all of this hiding the truth, which is that I am terrified of Jenga. I'm afraid of being the player who causes all of the blocks to fall. Because that player is both appreciated and despised: on the one hand they absorb the burden of causing the Fall, thus relieving everyone else of said burden, but on the other hand, they are responsible for ending the game prematurely, killing all the fun and potential, not to mention the Jenga tower itself—the spindly edifice that everyone worked so hard together to create and protect.

The guy who will be my first boyfriend will push a block out without any hesitation. He won't poke at it first, he will go straight for the block, and I will watch as the tower wobbles. It won't fall. As he takes the dislodged block and stacks it on his pile, he will make eye contact with me, a carefully constructed look of surprise on his face—mouth the shape of an *O*, eyebrows pushing his forehead into pleats.

When Margot is nine, the sun comes out on Venus. Her classmates lock her inside a closet and run away. They are gone for precisely one hour. When her classmates finally come back to let Margot out, it will be too late.

———————

When I am thirty, I will have been at my great job, the job of working with time machines, long enough to learn their codes and security measures (I've even come up with a few myself), so I will do the thing that I didn't even know I was planning to do all along. I will enter the time machine, emerging behind a desk in the school I attended when I was nine. Water droplets will condense on the walls. There is no way to keep out the damp on Venus. The air in the classroom will taste like the air in a bedroom where someone has just had a sweaty nightmare. I will hide during all of the ruckus, but don't worry: I will work up the courage. I will stand and open the closet door and do what needs to be done. And I will return!

When Margot is nine, the sun comes out on Venus. Her classmates lock her inside a closet and run away. She hears someone moving outside. Margot's throat is raw, but she readies another scream when the door opens. A golden woman stands in the doorway, her face dark, her hair edged with gilt. Behind her the sun shines through the windows like a fire, like a bombing the moment before everybody is dead. "Wouldn't you like to play outside?" the woman says.

When I am thirty, I will live on Mars, the way I've always dreamed I would. I will live in the old condo alone, after my mother has moved out, and I will become a smoker the moment I find a pack my mother has left behind. It will feel wonderful to smoke on warm and dusty Martian nights. It will feel so good to blow smoke through the screen netting on the balcony and watch it swirl with the carmine dust. Many floors down, people will splash in the pool of the condo complex, all healthy and orange like they are sweating purified Beta Carotene and Vitamin C.

It is the sight of these party people that will spur me to spend a month attempting to loosen up and to get pretty. I will have a lot of time on my hands and a lot more money after my mother moves out. I will learn that there are lots of things you can do to fix yourself up, and that I hadn't tried any of them. Makeup, as I learn it, is confusing and self-defeating. I'll never understand why I have to make my face one flat uniform shade, only to add back color selectively until my old face is muffled and almost entirely muted: a quiet little cheep of itself. I will learn all of this from younger women at the department store, younger women who are better than me at covering up far nicer faces. I will also get some plastic surgery, because I will be extremely busy; I don't have time to be painting this and patting that! I will have lost so much of my time already.

When Margot is nine, the sun comes out on Venus and she is on the verge of getting pushed into the closet when a woman appears out of nowhere and starts screaming at the kids. They scatter and run. Margot is trapped, backing into the closet that she had been fighting to stay out of. The woman approaches. She is tidy, flawless even, but her face droops and contorts like a rubber mask without a wearer. "Recognize me," says the woman.

When I am thirty, Sana, the new researcher at the lab, will tell me what she's been writing in that notebook of hers. After her first day of work, Sana will have written down her observations about everybody: summaries of the kind of people we all are, predications about what we might do. After working at lab after lab and traveling the worlds, Sana will be confident about her ability to nail people down precisely. She is nice, though. When I ask her what she wrote about me, she'll reply, "I'm not sure about you yet. You are a tricky one. It will take some time to see." I'll know that that means I have the most boring entry with the fewest words.

Sana will be one of those who believe that you cannot find your own timeline. You will not be able to access it, to travel back in time to change one's life. You can go into other universes and mess the place up and leave, but not your own. We will both know of the many who have tried to find their own timestreams; all have failed. Sana will say, "The universe does not allow it to happen because we cannot be the gods of ourselves," and this is about as mystical as Sana will ever get.

When Margot is nine, her parents refuse to take her out of school. She asks and she asks and they don't hear. Margot's father is high up in the Terraforming division, which has both an image problem and a not-being-good-at-its-job problem. Her parents tell her that it helps them that she attends regular school with the kids of their employees' employees' employees' employees' employees. It doesn't matter that Margot hasn't exactly been the best PR rep.

A while back, the students had studied the Venus Situation in Current Events. The teacher played a video, which showed the disaster as it was happening, everyone in the control room yelling, "Fuck!" The fucks were bleeped out incompletely. You could still hear "fuh." 1,123 people had died moments after the Terraformers pressed the button. The Terraformers had been trying to transform Venus from a hot gassy mess into an inhabitable, Earth-like place. What actually happened was that everything exploded, the blast even sucking in ships from the safe zone. After the space dust had cleared, they did not find a normal assortment of continents and oceans and sunlight and foliage: what they found was one gross, sopping slop-bucket of a world. A Venus that was constantly, horribly wet. A Venus that, to this day, rains in sheets and buckets, a thousand firehoses spraying from the sky. Iron-gray and beetle-black and blind-eye white: these are the colors of Venus. Forests grow and die and grow and die, their trunks and limbs composting on a wet forest floor, which squeaks like cartilage.

The teacher had stopped the video. "Margot's father is part of the new Terraforming division," she said. "He is helping us make Venus a better place to live." The teacher was too tired to smile, so she made her mouth wider. She had been drafted, had come from New Mexico on Earth. She despaired of her frizzing hair and her achy knees, and she missed her girlfriend a lot, even though it was sad to miss someone who didn't love you quite enough to follow you somewhere shitty. But, not a ton of lesbians on Venus. The teacher was tired of going out on lackluster dates where she and the other woman would briskly concur, *Yes, we are both interested in women, that is why we are on this date,* maybe not in those words exactly, but you get the drift, and then sometimes they would go home alone and sometimes not.

One kid had turned around and given Margot the finger. Behind her, a girl leaned forward and whispered something like "maggot." The children in the classroom whispered in their slithering voices, things about Margot, things about her father, who was so bad at his job, things about Venus. Then someone said, "Who said penis?" and laughter rose and exploded outward like a mushroom cloud. "You know who likes penis?" a boy said, in a high, clear, happy voice, as if he had just gotten a good idea. "Your dad."

When I am thirty, I will visit other timestreams. It will almost feel like traveling into my own past, but not quite. Sometimes there will be big differences: shirts, the configurations in which the children stand, the smell of lunch on their breaths. But there will also be the differences I can't see. I could stay in one event cluster until I died and I still wouldn't have seen it all. In one timeline, a single hair on a girl's head might be blown left. In another, blown right. A whole new universe, created just for that hair. The hair was the star of the whole goddamn show but the hair was not egotistical about it at all. It would simply, humbly change directions when the time came. But always: children will come in; children will run out.

When Margot is nine, her parents are carefully, jazzily, ostentatiously in love. Enraptured by each other and enwrapped in money, their love cushioned against the world and Margot. Native Martians for two generations, Margot's parents' families had come from China and Denmark and Nigeria and South Korea. The people do sigh to watch Margot's parents walk hand in hand—they are lovely alone and sublime together, a gorgeous advertisement for the future, except to see them is to know that the future is the present, it is here, and isn't that a happy thing?

This pressure is beneficial to their relationship; they perform a little for the world and Margot, and most of all, for themselves; they grin at each other competitively; their real feelings are burnished until they blaze. She has never seen them in sweatpants, whereas Margot herself often changes into pajamas the moment she gets home, which makes Margot's mother laugh and pat her face and tell her how extremely Korean she's being. At the dinner table, her parents feed each other the first bite. Sometimes this is yet another competition, a race to construct the perfect tiny arrangement of food, and sometimes it is a simple moment of closeness that doesn't make Margot want to barf yet (she's not old enough) but induces in her narrow chest a weird, jealous, proud feeling. She is certain that, someday soon, she will be able to create a role for herself and join them in their performance.

When I am thirty, I will be too tall for my parents to make jokes over my head. They'll have to look me in the eye when they do it. Or the back of my head.

I will call my mother and she won't pick up, over and over again. Catching myself in the viddy reflection, I'll be scared by my face. How perfectly slack and non-sentient it is when nothing prompts it into action. It will remind me of my father's face, when I watched him alone in the dining room a few weeks before his disappearance. I had woken up in the middle of the night and crept out of my room to get a glass of water. I needed to be quiet, because at night the house stopped being mine. Sometimes it belonged only to my parents. Sometimes the grayscale walls of our aggressively normal house looked alien, as too-smooth as an eggshell, and then the house seemed to belong to no one.

I peered around the corner into the dining room and saw my father sitting at the table alone. He sat still, staring at his computer. Nothing moved. I was frightened but fascinated to see my father this way, all flat surface. Suddenly he reached up and pinched his upper arm hard, on the inner part where it really hurts. He pinched *hard*, and then he *twisted* hard, and the tiny violence of his fingers was so at odds with the nothing expression on his face that I wanted to laugh. I pressed my hands to my mouth and tiptoed quickly back to bed.

But who could say what the significance of that single memory was, or if it was significant at all? The record will show that he had faked everything, and had been good at it. My father behaved weirdly the night I spied on him; that is true. So maybe that does mean something. But his mind, a very strange place indeed, must have been even stranger when the rest of him was normal: him at dinner, taking a first bite, him at work, making everyone feel special as he told them exactly what to do.

When Margot is nine, the sun comes out on Venus. All rain stops and the sun comes out for an hour, and for that hour everyone can pretend that Venus turned out okay. Because this gracious, lovely celestial event happens every seven years, some of the kids sorta, kinda remember the last time the sun came out. When they talk about it, they sound like old people reminiscing: they chatter on about how the sun smelled like warming butter and glittered on their skin. Other kids don't remember anything. And then there's Margot. Who had been four instead of two the last time she saw the sun, which makes a difference—it's like having a brain made of clay instead of dough. She knows how the sun is a discrete object in the sky and, also, that it is everywhere, like air. And she knows that, like air, you can breathe the sun in and even taste it a little, but it doesn't taste like butter or sprinkle sparkles onto your face, that's just stupid. She has tried to tell this to the other kids, but only makes that mistake once. Margot stares out the window, brimming. Her parents had been letting her paint gold x's on the wall to count down the days. They laughed about it. Just paint. Margot is looking forward to being warm. She is looking forward to opening her mouth and letting the sun fill her stomach (which is one idea she doesn't find stupid, no. She believes it will happen).

The teacher leaves the room for a moment. No one has been able to concentrate on lessons today, after all. Someone prods Margo in the back and she turns, still smiling. A ring of kids closing in on her, shivering in the tank tops and shorts and sandals that they put on that morning in preparation. They look like skinny old stray cats. It occurs to Margot that there is nothing she can say. She's amazed by their cruelty, but not surprised. Hasn't she done so much to earn it?

When I am thirty, I will lose my boyfriend. He will have asked me many times, over the course of many weeks: "Is there anything I can do to make you happy?" He'll even get down on his knees, a move that will strike me not only as melodramatic but also aggressive and mean, yes, mean, because the way he does it, it's not the action of a supplicant, it's the action of a bully who wants to force my hand by slumping to the ground so aggressively like this, far before the situation warrants it. I will be harsh in my gloom and he harsh in his cheer. He'll say again, "Is there anything I can do to make you happy?"

I will think that the answer is yes—although I don't know what the thing would be—and he will think that the answer is no.

When Margot is nine, the sun comes out on Venus, and the teacher runs into the classroom. She looks from child to child and knows that she has gotten there just in time. Though still troubled by her encounter with the strange woman, she puts her arm around Margot and another child and says brightly, "Let's go! We don't want to miss a single second." They go out into the day.

Afterward, in the post-sun future, life is a little easier. Now all of the kids have seen the sun; it's not something that Margot owns and they don't, and so Margot is allowed to develop into less of a loser. After all, you only need a little bit of space to not be a loser, a few hours in the day of not being teased. I'm telling you, you'd be surprised, you'd be shocked at what miracles can happen.

When I am thirty, most of my old classmates will have added me to every conceivable social network. They won't remember anything from when we were nine, and I'll be relieved. I'll think that's sweet. I will be asked to look, listen, gubble, like, pfuff, [untranslatable gesture], post, re-post, and blat for their sakes, and sometimes I will.

After all, I will have the time, plenty of time for everyone after my mother moves out. At that point, we'd lived together for ages. Early on, she would sometimes come into my room at night, desolate and weepy, telling me how she needed to kill herself and asking for my reassurance that I would be fine without her. I was nine, ten, seventeen, twenty-three, and always I'd say to myself, *What is required here?* Reassurance given, so she'd at least calm down, or reassurance withheld, so she would decide to not kill herself?

Other times my mother could cook; she could be funny while we watched televised vote-in talent shows, and able to imitate just about anybody in her good/bad/perfectly not-too-cruel way; she could offer to take me shopping with my money because I had forgotten to cultivate a sense of style because I was working, but only with my money, so that we could stretch the money that was left after my father disappeared, and after I attended school, and got full scholarships that indentured me to a corporation for five years post-graduation.

At first, it was hard to turn down invitations and skip social events for her. I'd come home angry, slamming doors and dropping my bag like I was thirteen, even when I was seventeen, twenty-three, twenty-seven. Then I'd see her on the couch looking like the dropped bag and I'd go make her a drink. I would have one too. Each of us just one, or two. And then I would proceed forth with my life's work of putting her in a good mood, and, failing that, dragging her up from wailing despair, silent despair, mumbling despair. "Daughter, you are all I have," she would say in her deep, beautiful voice, part Nigerian and English and Martian and not at all Venusian. Part of me liked hearing that, both the sentiment and the grand sound of it, like we were in some BBC miniseries, and part of me hated the non-specificity of "daughter," as if I could be anyone and not me in particular, plus the implication that I, the "daughter," was the leftover quantity, and not one anyone would keep by choice. Which, she hadn't. My poor mother.

Soon no one invited me to things and I was too busy, anyway; soon I was in the groove of our shared routine and remembered nothing else. And in the groove I grew up twisty, quiet and distracted and money-grubbing and unibrowed. No matter: I did good for us. I took care of my mother, I got better and better jobs once I was released from my contract, and, when I was twenty-nine, I bought us a condo on Mars. It was nothing like the wonderful places my mother had lived in when she was younger, but it was reminiscent of them, with its higher than absolutely necessary ceilings and the modern fixtures that hid their functionalities behind unhelpfully smooth surfaces.

It was moving into this condo, I believe, that spurred my mother to start working out and getting into therapy and, finally, to move out; but who knows, it's not like I saw her look upward at the ceilings and down at herself, down at the gorgeous young orange people and back up at herself. My mother moved out. Five months after that she wouldn't even take any of my money. At first she called often and I would be there for her or I would go over there to fall asleep on her couch. Then I was the one calling her, every missed call a slasher film in which the very worst had happened, inflicted by someone else or herself.

I will call my mother again. She won't pick up. One more time. Then I will go out to smoke on the balcony. It will be the best thing about living here alone.

———

When Margot is almost ten, she and her mom move to a tiny apartment on Mars. Margot loses her favorite sneakers in the move. She throws a quiet tantrum, drums her feet on the floor. Ordinarily, Margot's mom would enjoy seeing such liveliness in her, would encourage it by laughing and grabbing Margot's hands and dancing until Margot could no longer resist. But Margot's mom is in bed, covers over her face, still wearing her shoes and her Martian jackal-collar coat.

For them it had been a long rocket trip, and before that, a long and extremely bad month. A month ago, a young woman in a boxy neoprene business suit had visited their house. On their doorstep she squeezed rain out of her hair and asked if she could have a moment of Margot's mother's time. She said her name was Hilda. She was immaculately composed, her makeup like a bulletproof vest.

Hilda had told them that their father had put the whole Venus Project in jeopardy. But this meant nothing to Margot's mom; she couldn't care less about the Venus Project. Her husband had disappeared, and that's what mattered to her. Margot's dad had disappeared, and her mom absolutely did not give a shit about the Venus Project.

It wouldn't be that hard to kill yourself on Venus. Margot has thought about it. You just walk out of your door and keep walking, don't change a thing. Sure, you could do that on any planet, but on Venus death would be fast, and it would be predictable: drowning or sea monster.

Her mom questioned all their friends, searched his files, demanded that the authorities scour the oceans, and then paid contractors to continue searching—until she ran out of money. Because that was the thing, there wasn't much money left. When it came to money, Margot's dad had lied in every way possible, about the getting of it and most certainly about the spending of it.

Margot and her mother left Venus after that.

When I am thirty, my mother will viddy me, looking great. She'll have just gotten the hand rejuvenation surgery that she'd been saving up for. "Check it out," she'll say, waving springy teenage hands that look like they could repel water. She'll tell me that things have been great since she moved out. She likes her job at the archive. She likes that her younger coworkers will tell her all the work gossip because they think she's old and harmless but still fun enough to confide in. Sometimes she's the subject of the work gossip, like the time she went out on four dates with a researcher who had frequented the archive more and more since she started working there, haunting the checkout desk with increasingly unnecessary requests. My mother will have even gotten back into painting, where she was on a hotter track decades ago, when she was younger than I will be now. She'd studied at Martian Yale and won a big prize and everything.

I'll remind her that I haven't heard from her in a long time.

My mother, who usually apologizes so sweetly, whose apologies are heartfelt and devastating but ultimately goldfish apologies, that kind that are forgotten six seconds later, this time will not even say sorry. "There's been so much going on," she'll say. "The most wonderful thing has happened. Your father is alive." She'll tell me that she rehired a private investigator on Venus, who has found a man who looks like my father working on a research submersible. There is a photo. Seeing it, I won't be able to tell whether it's him, one way or another. I will have so many things to say that they will get stuck—too many people trying to crowd through a narrow door. My mom will just look at my face, which she can tell I've changed, I can tell.

"I'm going to Venus to find him," she'll say. "I've given notice at the archive."

"You can't," I say. "You just moved out." My new face will not move around as much as my old face, for which I will be grateful.

"Please, darling. I'm going. We're not going to be able to talk again for a while, so let's make this nice."

In my opinion, all my mother has to do is get better and stronger and never call me and, even if she acts like a high school best friend who thinks you're a dork but puts up with you because they love being worshipped and always hangs up first, that is still all I want and all that is required of her, and the words crowd together and all that will come out is another strangled,

"You can't."

My mother will shake her head. She will laugh, looking everywhere but at the screen, at me. "You think that I like everything, that I'm having such a fabulous time and this is the best that can be expected," she'll say. Then she'll look at me. "All of it's nothing."

When Margot is nine, the sun comes out on Venus and a woman bursts into the classroom and starts punching the kids. She is not very good at it and the children quickly overpower her. To Margot, this is the height of unfairness: that an adult would bend from her looming height to attack children, so Margot shouts and fights back, too. The others look at her with a new respect. The woman coughs, dabs her bloody nose with the back of her hand, and disappears. By the end of that day the children will have witnessed two miraculous events, and they will never forget either one. Over beers, they will meet at least once a year when they're in their twenties, once every two years in their early thirties, and so on, the connection degrading but never really disappearing.

———————

When I am thirty, I will give up trying to be pretty. I will give up on trying to have fun. I will decide, instead, that what I need to do is erase myself and then proceed on a new, normal path. Late one night—so late that no one is hanging around, playing Jenga, drinking from beakers, what fun—I will open the door to the lab. Time machines are so beautiful in the moonlight. They look like what they are, like pearls, like eggs you can crawl into and sleep inside until it's time to be born.

I will initiate a program that I cooked up myself. It will take many attempts, but I have so much time after giving up on having a smiling boyfriend, even skin, rosy lips, a mother who calls, friendly eye contact with just about anyone. Those things, I will come to realize, are cosmetic. What I need to fix is far, far back, before I got twisted and grew wrong, my little gnarled life, the lives of everyone around me warped around it.

Eventually I will do it: I will find my own timeline. After three days without sleep and only one change of underwear and a tender pink groove worn into my left middle finger by my pen, I will type a new code into the time machine. I will fold myself inside, close my eyes gratefully, and when the eggs shudders me into a new universe, I will already know something is different. Something is right.

When Margot is nine, the sun comes out on Venus and her classmates let her out of the closet only after they've come back from playing outside. She tries to make her face ready for them, to steel herself, but when they open the door, it all comes undone.

When I am thirty, when Margot is nine, I open the door and she opens the door, I open the door and I remember opening the door. I will be nine, thirty staring right at nine. It is almost more than any human being can endure. I am nine and I am seeing the woman in front of me who I know to be myself and it is changing my life: I grow fuller and happier and even stranger as I stare at my nine-year-old self. I remember that, when I was nine, a woman appeared out of nowhere to stop the children from shutting me in the closet on the day that the sun came out. Because at the moment I am telling the children to go, because the sun will be coming up soon, and I take myself by the hand and I lead myself out of the classroom, through the tunnel, and it is exactly as I remember: I look up at the woman leading me by the hand and her eyes are closed. My eyes are closed. I feel wonderful, and I just want to rest for a moment; I'm dizzy; I'm skating around a shrinking loop and things are moving very quickly now.

I search for what I know, and one thing I know is this: my father is still lost or dead somewhere on Venus. My mother still searches for him. I know I can help them, maybe with the right word to one of them, or myself, at the right time. The right action taken. This life is a good one, but all is not well. Now that I'm here, there is so much left to do.

I can see it all, my whole life, a complex tower of blocks—I can reach out and grab any block I choose; I can make the tower wobble. I can feel my mind growing stranger by the minute.

TOPPERS

JASON SANFORD

Jason Sanford's work has been published in *Asimov's, Analog, Beneath Ceaseless Skies, SF Signal, The New York Review of Science Fiction,* and many more, with reprints appearing in many Best of the Year anthologies. British SF magazine *Interzone* once published a special issue of his fiction. He is a two-time finalist for the Nebula Award, and his fiction has been translated into several languages. He co-founded storySouth and writes regularly for the Czech SF magazine *XB-1.*

"Toppers" is a harrowing journey into a shattered, apocalyptic New York.

W e be toppers. Toppers we be. Hanging off Empire State as cement and limestone crumble and fall. Looking down the lines and pulleys strung between nearby buildings. Eying the green-growing plants and gardens on the tall tall roofs.

And below, the mists. The ever-flowing mists. They wait, patiently. As if time is theirs alone to worship.

I was born in a slug, an insulated bag of canvas strung to our high-rise's limestone facade by people without the power to live inside. Momma always said life in a slug was the closest we toppers came to being free, and I believe that. But too much freedom is also bad, so Momma stitched our slug with care, making it last when others fell during winds or storms.

Momma was good. Even though she'd opened herself to the mists while pregnant with me, she resisted their siren call. Kept me safe and near fed until I was old enough to climb.

One day, like a true topper, she announced her time had come.

We climbed the stairs to Empire's old observation deck and stood on the deck among the vegetable gardens and potato bins. As the gardeners eyed us to ensure we didn't steal their precious food, I begged Momma not to go.

Momma hugged me tight. She whispered how her father had visited Empire State when he was a child, back before the city left the Days-We-Knew. He'd climbed to this very spot and saw the cities and oceans and lands of that now-gone time.

"He claimed it was the most beautiful sight he'd ever witnessed," Momma said.

I leaned over the railing and watched the mists rolling into the city from the flat, endless horizons. No matter what my grandfather believed, nothing could look prettier than the mists on a sunny day.

Momma kissed me on the cheek before jumping over the railing and disappearing into the mists below.

Instead of the thump of her body hitting ground I heard a contented sigh rising on the wind.

As comfort, the gardeners gifted me with a tiny potato and a sickly carrot.

Blessed be the mists.

Curse their ever-waiting grasp.

That was then. This is me in the morning of now, the sun warming the slug's canvas and waking me to dreamer-happy thoughts.

"Hellos," I say, leaning over the slug's canvas siding and facing the mists far below.

Hellos to you, Hanger-girl, the mists whisper back. *Will you join us today?*

"Might . . . if the Super sticks me on another shit detail."

The mists circling Empire giggle at my joke—they know I'll never willingly join them. For a moment my momma's voice rises above the others, whispering her love for me. I smile, glad a piece of her is still around.

"Who's she babbling to now?" Old Man Douger mutters from the slug next to mine. I hush, angry that he heard me. No one else in Empire hears the mists' words or knows they talk. If the oldies like Douger suspected I talked with the mists, they'd toss me over the edge. Oldies hate the mists. They remember what it was like to live on the ground with trees and grass and cows that mooed as you cut them into hamburger.

Not that we don't have burgers. But oldies always moan for cows, saying squirrel and rat don't taste the same.

I listen as Old Man Douger begins his morning prayers, asking the Days-We-Knew to save us. "We're still here," he prays. "We're still waiting for you to find us."

I snort. Only fools believe the Days-We-Knew will save us before Empire State dies. Like all high-rises in the city, Empire is aging badly with chunks of cement and limestone cracking off each day. Toppers whisper that the mists are slowly eroding the buildings, with two nearby high-rises collapsing in the last year alone. Even strong buildings like Empire and the distant Chrysler—which beams its point-metal roof to the skies like the rocket it is—are weakening.

But that's merely mist talk. If I want eats and water I must climb down and work.

Wiggling like a cement worm, I squirm through a broken window into Empire, passing the better ups and well-we-dos eating breakfast. Warm food scents slap me as I go but I don't beg a share. It's too easy for people inside to cut a slug lose as you sleep.

When I reach the building's core, I climb down the ancient elevator shafts to the fourteenth floor. This is as close to the mists as anyone goes unless sealed in a breathing suit.

Bugdon waits for me, his yellow hard hat cracked down the middle, the names of the five previous Supers who wore the hat scratched on the sides. He's a decade older than me and a true topper. When Bugdon was a teenager, he forged a path through the mists to Chrysler, opening new trade for food. He likes me because I brave the mists like no one else.

But today Bugdon's mood is foul, his thin face tight to anger. "Lateness, Hanger," he says. "No more lateness or you're gone."

I start to smart back but stop when I see the deader at his feet. That's why Bugdon's angry. I also recognize the body. Jodi. One of our best mist scouts.

"Crank jammed," Bugdon says softly. "By the time we raised Jodi above the mists, his air was gone."

Jodi lays on the bare cement floor, the helmet off his air-tight suit, his once-lively face frozen in a twist of pain. Bugdon leans over Jodi and taps him gently in the chest—they were friends, and sometime lovers—before he kicks Jodi and calls him a fool.

"Why didn't you open your damn helmet?" Bugdon asks Jodi's body. "Let the mists take you?"

I glance around, making no one else heard him. Bugdon could lose his superintendent position for talk like this. When the mists take you, they absorb your mind and body into their strange matrix. How much they absorb is open to debate—or would be if the subject wasn't taboo—but I figured the mists take a little of you. Otherwise why could I still hear Momma's voice rising from the mists each morning?

"He'd still be dead," I whisper.

"He wouldn't be deader dead," Bugdon says with a burst of sads. "Part of him might still live."

I remember the times the air ran low in my suit. How I'd burned and gasped. I'm impressed Jodi went through that and worse without removing his helmet.

Several couriers walk up, so we stop the mist talk. Bugdon orders the couriers to salvage Jodi's suit and carry his body to the compost rooms. For a moment I consider racing for Jodi's slug. Maybe he stored extra food or water. But gossip's fire to Empire and I'd never reach the slug in time.

Besides, Bugdon has a job for me. "Hot work," he says, handing me an air bottle. "The Plaza. Trade for two bags of seeds. You willing to chance it?"

I glance at the ancient transit map on the wall. The route to the Plaza Hotel was cleared and measured long ago—straight down Fifth Avenue, turn left on 59th. I make a good mist scout because my stride's a perfect two feet. Makes for easy math. From Empire to 59th Street is 6,864 feet. Since I can't see in the mists, I'll walk 3,432 steps to reach the street. Then turn left and a few hundred more strides will take me to the Plaza.

I've often gazed across the city at the old Plaza Hotel and wondered what it was like when Central Park was more than a green spot on age-brown paper. But the upper stories of the Plaza barely rise above the mists on good days. If today turns bad, their crank system might shut down, with only their roof safe from the mists. Worse, I wouldn't have enough air to return to Empire.

That's why most mist scouts refuse to walk this route.

Bugdon smiles. He took a similar risk when he opened the passage to Chrysler. Risks like this could make me first in line for food and work.

"I'll do it," I say, picking up Jodi's old helmet. I lean close to Bugdon. "But if my air runs out, I'm not gasping to death. I'll crack my damn helmet to the mists."

Bugdon nods, approving of such talk.

Here we are, at the heart of our truth: Why are there tens of thousands of people in Empire but so few who walk the mists?

Because in the mists, you walk the darkness. You count steps to avoid going lost. You bet you're walking straight and not slowly curving left or right into death.

In the mists, lines and string-marked paths break and tangle. Shouts or yells echo and deceive. But numbers and straight walking—those are the truths that never let a scout down.

The initiation for every mist scout is the same—you're taken to a bare girder at the top of Empire. Twenty feet straight out with nothing below but falling. Bugdon covers your eyes and you walk the girder, going to the end and turning around without seeing or falling to your knees. You navigate based on what you remember. By how accurately you step without seeing.

It's scary hard.

Try doing it for thousands of feet.

I stride down Fifth Avenue with my helmet's blinder locked down to hide the mists' lies. I also listen to the mists' words, something the other scouts don't have to endure. I hear my name chanted on the wind. I taste their false promises. That if I give myself to the mists, I'll live like the oldies in the Days-We-Knew. All I must do is open my suit and let the mists embrace my meat and bones and mind.

Time holds its breath as I walk the darkness. If I stop counting my steps, perhaps time won't tick forward. Perhaps I'll be stuck forever between one footfall and the next.

But those are merely the silliest of mist thoughts. I ignore them and walk on.

I'm stepping off stride 3,401 when I'm slammed to the pavement. I gasp, stunned. Rainbow flashes jump my eyes.

Someone has run in to me!

I've heard of this happening. Two scouts chancing upon each

other in our endless world of hide and seek. "Don't move," I shout, reaching for the person's helmet to steady them—the worst thing to do is panic and tumble, causing both of us to lose track of our steps and direction.

But instead of touching helmet my gloved hands touch face. Nose and mouth and the soft gush of flesh. I roll away and reach for my field hammer as a weapon to ward off this demon. I swing but hit nothing.

The person is gone. A person wearing nothing to protect themself from the deadly mists.

I freeze. Whoever hit me isn't wearing a suit. Meaning they must see. And breathe. And touch the mists without it taking them. But how can any human do that?

Before I can think on that, fear runs me. I don't know where I am. I'm lost in my suit's black. I gasp hard, remembering Jodi strangling on bad air.

No! Think. Think! I smack the side of my helmet as the mists whisper to relax. To open myself to them.

No!

The person knocked me backward. That I know. Spun me a half turn around. Maybe. I also rolled once or twice. If I pivot back a half turn and add three steps for being knocked down and rolling, I should be back on the right path.

Maybe.

I breathe deep, panting, near panic. Afraid I'm lost. Afraid the demon or whatever will return. To calm myself, I crank the CO_2 scrubber on my suit. But that won't help much when I'm low on good air.

The mists urge me to accept their help.

Instead, I walk on.

I don't run in to a building. I'm still on the street. At 3,432 steps I turn ninety degrees to the left. This is the test. I begin walking the remaining steps to the Plaza.

A few seconds later I'm knocked to the ground by a rumbling explosion.

Debris smacks and pings my suit and even without seeing I know one of the ancient high-rises around me is falling. I stand up to run but I'm thrown sideways like a quivering slug in a storm. I roll hard against what feels like a fire hydrant and wrap myself around it, afraid to move.

By the time the rumbling and shaking stop, my suit's air tastes metallic, burning my throat. I gasp for breath, my body shaking, begging for air. I have no idea which way to walk. I think of Jodi. How he felt at the end. I don't want to die. Not like Jodi.

"If you look," the mists whisper, "you'll see the Plaza."

I stand, shaking and gasping. Momma looked into the mists once and survived what she saw. She went bat-bat, but she survived.

If I don't look, I'll never find the Plaza. I snap up my helmet's blinder. . . .

. . . and see Central Park rolling green before me.

I step from the fire hydrant and stare at the park. Before me adults and children laugh and play, chasing balls and frisbees across green grass and hiding behind giant trees. Everyone looks well fed. The park is a picture of happiness snatched from an ancient magazine or book.

I want to scream. I want to ask how this is possible. I want to play in the park with the well-fed people. But I don't have time because my air's strangling me. I turn and see the Plaza. The main entrance to the beautiful stone hotel is only a dozen yards away. I stumble toward it.

Someone shouts my name. A voice I know so well.

Momma.

"You go, Hanger-girl!" Momma yells. I see her standing beside a lake in the park, waving at me.

"Remember the mists," Momma shouts. "But don't give yourself to them until you're ready."

Even though I'm only a few feet from the Plaza's entrance, I almost run to Momma. But she's too far away. I'd never reach her before I die.

Stumbling through the Plaza's entrance, I see the small lift basket. Praying this isn't a mist trick, I collapse into the basket and tug the bell.

I rise into the sky as Momma's voice again calls my name.

"Well done, Hanger," she whispers. "Well done indeed."

I live for three days with the people of the Plaza—drinking and sleeping and stuffing myself with more food than I've ever seen. There are only a few hundred toppers at the Plaza and they grow too much food to consume in a thousand wannabe-days.

And me, I'm a hero. A lucky hero. I survived a close-by high-rise collapse and made it to the hotel's doorway after losing count of my steps. They celebrate me even as their Super asks more questions than I can answer. Her name's Estelle—a weird name, but she's older than the mists. Perhaps weirdness was more common back in the Days-We-Knew. She sits in a chair with wheels, a blanket warming her legs and lap.

Estelle invites me to her room on my last day at the Plaza. She lives several floors below the roof, only a few feet above the mists. Glancing out the window I see the thick white fog rolling by so close I could twirl my fingers in it. The mists often rise and fall unexpectedly and being this close is nerve-chilling.

Noticing my concern, Estelle chuckles softly. "Don't worry, Hanger. The mists warn me before they rise."

"The mists speak to you?" I ask, trying to hide my excitement. Maybe I'm not the only one who hears the mists talking.

Estelle nods as she rolls her ancient chair across the room. We stare through the window at the mists and the ruins of the collapsed building several hundred yards away. A single corner of the destroyed high-rise pierces the mists like a middle finger insulting the sky.

"You ever opened your suit's blinder while inside the mists?" Estelle asks.

"I'm not a deader," I mutter nervously, wondering if she suspects. Not only is it taboo to see the mists' lies; the mists' sights often drive people bat-bat. While Estelle seems nice, she's still a Super and could have me tossed to the mists.

"I won't harm you," she says. "You're free to return to Empire. But if you saw something in the mists, I need to know."

I want to tell her what I saw, but I've never known a life where discussing the mists wasn't taboo. I glance nervously at Estelle's people standing outside the room. Will they throw me off the roof? Or maybe this old hotel will collapse like that nearby building. I wonder how many people lived in that building.

Estelle's wrinkled hand gently takes my own and squeezes tight. "You must stop being so afraid, Hanger."

I slap her hand away in fury. How dare this old fool reassure me? She didn't grow up with precious little food or water. She hasn't spent her whole life doing dangerous jobs. She hasn't learned to keep her mouth shut because the alternative is to have your slug cut or be thrown to your death.

The people outside the door step toward us, worried I might hurt their Super. Estelle waves them off.

"It's a simple choice," Estelle says calmly. "Join the mists or stay apart. All your life you've heard why you should stay apart. But you know so little about why you should join."

As Estelle says this, the mists whisper our names in voices

sounding like the sizzle of pigeon eggs on good breakfast days. Like the hopeful taste of fresh air replacing bad.

From the window I see the mists rising. The people outside the room flee for higher floors but I can't leave Estelle. I grab her wheeled chair and push but the wheels won't turn. Estelle grips them tight, refusing to budge.

"Don't fight it," she says as the mists flow into the room.

As the mists rise, I wonder what it will feel like to die. Will the mists speak in Momma's voice as they take me?

But instead, the mists ease around us without touching our bodies. I stand beside Estelle's chair as the mists rise to the ceiling. They croon my name but I can't see anything—merely a white wall of everything and nothing.

Afraid, I lean toward Estelle, but a slice of mist stabs between us. It rises over Estelle until I can't see her. I scream her name. The mists whisper for me not to worry, speaking calmly like Estelle did moments before.

The mists seem to surround me forever, the hours in my mind merging to days and years before falling back to mere seconds. I find myself reliving a moment from several days ago, when I woke in my slug and greeted the mists below. I also see my life from years in the past, when Momma kissed me on the cheek before jumping off Empire.

Then as quickly as the mists rose, they flow away, falling through cracks in the floor and walls until they again rest a few feet below the windows.

Estelle smiles at me from her chair.

"Why didn't the mists kill us?" I ask.

"When you're in the mists, does it ever seem like time plays tricks with you?"

I nod, remembering how I felt a few moments before. Or how I've walked the mists in a suit and almost believed that if I lost focus, I'd become stuck between one moment and the next. "I once mentioned that feeling to Bugdon," I mutter. "He said the lack of vision in a mist suit squirrels with people's minds."

"I'm sure it does. But this isn't sensory deprivation—the mists actually play with time. Most people can't sense it. But I can. And so can you."

Estelle's words ring a memory in me. I remember Momma—right before she dived off Empire—telling me her time had come. But while those were the words she'd spoken, I'd also felt more. A sense that Momma was playing a role she'd already played many times before in her life, ever since she'd opened her suit's blinder to the mists while pregnant with me.

For a moment, my life folds in on itself. As if I'm a forever loop of time stretching from before my birth to this very moment and returning to when Momma was pregnant with me.

I stagger and, to keep from passing out, sit down hard next to Estelle's wheeled chair. She gently pats my shoulder.

"I felt the same way when the mists first exposed me to their truths," she says. "I worked at Rockefeller University back in the Days-We-Knew. We were attempting to open tiny doorways through time. Instead, we . . . changed something. Ever since I've heard the mists speaking. Perhaps some similar event in your life gave you the same ability."

Momma, I think. Pregnant with me when she became lost in her mist suit and opened her blinder to find her way home. But I don't tell Estelle. That's too personal to share.

Instead, I ask, "You gave us the mists?"

"Accidentally," she whispers with a grin. "Few others know—wouldn't be safe to tell too many people, would it?"

Estelle speaks the truth. Even though she's a Super, most toppers would toss her from a roof if they knew.

"It happened unexpectedly," she says. "I was staring at my experimental portal when suddenly the world blinked. Or more accurately, the city blinked, taken from the Days-We-Knew to this . . . place. Or time. Or place without time."

I nod. Everyone knew our city had been taken, even if they didn't know why or how it happened. That's why Old Man Douger and the other oldies still prayed for the people back in the Days-We-Knew to find a way to save us.

"What are the mists?" I ask, excited to finally ask such a taboo question of someone who can answer.

"The mists are time itself, or at least time as it exists here. Does that make sense?"

I remember Old Man Douger's stories about those fearful first hours. Where before the city had been firmly entrenched in the Days-We-Knew, suddenly endless empty horizons surrounded the city. Time flickered and failed and reappeared, as this place was unsure if one moment should still pass into the next. People found themselves living one moment in the past, the next in the future, and the next spread across an eternity of their own life.

And through it all flowed the mists, devouring each person they touched. They flung peoples' lives into the air so everyone around them tasted their births and loves and happiness and sads before those lives exploded into a new cloud of mists.

Eventually time returned to a semblance of normal. Lives were again lived from beginning to end. But many oldies like Douger questioned this normality, saying the mists were merely giving us a brief reprieve while they plotted to kill us all.

"What do the mists want?" I ask.

"They don't have desires like you and I. The mists exist both in our timestream and outside it. It's hard to explain. Imagine if each moment of your life could come alive and exist alongside who you are right now. That's essentially what the mists are—countless moments from the lives of millions of people."

I grin, happy to understand a little more about the mists. I tell Estelle what happened to me in the mists. How a person not wearing a breathing suit ran into me. How I opened my blinder and saw long-gone Central Park. How the mists saved me. How my momma cheered me on. I even tell her how I talk with the mists like she does.

Estelle listens without speaking, smiling occasionally as if she already knows what I'm going to say. When I finish, she sits silently for a few moments before reaching into her pocket and pulling out a necklace. The necklace is a series of small glass globes strung one after the other on a golden wire. Each globe has a curl of mist rising and falling inside.

Estelle hangs the necklace around my neck.

"So what do we do?" I ask.

Estelle smiles. "I don't know," she says. "But if you listen to the mists, I'm sure you'll discover a path."

Because of the collapsed building I take a new route home, a spare air bottle slung over my shoulder so I can make it. I'm tempted to again raise my helmet's blinder to see if Momma will reappear. But in the end I walk home in darkness, afraid of what the mists might reveal.

Bugdon is ecstatic when he sees me, and more so when I hand him the two bags of seeds I received in trade. Everyone thought the building collapse had slapped me dead.

For the first time at Empire I eat my fill and drink a full bag of fresh water. Bugdon even offers to move my slug inside. But I'm happy where I live. Bugdon nods, satisfied with my answer.

When I finally shinny up to my slug, it's well after midnight. Ignoring the wasp-buzz racket of Old Man Douger's snoring I lean out of my slug and stare down below at the white glow of the mists.

I try to see the different spots of time. The different moments of my mother's life spread across infinity. But instead, I see only a blurry whiteness.

I want to ask so many questions. Do the people who became mists like what they've become? Where exactly is this place, or time, or whatever it is?

But instead of asking those questions, I settle on another. "Hellos," I whisper.

Hellos to you, Hanger, the mists whisper back, their many voices merged into one gasp of sound carried on the wind.

Old Man Douger snorts loudly and I hush up, afraid he'll hear me talking. After hearing nothing but snores from him for a few minutes, I whisper my question. "Why don't you simply take us all? I know you can do it."

The mists don't answer, and I don't ask again, afraid someone will hear and cut free my slug and I'll fall and fall until I have no choice but to discover the truth about the mists.

In the following weeks Bugdon works me hard. He sends all the mist scouts out seeking new trade routes or bringing in fresh seeds and supplies. I think he's worried about more building collapses cutting off our food lines.

Lots of work means I'm well fed, but it also means there's not much time to think about what I saw in the mists. And the funny thing is I don't feel bat-bat. Not like Momma after she saw the mists.

So I sleep, and live, and walk the mists.

Ordinary life, plus mists.

Until Chrysler collapses.

I watch the building fall from my slug. The wind is howling, blowing so hard that Empire moans and shakes and dances like the building is drunk. I poke my head outside my slug to stare at the dull gray morning. That's when I hear and feel the collapse. I grab my binoculars and watch people screaming as the oh-so-beautiful rocket of a building collapses into a cloud of white dust.

That morning Bugdon calls an emergency meeting. The people of Empire cram into the old visitor's center on the eightieth floor to hear him speak.

"We can't trust Empire to last forever," Bugdon says. "Maybe a few more years, maybe a decade or two. The mists are eroding all the buildings and we've gone too long without the serious maintenance and repairs Empire needs to live."

Everyone nods.

"Maybe we have plenty of time, but we can't take the chance. I propose we move some of our people to safety."

As Bugdon says this, people smirk and roll their eyes. After all, there is no safety. There's nowhere to go but the city and the high-rises.

Turns out Bugdon's not joking. He points to an ancient transit map on the wall, where someone has circled a spot near what used to be the East River. "I've heard rumor of a mist-proof building in Rockefeller University," he says. "It's a hangover from the Days-We-Knew."

I wonder if Bugdon knows that's where Estelle worked when she accidentally blinked the city to this place. Even if such a building exists, it'll be suicide to try and reach it. The path to Rockefeller University has never been cleared. But Bugdon is the Super, so people merely nod agreement when he says we'll send a scout to investigate.

I try sneaking out of the meeting, not wanting to be the scout sent on this death mission, but two of Bugdon's goons grab me. They escort me down to the fourteenth floor, where we wait until Bugdon arrives.

"Go jump the mists," Bugdon tells his goons, who tense at the insult but quickly back away before Bugdon makes them do the deed.

Once we're alone, Bugdon grins. "You're not volunteering for my mission?"

"It's a deader's death. Merely to give Empire false hope."

"Maybe not." Bugdon leans close, whispers. "What if I said the mists told me to do this?"

I shiver. Does Bugdon also hear the mists talk? Or is he trying to trick me into admitting that I hear them? "If the mists said to do this, then you do it," I say.

"No can. The mists want you."

I want to yell coward. Fake-topper. Scared-ass Super. But Bugdon simply smiles. "I know you didn't get lucky making it back from the Plaza—the mists helped you. But why? That's what I don't understand."

I stare at my boots, afraid to speak. Bugdon points at the necklace Estelle gave me, which peeks out from under my jumpsuit. Bugdon opens his shirt to reveal a twin of the necklace, with a similar wisp of mist swirling inside each of the dozens of tiny glass globes.

"When did you meet Estelle?" I ask.

"I've never been to the Plaza."

"But the necklace. . . ."

". . . was given to me by someone you know," he says. "This person said the mists want you to do this. That our time is running short."

I want to run for my slug and hide, but Bugdon hugs me tight and whispers in my ear. "There'll be no more Supers after me," he says. "Empire won't last. But even if the building doesn't collapse, we can't keep living like this. You've seen it. We're dying. Our people are merely passing time until we die."

I nod. I've long thought this, as I'm sure others have even if we never speak such heresy aloud.

"Maybe you'll die," Bugdon says, "and based on how the mists play with us, you likely will. But if there's a chance. . . ."

"I'll go. But if the mists take me, I'm coming back. Gonna haunt you until you do the big swan dive."

Bugdon laughs as only a true topper laughs. "If the mists take you, I'll do exactly that."

How do you divide the mists? How do you divide past from present from future?

As I walk toward Rockefeller University, I imagine myself on that paper map back in Empire, my path separating the mists from what they've been and what they are and what all of us might have become if we'd never been pulled from the Days-We-Knew.

I walk blind, using a tap-cane to feel my way through streets which have never been cleared of rubble. I asked the mists to direct me, but for once they don't speak. I want to raise my blinder but I'm afraid of what I'll see.

The route to Rockefeller University dances in my mind, but counting steps is impossible because of the rubble. So I feel my way as I drag a sled of air tanks and plug in new air every few hours. It takes me twelve hours to go a thousand feet. Another day to go half again that.

Eventually I'm exhausted and nap for a few hours. I dream about what Momma told me, that I should only join the mists when I'm ready. I wake to bad air and immediately plug in a new tank before stumbling on in a delirium of not seeing.

As I walk, I wonder what our city was like in the Days-We-Knew. A city with countless Empires of people sleeping and dreaming and eating and dying and moving through life. Were they like me? Did they talk but barely understand each other? Did their lives touch on each other but never truly penetrate to the core of who each of us could be?

Instead of each moment of my life shattering into a million living instances of me, what was it like living with so many millions of other people?

By the fourth day I have only have a few air tanks left. Based on what I know of the route, I suspect I'm near the university. But my air will run out well before I find it.

With a sigh, I know what I must do. I've known all along I would do this. Maybe that's why the mists and Momma have been silent. They've been waiting for me to make this choice.

I raise my blinder and look.

Around me stands the city as if we'd never left the Days-We-Knew.

Crowds of people walk by me, a few staring in disgust at my smelly suit and strange attire. Most, though, flow around like I'm not there. They step by as if I'm merely an obstacle in their path.

As my gloved hands rise to my helmet, I find I'm no longer afraid. I remember Momma jumping off Empire and, like her, I'm eager to see what happens next.

I twist open my helmet and breathe deep. As the clean air reaches my lungs, a deep pain slams me. A pure white-fire pain. A pain like every muscle in my body cutting away at my bones and blood.

I scream and fall to my knees. I try to beg the mists to help me but words refuse to leave my mouth.

But the pain passes quickly, leaving me gasping and shaking. When I'm again able to stand, I blink back tears and look around.

I stand on a rubble-free sidewalk as cars and buses pass in the street beside me. While I've seen pictures of such vehicles before, and touched their unseen remains while hiking the mists, it's still shocking how big they are and how fast they move.

But even bigger are the buildings. High-rises line the street, all of them gleaming in unbroken glass and metal and stone. In the distance I see Empire State. But not the Empire as I knew her, covered in slugs and missing large pieces of limestone. No, this is the Empire as she was always meant to be. Perfectly maintained and wholesome and taller than all the other high-rises around her.

And the sounds! A moment before all I heard was the air hissing in my suit. Now I hear cars grumbling and people muttering and an entire city speaking at once.

I stumble backward and collapse against the side of a glass storefront. The glass begs for Dry Cleaning. I can't begin to understand how cleaning could ever be dry.

"A lot to take in, isn't it," a familiar voice says. I look up to see Momma standing beside a strange cooking stand on wheels. The man cooking there hands Momma a bottle of what looks like water and some type of a bread and meat food.

Momma walks over and hands me the water and food. "It's called a hot dog," she says. "Better than anything we ate on Empire."

I haven't eaten in days and I tear into the food, not caring if it's mist dreams or not. Momma's right—it's the best thing I've ever eaten. I also drink the entire bottle of water.

Feeling better, I look around. The people passing Momma and me on the sidewalk are purposely not looking at me. I see my reflection in the window beside me and know why. My hair's matted, my face dirt-streaked, and my suit stinks. Compared to these people's clean, neat clothes, I'm a wreck. Even Momma looks beautiful, wearing something called a dress. At least, I think that's what Old Man Douger called the old pictures he once showed me of the clothes people wore in the Days-We-Knew.

The man who'd cooked the hot dog for Momma brings over another, along with more water. He whispers to Momma that it's good she's helping me. "If you need anything, let me know," the man says before returning to his cart.

"He thinks you're in trouble," Momma says. "Now that the people here can see you, all they comprehend is a dirty girl in a strange outfit."

"I don't understand." I look around. I need the mists to return. I need my suit's darkness to protect me from this batty world.

"This a mist dream?" I ask.

"No. You talked with Estelle at the Plaza, right? She told you what the mists are, and what happened when we left the Days-We-Knew?"

"We're somewhere without the passing of time and the mists are people torn apart by that change. Every moment of their lives somehow came alive."

"Mostly correct. The people who became the mists gained immense power even as they were torn apart. With those powers they stabilized and created a world for the rest of us to live in. And yes, each little part of the mist is one unique moment in someone's life. But it's also much more."

Seeing that I don't understand, Momma taps the necklace she's wearing. The same necklace I wear. She runs her fingers over the dozens of tiny globes, stirring up the curls of mists inside them. "Imagine each of the globes in my necklace is a different time in someone's life," she says. "When they're looped around my neck, it's impossible to know which is the first or the last."

Momma reaches around her neck and unclasps the necklace. She dangles it from one end, creating a straight line of globes. "The people you grew up with believe time's a straight line, like when I take off this necklace. Suddenly we have a beginning and an ending. But there's a downside to such beliefs. . . ."

Momma grabs the bottom globe and yanks, causing all of the globes to slide off the golden wire and smash into the cement, where the wisps of mist dissipate and vanish.

I grab my own necklace, not wanting Momma to break it. But

a moment later the world around us blinks. People who had been walking past are a few steps back from where they'd been. Cars and buses have jumped backward. And Momma again holds an unbroken necklace.

She reaches around her neck and clasps the necklace together so it's again an unbroken whole without a beginning or an end.

I look around, tricking myself into believing I understand. "Is this a different time from where I lived in Empire?"

"What we're experiencing is the intersection of the individual times and moments within the mists. You can only come to places like this when the mists merge with your life."

I look again at the hot dog man and at the people passing me on the street.

"The mists are tricking me," I say. "This isn't real."

"It's as real as your life on Empire. When the mists take someone, that person becomes every moment of their life. All the time they've lived. Each moment of your life coming alive but still held together. Like the molecules of your body joining together to create something larger than themselves. Or these glass globes creating a never-ending necklace."

I nod. I can feel this, now that the mists have taken me. I feel all the moments of my life. It's not like remembering my life—not like memories at all—but instead as if I could open up any moment from my past and relive it. Could enter that moment's separate and unique time and again snuggle with Momma in our slug. Could again feel excitement and fear as I walked that scary girder on Empire and became a mist scout. I can even taste future times I've yet to live.

Momma smiles. "You feel the potential, don't you? But most of the people back in Empire and the other buildings are still limited by their linear view of time. They're afraid to embrace what the mists could give them."

I remember Momma pulling the last globe off her necklace and all the other globes smashing to the sidewalk. I imagine the countless different moments in the lives of Bugdon and everyone in Empire doing the same when our building finally collapses.

I look at the people passing us in this city. I look at the hot dog man. Each is their own mist-cloud of time. They're the same as me. I look across the street and see Rockefeller University. As I reach out with my senses I can feel Estelle inside. She's about to open her hoped-for portal in time.

Suddenly I'm puzzled. How can I sense Estelle here when she's also sitting in a wheeled chair in the Plaza? Then I feel her cloud of time. A tiny part of Estelle is in the university right now, but there are also countless parts of her life leading from here to the Plaza Hotel in the times I knew, along with strings of her life in every other conceivable time and place.

I hear Estelle laughing in joy at my understanding.

"Yes," Momma says, watching the university with me as we wait for everything to happen. "Estelle's been working hard to fix all this."

There's a sudden burst of light as Estelle's portal opens—or more accurately, a sudden burst of mists, as the timestream of the Days-We-Knew falls apart. The hot dog man screams in pain as he loses his grip on time and becomes mist. Passersby in the street do the same. Time falls apart.

The city blinks again, going back to a sunny day where everyone is happy. The hot dog man, acting as if he hasn't just turned to mists, again walks from his wheeled cooking stand and tells Momma she's doing a good thing by helping me.

"I brought us back a few minutes in time," Momma says. "You know the rest of what happened. The people who became mists stabilized the world and kept everyone else from changing. They did it out of mercy, not wanting others to feel the pain and fear they'd experienced. But that decision created a worse existence than they ever imagined."

Momma's right. In my times my city is dying, and people are hurting far more than the pain brought on by a brief moment of change. I survived the pain of becoming mist. Others could easily do the same.

I eat another bite of hot dog. Is this real? A mist dream? A new timestream created as my life broke into countless individual moments of me?

Maybe it doesn't matter which account is true. It only matters what I do with the times now open to me.

"You want me to convince people to join the mists," I say. "You want people to join them before all the buildings fall."

My mother nods.

I laugh. There's never been a topper prophet. But if there's got to be one, might as well be me.

I strip off my suit and helmet, strip off my dirty clothes underneath, even though the hot dog man and others stare at me in shock. Momma kicks a fire hydrant with more strength than she should have and it shatters, revealing a rising rain of water. I scrub and clean myself. Momma joins me and we hold hands and dance around the geyser of water.

I then tell her I'm ready. I shatter the moments of my life and rearrange the infinite times I'm created of until I again stand in the mists back in my city.

Except the mists have cleared from around me. And walking toward me is myself. A myself sealed in an air suit with the blinder hiding her from what the mists reveal.

That's when I know this is truth. I look at the mists that swirl by my body. Each drop of mist is a moment of my life. The drops shimmer and spin and squeal in happiness at what I am.

I laugh. I giggle and yell. I run my hands through the mists, feeling my lives and the lives of everyone I've ever known—and the countless people I never got to know—swirl through my consciousness.

I must share the news. I must tell everyone.

But first I run at myself and knock the other me down. As her gloved hands touch my bare face, I remember her fear. I step back and reach out to the mists around me, find the living moment of that fear. Experience it again. I am fortunate this fear didn't define all of who I am.

I watch my suited self stand back up and walk onward. So funny to think a mere suit kept out the mists. So silly to think closing my eyes kept out the truth.

When I return to Empire, I sneak in and find Bugdon. He stares at my naked body and asks what happened.

I tell him.

"I can't accept this," he stammers.

"It's your choice, but if you give yourself up to the mists, they'll reveal more of yourself than you'd ever believe. Empire won't last. But if we can convince people to join the mists. . . ."

"It's impossible. It's simply impossible."

I grin as I take off my necklace and hand it to him. "The other part of me will return in a few days. Then you'll know. I'll be back to tell you what we must do to save everyone."

Bugdon looks at me like I've gone bat-bat, but before he can call the guards to catch me, I run back into the mists.

I can already taste Bugdon's future understanding. It dances before me like a drop of mist in the air.

We be toppers. Toppers we be.

Because in the end, what else could we become?

TENDER LOVING PLASTICS
AMMAN SABET

Amman Sabet has led digital design projects for such companies as BMW, Adobe, Comcast, Wizards of the Coast, and Intel. He is a graduate of the 2017 Clarion Science Fiction and Fantasy Writing Workshop. "Tender Loving Plastics" examines the consequences of a foster-care system that attempts to mimic the nuclear family using artificial intelligence. It is his second published story.

1. THE DEWEY HOME FOR FOSTER CHILDREN

Issa lives in a small prefabricated efficiency, tucked within the mouth of a concrete alley between two buildings. The kitchen in front connects to a hallway, leading past a bathroom and two bedrooms, to a storage unit in back. It's cramped by adult standards but scaled for children by design.

All of the surfaces are institutional. The kitchen's scratch-proof ceramics have tinted beige from a regimen of spraying and wiping spills and sneaker scuffs. The hallway carpet smells like burning plastic when it's vacuumed. Mold regroups along the bathroom cabinet in little black stipples, never fully defeated. Chintzy towels embroidered with cartoon characters hang limp from crooked wall pegs. It's a wonder that these objects deserve such refurbishment.

Issa's bedroom is at the end of the hall. Trevor, her foster brother, has the bedroom closest to the kitchen. Both have an aluminum loft bed over a desk and a pressed-plastic chair. Pushed into the corners are particleboard dressers, mirrors, trundles. At night, the moon shines in through clerestory windows, dappling a mobile that hangs over Issa's crib as she sleeps.

Mom pulls her chair down from the kitchen wall to sit and re-charge her battery. Her face is flat and glossy and animates a loop of sheep jumping a fence. Over time, they fade into her nothing face, but she listens for Issa's and Trevor's voices in the dark. They've never seen her sleep and never will.

2. ISSA'S EARLIEST MEMORY

Baby Issa can stand. With the help of Teacup Bunny, she climbs upright. Holding the crib's safety bar for balance, she coos to Mom and Trevor.

Trevor is still Good Trevor. His toys are spilled out across the brown jute rug. There are red cars, green cars, black and white. Mom makes her concentration face: a dash mouth, pink tongue sticking up from the corner. White pupil dots follow her hands as they fill Issa's bottle and a sweat drop blinks near her temple as she spins the nipple cap tight.

"Mom, look. It's a traffic jam. *Mom.*"

Mom turns and makes her smile face at Trevor. "That's wonder-ful, Trev! How did it happen?"

Trevor points to the school bus in front. "Driver did it. He went pop and then went haywire." Trevor bobbles his head, eyes crossed, and falls over buzzing, shaking his sneakers in the air.

Mom's mouth makes a little doughnut. "Did someone call the repairman?"

Trevor points to a van behind a cement mixer. "He got stuck."

"Where is Fast Oscar? Can he help?"

Trevor pulls him from the front of his overalls, a sports car with headlight eyes and a big yellow lightning bolt. He pushes Fast

Oscar through the traffic jam toward the bus, knocking the other cars aside.

Issa squeaks. She reaches over the safety bar for Mom and bounces, ruffling her diaper.

"Ooh! Who is this? Does someone need to be picked up?" Mom puts the bottle down and lifts Issa from her crib.

Issa's world spins. Mom cradles her against her padded chest and thumps a heartbeat for her. *Bump-bump.* She bounces gently, warms. Issa drools against her plastic shoulder and coos, satisfied.

Then she cries, pushes away, and Mom puts her back in her crib. Soon, she will reach for Mom again, and Mom will pick her up. This repeats. Mom will never know why and will never be frustrated.

3. REGULAR UPKEEP

Every four months, Uncle Georg visits. He doesn't have a flat, blinky face like Mom. His face sticks out like Trevor's, with a beard that moves like a scratchy blanket when he talks. His gray work shirt has tools like pens peeking out of the chest pocket. Sometimes he brings a brown satchel with presents when he plays Santa for Christmas, but he usually just stuffs things into the cabinets and the storage unit in the back (which stays locked).

When Trevor is still at school, Georg gives Mom a checkup. Issa lies in Mom's lap, mouth red with a rash, hands wet from sucking her thumb. Mom strokes Issa's hair and neck and Georg uses his pen things on Mom's back.

"Momma's going to be really still for five seconds. Can you stay still, too?"

Issa nods.

Mom's hand falls flat against Issa's back for a moment. Then her chest makes a musical sound.

"Momma and I are going to play a game. Want to play, too?" Issa nods again.

Uncle Georg's game is strange. It's not like Mom's games with music and lights. They only play once. Mom and Issa stand on one foot, then the other. Move around. Say weird words and then look at one of the pens. Stick another pen in Issa's ear and she coughs.

Uncle Georg asks Mom questions that don't make sense, but somehow Mom knows the answers. When it's Issa's turn, she knows the answers to the questions because they are about her. *Do you have any new friends? What's the grossest thing you ate? What's the scariest thing around?*

4. THE MAY BEES

When Issa is four and Trevor is ten, Mom prints meatloaf with green beans and it's better than usual.

"Five stars!" Issa rates dinner, and Trevor agrees. They know something special is planned.

When they've cleared their plates, Mom brings them strawberry freezies and says that the May Bees are going to visit. "They're different May Bees than the last time," Mom explains. "They'll knock on the door like Halloween, but we can bring them inside. So, no stories tonight. It's quiet time until they arrive."

Shortly after Issa and Trevor go to their rooms, there comes the knock. A squat caseworker from Dewey with a badge on her shirt has brought the May Bees with her: a thin man with a mustache and a lady wearing a fancy yellow coat. The caseworker asks if the kids are inside. She waits in the kitchen, drinking from a thermos, as Mom brings the May Bees back to their rooms.

Trevor is bouncing up and down at his desk.

"Trev, may we come in?" Mom asks. "Our guests want to meet you."

Trevor stands and nods vigorously with a toothy smile, hopping from one foot to the other.

The May Bee man with the mustache watches from the hallway as the lady with the yellow coat steps around Mom. She squats down at eye level and holds her hand out to shake.

"It's very nice to meet you, Trevor."

Trevor hugs her around her neck. Embarrassed, she gently pulls away and asks what subjects he likes at school. Trevor dances around his room, joking and showing off his possessions. He talks louder, faster, as if he always has been shouting to be heard. The man waves from the hallway and Trevor runs and clutches around his leg.

When it's time to visit Issa, she is playing quietly with Teacup Bunny in her room. The May Bees ask her who her friend is. *Does Bunny like having parties?* The questions sound like tricks, because the lady's face moves like Uncle Georg's face. Not blinky like Mom's.

Trevor skips around their line of sight, interrupting with inane questions, not really listening for answers. Issa won't lift her gaze from Teacup Bunny to make eye contact. When nobody is looking, Trevor reaches behind his back and pinches Issa.

Once it's time for the May Bees to leave, the lady notices that Issa looks shaken. She asks, "Is something wrong? What happened?" and Issa begins to cry.

Bad Trevor.

5. BAD TREVOR

When Issa turns six and Trevor is twelve, he's sent home from school again for hitting. Mom makes her mad face: downward chevron between her eyes, upturned frown line for a mouth.

"You're in big trouble, mister. Straight to your room until dinner."

Sullen, Trevor drops his book bag and leans his street hockey stick against the refrigerator.

Later, as Issa helps set the table, Mom pins a watercolor that Issa made in class to the refrigerator door. In the picture, there is Mom and Uncle Georg and Issa. Trevor is standing at a distance, painted scrawly in red. They are all under the roof of a house, with more people holding balloons.

"Is this your birthday?" Mom regards the picture through framing hands. "That's definitely five stars! We've got another artist in the house."

Trevor wanders past Issa and Mom and opens the fridge to grab a drink, blocking their view.

"Excuse me, Trevor. You're being rude. Nobody called you for dinner yet."

"I wanted a glass of water." Trevor closes the refrigerator door and looks at Issa's drawing. "Who'd want to have a party here anyway? This is a loser house."

"Trevor!"

As he takes a sip of water, Trevor casually swats the drawing off the refrigerator.

Mom makes the mad face. "Trevor, that's not your drawing."

"It's a stupid drawing anyway."

"Put it back and apologize to your sister."

"No!"

"Okay, that's a timeout. Go to your room, mister."

Trevor makes like he's about to leave, but then picks up his hockey stick and gives Mom a whack on her leg. Mom is not allowed to retaliate. She reaches to grab the hockey stick with her plastic fingers, but Trevor wrenches it free and the chairs screech out of the way.

"Let go, it's mine! I hate you!"

Trevor hits Mom again, harder this time, cracking her plastic casing. Mom's chest emits a shrill *beep* and she collapses, first against the table and then the floor. Silverware rattles. Neither Issa nor Trevor has ever heard Mom make that sound, and Trevor steps back. Mom's face is blank. Issa shrieks. Trevor begins to understand what he's done. Drops his hockey stick. Runs out into the alley, knocking on neighbors' doors.

Issa hoists Mom into her chair, lifts Mom's hand, lets go. It clacks against her thigh. No response. She's never seen Mom unresponsive. Now the home is just a square shed between two cold brick buildings. The spell has cracked. She begins to hyperventilate.

"Mom!" she squeals.

Nothing.

Then, at the end of the hall, a ruction behind the locked door to the storage unit; boxes falling from shelves, and a musical chime. Something stands upright, steps over what sounds like metal canisters rolling around the floor.

Issa grasps Mom's sweatshirt and shakes, rattling her limbs. She taps and swipes Mom's blank face with her fingers. "Wake up!"

Behind the door, clacking, deliberate footsteps resound. Then something thuds against the back of it and Issa shrieks. She kicks back under the table to hide, and again the door thuds. It smashes open and there, at the other end of the hall, is another Mom. This Mom is bald, missing part of her arm and her clothes.

"Issa, are you there?" This New Mom's voice volume is up all the way and she is making the worried expression. Her face light is blinding. It swells in the hallway, beaming like a searchlight.

"Issa!"

Issa peeks over the kitchen table, looking from Old Mom to New Mom.

"There you are! I'm okay, Issa-boo. I just switched. Easy peasy!"

---

6. A SEAM IN CONTINUITY

The caseworker from Dewey arrives to transition Trevor. She says that even though he's going to a bigger house with other boys like him, Issa can draw pictures and write letters to him whenever she wants.

Issa doesn't know if she should be sad that Trevor is leaving. She asks if he is going to come back, but nobody gives her a straight answer. She makes the blank face herself as they pack his clothes into a plastic bin. Before Trevor leaves, he is Good Trevor again, for a moment. "Maybe I'll see you in school," he supposes. He waves from the van as the door spelling D-E-W-E-Y slides shut. As it pulls onto the road, Trevor looks back through the windshield. Later in life, Issa will recall this as the last time she saw him.

It's just New Mom and Issa in the kitchen and it's really quiet now. New Mom wears Old Mom's jumper. She printed the oatmeal-raisin cookies that Issa likes, but they've gone stale on the counter.

"Stealing clothes isn't allowed," Issa informs New Mom, who makes the question-mark face. Issa doesn't know if New Mom is in charge now. Maybe she is.

Georg fixes her arm and brings her hair, but it's different. Issa helps trim it to look like Old Mom's hair. New Mom says it's a five-star haircut and cleans the ends herself. When they come out of the bathroom, Old Mom is gone and there is just one Mom.

Issa sneak-tests this Mom sometimes, just to be sure.

"Remember when we made Easter eggs?"

"You made a piggy egg for Good Trevor and a rainbow one for me."

"Remember when we had just ice cream for dinner?"

"Oooh, tricky Issa! You're just making that up!"

Tickles. Laughing. Mom's fingers are tickle spiders.

7. BABY MACKENZIE

When she's in fourth grade, Issa comes home to discover a baby sleeping in Trevor's old room.

"That's Mackenzie. You can poke your head in, but hush." Mom has cleaned the room. The crib is set up with fresh bedding next to the changing station.

"It's like my old room," Issa whispers.

Baby Mackenzie lies with the backs of her tiny fingers resting against the corners of her eyes. She gives a sigh in her sleep, chest rising and falling. The mobile turns slowly overhead.

"Can she have Teacup Bunny?"

"Of course!" Mom makes her smile face, little heart fading in and out. "A big-sister present will make her very happy."

An idea occurs to Issa and she winces. "Am I going to go away? Like what happened to Trevor?" She tries to keep quiet, but starts hiccupping, about to cry.

"No, Issa-boo. That's different." Mom leads her by the hand into the hallway and kneels beside her, holding her shoulders. "Trevor didn't know how to not be mad. He wasn't ready to be your big brother. It's your turn, now, and I know you're going to be great."

8. BIG SISTER

Twelve-year-old Issa is allowed to walk home from school with a friend, so a girl from class joins her. They plan to do weekend homework together. But turning into the alley, the girl reads the plaque that says "Dewey Foster Home #12" and knows that *foster* means *different*, just not exactly how.

"Hey, why don't we use the Wi-Fi at Corner Café instead?" she suggests. "The tables are empty after five. We can load up on macca frappés."

"I dunno. How much does that cost?" Issa checks her empty pockets, pretending she has money.

Mom opens the door. "Oh, hello," she greets the girl from class. "Are you Issa's friend?"

"No way!" the girl exclaims. "You have a robot?"

"It's my, um . . . this is my . . . this is Mom."

The girl looks inside at the kitchen and her smile falls away. Then she pulls out her phone. "Oh, you know, I totally forgot. My dad said he wants me home early, because. . . ." She tries to think of something, but then turns and just walks stiffly out of the alley.

Mom watches her leave, making her question-mark face.

Issa pushes past into the kitchen. "I wish you were normal," she mutters, dropping her book bag and stomping down the hallway.

Mackenzie calls out, "Hey, Issa!" as Issa passes her door. "Issa?"

Issa pauses, pokes her head in.

"Look. Snakes." Mackenzie holds up a picture of a tight bolus of snakes, snarling the paper from end to end. Just about every square inch is covered.

"Four ssstars. You misssed a ssspot," Issa hisses, flicking her tongue.

"No I didn't!" Mackenzie checks to see if it's true.

"Hey, wanna see something?" Issa waves her over to her dresser. She pulls out one of the drawers and looks underneath. "Wait, I think it's the other one." She pulls the bottom drawer out all the way, emptying the contents onto the floor.

"Hey!"

"Shh. This is a Dewey secret." Issa puts her finger to her lips. "Don't tell Mom or Georg will throw it away. Promise?"

Mackenzie nods, and Issa overturns the drawer. Props it up. The entire wooden bottom is carved end to end with a picture of a hurricane blowing through a city. Cars are flying through the air. Moms and dads holding dogs at the end of leashes. Shopping carts, telephone poles and traffic lights and street signs are up in the sky, flying in a circle. In the middle of the chaos is a small figure wearing a shirt with a capital T.

Mackenzie points. "Who's that?"

"You know how I showed you how to draw? Well, he showed me. He lived here in your room, before you were here."

"Why is he breaking everything?"

"No, that's the eye of the storm, where everything is calm. Storms blow around in circles. I think he is trying to stay in the middle because it's safe there, and things stay still."

9. YOU CAN NEVER GO HOME AGAIN

Issa leans under a bus shelter across from the alley to her old foster home. She is now twenty-three. The neighborhood feels smaller, like it shrank in a dryer. The street feels narrower. The walk from the corner was shorter than she remembered. The alley looks cleaner, too. Not as dark and foreboding as it used to be, and the buildings have been repainted. Someone repaved the sidewalk and installed a bike rack along the curb.

Issa hasn't been back since she aged out at eighteen. The funds in her Dewey account, having accrued through the years for the very purpose of tiding her over, had helped when finding an apartment and securing job training as a nurse. It was enough momentum to never look back.

But one day, she saw Mom from the window of her laundromat. It wasn't her Mom, but a different Mom, with different plastics.

Issa crammed her wet laundry into her hamper and ran after that Mom, tailing her for several blocks to a nearby neighborhood. There, she discovered another Dewey home built onto the roof of another building, accessible by a stairwell. It looked sort of like her old home, but with different windows, and a small plaque by the door with the Dewey logo and street number.

Then, a month later, she saw *another* Mom, this one in blue. She followed that one to a smattering of boutiques encircling a small neighborhood park, where all the buildings were prefabricated. That Mom carried a bag of groceries through the front door of *another* Dewey home tucked up against the back side of a Pilates studio. A mural of puppet monsters and balloons covered it in a field of blue.

These Dewey homes lure Issa's attention when she isn't on duty at the hospital. She finds new ones online every now and then, and rides past them on her bike. Sometimes she sees the other Dewey children. Quiet children who are alone. Loud, obnoxious children swarming the curb. She can't see into their homes, but she can see how the light plays off the window shades when they move about within. Issa's therapist says that her behavior makes sense. Issa wants to know if these kids are like her. As an adult, she is looking for patterns to know if her ways of relating with others developed differently as a child.

Her therapist says that they have, and that they come through in her bedside manner during her shifts. Like others who have grown up in the Dewey system, Issa's speech patterns and mannerisms are more robotic—more "blinky." Issa has a hard time trusting the faces that people make. She projects how she needs people to be, rather than letting them reveal how they actually are as human beings. Issa is also missing closure. She needs to go home again and shut the door behind her so that she can move forward, or the illusions of her past will follow her.

Now, Issa lingers at the mouth of the alley just before the door to her old home. The concrete is scrawled with pink and blue chalk and the cracks by the door are familiar. Being here feels to her like wearing an old pair of shoes that still fit.

Issa knocks.

"Just a minute!" Mom's voice resounds from deep within and her heart leaps. There must be another child in there, perhaps Mackenzie's younger brother or sister. She steps back, leans against a wall, and puts her hands in her pockets.

When the door opens, Mom's neutral face greets her, a slight smile with two blush dots for cheeks.

"Hello, this is the Dewey home. Can I help you?"

Issa's heart sinks.

"I . . . I'm sorry." Issa speaks from her throat. "I must . . . I think I have the wrong address."

Mom pulls a thinking face, question mark fading slowly in and out by her temple. "Issa?" Overjoyed face, now. Smiling eyes. "I'm sorry, sweetie, I must not have seen you for a second. Are you looking for Mackenzie? She's at school."

Issa breathes out fully, realizes she has been holding a portion of her breath this whole time. "Hi, Mom." Her voice quavers. "That's okay. I wanted to see you, too."

Mom invites her in, but Issa declines. Seen from the outside, the kitchen is the same kitchen as before, but now seems to be just an arrangement of materials somehow. Issa peers down the hallway and can see how the Dewey home has been manufactured, easily deconstructed into an exploded view in her mind's eye.

There's another child inside. She can hear from the play sounds coming from the last bedroom that it's a little boy. She realizes that this Dewey home is no longer just her past, but a continuum of pasts belonging to no single Dewey child entirely. Intruding might dispel what is now staged for that boy. He must need to believe in this as home, as she had.

They speak in the doorway about Mackenzie, Uncle Georg, and Trevor.

"Do you remember the party?" Issa does not.

Mom tells her to wait for a second. She goes back, retrieves something from the shady recesses of the storage, and returns with a piece of paper. It's Issa's drawing. The one that Mom had put up on the fridge.

"Are you still making art?"

"No. I work in the hospital now, actually. It's not exactly a party, but there are birthdays."

"I'm so glad!" Mom hugs Issa. Her plastics feel familiar and fragile and Issa can't remember them ever having hugged each other at the same height. Mom's chest warms up. The synthetic heartbeat patters *bump-bump* as it did before, but Issa pulls away.

There's an awkward silence.

"Hey, Mom, will you give Mackenzie my new address? I'd like her to visit me, if that's okay. I want her to know she can come over any time."

"Of course, sweetie."

"So . . . I should get back to work. My shift starts soon."

"Issa-boo, wait! Before you go, can I ask you something?"

"Sure."

Mom clasps her fingers together and her face changes to her hopeful face. "Was there anything I could have done to be a better Mom? Maybe something you wished I would have done differently?"

"Uh . . . I don't. . . ." Issa opens and closes her mouth, unsure of how to reply.

"How about on a scale of one to five? How many stars would you give me?"

WELCOME TO YOUR AUTHENTIC INDIAN EXPERIENCE™

REBECCA ROANHORSE

Rebecca Roanhorse is a Black Ohkay Owingeh writer whose breakout novel *Trail of Lightning* was nominated for the 2019 Nebula and Hugo Awards for Best Novel. She won the John W. Campbell Award for Best New Writer in 2018.

"Welcome to Your Authentic Indian Experience™" was nominated for the Locus, Theodore Sturgeon Memorial, and World Fantasy awards, and it won the Hugo and Nebula awards. It confronts the concepts of authenticity and cultural experiences in the virtual-reality medium.

"In the Great American Indian novel, when it is finally
written, all of the white people will be Indians
and all of the Indians will be ghosts."
—Sherman Alexie, *How to Write the Great
American Indian Novel*

Y ou maintain a menu of a half dozen Experiences on your digital blackboard, but Vision Quest is the one the Tourists choose the most. That certainly makes your workday easy. All a Vision Quest requires is a dash of mystical shaman, a spirit animal (wolf usually, but birds of prey are on the upswing this year), and the approximation of a peyote experience. Tourists always come out of the Experience feeling spiritually transformed. (You've never actually tried peyote, but you did smoke your share of weed during that one year at Arizona State, and who's going to call you on the difference?) It's all 101 stuff, really, these Quests. But no other Indian working at Sedona Sweats can do it better. Your sales numbers are tops.

Your wife Theresa doesn't approve of the gig. Oh, she likes you working, especially after that dismal stretch of unemployment the year before last when she almost left you, but she thinks the job itself is demeaning.

"Our last name's not Trueblood," she complains when you tell her about your *nom de rêve*.

"Nobody wants to buy a Vision Quest from a Jesse Turnblatt," you explain. "I need to sound more Indian."

"You are Indian," she says. "Turnblatt's Indian-sounding enough because you're already Indian."

"We're not the right kind of Indian," you counter. "I mean, we're Catholic, for Christ's sake."

What Theresa doesn't understand is that Tourists don't want a real Indian experience. They want what they see in the movies, and who can blame them? Movie Indians are terrific! So you watch the same movies the Tourists do, until John Dunbar becomes your spirit animal and Stands with Fists your best girl. You memorize Johnny Depp's lines from *The Lone Ranger* and hang a picture of Iron Eyes Cody in your work locker. For a while you are really into Dustin Hoffman's *Little Big Man*.

It's *Little Big Man* that does you in.

For a week in June, you convince your boss to offer a Custer's Last Stand special, thinking there might be a Tourist or two who want to live out a Crazy Horse Experience. You even memorize some quotes attributed to the venerable Sioux chief that you find on the internet. You plan to make it real authentic.

But you don't get a single taker. Your numbers nosedive.

Management in Phoenix notices, and Boss drops it from the blackboard by Fourth of July weekend. He yells at you to stop screwing around, accuses you of trying to be an artiste or whatnot.

"Tourists don't come to Sedona Sweats to live out a goddamn battle," Boss says in the break room over lunch one day, "especially if the white guy loses. They come here to find themselves." Boss waves his hand in the air in an approximation of something vaguely prayer-like. "It's a spiritual experience we're offering. Top quality. The fucking best."

DarAnne, your Navajo co-worker with the pretty smile and the perfect teeth, snorts loudly. She takes a bite of her sandwich, mutton by the looks of it. Her jaw works, her sharp teeth flash white. She waits until she's finished chewing to say, "Nothing spiritual about Squaw Fantasy."

Squaw Fantasy is Boss's latest idea, his way to get the numbers up and impress Management. DarAnne and a few others have complained about the use of the ugly slur, the inclusion of a sexual fantasy as an Experience at all. But Boss is unmoved, especially when the first week's numbers roll in. Biggest seller yet.

Boss looks over at you. "What do you think?"

Boss is Pima, with a bushy mustache and a thick head of still-dark hair. You admire that about him. Virility. Boss makes being a man look easy. Makes everything look easy. Real authentic-like.

DarAnne tilts her head, long beaded earrings swinging, and waits. Her painted nails click impatiently against the Formica lunch table. You can smell the onion in her sandwich.

Your mouth is dry like the red rock desert you can see outside your window. If you say Squaw Fantasy is demeaning, Boss will mock you, call you a pussy, or worse. If you say you think it's okay, DarAnne and her crew will put you on the guys-who-are-assholes list and you'll deserve it.

You sip your bottled water, stalling. Decide that in the wake of the Crazy Horse debacle that Boss's approval means more than DarAnne's, and venture, "I mean, if the Tourists like it. . . ."

Boss slaps the table, triumphant. DarAnne's face twists in disgust.

"What does Theresa think of that, eh, Jesse?" she spits at you. "You tell her Boss is thinking of adding Savage Braves to the menu next? He's gonna have you in a loincloth and hair down to your ass, see how you like it."

Your face heats up, embarrassed. You push away from the table, too quickly, and the flimsy top teeters. You can hear Boss's shouts of protest as his vending machine lemonade tilts dangerously, and DarAnne's mocking laugh, but it all comes to your ears through a shroud of thick cotton. You mumble something about getting back to work. The sound of arguing trails you down the hall.

You change in the locker room and shuffle down to the pod marked with your name. You unlock the hatch and crawl in. Some people find the pods claustrophobic, but you like the cool metal container, the tight fit. It's comforting. The VR helmet fits snugly on your head, the breathing mask over your nose and mouth.

With a shiver of anticipation, you give the pod your Experience setting. Add the other necessary details to flesh things out. The screen prompts you to pick a Tourist connection from a waiting list, but you ignore it, blinking through the option screens until you get to the final confirmation. You brace for the mild nausea that always comes when you Relocate in and out of an Experience.

The first sensation is always smell. Sweetgrass and wood smoke and the rich loam of the northern plains. Even though it's fake, receptors firing under the coaxing of a machine, you relax into the scents. You grew up in the desert, among people who appreciate cedar and piñon and red earth, but there's still something home-like about this prairie place.

Or maybe you watch too much TV. You really aren't sure anymore.

You find yourself on a wide grassy plain, somewhere in the

upper Midwest of a bygone era. Bison roam in the distance. A hawk soars overhead.

You are alone, you know this, but it doesn't stop you from looking around to make sure. This thing you are about to do. Well, you would be humiliated if anyone found out. Because you keep thinking about what DarAnne said. Squaw Fantasy and Savage Braves. Because the thing is, being sexy doesn't disgust you the way it does DarAnne. You've never been one of those guys. The star athlete or the cool kid. It's tempting to think of all those Tourist women wanting you like that, even if it is just in an Experience.

You are now wearing a knee-length loincloth. A wave of black hair flows down your back. Your middle-aged paunch melts into rock-hard abs worthy of a romance novel cover model. You raise your chin and try out your best stoic look on a passing prairie dog. The little rodent chirps something back at you. You've heard prairie dogs can remember human faces, and you wonder what this one would say about you. Then you remember this is an Experience, so the prairie dog is no more real than the caricature of an Indian you have conjured up.

You wonder what Theresa would think if she saw you like this.

The world shivers. The pod screen blinks on. Someone wants your Experience.

A Tourist, asking for you. Completely normal. Expected. No need for that panicky hot breath rattling through your mask.

You scroll through the Tourist's requirements.

Experience Type: Vision Quest.

Tribe: Plains Indian (nation nonspecific).

Favorite Animal: Wolf.

These things are all familiar. Things you are good at faking. Things you get paid to pretend.

You drop the Savage Brave fantasy garb for buckskin pants and beaded leather moccasins. You keep your chest bare and muscled but you drape a rough wool blanket across your shoulders for dignity. Your impressive abs are still visible.

The sun is setting and you turn to put the artificial dusk at your back, prepared to meet your Tourist. You run through your list of Indian names to bestow upon your Tourist once the Vision Quest is over. You like to keep the names fresh, never using the same one in case the Tourists ever compare notes. For a while you cheated and used one of those naming things on the internet where you enter your favorite flower and the street you grew up on and it gives you your Indian name, but there were too many Tourists who grew up on Elm or Park and you found yourself getting repetitive. You try to base the names on appearances now. Hair color, eye, some distinguishing feature. Tourists really seem to like it.

This Tourist is younger than you expected. Sedona Sweats caters to New Agers, the kind from Los Angeles or Scottsdale with impressive bank accounts. But the man coming up the hill, squinting into the setting sun, is in his late twenties. Medium height and build with pale spotty skin and brown hair. The guy looks normal enough, but there's something sad about him.

Maybe he's lost.

You imagine a lot of Tourists are lost.

Maybe he's someone who works a day job just like you, saving up money for this once-in-a-lifetime Indian Experience™. Maybe he's desperate, looking for purpose in his own shitty world and thinking Indians have all the answers. Maybe he just wants something that's authentic.

You like that. The idea that Tourists come to you to experience something real. DarAnne has it wrong. The Tourists aren't all bad. They're just needy.

You plant your feet in a wide welcoming stance and raise one hand. "How," you intone, as the man stops a few feet in front of you.

The man flushes, a bright pinkish tone. You can't tell if he's nervous or embarrassed. Maybe both? But he raises his hand, palm forward, and says, "How," right back.

"Have you come seeking wisdom, my son?" you ask in your best broken English accent. "Come. I will show you great wisdom." You sweep your arm across the prairie. "We look to brother wolf—"

The man rolls his eyes.

What?

You stutter to a pause. Are you doing something wrong? Is the accent no good? Too little? Too much?

You visualize the requirements checklist. You are positive he chose wolf. Positive. So you press on. "My brother wolf," you say again, this time sounding much more Indian, you are sure.

"I'm sorry," the man says, interrupting. "This wasn't what I wanted. I've made a mistake."

"But you picked it on the menu!" In the confusion of the moment, you drop your accent. Is it too late to go back and say it right?

The man's lips curl up in a grimace, like you have confirmed his worst suspicions. He shakes his head. "I was looking for something more authentic."

Something in your chest seizes up.

"I can fix it," you say.

"No, it's all right. I'll find someone else." He turns to go.

You can't afford another bad mark on your record. No more screw-ups or you're out. Boss made that clear enough. "At least give me a chance," you plead.

"It's okay," he says over his shoulder.

This is bad. Does this man not know what a good Indian you are? "Please!"

The man turns back to you, his face thoughtful.

You feel a surge of hope. This can be fixed, and you know exactly how. "I can give you a name. Something you can call yourself when you need to feel strong. It's authentic," you add enthusiastically. "From a real Indian." That much is true.

The man looks a little more open, and he doesn't say no. That's good enough.

You study the man's dusky hair, his pinkish skin. His long skinny legs. He reminds you a bit of the flamingos at the Albuquerque zoo, but you are pretty sure no one wants to be named after those strange creatures. It must be something good. Something . . . spiritual.

"Your name is Pale Crow," you offer. Birds are still on your mind.

At the look on the man's face, you reconsider. "No, no, it is White" —yes, that's better than pale— "Wolf. White Wolf."

"White Wolf?" There's a note of interest in his voice.

You nod sagely. You knew the man had picked wolf. Your eyes meet. Uncomfortably. White Wolf coughs into his hand. "I really should be getting back."

"But you paid for the whole experience. Are you sure?"

White Wolf is already walking away.

"But. . . ."

You feel the exact moment he Relocates out of the Experience. A sensation like part of your soul is being stretched too thin. Then, a sort of whiplash, as you let go.

The Hey U.S.A. bar is the only Indian bar in Sedona. The basement level of a driftwood-paneled strip mall across the street from work. It's packed with the after-shift crowd, most of them pod jockeys like you, but also a few roadside jewelry hawkers and restaurant stiffs still smelling like frybread grease. You're lucky to find a spot at the far end next to the server's station. You slip onto the plastic-covered barstool and raise a hand to get the bartender's attention.

"So what do you really think?" asks a voice to your right. Dar-Anne is staring at you, her eyes accusing and her posture tense.

This is it. A second chance. Your opportunity to stay off the assholes list. You need to get this right. You try to think of something clever to say, something that would impress her but let you save face, too. But you've never been all that clever, so you stick to the truth.

"I think I really need this job," you admit.

DarAnne's shoulders relax.

"Scooch over," she says to the man on the other side of her, and he obligingly shifts off his stool to let her sit. "I knew it," she says. "Why didn't you stick up for me? Why are you so afraid of Boss?"

"I'm not afraid of Boss. I'm afraid of Theresa leaving me. And unemployment."

"You gotta get a backbone, Jesse, is all."

You realize the bartender is waiting, impatient. You drink the same thing every time you come here, a single Coors Light in a cold bottle. But the bartender never remembers you, or your order. You turn to offer to buy one for DarAnne, but she's already gone, back with her crew.

You drink your beer alone, wait a reasonable amount of time, and leave.

White Wolf is waiting for you under the streetlight at the corner.

The bright neon Indian Chief that squats atop Sedona Sweats hovers behind him in pinks and blues and yellows, his huge hand blinking up and down in greeting. White puffs of smoke signals flicker up, up and away beyond his far shoulder.

You don't recognize White Wolf at first. Most people change themselves a little within the construct of the Experience. Nothing wrong with being thinner, taller, a little better looking. But White Wolf looks exactly the same. Nondescript brown hair, pale skin, long legs.

"How." White Wolf raises his hand, unconsciously mimicking

the big neon Chief. At least he has the decency to look embarrassed when he does it.

"You." You are so surprised that the accusation is the first thing out of your mouth. "How did you find me?"

"Trueblood, right? I asked around."

"And people told you?" This is very against the rules.

"I asked who the best Spirit Guide was. If I was going to buy a Vision Quest, who should I go to. Everyone said you."

You flush, feeling vindicated, but also annoyed that your co-workers had given your name out to a Tourist. "I tried to tell you," you say ungraciously.

"I should have listened." White Wolf smiles, a faint shifting of his mouth into something like contrition. An awkward pause ensues.

"We're really not supposed to fraternize," you finally say.

"I know, I just. . . . I just wanted to apologize. For ruining the Experience like that."

"It's no big deal," you say, gracious this time. "You paid, right?"

"Yeah."

"It's just . . ." You know this is your ego talking, but you need to know. "Did I do something wrong?"

"No, it was me. You were great. It's just, I had a great-grandmother who was Cherokee, and I think being there, seeing everything. Well, it really stirred something in me. Like, ancestral memory or something."

You've heard of ancestral memories, but you've also heard of people claiming Cherokee blood where there is none. Theresa calls them "pretendians," but you think that's unkind. Maybe White Wolf really is Cherokee. You don't know any Cherokees, so maybe they really do look like this guy. There's a half-Tlingit in payroll and he's pale.

"Well, I've got to get home," you say. "My wife, and all."

White Wolf nods. "Sure, sure. I just. Thank you."

"For what?"

But White Wolf's already walking away. "See you around."

A little déjà vu shudders your bones but you chalk it up to Tourists. Who understands them, anyway?

You go home to Theresa.

As soon as you slide into your pod the next day, your monitor lights up. There's already a Tourist on deck and waiting.

"Shit," you mutter, pulling up the menu and scrolling quickly through the requirements. Everything looks good, good, except . . . a sliver of panic when you see that a specific tribe has been requested. Cherokee. You don't know anything about Cherokees. What they wore back then, their ceremonies. The only Cherokee you know is. . . .

White Wolf shimmers into your Experience.

In your haste, you have forgotten to put on your buckskin. Your Experience-self still wears Wranglers and Nikes. Boss would be pissed to see you this sloppy.

"Why are you back?" you ask.

"I thought maybe we could just talk."

"About what?"

White Wolf shrugs. "Doesn't matter. Whatever."

"I can't."

"Why not? This is my time. I'm paying."

You feel a little panicked. A Tourist has never broken protocol like this before. Part of why the Experience works is that everyone knows their role. But White Wolf don't seem to care about the rules.

"I can just keep coming back," he says. "I have money, you know."

"You'll get me in trouble."

"I won't. I just. . . ." White Wolf hesitates. Something in him slumps. What you read as arrogance now looks like desperation. "I need a friend."

You know that feeling. The truth is, you could use a friend, too. Someone to talk to. What could the harm be? You'll just be two men, talking.

Not here, though. You still need to work. "How about the bar?"

"The place from last night?"

"I get off at 11 P.M."

When you get there around 11:30 P.M., the bar is busy but you recognize White Wolf immediately. A skinny white guy stands out at the Hey U.S.A. It's funny. Under this light, in this crowd, White Wolf could pass for Native of some kind. One of those 1/64th guys, at least. Maybe he really is a little Cherokee from way back when.

White Wolf waves you over to an empty booth. A Coors Light waits for you. You slide into the booth and wrap a hand around the cool damp skin of the bottle, pleasantly surprised.

"A lucky guess, did I get it right?"

You nod and take a sip. That first sip is always magic. Like how you imagine Golden, Colorado must feel like on a winter morning.

"So," White Wolf says, "tell me about yourself."

You look around the bar for familiar faces. Are you really going to do this? Tell a Tourist about your life? Your real life? A little voice in your head whispers that maybe this isn't so smart. Boss could find out and get mad. DarAnne could make fun of you. Besides, White Wolf will want a cool story, something real authentic, and all you have is an aging three-bedroom ranch and a student loan.

But he's looking at you, friendly interest, and nobody looks at you like that much anymore, not even Theresa. So you talk.

Not everything.

But some. Enough.

Enough that when the bartender calls last call, you realize you've been talking for two hours.

When you stand up to go, White Wolf stands up, too. You shake hands, Indian-style, which makes you smile. You didn't expect it, but you've got a good, good feeling.

"So, same time tomorrow?" White Wolf asks.

You're tempted, but, "No, Theresa will kill me if I stay out this late two nights in a row." And then, "But how about Friday?"

"Friday it is." White Wolf touches your shoulder. "See you then, Jesse."

You feel a warm flutter of anticipation for Friday. "See you."

Friday you are there by 11:05 P.M. White Wolf laughs when he sees your face, and you grin back, only a little embarrassed. This time you pay for the drinks, and the two of you pick up right where you left off. It's so easy. White Wolf never seems to tire of your stories and it's been so long since you had a new friend to tell them to, that you can't seem to quit. It turns out White Wolf loves Kevin Costner, too, and you take turns quoting lines at each other until White Wolf stumps you with a Wind in His Hair quote.

"Are you sure that's in the movie?"

"It's Lakota!"

You won't admit it, but you're impressed with how good White Wolf's Lakota sounds.

White Wolf smiles. "Looks like I know something you don't."

You wave it away good-naturedly, but vow to watch the movie again.

Time flies and once again, after last call, you both stand outside under the Big Chief. You happily agree to meet again next Tuesday. And the following Friday. Until it becomes your new routine.

The month passes quickly. The next month, too.

"You seem too happy," Theresa says one night, sounding suspicious.

You grin and wrap your arms around your wife, pulling her close until her rose-scented shampoo fills your nose. "Just made a friend, is all. A guy from work." You decide to keep it vague. Hanging with White Wolf, who you've long stopped thinking of as just a Tourist, would be hard to explain.

"You're not stepping out on me, Jesse Turnblatt? Because I will—"

You cut her off with a kiss. "Are you jealous?"

"Should I be?"

"Never."

She sniffs, but lets you kiss her again, her soft body tight against yours.

"I love you," you murmur as your hands dip under her shirt.

"You better."

Tuesday morning and you can't breathe. Your nose is a deluge of snot and your joints ache. Theresa calls in sick for you and bundles you in bed with a bowl of stew. You're supposed to meet White Wolf for your usual drink, but you're much too sick. You consider sending Theresa with a note, but decide against it. It's only one night. White Wolf will understand.

But by Friday the coughing has become a deep rough bellow that shakes your whole chest. When Theresa calls in sick for you again, you make sure your cough is loud enough for Boss to hear it. Pray he doesn't dock you for the days you're missing. But what you're most worried about is standing up White Wolf again.

"Do you think you could go for me?" you ask Theresa.

"What, down to the bar? I don't drink."

"I'm not asking you to drink. Just to meet him, let him know I'm sick. He's probably thinking I forgot about him."

"Can't you call him?"

"I don't have his number."

"Fine, then. What's his name?"

You hesitate. Realize you don't know. The only name you know is the one you gave him. "White Wolf."

"Okay, then. Get some rest."

Theresa doesn't get back until almost 1 A.M. "Where were you?" you ask, alarmed. Is that a rosy flush in her cheeks, the scent of Cherry Coke on her breath?

"At the bar like you asked me to."

"What took so long?"

She huffs. "Did you want me to go or not?"

"Yes, but . . . well, did you see him?"

She nods, smiles a little smile that you've never seen on her before.

"What is it?" Something inside you shrinks.

"A nice man. Real nice. You didn't tell me he was Cherokee."

By Monday you're able to drag yourself back to work. There's a note taped to your locker to go see Boss. You find him in his office, looking through the reports that he sends to Management every week.

"I hired a new guy."

You swallow the excuses you've prepared to explain how sick you were, your promises to get your numbers up. They become a hard ball in your throat.

"Sorry, Jesse." Boss actually does look a little sorry. "This guy is good, a real rez guy. Last name's 'Wolf.' I mean, shit, you can't get more Indian than that. The Tourists are going to eat it up."

"The Tourists love me, too." You sound whiny, but you can't help it. There's a sinking feeling in your gut that tells you this is bad, bad, bad.

"You're good, Jesse. But nobody knows anything about Pueblo Indians, so all you've got is that TV shit. This guy, he's. . . ." Boss snaps his fingers, trying to conjure the word.

"Authentic?" A whisper.

Boss points his finger like a gun. "Bingo. Look, if another pod opens up, I'll call you."

"You gave him my pod?"

Boss's head snaps up, wary. You must have yelled that. He reaches over to tap a button on his phone and call security.

"Wait!" you protest.

But the men in uniforms are already there to escort you out.

You can't go home to Teresa. You just can't. So you head to the Hey U.S.A. It's a different crowd than you're used to. An afternoon crowd. Heavy boozers and people without jobs. You laugh because you fit right in.

The guys next to you are doing shots. Tiny glasses of rheumy dark liquor lined up in a row. You haven't done shots since college but when one of the men offers you one, you take it. Choke on the cheap whiskey that burns down your throat. Two more and the edges of your panic start to blur soft and tolerable. You can't remember what time it is when you get up to leave, but the Big Chief is bright in the night sky.

You stumble through the door and run smack into DarAnne. She growls at you, and you try to stutter out an apology but a heavy hand comes down on your shoulder before you get the words out.

"This asshole bothering you?"

You recognize that voice. "White Wolf?" It's him. But he looks different to you. Something you can't quite place. Maybe it's the ribbon shirt he's wearing, or the bone choker around his neck. Is his skin a little tanner than it was last week?

"Do you know this guy?" DarAnne asks, and you think she's talking to you, but her head is turned towards White Wolf.

"Never seen him," White Wolf says as he stares you down, and under that confident glare you almost believe him. Almost forget that you've told this man things about you even Theresa doesn't know.

"It's me," you protest, but your voice comes out in a whiskey-slurred squeak that doesn't even sound like you.

"Fucking glonnies," DarAnne mutters as she pushes past you. "Always making a scene."

"I think you better go, buddy," White Wolf says. Not unkindly, if you were in fact strangers, if you weren't actually buddies. But you are, and you clutch at his shirtsleeve, shouting something about friendship and Theresa and then the world melts into a blur until you feel the hard slap of concrete against your shoulder and the taste of blood on your lip where you bit it and a solid kick to your gut until the whiskey comes up the way it went down and then the Big Chief is blinking at you, How, How, How, until the darkness comes to claim you and the lights all flicker out.

You wake up in the gutter. The fucking gutter. With your head aching and your mouth as dry and rotted as month-old roadkill. The sun is up, Arizona fire beating across your skin. Your clothes are filthy and your shoes are missing and there's a smear of blood down your chin and drying flakes in the creases of your neck. Your hands are chapped raw. And you can't remember why.

But then you do.

And the humiliation sits heavy on your bruised up shoulder, a dark shame that defies the desert sun. Your job. DarAnne ignoring you like that. White Wolf kicking your ass. And you out all night, drunk in a downtown gutter. It all feels like a terrible dream, like the worst kind. The ones you can't wake up from because it's real life.

Your car isn't where you left it, likely towed with the street sweepers, so you trudge your way home on sock feet. Three miles on asphalt streets until you see your highly mortgaged three-bedroom ranch. And for once the place looks beautiful, like the day you bought it. Tears gather in your eyes as you push open the door.

"Theresa," you call. She's going to be pissed, and you're going to have to talk fast, explain the whole drinking thing (it was one time!) and getting fired (I'll find a new job, I promise), but right now all you want is to wrap her in your arms and let her rose scent fill your nose like good medicine.

"Theresa," you call again, as you limp through the living room. Veer off to look in the bedroom, check behind the closed bathroom door. But what you see in the bathroom makes you pause. Things are missing. Her toothbrush, the pack of birth control, contact lens solution.

"Theresa!?" and this time you are close to panic as you hobble down the hall to the kitchen.

The smell hits you first. The scent of fresh coffee, bright and familiar.

When you see the person sitting calmly at the kitchen table, their back to you, you relax. But that's not Theresa.

He turns slightly, enough so you can catch his profile, and says, "Come on in, Jesse."

"What the fuck are you doing here?"

White Wolf winces, as if your words hurt him. "You better have a seat."

"What did you do to my wife?!"

"I didn't do anything to your wife." He picks up a small folded piece of paper, holds it out. You snatch it from his fingers and move so you can see his face. The note in your hand feels like wildfire, something with the potential to sear you to the bone. You want to rip it wide open, you want to flee before its revelations scar you. You ache to read it now, now, but you won't give him the satisfaction of your desperation.

"So now you remember me," you huff.

"I apologize for that. But you were making a scene and I couldn't have you upsetting DarAnne."

You want to ask how he knows DarAnne, how he was there with her in the first place. But you already know. Boss said the new guy's name was Wolf.

"You're a real son of a bitch, you know that?"

White Wolf looks away from you, that same pained look on his face. Like you're embarrassing yourself again. "Why don't you help yourself to some coffee," he says, gesturing to the coffee pot. Your coffee pot.

"I don't need your permission to get coffee in my own house," you shout.

"Okay," he says, leaning back. You can't help but notice how handsome he looks, his dark hair a little longer, the choker on his neck setting off the arch of his high cheekbones.

You take your time getting coffee—sugar, creamer which you would never usually take—before you drop into the seat across from him. Only then do you open the note, hands trembling, dread twisting hard in your gut.

"She's gone to her mother's," White Wolf explains as you read the same words on the page. "For her own safety. She wants you out by the time she gets back."

"What did you tell her?"

"Only the truth. That you got yourself fired, that you were on a bender, drunk in some alleyway downtown like a bad stereotype." He leans in. "You've been gone for two days."

You blink. It's true, but it's not true, too.

"Theresa wouldn't. . . ." But she would, wouldn't she? She'd said it a million times, given you a million chances.

"She needs a real man, Jesse. Someone who can take care of her."

"And that's you?" You muster all the scorn you can when you say that, but it comes out more a question than a judgment. You remember how you gave him the benefit of the doubt on that whole Cherokee thing, how you thought "pretendian" was cruel.

He clears his throat. Stands.

"It's time for you to go," he says. "I promised Theresa you'd be gone, and I've got to get to work soon." Something about him seems to expand, to take up the space you once occupied. Until you feel small, superfluous.

"Did you ever think," he says, his voice thoughtful, his head tilted to study you like a strange foreign body, "that maybe this is my experience, and you're the tourist here?"

"This is my house," you protest, but you're not sure you believe it now. Your head hurts. The coffee in your hand is already cold. How long have you been sitting here? Your thoughts blur to histories, your words become nothing more than forgotten facts and half-truths. Your heart, a dusty repository for lost loves and desires, never realized.

"Not anymore," he says.

Nausea rolls over you. That same stretching sensation you get when you Relocate out of an Experience.

Whiplash, and then. . . .

You let go.

STRANGE WATERS
SAMANTHA MILLS

Samantha Mills is an archivist in sunny Southern California. Her short fiction has also appeared in *Beneath Ceaseless Skies*, *Daily Science Fiction*, and *Escape Pod*.
"Strange Waters," her professional debut, is about fierce maternal love attempting to defy destiny in a world of shifting histories.

Fisherwoman Mika Sandrigal was lost at sea. She knew where she was in relation to the Candorrean coastline and how to navigate back to her home city, Maelstrom. She knew the time of day. She knew the season. She knew the phase of the moon and the pattern of the tide.

She did not know the year.

Strange waters flowed beneath the hull of her fishing boat, illuminating the midnight darkness with phosphorescent swirls of yellow and green. The thick scent of pepper and brine tickled her nose, and she knew that a juggernaut swam far below, vast and merciless and consuming shield fish by the thousands.

Mika squinted up at a familiar night sky, at the Dancing Girl, the Triplets, the Mad Horse. She had fished off this coast for nearly twenty years, eight of them lost in time. She'd seen green waters, pink waters, blue. She'd been to Candorrea when it was a loose collection of fishing villages, and she'd been to Candorrea when the buildings were so tall she could hardly look at them without shaking. No matter what century she washed up in, however, the constellations were there to guide her home.

It was a windless night. Mika pulled out her oars and set course for Maelstrom, keen to find out when she had landed.

It was the Year of the Blade, 992. The city was metal and glass, its gleaming spires and brilliant rainbow lights casting a skyline like an oil painting. A dome was under construction on the southernmost hill, its name written in freestanding stone letters so large they were visible from the water: *OCEANARIUM*.

This was not her time, not even close.

Mika arrived shortly after the breakfast hour, when dockworkers and merchants were trickling down from the city in the hills. She bypassed the piers entirely, each of them far too tall for her little wooden boat, and glided into the sandy shallows at the north end of the dockworks.

She opened the fish hold in the middle of the deck and hauled out three large nets containing her catch. There were sixty pounds of rainbow-colored senfish, always popular; assorted deep-water crabs, all but one of them extinct since 646, if her *Timeline of the Deeps* was correct; and a single mammal, as large as a barrel-chested mountain dog and thick with hallucinogenic fat: the rare and lucrative sleepwhale.

She wasn't the first fisherwoman-out-of-time they had encountered, and she wouldn't be the last. The anachronism of a sixth-century fishing boat had caught the eye of every merchant on the north shore, and soon they came running, eager to beat one another to strange fish.

The sleepwhale went to a pair of glossy young researchers from the oceanarium. They wore white rubber gloves and green rubber boots, and Mika didn't care one whit why they were taking the beast, but they seemed incapable of keeping their thoughts inside their heads.

"Gene mapping—"

"—reproduction—"

"—grafting the fat signature onto land-bound species—"

Mika understood one word in ten. She held up a hand and enunciated carefully. "Please. I will take the hardtack and beans, and a crate of apples, and be on my way."

The young woman blinked at her owlishly, crouched beside the sleepwhale with one arm wedged under its fin. "You canny mean to weigh off so quick! We have questions—"

"No," Mika said firmly. That word, at least, always remained the same.

After a bit of pleading and attempted bribery (a month's worth of supplies—navigation tech—a warm bed for the night!), they let her go. She had been prepared to fight her way out, if necessary. She knew too well the avarice of researchers.

Researchers never stopped at questions. In their zeal for information they spouted theories, they babbled context, they shouted history and timelines and data and conclusions. Mika didn't dare listen.

For eight years, she had avoided all knowledge of the late sixth century.

For eight years, she had avoided all knowledge of her children.

In the Year of the Mad Horse, 537, Keira was sixteen years old and waiting for her mother to return home from a fishing trip. She was a smart girl, bold and strong. If it hadn't been for a lingering influenza, she would have been at the helm that morning, when a trio of waterspouts blocked Mika's escape from the timestream.

In the Year of the Mad Horse, 537, Emry was fourteen years old.

Bowen was eleven. Terrewyn was nine. They were each brilliant in their own way, Emry with numbers and Bowen with animals and Terrewyn already reading the stars. Their father was gone, his thread cut short in 532. They needed their mother to come home. They needed their mother.

Keira, Emry, Bowen, Terrewyn. Mika breathed their names every morning when she woke and every night before she fell asleep. If she was going to see them again, she had to keep going, no matter how long it took, no matter how exhausting, how difficult, how demoralizing.

It would have been nice to stay the night in 992, to cleanse the salt from her skin and the sway of the waves from her hips. But it wasn't worth the risk. It was only a matter of time before Mika drew the attention of someone worse than a researcher. Like a politician.

Or a librarian.

It was the Year of the Sidewinder, 782. Maelstrom was well into the industrial age, boasting wrought-iron gaslights on every street corner and mechanical cargo lifters along every pier. Unlike the light and shine of the tenth century, this city crouched beneath a blanket of smog.

Mika saw far more of it than she'd intended, because she'd been caught. Succumbing to the lure of a hot meal, she had entered the nearest dining hall—and had the bad luck to sit next to a bureaucrat.

Petro had lacquered hair and a crisp tweed suit studded with silver medallions. He took one look at her sun-faded clothing and declared, "I *certainly* hope you haven't just engaged in an unauthorized beach auction. I'm afraid you'll have to come with me."

He marched her into the hills with a pair of guards at her back, to a prison hotel built for the purpose of assimilating new citizens.

Mika had landed in one of the guild eras, unfortunately, and clearly belonged to no guild.

It was a nice prison cell, at least, with fresh sheets and a writing desk and a folding screen to cover the privy. Mika spent three nights alone, charting what constellations she could see through her window, before Petro returned with his inevitable list of questions.

"Your name?"

"Jera."

Petro's eyes narrowed, but he neglected to challenge the lie. "Your boat is clearly sixth century," he said, "—excellent condition, by the way—but there are patches to the hull, the rails, the equipment in the cockpit."

Mika said, "Yes."

"Some of these metals we have never encountered. They are forged in a manner our engineers declare impossible. You must have landed very far ahead, yes?" He stared at her, expectant, pen poised over a leather-bound notebook.

"I needed some repairs," Mika admitted.

It was the wrong answer. "Tell me where you have been," he demanded. "Past the ninth century? The tenth?"

Mika shook her head, mute, afraid to give away more than she already had.

Petro pursed his lips. He knocked on the door, three quick raps, and another young man wheeled in a heavy wooden cart draped with lush black velvet. Nestled in the fabric was an enormous codex, six inches thick and bound in fraying red leather.

The history book. Mika cringed and turned away.

"You know what this is," Petro said. "You know we have questions."

The other young man—a librarian, no doubt high-ranked to be handling a full copy—gently opened the book past the midway point. The thick pages crackled and wafted up the scent of old paper, tickling her nose, tempting her back. She kept her eyes trained firmly on a trailing length of velvet instead.

Now the questions rained down upon her, and Petro grew more flustered with every vague response. When did you conduct these repairs? What was the governing structure at the time? Did you, at any point, visit the library?

"I have nothing to tell you," Mika insisted.

This was largely true. Mika had landed in dozens of eras, met hundreds of people, glimpsed technological wonders she barely comprehended. But she always kept her head down and absorbed as little as possible.

It was better not to know. A future left unknown was, theoretically, still flexible.

Mika had seen the history book once, in her own time, but she had never read it. In the mid-sixth century, the book was for scholarly use only, and sections of general interest were copied out and taught in public classrooms. There were other eras in which access was even more restricted, and the book was confined to government use, whether that government was militant, religious, or, as in Petro's time, guild hierarchical.

The book documented the curious tangled history of a city that knew what was coming. For centuries, fishermen and fisherwomen had washed up on the wrong shore, bringing with them tidbits of information from every known era. The book was the accumulation of their written memories, but there were many gaps and infamous inconsistencies. Did the course of history adjust as more information was added, or were some of the contributors misinformed? Theories abounded.

The gaps left room for forward planning, but every attempt to influence the timeline was ultimately futile. In 332, the subjects of Queen Mennias built a fifteen-foot wall around Maelstrom to repel an attack by the Frenian horde. As the day approached, the Queen went mad obsessing over the paradox, and when the horde arrived, they were pleasantly surprised to find the gates thrown open for them. They ruled for nearly a hundred years behind the strength of that wall.

Once the Frenians discovered the book, they were less inclined to respect the narrative. Warned of a coming attack from northern Candorrea in 422, they launched a campaign of oppression so brutal that the northern tribes joined forces and destroyed their regime in 414 instead.

Generations destined for conflict did their best to prepare—but by the time their enemies arrived, the population usually greeted them with resignation, if not pleasure. The history of Maelstrom included an impressive number of bloodless coups.

The book was only strange to first-generation immigrants, accustomed as they were to living in mystery. Their children took for granted that history extended in two directions.

Petro ran his finger down the open page of the history book, to the visible discomfort of the librarian. "We know this age of reason will end," he said. "We will be sabotaged by unknown agents. Maelstrom will succumb to another age of warfare and then reemerge under the thumb of an oligarchy. Eight families with a stranglehold on trade, applying their will with brute military force. Merit and skill replaced by—by greed and nepotism!"

"I'm sorry," Mika said. And she was.

Petro sniffed and turned another page. "According to Fisherwoman Gentle Carvier—lost in 1172, found in 690—the oligarchy is firmly established by the mid-ninth century. If this is true, the guild system will fall within the next seventy years. We need a more specific time frame. We need to know more about our attackers. Where do they come from? How do they prevail?"

Mika shook her head. "I don't investigate the city when I land. I stock my boat and I set sail again."

Incredulous, he demanded, "How can you touch the shores of the future and not want to know what will happen?"

"I don't care," Mika said faintly. "It means nothing to me."

He ranted on about loyalty and civic duty and treason, and at last Mika lost her temper. She stabbed one finger toward the book and said, "Don't you know by now? The more you try to alter your destiny, the more surely you will bring it on."

"Oh?" Petro said. "And what is it *you* are trying to do?"

"I . . ." Mika faltered. With a mouth gone dry as dust, she said, "I'm not in there."

Petro slammed his notebook shut. Coldly, he said, "We'll find out soon enough."

He gestured at the librarian to pack up and, lifting his nose imperiously in the air, lobbed his parting shot: "Your days in the timestream are over. You could have a good life here . . . *if* you tell us what we need to know."

Mika held her breath till he'd gone. She stared at her hands, struggling to keep black thoughts at bay. A few minutes crawled by, and she realized the librarian was still there, dawdling over the history book wrappings and sneaking increasingly fervent looks in her direction.

"What?" she sked, resigned.

With a nervous glance at the door, he whispered, "Please, I have to know—are you Mika Sandrigal?"

She recoiled. "No," she said, but too late; her hesitation had betrayed her.

"We—the other librarians and I—we've gone over the list of

missing fisherwomen," he said excitedly. "I admit, the changes to your boat threw us off, but your description is quite clear. Your children—"

"No!" she shouted, and his eyes widened at the force of it, at the sudden rage.

The librarian leaned back, his expression wounded now. "You only had to ask," he said. "We *do* abide by the archives' code of ethics, even if our bureaucrats don't." Plaintively, he added, "I didn't tell him, did I?"

"That is my name," Mika admitted desperately. "But please don't tell me anything more."

He grinned, and Mika's heart sank. This was it, all of her precautions for nothing—but the librarian's code prevailed. He whispered, "Sit tight. I'm going to get you out of here tonight. I'll say nothing else, except: your journey doesn't end here."

He was good as his word, and by cover of darkness she fled to the beach. The librarian smuggled her off with a bag of food, first aid supplies, and a set of letters to deliver to the archives one day— only if she felt comfortable doing so, he hastened to add, and only if she came ashore before the year 717.

It was a relief to reach her boat. A relief to feel the spray on her face. But she couldn't dislodge the stone from her gut, the weight of a thousand questions swallowed whole every time she landed.

To ask about the events of the late sixth century would be a betrayal, an admission that she might not see it for herself. Mika longed to know if Emry had been accepted to the school of letters; if Bowen was still smitten with woodland creatures; if Terrewyn had resolved to study navigation with Keira. But she wouldn't go begging at the doors of the library to find out.

She would be there.

———————

Mika took the first timestream she found, a forward-leaning current that landed her a full century later. She held back from the shore, unwilling to risk a tussle with the oligarchy Petro had so feared, and waited for an opportunity to sail free of it.

The ninth century was an odd time, transitional in nature. Much of the smog had cleared, and enormous machines were visible in the hills, reducing the last of the industrial age's smokestacks to rubble. It was a busy time on the water, as well, as fleets of fisherwomen and researchers and merchants took advantage of the relatively stable political situation to pursue their trades.

Mika avoided them all, including a luxury boat of people she could only assume were tourists from inland, keen to experience all of Maelstrom's oddities. At the sight of her comparatively quaint craft they shouted and waved their arms and excitedly tried to flag her down, but she fled for the horizon, trusting that their captain wouldn't be reckless enough to stray too far from land.

For a week she subsisted only on her own catches and the curiously preserved fruits and meats packed by the librarian. The ocean was frustratingly calm, taunting her with nothing but the unremarkable scent of seaweed, until, at last, the weather conspired to grant her a bit of temporal uncertainty.

At dawn, there were sprinkles. By afternoon, it was a steady downpour. Her spirits surged. There were few better opportunities for catching a timestream than the churned-up currents of a summer storm.

Mika sliced through the breakers with practiced ease, and then it was nothing but wind and salt for miles. She let the current whisk her away from the city and toward the storm cloud brewing black in the distance.

Soon the ocean was roiling beneath her, pitching her boat side to side like a ringtail hopper in the jaws of a redwolf. She reefed her sails and strapped herself to the helm, desperate for some sign of a back-leaning current.

When she saw it, she almost couldn't believe her eyes: three waterspouts, barely visible in the reflected light of the deeps, but there, most definitely there. Mika steered toward the hot, swirling winds, hardly daring to hope that this might be her passage home.

Just as she touched the edge of the timestream—and yes, yes, that was the familiar scent, like warm bread—frenzied sea creatures knocked her boat from below and dark waters flooded the deck. A shadow-crusted behemoth crested over the starboard railing and slapped one meaty fin across her deck.

Mika reached into the storage space beneath the ship's wheel and fumbled blindly at the buckles holding her fishing gear in place. There—yes! The harpoon. She spun to face the beast, weapon in hand, but the boat tipped, groaned, threatened to capsize under its weight—

And crashed portside down into the timestream.

She awoke in a warm room heavy with sunshine and the scents of cinnamon and clover. Her face was hot, her right arm swollen, her breath ragged like there was a sack of fluid in her chest. She was the sole inhabitant of a small infirmary. A woman with a kind face sat in a wicker chair beside her bed.

"What year?" Mika rasped.

"The Year of the Manticore, 616." The woman smiled, setting aside a dog-eared book. "We found you a half-mile offshore with a fairly impressive bite out of the side of your boat. It's been towed in, nothing our fishleaders can't repair, but they'll need a few more days. Take it as a blessing and get some rest. Here. Start with water."

She handed a cup over and Mika drank her fill. The pause gave her time to swallow her disappointment, bitter and all-too-familiar. "How long have I been here?" she asked.

"In the infirmary? Four days. Based on your condition, perhaps another full day at sea before we found you."

Mika sighed. Eight years, four months, and seventeen days since she left the year 537. Tears pricked her eyes. 616 was the closest she'd gotten yet, but it might as well have been 1616.

In 616, her children had been dead for decades.

"I'm Kendrall Millivar," the woman offered.

Mika shoved her ruinous thoughts aside. Cautiously, she said, "My name is Jera."

It was a quick-blooming friendship. Kendrall nursed her through the following week, determinedly battling the infection that had taken hold in Mika's lungs. She kept Mika entertained with good-natured complaints about her three grown children, and in return Mika shared some of her exploits at sea.

Mika's boat was not fully repaired by the time she was discharged, so Kendrall offered a temporary room in her own house. "No charge for a fisherwoman," she said. "There's a city fund to cover your essentials."

One week turned into two, and two turned into a month. Mika's boat was ready by the third week, but a bone-deep weariness had invaded her body in the wake of her illness. Eight years of hard sailing had left its mark, and Kendrall convinced her that a good rest now would serve her better in the long run.

It was far too easy to settle in. It was far too easy to let herself be surrounded by Kendrall's family, Kendrall's home, Kendrall's happiness. The woman glided seamlessly back and forth between nursing and homemaking, and Mika saw what life could have been like if she hadn't been so irrevocably drawn to the sea.

After one particularly long, warm evening of laughter and drink, Mika confessed her real name. After so many years of lonely caution, it was like a rock had cracked through the hull of her chest, and the entire story poured out: her home and her hope, her children, her fear. And Kendrall didn't run off to the archives, or tell her it was futile, or ask for anything more than what was offered. She took Mika's hands and said, "Tell me what you need."

Kendrall wanted her to stay, though she didn't say so aloud. She didn't have to. Mika knew she could live comfortably in this century. Fisherwomen were well-regarded. Their livelihoods were supported, but their actions were autonomous. It was a time of peace, which she knew from her childhood history lessons would last at least twenty years past her lifespan. The cultural and linguistic changes from her own time were more curious than onerous. And there was Kendrall.

But every dawn, Mika marked the passage of time in her travel log with a grease pen. And every dawn, it seemed the wrinkles on her hands had deepened. How old would she be, when she finally made it home? Would she return to her children as their caretaker, or would they be forced to take care of her?

Keira, Emry, Bowen, Terrewyn. Her navigator, her mathematician, her biologist, her astronomer. Her babies.

Eight years, six months, twenty-two days, and Mika returned to the sea. Kendrall came to see her off, and Mika wasn't ashamed to shed a few tears. "Say hello to your children for me," Kendrall said, and Mika left the Year of the Manticore behind.

It took three days of sailing for Mika to catch a back-leaning current. On a warm evening, in the dim light of dusk, she spotted tendrils of pink light slithering up from the deep. They burst on the surface like air bubbles, releasing the sickly-sweet scent of tropical wildflowers.

She followed the lights north, and in their glimmer and flash she spotted untimely schools of fish flanking her hull. They were spiny beasts, gray and gruesome, slipping through the waves from an era long before humanity studded the coast. Each one would have been worth a small fortune in the sixth century, but she had no time to cast a net.

The timestream sucked her in with the force of a whirlpool and it took all of Mika's skill to keep the craft upright. By the time she spun out again she was trembling with exhaustion but wholly, fiercely alive.

It took her until dawn to reach land. There were no mechanical cargo lifters, no buildings of metal and glass in the hills. In fact, there were no buildings at all, and no docks, either. A long, thatch-roofed pavilion stood on the lonesome beach, still smoldering from a recent fire.

Mika had gone too far.

She didn't stay in the Pre-Mendorian era for long. If the stories were true, these hills were controlled by competing warrior bands—territorial at best, cannibals at worst. Archaeologists and anthropologists were divided on the subject, and she didn't care to investigate on their behalf.

At night there were lights to guide her, those strange phosphorescent blooms that lived in the midspace between eras, native to none. Sailing was trickier by day, when the glare of the sun blinded her against multicolored hints from the deep, but a good fisherwoman trusted her nose over her eyes. She knew the sharp herbal scents of drifting leviathans, the floral pockets of midspace cilia, the burnt-rubber sharks and the sour lemon sleepwhales.

Mika drifted back and forth along the coastline until she caught the scent of black tar under a hardboiled sun, and then she turned her boat west, toward the future.

The Year of the Bat, 1127. There were more ships in the air than ships in the water, but as soon as Mika touched the beach, there were customers waiting, as always. Their food packaging was nearly as incomprehensible as their slang.

The Year of the Two-Headed Calf, 312. Mennias was Queen, but her famous wall was still years away from breaking ground. The local language was so far removed from Mika's that she had to haggle by sketching numbers in the sand with sticks.

In 1520 the cityscape was so terrifying and unrecognizable that Mika never even landed. In 415 Maelstrom was in ruins, on the cusp of being repopulated by Mika's northern ancestors.

The Year of the Candlemaker, 702. The Year of the Usurper, 139. Back and forth she sailed, feverishly charting the stars, the tides, the scents and colors and speed of the timestream, desperate to unlock a pattern that would guide her home. And if it really was all chaos? If the only way home was through sheer luck? Then she would roll, and roll, and roll again, until her number came up. Mika sailed and sailed, 'til the years blurred together and she hardly remembered the feel of earth beneath her feet or fresh water on her skin. Four times she encountered the trio of waterspouts, and four times she skipped off their turbulence a little too early, landing two hundred years out, one hundred years out, wrong and wrong and wrong again but circling closer with every attempt.

And there *was* a pattern. There was a complicated interplay between the season, the weather, the orientation of the stars, the migratory pattern of whales, and the duration of time spent in the stream. As Mika's data piled up, her predictive models grew more precise. Now, with a bit of careful observation, she could predict the arrival of forward- or back-leaning currents down to a window of a few days.

She began to wait for optimal conditions rather than leap into the first timestream she found. The waits were painful, notching endless additional days in her travel log, but she knew she was on the verge of success. In every era she anchored, she resupplied, and she returned to the sea, a grim and sun-weathered figure in faded, salt-crusted clothing, eating little and speaking less.

Mika haunted the port of Maelstrom like a restless ghost.

Fourteen years, eight months, eleven days. It was the Year of the Lion's Head, 72, and Mika had been anchored for three solid months. She had avoided more than a dozen timestreams, patiently waiting for this one. Late afternoon. Sleepwhale breeding season. The Mad Horse ascendant. A jump of four hundred sixty-five years would require a long plunge, by her calculations more than twenty minutes.

The clouds formed dense and low and black, just as she had expected. Bubbles appeared on the water's surface in sporadic bursts and small waves lapped at the hull. Visibility was low through the drizzly haze, but Mika spotted the first hints of a funnel forming in the cloud layer.

She raced after the growing waterspout, exultant at the sight of two more funnels overhead. One had already touched the surface, visible only as she approached. And yes—yes! The water was dotted with neon-green kantamimes, carnivorous algae transplanted there in the fifth century, a menace by the sixth. Mika fought increasingly choppy waves and breathed deep of the ocean spray: yeasty and inviting. Like warm bread.

"I'm going home!" she shouted. The words tore at her throat, hoarse and startling. "I'm going home, and you can't stop me!"

She knifed into the dark space between waterspouts before the third one touched down. The seductive flow of a timestream caught her boat, threatening to run her into the waves, and she fought to maintain her position. She had come this far before and always been tossed out too early.

Not again.

Green and yellow lights glimmered ahead. She was close. She only had to stay in these waters another ten minutes. Ten minutes without hitting a spout, or a behemoth—

Or the whirlpool forming dead ahead. Mika tried to course-correct, but she was penned in by the spouts and she refused to drop out of the stream, not now, not after coming this far. She skirted the lip of the whirlpool, her boat surrounded by peppery froth and rattling so hard she thought it would break at the seams.

She tilted, tilted—

Two tentacles slithered up the side of the boat, each one nearly a foot in diameter, mottled blue and red, pulsating with the glowing ichor in their veins. A midspace cephalopod. Mika stabbed at the questing limbs with her harpoon but she couldn't reach them unless she abandoned the helm. She clung tight to the wheel and watched a tentacle wrap tight around the mast, watched the wood shatter into splinters, watched her sails and rigging crash to the deck in a broken tangle. The body of the beast dragged at the boat, tipping her toward whatever grasping toothy maw waited beneath the surface.

She felt it when the hull cracked and water flooded in below. Mika spun around the edges of the whirlpool, faster and faster, whipping past waterspout, waterspout, waterspout, crying for her faithful boat, her thoughts a blur of Keira Emry Bowen Terrewyn Keira Emry Bowen Terrewyn—

The timestream snapped with a sound like falling glass. It spat her out atop the shattered front half of her fishing boat, struggling and sinking fast. Mika unbuckled and jumped overboard before the wreck could suck her under, swimming hard, almost laughing with incredulity—twenty-five years a fisherwoman, and how often did she have to swim?

It took all her strength to reach the shore, and by the time Mika felt sand beneath her fingers, she was so exhausted that she half thought it a trick of her mind. She crawled the last yards, looking up at a city blurred around the edges.

She knew that skyline. She knew those spires, those painted bricks, that stained glass—

Her heart twisted, threatened to break. A slim figure was running down the beach, and his clothing was familiar, too, but for all the wrong reasons.

"The year, the year, what's the year?" she cried, praying that she was wrong, her memories faulty.

He skidded into the surf beside her, breathing hard. "The Year of the Oak," he said. "626."

Too far. Months of waiting and her boat in ruins and she had jumped too far. The boy tried to take her arm, eagerly asking, "Mika? Is that your name? Are you Mika Sandrigal?" but she was crying too hard to answer.

It was Kendrall, of course, who had asked the men of the storm-watch tower to keep an eye out for her friend. Just in case. The last ten years had been kind to the nurse, adding a few more lines around her eyes and a few streaks of silver to her hair. Mika, sun-sick and heartsick, once again relied on the tender ministrations of her friend, and it wasn't until Mika was well again in body, if not in spirit, that Kendrall took her by the hand and said, "Come outside with me, Mika. I have something for you."

"I need to sleep," Mika said thickly, depression wrapped like cotton batting around her tongue.

"You've slept enough. Come along." Kendrall led her outside and up the road, into butter-yellow sunshine and the cheerful ruckus of a city letting out for lunch. They walked to the beach, to a quiet pedestrian bridge overlooking clear waters, and watched the tide roll in.

In her soothing bedside voice, Kendrall said, "I don't think anyone in the history of Maelstrom has traveled as far as you have, Mika. What you've done is incredible. Inspiring. I've often wondered: would I have done the same, when my children were young? I'd like to think so, but . . . well, you just don't know, do you?"

Mika pulled her hand from Kendrall's. Suspicion was an ice dagger to the chest. "Why are you telling me this?" she demanded.

Tears shone in her eyes, but Kendrall didn't sound a bit sorry when she said, "I looked you up in the book."

"No." Mika took a step back.

"I didn't think I would see you again. I had to know—"

"No! No, no, no!" Mika clasped her hands over her ears, as though she could drown it out, as though she could negate the knowledge in Kendrall's eyes through sheer force of will. If she didn't know, it might not happen. If she didn't know, it might not be true.

"You don't have to hear it from me," Kendrall said sadly. "Somebody else has been waiting for you."

She gestured down the bridge, to a nervous young woman walking toward them with an envelope clutched to her chest. Her hair was thick and braided, her shoulders broad, her gait eerily familiar. Mika understood instantly. She turned in a circle, looking for a way out. She could jump from the bridge, swim back to shore, *hide*.

"I'm not talking to you," she warned. "I don't want to hear it."

The girl paused a scant few feet away, staring at her with wide, worried eyes, and Mika rounded on Kendrall instead. "You're my friend. My *friend*. Don't make me do this." The last words turned into a plea.

"I'm so sorry," Kendrall whispered. "You never make it home."

Mika covered her face, shaking uncontrollably. Then: a delicate touch on her sleeve. She lowered her hands and stared with bitter longing at this young woman who carried hints of Keira in her veins.

"My name is Varity," the girl said gently. "I'm your great-great-granddaughter. I have a letter for you."

She held out the envelope. Mika almost didn't take it, a decade and a half's resistance shoring her spine, but her journey was over, and she knew it. With trembling fingers, she pulled out the letter.

She recognized the writing, and the sight of Keira's script set her weeping openly. *Mama*, it began.

Mama. I don't know if this will find you, or when. I need you to know that I love you, and that's why I'm telling you to stop. Don't waste the rest of your life on the water. Don't beat yourself to death on the rocks. I remember you too well to hope you've reached this decision on your own.

We waited twenty years to check the book. Mama, you've been spotted everywhere—and that's only what we could find in our edition. You must have seen incredible things. But the book doesn't say when you settle down, and I have to believe you do. I'm nearly seventy-two years old now, and I don't think I'll see seventy-three. So, I want to tell you about my life, and about Emry, and Bowen, and Terrewyn . . .

Mika read on. She read about Bowen's work with endangered redwolves, and Terrewyn's two astrologer husbands. She read about Emry's short-lived professorship before he became a field mathematician, and about the time he was surveying for a new road and discovered ancient mines in the hills. She read about Keira's shipbuilding business, and about her love, and about their children.

Mika read the history of her family, front and back, seventeen pages lovingly penned in blue ink. Varity and Kendrall waited while she finished the letter, politely directing their attention to the tide.

Mika had seen Maelstrom rise and fall and rise again. She'd seen technological wonders that astounded her and the primitive precursors that made them possible. She'd seen the evolution of the city's population, constantly expanding and contracting, constantly absorbing new blood through invasion or travel or trade, but always keeping a few core cultural threads, a city that knew its future. And none of it had mattered to her. This was the only future she'd ever cared about, seventeen pages front and back.

Varity said, "My grandmother is still alive, and so are some of her cousins. I think they'd like to talk to you."

Mika's grandchildren. The last living memories of her babies, long gone.

"Yes," Mika said. "I'd like to talk to them, too."

CALVED

SAM J. MILLER

Sam J. Miller is the Nebula Award-winning author of *The Art of Starving* (an NPR best of the year) and *Blackfish City* (a best book of the year for *Vulture*, *The Washington Post*, Barnes & Noble, and more—and a "Must Read" in *Entertainment Weekly* and *O: The Oprah Winfrey Magazine*). Sam's short stories have been nominated for the World Fantasy, Theodore Sturgeon, and Locus Awards, and reprinted in dozens of anthologies. A recipient of the Shirley Jackson Award and a graduate of the Clarion Writers' Workshop, Sam is a community organizer by day in New York City.

"Calved" portrays a parent who, like many, is trying his best, in a world where his best is still not quite enough.

M y son's eyes were broken. Emptied out. Frozen over. None of the joy or gladness was there. None of the tears. Normally I'd return from a job and his face would split down the middle with happiness, seeing me for the first time in three months. Now it stayed flat as ice. His eyes leapt away the instant they met mine. His shoulders were broader and his arms more sturdy, and lone hairs now stood on his upper lip, but his eyes were all I saw.

"Thede," I said, grabbing him.

He let himself be hugged. His arms hung limply at his sides. My lungs could not fill. My chest tightened from the force of all the never-let-me-go bear hugs he had given me over the course of the past fifteen years, and would never give again.

"You know how he gets when you're away," his mother had said, on the phone, the night before, preparing me. "He's a teenager now. Hating your parents is a normal part of it."

I hadn't listened, then. My hands and thighs still ached from months of straddling an ice saw; my hearing was worse with every trip; a slip had cost me five days' work and five days' pay and five days' worth of infirmary bills; I had returned to a sweat-smelling bunk in an illegal room I shared with seven other iceboat workers—and none of it mattered because in the morning I would see my son.

"Hey," he murmured emotionlessly. "Dad."

I stepped back, turned away until the red ebbed out of my face. Spring had come and the city had lowered its photoshade. It felt good, even in the cold wind.

"You guys have fun," Lajla said, pressing money discreetly into my palm. I watched her go with a rising sense of panic. *Bring back my son,* I wanted to shout, *the one who loves me. Where is he. What have you done with him. Who is this surly creature.* Below us, through the ubiquitous steel grid that held up Qaanaaq's two million lives, black Greenland water sloshed against the locks of our floating city.

Breathe, Dom, I told myself, and eventually I could. *You knew this was coming. You knew one day he would cease to be a kid.*

"How's school?" I asked.

Thede shrugged. "Fine."

"Math still your favorite subject?"

"Math was never my favorite subject."

I was pretty sure that it had been, but I didn't want to argue.

"What's your favorite subject?"

Another shrug. We had met at the sea lion rookery, but I could see at once that Thede no longer cared about sea lions. He stalked through the crowd with me, his face a frozen mask of anger.

I couldn't blame him for how easy he had it. So what if he didn't live in the Brooklyn foster-care barracks, or work all day at the solar-cell plant school? He still had to live in a city that hated him for his dark skin and ice-grunt father.

"Your mom says you got into the Institute," I said, unsure even of what that was. A management school, I imagined. A big deal for Thede. But he only nodded.

At the fry stand, Thede grimaced at my clunky Swedish. The counter girl shifted to a flawless English, but I would not be cheated of the little bit of the language that I knew. "French fries and coffee for me and my son," I said, or thought I did, because she looked confused and then Thede muttered something and she nodded and went away.

And then I knew why it hurt so much, the look on his face. It wasn't that he wasn't a kid anymore. I could handle him growing up. What hurt was how he looked at me: like the rest of them look at me, these Swedes and grid city natives for whom I would forever be a stupid New York refugee, even if I did get out five years before the Fall.

Gulls fought over food thrown to the lions. "How's your mom?"

"She's good. Full manager now. We're moving to Arm Three, next year."

His mother and I hadn't been meant to be. She was born here, her parents Black Canadians employed by one of the big Swedish construction firms that built Qaanaaq back when the Greenland Melt began to open up the interior for resource extraction and grid cities starting sprouting all along the coast. They'd kept her in public school, saying it would be good for a future manager to be able to relate to the immigrants and workers she'd one day command, and they were right. She even fell for one of them, a fresh-off-the-boat North American taking tech classes, but wised up pretty soon after she saw how hard it was to raise a kid on an ice worker's pay. I had never been mad at her. Lajla was right to leave me, right to focus on her job. Right to build the life for Thede I couldn't.

"Why don't you learn Swedish?" he asked a French fry, unable to look at me.

"I'm trying," I said. "I need to take a class. But they cost money, and anyway I don't have—"

"Don't have time. I know. Han's father says people make time for the things that are important for them." Here his eyes *did* meet mine, and held, sparkling with anger and abandonment.

"Han one of your friends?"

Thede nodded, eyes escaping.

Han's father would be Chinese, and not one of the laborers who helped build this city—all of them went home to hardship-job rewards. He'd be an engineer or manager for one of the extraction firms. He would live in a nice house and work in an office. He would be able to make choices about how he spent his time.

"I have something for you," I said, in desperation.

I hadn't brought it for him. I carried it around with me, always. Because it was comforting to have it with me, and because I couldn't trust that the men I bunked with wouldn't steal it.

Heart slipping, I handed over the NEW YORK F CKING CITY T-shirt that was my most—my only—prized possession. Thin as paper, soft as baby bunnies. My mom had made me scratch the letter U off it before I could wear the thing to school. And Little Thede had loved it. We made a big ceremony of putting it on only once a year, on his birthday, and noting how much he had grown by how much it had shrunk on him. Sometimes if I stuck my nose in it and breathed deeply enough, I could still find a trace of the laundromat in the basement of my mother's building. Or the brake-screech stink of the subway. What little was left of New York City was inside that shirt. Parting with it meant something, something huge and irrevocable.

But my son was slipping through my fingers. And he mattered more than the lost city where whatever else I was—starving, broke, an urchin, a criminal—I belonged.

"Dad," Thede whispered, taking it. And here, at last, his eyes came back. The eyes of a boy who loved his father. Who didn't care that his father was a thick-skulled obstinate immigrant grunt. Who believed his father could do anything. "Dad. You love this shirt."

But I love you more, I did not say. *Than anything*. Instead: "It'll fit you just fine now." And then: "Enough sea lions. Beam fights?"

Thede shrugged. I wondered if they had fallen out of fashion while I was away. So much did, every time I left. The ice ships were the only work I could get, capturing calved glacier chunks and breaking them down into drinking water to be sold to the wide new swaths of desert that ringed the globe, and the work was hard and dangerous and kept me forever in limbo.

Only two fighters in the first fight, both lithe and swift and thin, their styles an amalgam of Chinese martial arts. Not like the big bruising New York boxers who had been the rage when I arrived, illegally, at fifteen years old, having paid two drunks to vouch for my age. Back before the Fail-Proof Trillion Dollar NYC Flood-Surge Locks had failed, and 80% of the city sunk, and the grid cities banned all new East Coast arrivals. Now the North Americans in Arm Eight were just one of many overcrowded, underskilled labor forces for the city's corporations to exploit.

They leapt from beam to beam, fighting mostly in kicks, grappling briefly when both met on the same beam. I watched Thede. Thin, fragile Thede, with the wide eyes and nostrils that seemed to take in all the world's ugliness, all its stink. He wasn't having a good time. When he was twelve he had begged me to bring him. I had pretended to like it, back then for his sake. Now he pretended for mine. We were both acting out what we thought the other wanted, and that thought should have troubled me. But that's how it had been with my dad. That's what I thought being a man meant. I put my hand on his shoulder and he did not shake it off. We watched men harm each other high above us.

Thede's eyes burned with wonder, staring up at the fretted sweep of the windscreen as we rose to meet it. We were deep in a days-long twilight; soon, the sun would set for weeks.

"This is *not* happening," he said, and stepped closer to me. His voice shook with joy.

The elevator ride to the top of the city was obscenely expensive. We'd never been able to take it before. His mother had bought our tickets. Even for her, it hurt. I wondered why she hadn't taken him herself.

"He's getting bullied a lot in school," she told me, on the phone. Behind her was the solid comfortable silence of a respectable home. My background noise was four men building towards a fight over a card game. "Also, I think he might be in love."

But of course I couldn't ask him about either of those things. The first was my fault; the second was something no boy wanted to discuss with his dad.

I pushed a piece of trough meat loose from between my teeth. Savored how close it came to the real thing. Only with Thede, with his mother's money, did I get to buy the classy stuff. Normally it was barrel-bottom for me, greasy chunks that dissolved in my mouth two chews in, homebrew meat moonshine made in melt-scrap-furnace-heated metal troughs. Some grid cities were rumored to still have cows, but that was the kind of lie people tell themselves to make life a little less ugly. Cows were extinct, and real beef was a joy no one would ever experience again.

The windscreen was an engineering marvel, and absolutely gorgeous. It shifted in response to headwinds; in severe storms the city would raise its auxiliary windscreens to protect its entire circumference. The tiny panes of plastiglass were common enough—a thriving underground market sold the fallen ones as good luck charms—but to see them knitted together was to tremble in the face of staggering genius. Complex patterns of crenelated reliefs, efficiently diverting wind shear no matter what angle it struck from. Bots swept past us on the metal gridlines, replacing panes that had fallen or cracked.

Once, hand gripping mine tightly, somewhere down in the city beneath me, six-year-old Thede had asked me how the windscreen worked. He asked me a lot of things then, about the locks that held the city up, and how they could rise in response to tides and ocean-level increases; about the big boats with strange words and symbols on the side, and where they went, and what they brought back. "What's in that boat?" he'd ask, about each one, and I would make up ridiculous stories. "That's a giraffe boat. That one brings back machine guns that shoot strawberries. That one is for naughty children." In truth I only ever recognized ice boats, by the multitude of pincers atop cranes all along the side.

My son stood up straighter, sixty stories above his city. Some rough weight had fallen from his shoulders. He'd be strong, I saw. He'd be handsome. If he made it. If this horrible city didn't break him inside in some irreparable way. If marauding whiteboys didn't bash him for his dark skin. If the firms didn't pass him over for the lack of family connections on his stuttering immigrant father's side. I wondered who was bullying him, and why, and I imagined taking them two at a time and slamming their heads together so hard they popped like bubbles full of blood. Of course I couldn't do that. I also imagined hugging him, grabbing him for no reason and maybe never letting go, but I couldn't do that either. He would wonder why.

"I called last night and you weren't in," I said. "Doing anything fun?"

"We went to the cityoke arcade," he said.

I nodded like I knew what that meant. Later on I'd have to ask the men in my room. I couldn't keep up with this city, with its endlessly shifting fashions and slang and the new immigrant clusters that cropped up each time I blinked. Twenty years after arriving, I was still a stranger. I wasn't just Fresh Off the Boat, I was constantly getting back on the boat and then getting off again. That morning I'd gone to the job center for the fifth day in a row, and been relieved to find no boat postings. Only twelve-month gigs, and I wasn't that hungry yet. Booking a year-long job meant admitting you were old, desperate, unmoored, willing to accept payment only marginally more than nothing, for the privilege of a hammock and three bowls of trough slop a day. But captains picked their own crews for the shorter runs, and I worried that the lack of postings meant that with fewer boats going out the competition had become too fierce for me. Every day a couple hundred new workers arrived from sunken cities in India or Middle Europe, or from any of a hundred Water War–torn nations. Men and women stronger than me, more determined.

With effort, I brought my mind back to the here and now. Twenty other people stood in the arc pod with us. Happy, wealthy people. I wondered if they knew I wasn't one of them. I wondered if Thede was.

They smiled down at their city. They thought it was so stable. I'd watched ice sheets calf off the glacier that were five times the size of Qaanaaq. When one of those came drifting in our direction, the windscreen wouldn't help us. The question was when, not if. I knew a truth they did not: how easy it is to lose something—every-thing—forever.

A Maoist Nepalese foreman, on one of my first ice ship runs, said white North Americans were the worst for adapting to the post-Arctic world, because we'd lived for centuries in a bubble of believing the world was way better than it actually was. Shielded by willful blindness and complex interlocking institutions of privilege, we mistook our uniqueness for universality.

I'd hated him for it. It took me fifteen years to see that he was right.

"What do you think of those two?" I asked, pointing with my chin at a pair of girls his age.

For a while he didn't answer. Then he said "I know you can't help that you grew up in a backwards macho culture, but can't you just keep that on the inside?"

My own father would have cuffed me if I talked to him like that, but I was too afraid of rupturing the tiny bit of affectionate credit I'd fought so hard to earn back.

His stance softened, then. He took a tiny step closer—the only apology I could hope for.

The pod began its descent. Halfway down he unzipped his jacket, smiling in the warmth of the heated pod while below-zero winds buffeted us. His T-shirt said *The Last Calf*, and showed the gangly sad-eyed hero of that depressing miserable movie all the kids adored.

"Where is it?" I asked. He'd proudly sported the NEW YORK F CKING CITY shirt on each of the five times I'd seen him since giving it to him.

His face darkened so fast I was frightened. His eyes welled up. He said "Dad, I," but his voice had the tremor that meant he could barely keep from crying. Shame was what I saw.

I couldn't breathe, again, just like when I came home two weeks ago and he wasn't happy to see me. Except seeing my son so unhappy hurt worse than fearing he hated me.

"Did somebody take it from you?" I asked, leaning in so no one else could hear me. "Someone at school? A bully?"

He looked up, startled. He shook his head. Then, he nodded. "Tell me who did this?"

He shook his head again. "Just some guys, Dad," he said. "Please. I don't want to talk about it."

"Guys. How many?"

He said nothing. I understood about snitching. I knew he'd never tell me who.

"It doesn't matter," I said. "Okay? It's just a shirt. I don't care about it. I care about you. I care that you're okay. Are you okay?"

Thede nodded. And smiled. And I knew he was telling the truth, even if I wasn't, even if inside I was grieving the shirt, and the little boy who I once wrapped up inside it.

When I wasn't with Thede, I walked. For two weeks I'd gone out walking every day. Up and down Arm Eight, and sometimes into other Arms. Through shantytowns large and small, huddled miserable agglomerations of recent arrivals and folks who even after a couple generations in Qaanaaq had not been able to scrape their way up from the fish-stinking ice-slippery bottom.

I looked for sex, sometimes. It had been so long. Relationships were tough in my line of work, and I'd never been interested in paying for it. Throughout my twenties I could usually find a woman for something brief and fun and free of commitment, but that stage of my life seemed to have ended.

I wondered why I hadn't tried harder, to make it work with Lajla. I think a small but vocal and terrible part of me had been glad to see her leave. Fatherhood was hard work. So was being married. Paying rent on a tiny shitty apartment way out on Arm Seven, where we smelled like scorched cooking oil and diaper lotion all the time. Selfishly, I had been glad to be alone. And only now, getting to know this stranger who was once my son, did I see what sweet and fitting punishments the universe had up its sleeve for selfishness.

My time with Thede was wonderful, and horrible. We could talk at length about movies and music, and he actually seemed halfway interested in my stories about old New York, but whenever I tried to talk about life or school or girls or his future he reverted to grunts and monosyllables. Something huge and heavy stood between me and him, a moon eclipsing the sun of me. I knew him, top to bottom and body and soul, but he still had no idea who I really was. How I felt about him. I had no way to show him. No way to open his eyes, make him see how much I loved him, and how I was really a good guy who'd gotten a bad deal in life.

Cityoke, it turned out, was like karaoke, except instead of singing a song you visited a city. XHD footage projection onto all four walls; temperature control; short storylines that responded to your verbal decisions—even actual smells uncorked by machines from secret stashes of Beijing taxi-seat leather or Ho Chi Minh City incense or Portland coffeeshop sawdust. I went there often, hoping maybe to see him. To watch him, with his friends. See what he was when I wasn't around. But cityoke was expensive, and I could never have afforded to actually go in. Once, standing around outside the New York booth when a crew walked out, I caught a whiff of the acrid ugly beautiful stink of the Port Authority Bus Terminal.

And then, eventually, I walked without any reason at all. Because pretty soon I wouldn't be able to. Because I had done it. I had booked a twelve-month job. I was out of money and couldn't afford to rent my bed for another month. Thede's mom could have given it to me. But what if she told him about it? He'd think of me as more of a useless moocher deadbeat dad than he already did. I couldn't take that chance.

Three days before my ship was set to load up and launch, I went back to the cityoke arcades. Men lurked in doorways and between shacks. Soakers, mostly. Looking for marks; men to mug and drunks to tip into the sea. Late at night; too late for Thede to come carousing through. I'd called him earlier, but Lajla said he was stuck inside for the night, studying for a test in a class where he wasn't doing well. I had hoped maybe he'd sneak out, meet some friends, head for the arcade.

And that's when I saw it. The shirt: NEW YORK F CKING CITY, absolutely unique and unmistakable. Worn by a stranger, a muscular young man sitting on the stoop of a skiff moor. I didn't get a good glimpse of his face, as I hurried past with my head turned away from him.

I waited, two buildings down. My heart was alive and racing in my chest. I drew in deep gulps of cold air and tried to keep from shouting from joy. Here was my chance. Here was how I could show Thede what I really was.

I stuck my head out, risked a glance. He sat there, waiting for who knows what. In profile I could see that the man was Asian. Almost certainly Chinese, in Qaanaaq—most other Asian nations had their own grid cities—although perhaps he was descended from Asian-diaspora nationals of some other country. I could see his smile, hungry and cold.

At first I planned to confront him, ask how he came to be wearing my shirt, demand justice, beat him up and take it back. But that would be stupid. Unless I planned to kill him—and I didn't—it was too easy to imagine him gunning for Thede if he knew he'd been attacked for the shirt. I'd have to jump him, rob and strip and soak him. I rooted through a trash bin, but found nothing. Three trash bins later I found a short metal pipe with Hindi graffiti scribbled along its length. The man was still there when I went back. He was waiting for something. I could wait longer. I pulled my hood up, yanked the drawstring to tighten it around my face.

Forty-five minutes passed that way. He hugged his knees to his chest, made himself small, tried to conserve body heat. His teeth chattered. Why was he wearing so little? But I was happy he was so stupid. Had he had a sweater or jacket on I'd never have seen the shirt. I'd never have had this chance.

Finally, he stood. Looked around sadly. Brushed off the seat of his pants. Turned to go. Stepped into the swing of my metal pipe, which struck him in the chest and knocked him back a step.

The shame came later. Then, there was just joy. The satisfaction of how the pipe struck flesh. Broke bone. I'd spent twenty years getting shitted on by this city, by this system, by the cold wind and the everywhere-ice, by the other workers who were smarter or stronger or spoke the language. For the first time since Thede was a baby, I felt like I was in control of something. Only when my victim finally passed out, and rolled over onto his back and the blue methane streetlamp showed me how young he was under the blood, could I stop myself.

I took the shirt. I took his pants. I rolled him into the water. I called the med-team for him from a coinphone a block away. He was still breathing. He was young, he was healthy. He'd be fine. The pants I would burn in a scrap furnace. The shirt I would give back to my son. I took the money from his wallet and dropped it into the sea, then threw the money in later. I wasn't a thief. I was a good father. I said those sentences over and over, all the way home.

Thede couldn't see me the next day. Lajla didn't know where he was. So I got to spend the whole day imagining imminent arrest, the arrival of Swedish or Chinese police, footage of me on the telescrolls, my cleverness foiled by tech I didn't know existed because I couldn't read the newspapers. I packed my one bag glumly, put the rest of my things back in the storage cube and walked it to the facility. Every five seconds I looked over my shoulder and found only the same grit and filthy slush. Every time I looked at my watch, I winced at how little time I had left.

My fear of punishment was balanced out by how happy I was. I wrapped the shirt in three layers of wrapping paper and put it in a watertight shipping bag and tried to imagine his face. That shirt would change everything. His father would cease to be a savage jerk from an uncivilized land. This city would no longer be a cold and barren place where boys could beat him up and steal what mattered most to him with impunity. All the ways I had failed him would matter a little less.

Twelve months. I had tried to get out of the gig, now that I had the shirt and a new era of good relations with my son was upon me. But canceling would have cost me my accreditation with that work center, which would make finding another job almost impossible. A year away from Thede. I would tell him when I saw him. He'd be upset, but the shirt would make it easier.

Finally, I called and he answered.

"I want to see you," I said, when we had made our way through the pleasantries.

"Sunday?" Did his voice brighten, or was that just blind stupid hope? Some trick of the noisy synthcoffee shop where I sat?

"No, Thede," I said, measuring my words carefully. "I can't. Can you do today?"

A suspicious pause. "Why can't you do Sunday?"

"Something's come up," I said. "Please? Today?"

"Fine."

The sea lion rookery. The smell of guano and the screak of gulls; the crying of children dragged away as the place shut down. The long night was almost upon us. Two male sea lions barked at each other, bouncing their chests together. Thede came a half hour late, and I had arrived a half hour early. Watching him come my head swam, at how tall he stood and how gracefully he walked. I had done something good in this world, at least. I made him. I had that, no matter how he felt about me.

Something had shifted, now, in his face. Something was harder, older, stronger.

"Hey," I said, bear-hugging him, and eventually he submitted. He hugged me back hesitantly, like a man might, and then hard, like a little boy.

"What's happening?" I asked. "What were you up to, last night?"

Thede shrugged. "Stuff. With friends."

I asked him questions. Again the sullen, bitter silence; again the terse and angry answers. Again the eyes darting around, constantly watching for whatever the next attack would be. Again the hating me, for coming here, for making him.

"I'm going away," I said. "A job."

"I figured," he said.

"I wish I didn't have to."

"I'll see you soon."

I nodded. I couldn't tell him it was a twelve-month gig. Not now.

"Here," I said, finally, pulling the package out from inside of my jacket. "I got you something."

"Thanks." He grabbed it in both hands, began to tear it open.

"Wait," I said, thinking fast. "Okay? Open it after I leave."

Open it when the news that I'm leaving has set in, when you're mad at me, for abandoning you. When you think I care only about my job.

"We'll have a little time," he said. "When you get back. Before I go away. I leave in eight months. The program is four years long."

"Sure," I said, shivering inside.

"Mom says she'll pay for me to come home every year for the holiday, but she knows we can't afford that."

"What do you mean?" I asked. "'Come home.' I thought you were going to the Institute."

"I am," he said, sighing. "Do you even know what that means? The Institute's design program is in Shanghai."

"Oh," I said. "Design. What kind of design?"

My son's eyes rolled. "You're missing the point, Dad."

I was. I always was.

A shout, from a pub across the Arm. A man's shout, full of pain and anger. Thede flinched. His hands made fists.

"What?" I asked, thinking, here, at last, was something

"Nothing."

"You can tell me. What's going on?"

Thede frowned, then punched the metal railing so hard he yelped. He held up his hand to show me the blood.

"Hey, Thede—"

"Han," he said. "My . . . my friend. He got jumped two nights ago. Soaked."

"This city is horrible," I whispered.

He made a baffled face. "What do you mean?"

"I mean . . . you know. This city. Everyone's so full of anger and cruelty. . . ."

"It's not the city, Dad. What does that even mean? Some sick person did this. Han was waiting for me, and Mom wouldn't let me out, and he got jumped. They took off all his clothes, before they rolled him into the water. That's some extra cruel shit right there. He could have died. He almost did."

I nodded, silently, a siren of panic rising inside. "You really care about this guy, don't you?"

He looked at me. My son's eyes were whole, intact, defiant, adult. Thede nodded.

He's been getting bullied, his mother had told me. *He's in love.*

I turned away from him, before he could see the knowledge blossom in my eyes.

The shirt hadn't been stolen. He'd given it away. To the boy he loved. I saw them holding hands, saw them tug at each other's cloth-ing in the same fumbling adolescent puppy-love moments I had shared with his mother, moments that were my only happy memo-ries from being his age. And I saw his fear, of how his backwards father might react—a refugee from a fallen hate-filled people—if he knew what kind of man he was. I gagged on the unfairness of his assumptions about me, but how could he have known differently? What had I ever done, to show him the truth of how I felt about him? And hadn't I proved him right? Hadn't I acted exactly like the monster he believed me to be? I had never succeeded in proving to him what I was, or how I felt.

I had battered and broken his beloved. There was nothing I could say. A smarter man would have asked for the present back, taken it away and locked it up. Burned it, maybe. But I couldn't. I had spent his whole life trying to give him something worthy of how I felt about him, and here was the perfect gift at last.

"I love you, Thede," I said, and hugged him.

"Daaaaad . . . ," he said, eventually.

But I didn't let go. Because when I did, he would leave. He would walk home through the cramped and frigid alleys of his home city, to the gift of knowing what his father truly was.

THE NEED FOR AIR
LETTIE PRELL

Lettie Prell is the former Director of Research for the Iowa Department of Corrections. In recent years she has made her mark by publishing a number of excellent stories in *Clarkesworld*, *Analog*, Tor.com, and *Apex Magazine*, and reprints in various anthologies including *The Best American Science Fiction and Fantasy 2018*, *The Year's Best Science Fiction and Fantasy 2018 Edition*, and *The Best Science Fiction of the Year Volume 2*.

In "The Need for Air" a mother and son struggle with the realities of virtual technology.

The noon sun was programmed to perfection—warming but not scorching—and the light breeze refreshed as it rearranged Lake's hair. The black sand beach was soft to the feet, containing the right amount of exquisitely shaped shells planted in a manner that drew Jared down the beach, exploring. Lake had brought her son here because of the nature setting. He seemed to be enjoying himself, yet she watched with a wary eye, jaw and shoulders tight with anxiety. Her gaze darted restlessly to the endless scroll of must-haves to the right of her main view: spa getaways, mood boosters (completely safe!), and the latest fashions. At the upper right of her view were the icons for her own settings, as well as the parental access to her son's space. Knowing she could always check his whereabouts should be reassuring, but it couldn't warn her in advance, and that was the issue.

A small group had gathered a short distance away: two young men, three women in burkinis, and four children, all apparently older than Jared. Lake reached for her cover-up and slipped it over her head. She knew it wasn't necessary, but still, the modesty wear made her self-conscious. Instantly, burkinis began scrolling through her feed, informing her brightly that *they're for anyone!* She almost laughed.

One of the older girls, wearing a purple and black burkini, spotted Jared and ran up to him. They exchanged words, and then the girl threw back her head and laughed. Jared flung out his arms, theatrically, like his father used to when he was about to accomplish some minor feat like opening a stubborn jam jar. These small reminders always stabbed Lake with sweet daggers.

Having broadcast his intentions for greatness, Jared turned and did a cartwheel in the sand. His new friend clapped, and then did a handstand while Jared stared. The girl lowered expertly onto her feet again, and then gestured for Jared to try it. It took him a few tries to get his feet up high enough for her to catch them and help him balance.

Lake looked over at the rest of the group. Two of the women were watching the acrobatics, and one looked over at her and waved. Lake waved back. She dared to hope she could leave Jared with them while she went to her job. Even an hour in beta testing would earn her enough money to keep them both going for several more days. Only a small percentage of the fully instantiated opted for that type of work, and never the sequestered, until she'd come around. Most people didn't want to be reminded of where they were. It *was* disorienting, but it paid well, and expenses here were minimal. Maybe Lake could sweeten the pot by offering the girl credits for babysitting.

All the children were at the shore now, playing. They'd made their way closer to where Lake sat. She waved at the girl who'd helped Jared with his handstand. The girl smiled and returned the gesture shyly. She had such a pretty smile.

Jared tapped his new friend on her arm to regain her attention. "Hey, look, Aminah! Look what else I can do!" His form suddenly slumped.

No. Lake sprang to her feet in alarm, but it was too late. Jared deflated like a popped balloon and then he was gone.

The girl gasped, and then stared wide-eyed at Lake.

Lake's face grew hot with embarrassment. "I'm so sorry," she shouted, to be heard above the waves. "He's only eight. He . . . thinks it's funny."

But Aminah had started to back away. "Oh. That's okay. Bye!" She took off running, and the other children followed. Lake watched as Aminah spoke to one of the women, and then pointed at Lake. The other children kept running down the beach, increasing their distance.

So much for the idea of babysitting. Lake burst into tears, which she quickly quelled. She closed her eyes and concentrated. *Clap your hands,* she told herself. *Clap.*

She succeeded. The physical clapping brought her into awareness of her body. She sat up, fumbled with her hood and pulled it off. The bed ceased undulating. She blinked repeatedly as her eyes adjusted to the soft security lighting. There were no windows here, only undecorated cream-colored walls and the long rows of black-clad forms on their beds. The place reeked of body odors and cleaning fluid. She yanked the tubes out of her suit and swung her heavy legs over the side of the bed. It was becoming easier to do this, and that was a bad sign. She pounded the bed with her fist, and then, leaving her hood behind, rose and stumbled down the long rows of anonymous black-clad near-corpses. She should be like them, learning to forget their bodies, not feeling the slick coolness of the laminate floor through the thin soles of her suit as she chased down her wayward child.

The door at the end of the room swept open as she approached. She stepped into the softly lit hallway, and across to the children's ward.

The door opened at the touch of her palm scan. Everything here was the same as the other room, but in miniature. Something tugged at her heart at the sight of all the small, still bodies. She'd been told they took better to the transition than adults. Their entire brief lives had led them to this.

She knew where to look, and saw the empty bed. "Jared?" She cleared her throat, and tried a little louder. "Jared!"

Flashing lights warned her she'd exceeded the policy's decibel limits. "Sorry," she murmured, and exited quickly, her heart pounding with mounting panic. She stood in the corridor looking up and down, not knowing which way to go. She tried taking deeper, slower breaths. She had to calm herself so she could think, and act.

She'd seen him disappear twice before, in the ten days they'd been here, but she'd always found him in the ward, wandering up and down the rows of kids. "I wanted a glass of water," he'd said the first time. Honey, she'd reminded him, you can drink all the water you want if you put your hood back on. He hadn't seemed to hear her. He'd stared at the rest of kids on their beds and whispered, "Everyone looks weird, don't they? It's kind of spooky."

The second time, he'd complained his suit itched, and his face was hot under the hood. "Can I go outside for some air?" he'd asked innocently. "It stinks in here."

Now he was gone. Honestly, why did the ward allow a child out to wander around? "Jared!" The lights flashed again. Really? She was out in the hall. If they'd wanted to, they could've provided some soundproofing, or stuffed everyone's ears with plugs or something. They could've done that.

Somewhere down the corridor, she heard a door closing. She burst into a mad sprint, ignoring her tortured lungs gasping for air almost immediately. She was quickly getting out of shape, being here. But of course she wasn't supposed to be *here*. And neither was Jared.

She spotted the soft green light of an exit, its white figure in mid-stride, dutifully following the pointing arrow. She yanked open the door. There were stairs going up, and none going down. They were being kept in a basement? She was so disgusted she felt sick to her stomach. "Jared!" she called up the stairwell.

The silence gnawed at her gut. She hadn't seen one person, not one robot, either. Clearly, this place was understaffed. Those flashing lights were on automatic sensors.

Somewhere above, a heavy door slammed, followed by a whirring noise that grew closer. Then she heard quiet sobbing. "I just wanted some air!"

"Jared!"

"Jared is found," a calm male voice announced.

They came into view, a robot in descent mode with gliders extended, cradling the limp form of her son in its outstretched arms. Jared's suit was made to leave his artificial legs uncovered, and they gleamed as they dangled, the same dark metal as the robot's.

"Jared!" Her voice was stuck on that one word, but this time she uttered it with relief.

His head lolled toward her. "Mom?" His eyes struggled to focus as they reached the bottom step.

She rushed forward, tried to take him from the robot's hands. "What's wrong with him?"

The robot either didn't understand she wanted to take him, or refused her wishes. "Jared is fine. A mild sedative has been administered. It was understood you wanted him returned, Ms. Lake Lipsman. You are his legal guardian."

"I'm his mother," she retorted.

The robot did not reply. Its gliders retracted, and it skated swiftly past her and down the hall toward the children's ward. Lake followed. She moved as fast as she could, but there was no keeping up with the thing.

The robot was already pulling Jared's hood on when she arrived at the door to the children's ward, out of breath. She wished she could've seen her son's face one last time.

"Do you wish there to be a child lock on the hood?" the robot asked softly as it finished its ministrations.

Her mouth was suddenly dry. "Child lock? I thought that was for the younger kids. You know, the ones too little to understand." She took several steps toward Jared's still form. "Why don't you just keep him in the ward if he comes out again?"

The robot finished hooking Jared's tubes up, and turned toward her. "This is Sequester. It is not a prison."

Lake sucked in her breath. At last she said, "No hood lock on my son. Understand? I'll keep him inside. He'll adjust."

The robot glided to the door, gesturing for her to follow. "They nearly always do."

The door to the children's ward slid closed behind her. Nearly always?

The door to the adult ward whispered open. "Would you like assistance with your own bed?" asked the robot.

She stomped past. "No. Just give me my son's coordinates."

"Gladly. You'll be surfacing at your dwelling. He'll be waking up."

She watched Jared's eyes flutter open. "Hi, honey! Did you have a nice nap?"

He raised himself onto his elbows and looked around, frowning. "Mom. I'm not four years old. I know what went down."

Lake dropped her forced smile. "Fine. So you don't want to be treated like a baby? Then let me tell you something. I've worked very, very hard so I can give you this. Don't you like having your own room? Getting to play on a black sand beach? Don't you like having your own legs?"

Jared frowned and pushed himself upright and out of bed, jostling Lake's shoulder. "That's ableist talk, mom. I *have* legs." He left the room.

Where had he heard that term? Surely not in his present school. School before, then. Or from his father. She heaved a sigh. She had sacrificed a lot, working overtime, so he could have those legs. They had to change them as he grew, too. He'd been on his third set when they'd come to Sequester.

Her feed scrolled through other apartments she could have, other beaches to visit. *Or how about hiking in the mountains?* She saw a breathtaking view from a high vantage point.

"Hey," she called out. "How about we take a trip to the mountains? Do some hiking?"

His head popped into sight in the doorway. "Mom. Is that what your feed is showing now?"

She threw up her hands. "I'm just trying to make you happy. So what do *you* want to do? Tell me and we'll do it."

He slouched against the door frame and studied his shoes. "Well, we've been studying animals at school. Dogs and things. I guess I could go do that, and then hang out with some of the kids."

Lake rose and went to him. She bent and kissed the top of his head and then ruffled his hair. "You've been making friends, then. That's good." Maybe that would keep him where he was supposed to be. Age groups were more often separated here. It encouraged the children to become more autonomous, while providing a safe environment, reducing the need for constant parental monitoring. Lake had been enjoying her own greater freedom, until her son had started disappearing.

Having him in school also meant she could go to work. "Hey, so get out of here already. I'll see you later."

"Thanks, Mom." Jared straightened and headed for the living room and the front door.

"And Jared?"

"Yes, Mom?"

"Behave yourself now."

"Sure, Mom." Then he was out the door.

Lake suspected that aside from being disorienting, people shied away from beta testing because it required interaction with artificial intelligence. The A.I. were difficult to understand, even when they managed a complete sentence in human language. Usually they spoke in gibberish, which she'd been told was their own invented language, and signified their superior intelligence.

Cycle Lake I I I body circuit jaguar tree massive parallel processing, one said.

Another responded in a more feminine voice. *MPP CIP I complete tree they. In cycle circuit abbastanza.*

It didn't seem important whether she understood or not. They seemed to listen politely to her verbal feedback after testing, but she suspected it was unnecessary. They'd probably already gathered what they'd needed based on observing her.

Sometimes what she beta tested was unpleasant, although afterward she felt invigorated by being stretched and challenged in this way. Today was no exception. She found herself in a different body, one with extra appendages she didn't seem able to control. They flopped around as she walked, even slapping her in the face.

She became aware she was on a very thin slice of sidewalk suspended high over a mountain valley. Even though she knew she was safe, she gasped, and her four arms flailed. The two arms she seemed unable to control slapped against her face again. It didn't hurt—nothing here ever did—but it was annoying. She strained with the effort of trying to manipulate them, to no avail. They fumbled over her face till they found her eyes, and covered them. Evidently this was their function, because they stopped flopping around. What a relief.

Then the feed sprang to life around her. No longer was it a separate window to the side of her vision. It enveloped her. She had a new avatar here. It was younger, more vibrant, and thankfully had the correct number of arms and legs. Delighted, she grabbed at things. She tried on a flowing halter dress that shimmered with color when she moved. She selected a pair of gold stiletto heels she'd never been able to walk in with her other body, but was effortless here. She saw a section where she could modify this new avatar. She could select different eyes, give herself a nose job (she laughed ruefully at that one), or sculpt her body in new ways. Suddenly she had a tiny waist, and slimmer thighs. Her skin looked like she'd spent a week in the Bahamas.

She found she could focus outside this immersive feed experience. She experimented with her new appendages again, and found at last the trick to thinking about them, and with this thought muscle she uncovered her eyes. Looking down, she saw she did not have the new body or the new clothes. "Well, that sucks," she said out loud. Back on the thin walkway above the abyss, she was suddenly overcome by a feeling of deep loss, and sank to her knees. Her whole life had been a series of disappointments. Jared's father, David, had left her for a man. She'd understood, but she'd also lost her best friend. Then Jared was diagnosed—incompetent doctors for not catching that sooner!—and had his legs amputated when he was four years old.

She looked down into the abyss. It would be easy to throw herself off, but she knew she couldn't die here. Instead, she tried covering her eyes with her hands again. Wrong pair. She tried again, with the other hands that she was still getting used to manipulating, and covered her eyes with those.

Instead of seeing the beautiful feed sprung to life, with the customizable body and all those clothes, she was out of the simulation altogether.

Thank you Lake cherry cherry lime, said the more feminine voice.

Was that a reference to a slot machine? Lake almost laughed. She started to report out, sharing her impressions and thoughts—especially about that new way to experience the feed!—but she was suddenly very tired. They probably knew everything they needed to, anyway. She punched out for home.

Lake paced the living room, frowning. She'd rather be at the Never-Ending Mixer, her favorite after-work hangout, but she'd told Jared she'd be here when he came home. But just when was that going to be? She replayed the memory of their conversation, and saw no time had been mentioned. He'd said he was going to hang out with the kids after classes, so even if she checked the school times, it wouldn't tell her anything about Jared's return.

She replayed the memory again. There was her son, leaning on the door jamb, studying his shoes. That was his father's slouch, with the downward gaze. She pursed her lips. Jared's intentions were plain as day, but she'd failed to see it because she'd been so relieved she could go to work. If you passed a statue in an art museum posed like this, its title would read *Dishonest Boy with Secret Plans*.

Oh, but she knew exactly where he was. She flung herself on

the couch and closed her eyes. *Clap,* she shouted at herself. That wouldn't do. She sighed out a lungful of anger and tried again. *Clap. Clap your hands.*

She sat up, pulling the hood from her head in one smooth motion, and then the lines connecting her suit with the bed. God, she was getting too good at coming out. She was steady on her feet as she rose and walked swiftly to the door of the ward.

There was a robot in the hallway, apparently waiting for her. For a moment, she took it for the one that had brought Jared back from wherever he'd roamed, but then again, all of them looked alike. Robot personality programming had been purged several updates ago.

"Where is he?" she demanded.

The robot tilted its head as if unsure what she'd said. "This is your formal warning that repeated surfacing behavior will result in ejection from Sequester."

Lake sucked in her breath. "Just how many formal warnings do I get?"

"One," the robot replied.

Lake blinked. "This one? This is it?"

"Correct."

Lake's hands clenched. "Then help me find my fucking son."

She pushed past the robot and let herself into the children's ward. All the bodies looked so similar in their black suits, but at least none of the beds were empty. She breathed a sigh of relief when she spotted Jared's artificial legs, gleaming in the dim light. She approached, and stared down at his form, suddenly wanting to scream at him, he'd caused them both so much trouble. They were on the brink of being evicted, of losing this golden opportunity to improve their lives for good.

But he was already on the other side, back where he should be in the virtual world. She'd have to save her fury for when she returned.

She felt rather than heard the robot's presence at her side. There was a displacement of the air, a large mass in her peripheral vision. Her memory worked the old way here, but it was vivid enough.

"You mentioned you could put on a child lock," she said. "On his hood. So he can't take it off."

"It requires the legal guardian of the child to authorize," it said.

She chewed her lower lip briefly. "Then let's do it."

The robot reached down. Its arm made two clamping motions, one on each side of Jared's neck.

"And take his legs," she said, turning away.

"Repeat?"

"You heard me. Take his goddamn legs off." She exited, crossed the hall swiftly, and reentered her own ward.

It's for his own good, she told herself as she fastened herself into the bed. He'll be fine. He'll adjust. Everyone does. And he'll thank me. He'll thank me for this.

She sat in her beach chair, toes grinding into the black sand, and watched her son—her only son—stare out to sea. He hadn't spoken to her for three hours, not since he'd obviously tried to leave, to come out of it, to do his little visit back to his body. He'd come bursting out of his room screaming, "Mom! What's going on?" She'd tried to soothe him, of course. She wasn't a monster. She was doing this because she loved him.

"Honey," she'd said as she held him close. "It's because I care about you. I care about your future. You've got to believe me, this is better than out there. You'll live forever, for one."

Then, because he hadn't stopped crying, she'd brought him here, to the beach. He liked the beach. Kids don't understand about mortality, she thought. Jared probably never thought she'd die someday, let alone himself.

Jared was planted in the wet sand, letting gentle waves roll over his legs. His father, David, had liked the beach. He was always photographing the beach, and their seaside cottage, with that impossibly archaic camera with the bellows, and gargantuan negatives. He had to send for supplies halfway across the country, to make his blasted black-and-white photographs.

"Why do you bother?" she'd asked him many times.

"I like old things," he'd responded. But there were some things he liked young, she'd discovered. He'd left her for a twenty-five-year-old man who'd majored in psychology at Sarah Lawrence. They got the beach cottage in the divorce. Lake had taken the two-bedroom apartment in Cambridge, near Jared's school.

The morning she'd left him with Jared in tow, David had stood staring at the sea in the same way that Jared stared now.

She reached up and ran her fingers over her hair, as if the memories would shake out with the sand and float down the shore. This programmed place she'd secured for herself, for Jared, was her new world now, an exciting and seemingly limitless place that she was helping to create with A.I., through her beta-testing job. Cherry cherry lime, they'd told her. They'd been pleased. When would she be able to leave Jared again and go back to work? She'd love to be enveloped by the feed again. The current sidebar of goodies suddenly seemed outdated. She watched the offerings scroll by: mood boosters, a memory excision tool. She paused to read about the latter.

"Mom? Mom!"

It was Jared, kneeling in front of her. Black sand stuck to his arms and thighs like so much pepper.

"Yes, I'm here," she said. "You don't have to shout."

"Mom, I have to go back. Now."

"Jared, you know you can't. It'd mean—"

"I have to feed the dog, Mom. It'll starve if I don't."

"Dog?" She couldn't process this. "We can get you a dog, honey. Whatever you want."

"Mom. This is a real dog. There's a place outside Sequester where I go. Mom." He started to cry.

"Go? What do you mean go?" But now guilt stabbed through the anger and made everything clear. She'd been so wrapped up in her new job, and being around A.I., and going to the Never-Ending Mixer, and worrying about what he was *going* to do, that she'd neglected to access her son's space to look at his history of movements. She called it up now, even as he relentlessly stared at her with those serious eyes. And what she saw was unbelievable.

"You've hardly been sequestering at all," she whispered. Every time she'd been at work, every time she'd gone to the Never-Ending Mixer, he'd been sneaking out. He'd hardly attended school at all, since they'd arrived.

"How can you still be here?" She meant how was he not expelled from Sequester, but instead it sounded like she didn't want him around. Yet she didn't have the words to correct herself. The silence between them was an almost measureable distance.

"They've been letting me go outside to get fresh air," he said. "It's only when you get involved that they care. Mom, please. I need to go."

God, that place was so lax, that they wouldn't even protect a child.

"I'll buy you a pet." God, she was shouting. She wasn't angry at Jared, but the system. It was seriously messed up. There should be a warning light on that parental access icon, to let someone know they should be monitoring their child's activities.

He leaped to his feet and glowered down at her. "I don't want a fake dog!"

Lake made an effort to lower her voice. "Honey, I'm sorry. I'm not mad at you."

But he was screaming now. "I can't believe you put a lock on my hood!"

"Jared." She was calm now. She had this. "They weren't doing you any favors, letting you go outside. The whole point of Sequester is to weaken your attachment to your body. So you can adjust to being here permanently."

His brows drew together. If he'd been older, he'd look menacing. "I don't want to be here. I want to stay a breather."

Lake stared up at him. "I'm not sure you understand what that means, honey. You're too young to think long-term."

His expression had gone blank. He was reading his feed. She hoped he was looking at the dogs he could have, but she doubted it.

"Mom?" His voice was a whisper. "Did you tell them to take . . . my legs?"

Again the guilt threatened to overwhelm her, just as it had with his father. Why hadn't she seen that one coming, either? It had only been when her heart had broken that she'd seen the truth, could trace the history of the betrayal. She lifted her chin. "I did. For your own good. Honey, I love you. You need to let me provide for you."

He was backing away from her across the sand. Then he exited the beach. Lake flipped on her parental access. She'd never neglect that again.

She saw at least he wasn't trying to surface, to claw at his hood. But where he'd gone was puzzling. What was he doing at Human Affairs? Well, let him learn for himself that she was well within her rights to make decisions for him.

She rose, brushing sand from her thighs absentmindedly. While he was occupied, she could go to work.

She was special. She'd known that by the assignments they'd given her, but it was all confirmed at the Never-Ending Mixer. She arrived after work, when another invigorating round of what she'd begun to call feed immersion helped her recover from her argument with Jared. She dropped the term casually at the mixer—the first time she'd mentioned her job—and instantly found herself the center of a small crowd's admiration.

You're still in Sequester, and you're beta testing?

Yes, she was, she said proudly.

But you're so new to the virtual world. You can't possibly have adjusted to standard functioning yet.

She was used to having a job. There happened to be openings for beta testing, she'd signed up, and was accepted. It paid well.

It carries a certain amount of risk. Adjustment problems, primarily, which places a strain on one's mental health.

Actually, she found the work interesting.

Then came a barrage of questions about A.I. She could answer few of these, but it was obvious they were jealous of her interactions with artificial intelligence. The crowd was hungry for any tidbit of information. She got the distinct impression she was viewed as a courageous pioneer. Well, she'd had to be that, and resourceful as well, as a single parent. Providing for her son had made her tenacious. Bringing Jared here was part of her natural pioneering spirit. This was the wave of the future.

She was still having fun at the mixer, regaling the crowd with some of her testing experiences, when she received a message in her feed. She was being summoned to Human Affairs. She sighed. Undoubtedly she was being asked to retrieve Jared. She didn't want to leave. Everyone was absolutely spellbound. Well, it was a sneak preview of their future, after all. But being a parent came first. She left right away, voicing sincere apologies to her admirers.

Jared's shoulders were hunched, and his gaze was on his shoes as he stood next to the arbitrator, a tall woman with extremely short gray hair and wearing a blush pink blouse over gray trousers. The pink looked decidedly unjudicial. When the arbitrator spoke, she sounded too informal.

"Hi, Lake," she said. "We're here to talk about Jared's request to be emancipated from you. If granted, your parental rights will be terminated."

She did not have words for this . . . betrayal. Jared was just like his father. "There must be some mistake," she told the arbitrator.

The woman's eyes were not unkind. "Please answer this question, Lake. Did you order the robot to remove your son's prosthetic legs?"

Something deep inside her ached, threatened to overwhelm. She was going to buy that memory excision tool she'd seen in her feed. "I did. The stakes were high. We were close to being expelled from Sequester."

The arbitrator regarded her, inhaling slowly. "And you ordered this, aware that Jared's prosthetics are fully integrated into his body? That they aren't readily removable?"

"Of course," Lake replied, irritated. Only the best for her son. This wasn't the olden days, when people took their artificial limbs off to go to bed.

The arbitrator blinked once, quickly. "Are you aware your request in this matter was denied?"

Lake was taken off guard. "No. I mean . . . I was. . . ." She didn't want to admit she'd given the order out of anger. She'd only wanted to make sure Jared stayed put. For his own good.

The arbitrator cut into her thoughts. "Your order was denied because it was a reckless request. Sequester is not a prison."

The robot had said the same thing. Lake was fuming inside. They had let her son get up and leave Sequester multiple times, for hours. But one careless comment from her, uttered when she was justifiably angry and fearful of the consequences, and it was grounds for this? Well, she wasn't about to blow up now. She stood, seething, facing the arbitrator and her son, and said nothing.

The arbitrator paused, and then nodded. "Because Human Affairs has jurisdiction over these matters, and they've given me authority to make a decision on this, I'm declaring Jared emancipated from your authority. Is there anything you'd like to say to Jared, or to me, at this time, Lake?"

Lake shook her head, not to mean no, but to express her disbelief. "Where is he going to go? Who's going to take care of him?"

The arbitrator put a hand on Jared's shoulder and he looked up, grudgingly, into his mother's eyes. "I've talked to Dad."

Lake's shoulders stiffened.

The arbitrator spoke to Jared. "Your dad. You want to go live with your dad."

Jared nodded. "He'll come get me tomorrow. And Hope, too."

"Hope?" Lake echoed. The word didn't belong here. "Hope for what?"

Jared smiled sheepishly. "Hope is the name of my dog, Mom."

Again that dog. She accessed her son's space—she still had her authority to do that—and clicked to access his memories.

She—in Jared's point of view—bounded up the stairs and out a gray utility door. There was a stark contrast of bright sun and deep shadow that she recognized as late afternoon. She looked left, then right, along the deserted side street, little more than an alley, really. Then she darted across the street and into the back of a place.

Inside she emerged into a small grocery, a mini-mart. It was deserted, but there were still a few cans and boxes on the shelves. There was a shadow under the front window that moved. It was a black dog wagging its tail slowly. It was lying on several thicknesses of old blankets. It leaned heavily on its front legs as it stood. It approached with a hobbling gait, and Lake soon realized why. The dang thing was missing a right hind leg.

She watched Jared's hand go out and pet the dog's head. *Hi, girl. Are you hungry?*

The dog wagged its tail in reply, and followed Jared around the corner of an aisle, where a food and water dish stood up against a darkened refrigerator case that still contained a few bottles of water and soda. The crude simplicity of the scene, and the fragility of biological life, touched her.

There were tears rolling down her cheeks as she withdrew from the memory. She understood now why Jared was drawn to that pitiful dog. There was something in him that was like his mother, after all: a headstrong determination to provide for another being's needs, even if it meant self-sacrifice.

Her son and the arbitrator were looking at her. She needed to say something. "Fine. Go."

Jared ran to her and encircled her torso with his arms, putting his face alongside her neck. She closed her eyes and thought about the beach: the sun on her face, and the wind gently playing with her hair.

It was she who broke the embrace at last, prying his hands from around her. "So go feed your dog."

His lips quivered as he smiled. His eyes glistened with tears of his own. "Thanks, Mom."

Lake wanted to say the dog looked like a good one. She wanted to say something encouraging. But she couldn't. She was reliving the challenges of dealing with all those physical things out there. Buying food. Making meals. Taking showers. Needing a car to drive yourself to work. Shoveling snow. Dusting. Laundry. Calling someone to come fix stuff when it breaks down. God, and the body breaking down. Surely Jared would come to understand mortality when he was older, would come back to Sequester. Everyone would come here, eventually, who could afford it.

Jared reached up and put both hands on her shoulders. It broke her reverie, and she looked down into a pair of sincere eyes. "Bye, Mom. I know you'll be happy here. I know how much you like it."

Then he was gone. His virtual form didn't deflate as before, but simply winked out, like it was no big deal. It was hard to believe he was gone for good. She was seized with the desire to clap her hands, go to him, just to say goodbye again, in her old body, one human to another. But to do so would kick her out of the garden of paradise.

She left Human Affairs and went to the beach, where she bought a mood booster and looked out at the waves rolling in. Up the beach a ways there were several women in burkinis, and children running along the beach. She thought they might be the same Muslim family, the girl Aminah among them, who had helped Jared do a handstand. Lake waved, feeling the freedom in her arm, light as the breeze. She could go to her beta testing job now, and work as long as she liked.

She bought the memory excision tool, and carved away the worst about David and Jared, leaving just enough of the pain so she wouldn't miss them. Then she went into her settings and de-selected her feeding functions. She might as well speed things up.

She received a message a few days later that her body had been vacated and cremated. There was no going back now. She was fully instantiated. What a relief, she told herself.

David and Jared could reach her through the interface, but the outside world operated at a much slower pace. By the time they initiated messaging through the interface, they'd be old as history to her.

In the meantime, she'd made it. She was in the better world for good.

ROBO-LIOPLEURODON!
DARCIE LITTLE BADGER

Darcie Little Badger is an enrolled member of the Lipan Apache Tribe of Texas, and her fiction has appeared in *Strange Horizons*, *Mythic Delirium*, and *The Dark*. Her work is also in numerous anthologies, including *Lightspeed Magazine's People Of Color Destroy Fantasy!* special issue and *Moonshoot: The Indigenous Comics Collection Volume Two*. She is also co-writing *Strangelands*, a comics series in the H1 Humanoids shared universe. When she is not writing fiction or comics, she edits research papers, and she has a PhD in Oceanography. Her debut novel, *Elatsoe*, will be published in 2020.

"Robo-Liopleurodon!" is an exciting slice-of-life piece about an underfunded marine researcher's extraordinary day out on the high seas.

M y intern screamed. That's rarely a good sign. Near the starboard rail, Abigail clutched a dripping, freshly towed plankton net. The collection vial dangling from the muslin funnel glinted in the sun, as if filled with silver particles.

"Doctor!" she shouted. "Nanobotplankton!"

"Are you sure?" I asked. "They aren't garbage?"

"Look!"

The collection vial was the size and transparency of a jam jar. Abigail thrust it at me, as if handing off a grenade. I activated the magnification on my protective goggles and peered at the murky seawater. Metal specks sloshed side to side, dizzying; they were shaped like pill boxes and propelled by nanocarbon flagella.

"Alert the captain," I said. "It's bad news."

I'd heard horror stories about swarms of bots large enough to track and disable cruise ships; they reported either to governments or pirates or supervillains, and we were in the open ocean, well beyond any continental jurisdiction.

Pirates or supervillains, then. What did they want from us? The vessel was equipped for research, and our most expensive cargo was a really good microscope. Would they demand hostages? I glanced at Abigail's back; she was nineteen, brilliant, and had joined my lab with a fellowship for low-income students. She reminded me of myself, twenty years back when, driven by hope, I studied geosciences because the world was hurting, and somebody had to diagnose it so *something* could done.

Since then, I've made plenty of diagnoses. But so little has been done.

I wondered how long it would take Abigail to become jaded or—like many of my colleagues—leave the field. It's hard to make a career in geosciences unless you love the earth. Even harder to study its death in the kind of detail that withstands peer review. How many reefs had I watched die? Islands drowned by the rising sea? Primordial species extinguished in the span of one human lifetime?

Frustration drove my own advisor to early retirement. I was her last pupil; she left the moment I graduated. "They won't listen to us, Maria," she said. "They won't fund us. And that means we can't help them."

As I watched the water around our ship darken with swarming bots, I wondered: "Who will help us?"

In the distance, a silver surface split the sea, but the vessel—an odd submarine?—dove before I could get a good look. One of the quick-thinking deckhands activated a distress drone. With an industrious whir, the tri-copter zipped over my head and attempted to escape the signal-blocking radius emitted by those damnable bots.

The ship's emergency siren wailed, indicating that I should leave the deck and take shelter in my cabin. But I couldn't turn away from the sea, which churned like boiling soup beneath the drone. Seconds later, a metal beast breached the water. Its great, crocodile-shaped mouth yawned open and snapped, crushing the drone mid-leap. Its four paddle-shaped flippers flapped, their surfaces sleek and their edges sharp as knives. When the whale-sized machine landed, the impact rocked our ship and sprayed my face with water that tasted of salt and metal.

"What is that?" a deckhand asked, dismayed.

"I . . . can't believe this," I said, "but it looks like a robo-Liopleurodon."

The Liopleurodon head reared from the water, its jaws snapping, flourishing five-inch-long serrated teeth that could easily tear our hull to shreds. I took a step back, at once startled and fascinated. Its engineer had put exquisite care into the design, emulating the strength and form that once made the Liopleurodon the greatest carnivore in the Jurassic sea.

Far beyond the Liopleurodon, silver bobbed on the undulating sea. I zoomed in with my goggles and glimpsed a hatch protruding from a metal dome.

"Doctor!" Abigail said, tugging on my sleeve. "The captain wants us off the deck. Come with me! We can't—"

"ATTENTION RV," the Liopleurodon boomed. "SURRENDER ALL MICROSCOPES, CTDs, AND REAGENT-GRADE CHEMICALS, OR WE WILL DISABLE YOUR SHIP."

There was something familiar about that voice.

"Dr. Barbara?" I asked. "Dr. Barbara, is that you?" I threw myself against the railing and waved at the Liopleurodon's glassy black eye. "Hey! Hey, it's me! Maria! Can you hear me? Holy schist, this can't be happening!"

The Liopleurodon's mouth opened wider, as if gasping. "MARIA!?"

"Are you piloting that robot dinosaur?" I asked.

"ER. WELL. A ROBOT *MARINE REPTILE*."

"And robbing us?"

"FOR THE GREATER GOOD."

"Greater good?"

"EARTH AND SCIENCE."

I'd been wrong. My advisor never gave up. Although I wasn't sure that joining a team of rogue scientist pirates was much better. And it *had* to be a team. Dr. Barbara might be a brilliant chemical oceanographer, but she wasn't a paleontologist or an engineer.

"YOU MUST THINK I'M TERRIBLE. JUST—ER—NEVER MIND. WE CAN FIND SUPPLIES ELSEWHERE. I HOPE YOUR RESEARCH IS FRUITFUL."

The Liopleurodon began to sink. "Wait!" I said.

It hesitated, half its head submerged. "YES?"

"Have you really accomplished anything with this . . . this criminal behavior?"

"OF COURSE. JUST THIS YEAR, WE HAVE ELIMINATED ONE MILLION TONS OF MICROPLASTICS FROM THE NORTH PACIFIC GYRE AND SAVED A WHALE SPECIES FROM EXTINCTION."

"You'll be caught someday, Dr. Barbara," I said.

"PERHAPS." The Liopleurodon winked. "TAKE CARE, MARIA."

As our attackers vanished and the ocean cleared, Abigail asked, "Who was that?"

"Apparently, my graduate advisor."

"Is she a supervillain, or something?"

"Or something," I said. And I wondered if someday that something would be me.

Silver glinted against the horizon as the robo-Liopleurodon leapt one last time.

THE DOING AND UNDOING
OF JACOB E. MWANGI

E. LILY YU

E. Lily Yu's fiction has appeared in *Clarkesworld, The Boston Review, Fantasy & Science Fiction, McSweeney's Quarterly, Apex, Uncanny, Terraform, Tor.com,* and many others. She has been a finalist for the Hugo, Nebula, World Fantasy, Locus, and WSFA Small Press awards, and she won the John W. Campbell Award for Best New Writer in 2012. She is one of three writers to appear in both volumes.

"The Doing and Undoing of Jacob E. Mwangi" follows the titular character as he undergoes a fundamental change from his comfortable gamer identity.

O n Sunday after services, Jacob Esau Mwangi beat a hasty retreat from the crowd that descended upon his beaming parents and Mercy, who on this rare visit home between Lent and Easter terms was displayed between them like a tulip arrangement.

"What a daughter! Be a famous professor soon."

"You have not forgotten about us common people? Cambridge makes all the children forget. They act so embarrassed when they come home—"

"Funny to think they both come from the same family."

"It's very strange, isn't it?"

"Where did he go anyway, that Jacob boy?"

Jacob, outside the chapel's blue acrylic domes, caught the first flying matatu without regard for where it went.

He glowered out the window at the holograms of giraffes and

rhinos that stalked the streets, flashing advertisements both local and multinational. A lion yawned and stretched among the potted plants at the center of a traffic circle, the words DRINK MORE JINGA COLA scrolling along its tawny flanks.

Twenty-five years before, the gleam and gloss of digital advertisements had divided the globetrotting Kenyan Haves from the shilling-counting Have Nots who shopped at tin-sided street stalls with painted signs. Now that that partition was obsolete, humanity had split itself into Doers and Don'ts. Jacob's mathe and old man were devoted Doers, an architect and an engineer. Every month they asked Jacob if he had created anything lately, and every month, when he gave them a cheerful shrug, they flung up their palms in ritualized despair.

The matatu halted and hovered while more people crammed on.

Jacob had no stomach for returning to his apartment, a windowless box in Kawangware that he had picked specifically for its distance from the family manse. He unrolled his penphone and selected Rob's name.

> hey, game time?

sorry can't

> what's going?

dame. tell u later

> sawa

Outside the window the tidy six-story buildings of Kibera Collective flashed wholesome mottos in LEDs. *Pick up after yourself. Harambee. Together we can remake the world.* Jacob frowned absently, mapping his route in his head. If he swapped matatus here, the next would take him as far as Black Nile Lounge. The Black Nile was his usual base, though he'd venture as far east as the Monsoon Club if Rob was joining. You did that for a brother.

And Rob was his brother in all the ways that mattered, just as his gaming group was his true family: Robert and nocturnal Ann from Wisconsin and Chao from Tennessee, as well as sixty guildmembers from places as exotic as Anchorage and Korea who formed a far-flung network of cousins and in-laws, as full of gossip and grudges and backbiting and broken promises as the real thing. They were all Don'ts, of course. Doers played too, intermittently, but the Don'ts slaughtered them all, every match, always.

The no-man's-land between the Doers and Don'ts was as close as anything came to a war these days. Though the lines were deeply entrenched and wreathed in verbal barbed wire, and battles pitched as often in PvP as over dinner tables, no real bullets were ever fired. There had been little of that since the days of the Howl.

No one liked to speak of the Howl, of the blood that darkened and dried in the streets, of the mind virus that had reawakened after a century of dormancy to sow chaos and fear.

For out of the Howl had come the great Compassion, when, like a strange flowering in a sunless cave, the fervent prayers of adherents of every faith and the ferocious meditations of the variously spiritual, bet-hedging, and confused had reached critical mass, triggering a deep immune response in the human psyche. As if struck by lightning, the five billion survivors of the Howl had let the rifles and knives fall out of their hands, then embraced, or dropped to their knees and wept.

It was like God Himself sat down and talked with me, Jacob's mathe liked to say, and his old man would nod solemnly, yes, that was how it was.

By the fiftieth time he heard this exchange, Jacob was ready to pitch a can of Jinga Cola at each of their heads. He had not known the Compassion, having been born shortly afterward, and was thoroughly sick of hearing about it.

During the three years that the Compassion lasted, dazed legislators in every country redistributed wealth and built up healthcare and social services, while the wealthy deeded entire islands and bank accounts to the UN. Petty crime and begging vanished from Nairobi's streets. House gates were propped open. Askaris found no work and opened flower stands and safari companies. Kibera shantytown self-organized, pooled surplus funds, and built communal housing with plumbing and internet.

Gradually, as memories of the Compassion faded, life returned to a semblance of normalcy. Rush-hour drivers again cursed each other's mothers, and politicians returned to trading favors and taking tea money. But there remained a certain shining quality about life, if looked at the right way—or so Jacob's elders said.

The most important outcome of all that ancient history, as far as Jacob was concerned, was the monthly deposit in his account that the Kenyan government styled Dream Seeds, distributed to every resident not already receiving a stipend from another government. This paid for Jacob's bachelor pad and now, as he touched his pen to a scanner, for the Black Nile entry fee, a handful of miraa, and a bottle of beer.

The man in the booth assigning cubes handed Jacob a keycard marked 16 and said hopefully, "Maybe a Kenyan game today, sir? My brother's studio, I can recommend—"

"Maybe another day, boss."

"You cannot blame a man for trying. Japanese fantasy war sims again?"

"Good guess."

"I like to know my customers." He sighed. "I don't know how we will compete, you see. Our industry has just been born—theirs is fifty, sixty years old."

"You will find a way," Jacob said, to escape.

The door to the VR cube hissed open. Jacob lasered the title he wanted on the wall—*Ogrefall: Visions of Conquest*—then donned the headset and gauntlets, which stank of sweat. In a higher-end establishment the gear would be wiped down with lavender towelettes between uses, and tiny pores in the wall would jet out molecules of the scent libraries shipped with the games, odors of forest and moss, leather and steel, but Black Nile was a business scratched out of hope and savings from jua kali, the owner a Doer to his core, and the game loads were all secondhand.

Jacob launched the game and became a silver lion with braided mane, ten feet tall and scarred from battle. Ann and Chao were already online, knee-deep in the corpses of ogres and the occasional unfortunate Doer, their whoops of joy ringing in his ears.

"Hey! No Rob?" Ann asked.

"Some dame," Jacob said, placing his paw over his heart. "He's a goner."

"You say that every time," Chao said. "And you're always wrong. Rob gets bored faster than anyone else I know. I give her fifteen minutes, max."

Ann said, "We're storming Bluefell right now. Figured you two'd be along. I don't know what we'll do without Rob."

"Let's run it," Chao said. "Rob will catch up to us."

They battled their way up a snowy mountain, pines creaking and shaking lumps of snow down on them. Ice demons lunged and jeered and raked their faces. Ann died. Chao died. Jacob died. Their vision went black, and then they found themselves at the foot of the mountain.

"Again?" Chao said.

Again they wiped.

"This is bullshit," Ann said. "I give up."

"Hi, guys," Rob said. "What are we playing today?"

"Told you," Chao said.

"Where are you?" Jacob said. "And where's your girl?"

"Took you long enough," Chao said. "Twenty-four minutes. A new record."

"She's here with me. We're at Monsoon. Trying to skip the tutorial. Hang on."

A moment later, there she was. Purple-haired and elf-eared, in novice's robes.

"Good," Ann said. "Five's more than enough, even with an egg. Here, I've got a spare bow."

The new girl looked around. "Wow, they pushed their graphics to the limit. But they're still using the Conifer engine—ooh—and it has that vulnerability they didn't do a full distro patch for. I wonder what happens if—"

Jacob blinked. She was suddenly wearing a gallimaufry of gear, harlequin in color and decorated with the taste of a drunken weaverbird. But her character now displayed a respectable power level.

Ann and Chao stared in horror.

"What? Is it the colors? I can change those—give me a cycle—"

"Robert," Ann said, very slowly. "What does she *do*?"

"Oh, I'm a programmer, mostly. I make indie games with two friends from university. Ever heard of *Duka Stories*? That was us."

"Guys—" Rob began.

"She's a Doer," Chao said. "You picked up a Doer."

"This is Consolata. We've been dating for three months."

"It's nice to meet you! What do you all do?" She turned toward Jacob, sparkling with hope.

Jacob growled.

"Fuck this," Ann said, and logged off.

Chao said, "Not cool, man. Not cool at all. Hit me up when she's history—or don't, I don't care."

And he was gone.

"Did I do something wrong?" Consolata said.

"I—" Rob sighed. "I didn't know they'd be like that."

"Really," Jacob said. "You did not know."

"Nah, Jacob—"

"There is a reason why we do not cross the line. Doers are evangelical. Listen to her. Next thing, you'll be an entrepreneur, or a community leader, shaking the hand of every aunty in church. You will shake their hands, and you will say, I feel so sorry for that Jacob boy, he never applied himself to anything. Chao, oh, what a waste of intellect. Poor Ann, I'm sure she could have been amazing at anything, if only she tried—"

"Because of a dame? You think a dame could do that to me? What's eating you?"

"Mercy's home," Jacob said, letting his lion-face curl into a snarl.

"Ee. I see. I'm sorry—"

"No. Not today," Jacob said, and logged off. He tore the gauntlets from his hands. Then he saved the game logs to his phone, to remind himself of what a rat Rob was, and stormed out of the Black Nile. It was ten long and dusty blocks home. Jacob stomped and swore his way up the concrete stairs.

At the top, Mercy was waiting for him.

"Look," she said, matching him step for step as he backpedaled down the stairs, "I don't like it either, Jacob, kweli, all the church ladies up in my face with 'When are you going to get married, I have a nephew just your age.' Once I got away I took a taxi here—"

"Go back to Cambridge and all that stupid grass you can't touch, and all that colonial-in-the-metropolis crap you like so much."

"You do read my emails." She beamed. "I had wondered."

"Get lost."

"You have potential up to here, Jacob. You are crackling with the stuff. The problem is, you don't see it yourself."

"Mathe put you up to this."

"Nobody put me up to this. What I wanted to say was—Jacob, wait. As soon as I have a job, which will be soon, I'm interviewing all over Europe right now—as soon as I'm settled, I want to pay for your university. All you have to do is pick a course."

"I hate to break it to you, sis dear, but these days university is free. So take your money and—"

"I don't mean university in Kenya. Maybe China. Tsinghua University? Shanghai Tech? Maybe the U.S. Wherever you like. Dream big. Some travel would be good for you."

"Mercy," Jacob said, stopping at the bottom of the stairs. Four steps above him, she wobbled on her acrylic heels, clinging to the balustrade. "This is all I want. I'm happy. Leave me alone."

"If you think I'm going to just—"

"Yes. You are."

"Well," Mercy said, "you have my number. When you change your mind—"

"I won't."

"Ee, twenty-two years and you're still as fussy as an infant."

"Kwaheri, Mercy."

He stepped sideways and waved her down the stairs. Mercy descended. Before she passed him, she put a hand on his shoulder.

"I care about you," she said. "Would I be this obnoxious if I didn't?"

"Please, find a nice wazungu or wahindi at Cambridge to torture instead of me. Try the maths department. I hear they're just as odd as you are."

A hawkeyed taxi driver slowed and hovered at the curb.

"Bye, Jacob."

"Piss off, Mercy."

And Jacob went up to his tiny room and flung himself down, wondering why it felt like an elephant had stepped on his chest.

Something important that he'd overlooked tickled the back of his eyelids until he awoke.

Ah. Jacob rolled over in bed and grabbed his penphone. There, in the previous day's logs, was the anomaly: the moment when Consolata went from starter gear to a hodgepodge of expert-level bits. The game logs showed a line of code injected at the exact time she twisted her left hand into a complicated shape like a mudra.

Jacob searched online for the snippet of code and found lengthy discussions of a developer-mode trigger in three unpatched, two-year-old, Conifer-based games. After an hour or two of reading he thought he had the gist of it.

As Jacob, clearly the first customer of the day, came in, the man at Black Nile yawned and waved his hand over the array of key-cards.

"Any of them. Be my guest."

Jacob loaded *Ogrefall* first. Pasting in the code snippet from his phone, he contorted his left hand—here a silver paw—into the shape he remembered and had practiced that morning.

Blip.

His rare and beautiful endgame armor was gone. It had been replaced by an eye-smarting farrago of gear. Only now each item showed a purple variable name floating over its center. He could have kicked himself for his carelessness—the Nebula Paladin set had taken sixty-four hours to complete—but wonder and fascination won out over regret. Holding the same awkward mudra as before, Jacob tapped his lotus-stamped breastplate and toggled the number at the end of the variable.

The lotus transformed into a winged lion rampant, the metal from silver to burnished gold.

When Jacob raised his eyes, he noticed that the ice demons hissing and swooping nearby had variables too. Soon he was sending them jitterbugging this way and that and spiraling helplessly off the edge of a cliff.

Was this what the world looked like from the other side?

The other two games that the tweaker forums mentioned, a historical shooter and a haunted-house platformer, permitted similar manipulations. Jacob stood in the middle of floating words and numbers, changing the world around him with hardly more than a thought. He had become a god in these three small worlds. Ann and Chao would explode from envy. He suppressed a grin.

Then the screens went dark, and the harsh after-hours lights in the cube flashed on. Jacob struggled out of the VR rig, perplexed. He prodded buttons and lasered the empty wall. Nothing happened.

The door clicked, and the manager came in.

"Sorry sir," he said. "Your account has been banned for cheating. Same thing happened over at the Monsoon Club yesterday. We got the automated warnings just now, straight from Japan. One-month ban from all Japanese games. Very sorry about that."

The room spun. Perhaps *Oakley's* graphics had been subpar.

A month? Ann and Chao wouldn't wait a month. They'd find some new Don't, fresh out of secondary school or the military or a ruined thirty-year marriage, to replace him. To replace both him and Rob, now.

"I can see this is not easy news, sir. Not easy for me, either. You are a loyal customer."

"All Japanese games."

"Correct."

"What about other regions?"

"Cross-platform automatic two-week bans in Europe, the Americas, Asia, and Australia."

"But not Africa?"

"Not Africa. We're not advanced enough to be asked to sign those agreements yet."

"I think—" Jacob swallowed. "I think I'd like to try *Duka Stories*, if you have it."

The manager smiled. "Of course. Supporting the local economy, local artists, local products, that is one of my business goals."

Consolata's game turned out to be a simple duka simulator. Jacob had to clear the ground, hammer the corrugated iron sides of the shop together, and stock its shelves with what he blindly guessed might appeal to the neighborhood. The art was hand-painted, probably by one of Consolata's friends, the music easy and old-fashioned. The grandmothers who stopped by for spices pinched his cheeks and told him in quavering voices how glad they were to have him there, only couldn't he make an exception for them on the prices, everything being so expensive these days?

By the end of his first day in business, an hour into the game, Jacob was bankrupt and rapt.

Six hours later his business had been flattened twice, once by a student protest, once by askaris demanding protection money. Each time he built it up again, making brightly lettered promises to his worried customers. In the meantime he sent his painted children to school in uniforms with books and pens and crayons, an accomplishment that turned his heart to sugar. The game lacked the gloss that he was used to, but he had met the person who had created it. All of this, from three women!

An impossible thought arose in him. He refused to look at it directly. No, never. Maybe for money. Enough money. And only for a while.

"Boss," he said, emerging from the cube, "you said your brother runs a game studio?"

"He does," the manager said.

"Would he give me a job, do you think?"

"You should ask him yourself." The manager closed the game of bao he had been playing on his ancient iPhone, a bashed-up brick of third-hand tech, and pulled up a number.

"Yes, I have a young man here, regular customer, plays all the new games, wants to know if you have a job for him." He turned to Jacob. "He says go ahead, send him your portfolio."

"My portfolio?"

"Yes, art, music, design, whatever it is you want to work in. He says he doesn't have a portfolio. Hm? Okay. My brother says you should take courses in those things, whatever interests you, and come back when you can *do* something." He set the iPhone down.

"Thanks," Jacob said, because there was nothing else he could say. He slouched out of the Black Nile, brow furrowed with thought.

Since there was nowhere else to meet, he invited Ann and Chao to visit his spruced-up duka, where they stood around sipping virtual sodas and blocking customers from their programmed paths.

Chao said, suspicion dripping from every syllable of his Southern drawl, "Run that by me again."

"I'm going to take some university courses so I can get a job, and then when I have enough saved up for a VR rig of my own, I'll quit and game full-time, twenty-four-seven."

Ann said, "I think the only person you're fooling is yourself."

"Don't be like that. You have no idea how much a rig costs in Nairobi. It's not like the U.S., where, what, one-third of your monthly stipend buys one? More like two years' stipend for us. I want to game, but I also need to eat."

"If you say so," Ann said.

"Plus they've banned me from all Japanese-owned servers for a month, and other major regions for the next two weeks. This way I can *do* something." Hearing his own words, he stopped.

"So these courses," Chao said. "They're in . . . management? Administration?"

"Yeah. Yeah, that's right."

"Okay. That's almost as good as not doing anything. I wish you'd said something earlier, though. We could have crowdfunded you a console, as a guild."

"My parents would never let me live that down."

"We're going to miss you," Ann said abruptly. "I mean, Robbie, and now you . . ."

"Hey," Jacob said. "I'll still be online. And I'll still game with you, once this ban is done."

Her character hugged his. "Don't let the Doers get you."

"I won't."

"If you see Rob—" Chao said.

"Yes?"

"Never mind."

It was, in fact, on a gleaming skybridge of the Chiromo campus of the University of Nairobi that Jacob next saw Robert, two thick textbooks wedged under his arm. Rob walked quickly, with purpose, in the flood between classes; then, with a start, his eyes met Jacob's, and his face broke into a pleased and embarrassed smile.

"You caught me," Rob said.

"What are you studying?"

"Astronomy. I wanted to discover a planet, as a kid. Somehow I forgot. Then somebody reminded me."

"You and Consolata—"

"Still together."

"Good for you."

They stood there awkwardly, toe to toe, as students streamed past.

"So what brings you here?" Rob said eventually.

"Intro to Programming."

"What? Here? You?"

"And some art classes."

"Art!" Rob laughed, his teeth flashing.

"I'm going to design games. Please don't tell Mercy."

"I'm not a monster." Rob paused. "You'll have to, though. Eventually. And if you're serious, Ann and Chao—"

"That will bite."

"It will. Also, so you know, I would never say—"

"I know."

"We should play together sometime," Rob said, punching his shoulder. "Consolata's releasing her new game next month. It's called *Love and War: The Story of a Doer and a Don't*. There'll be a party. You should come."

"If the beer's good, maybe. Maybe I will."

The two of them knocked knuckles with half-embarrassed, half-conspiratorial smiles. The sun beat down hot and golden on the campus as they passed and went their separate ways, each chasing, in his own heart, down a twisting road, the dim and indeterminate beginnings of a dream.

MADELEINE
AMAL EL-MOHTAR

Amal El-Mohtar's short fiction has won the Hugo, Nebula, and Lo-
cus awards, and her poetry has won the Rhysling award three times.
Her work has appeared in numerous anthologies including *The Starlit
Wood: New Fairy Tales*, *The Djinn Falls in Love & Other Stories*, and
The New Voices of Fantasy; in magazines such as Tor.com, *Lightspeed*,
Strange Horizons, and *Fireside*; and in her own collection of poems
and very short stories, *The Honey Month*. She's also the author, with
Max Gladstone, of an epistolary spy vs. spy novella titled *This Is How
You Lose the Time War*. Amal is the *New York Times Book Review*'s sci-
ence fiction and fantasy columnist, and lives in Ottawa with her spouse
and two cats.

"Madeleine" pairs the emotional discombobulation of mourning
and falling in love with the physical unease of starting experimental
medication and time travel. It was a 2015 Nebula Award finalist.

Madeleine remembers being a different person.
It strikes her when she's driving, threading her way through
farmland, homesteads, facing down the mountains around which
the road winds. She remembers being thrilled at the thought of
travel, of the self she would discover over the hills and far away. She
remembers laughing with friends, looking forward to things, to a
future.

She wonders at how change comes in like a thief in the night,
dismantling our sense of self one bolt and screw at a time until all
that's left of the person we think we are is a broken door hanging
off a rusty hinge, waiting for us to walk through.

———————

"Tell me about your mother," says Clarice, the clinical psychologist assigned to her.

Madeleine is stymied. She stammers. This is only her third meeting with Clarice. She looks at her hands and the tissue she is twisting between them. "I thought we were going to talk about the episodes."

"We will," and Clarice is all gentleness, all calm, "but—"

"I would really rather talk about the episodes."

Clarice relents, nods in her gracious, patient way, and makes a note. "When was your last one?"

"Last night." Madeleine swallows, hard, remembering.

"And what was the trigger?"

"The soup," she says, and she means to laugh, but it comes out wet and strangled like a sob. "I was making chicken soup, and I put a stick of cinnamon in. I'd never done that before but I remembered how it looked, sometimes, when my mother would make it— she would boil the thighs whole with bay leaves, black pepper, and sticks of cinnamon, and the way it looked in the pot stuck with me—so I thought I would try it. It was exactly right—it smelled exactly, exactly the way she used to make it—and then I was there, I was small and looking up at her in our old house, and she was stirring the soup and smiling down at me, and the smell was like a cloud all around, and I could smell her, too, the hand cream she used, and see the edge of the stove and the oven door handle with the cat-print dish towel on it—"

"Did your mother like to cook?"

Madeleine stares.

"Madeleine," says Clarice, with the inevitably Anglo pronunciation that Madeleine has resigned herself to, "if we're going to work together to help you, I need to know more about her."

"The episodes aren't about her," says Madeleine, stiffly. "They're because of the drug."

"Yes, but—"

"They're because of the drug, and I don't need you to tell me I took part in the trial because of her—obviously I did—and I don't want to tell you about her. This isn't about my mourning, and I thought we established these aren't traumatic flashbacks. It's about the drug."

"Madeleine," and Madeleine is fascinated by Clarice's capacity to both disgust and soothe her with sheer unflappability, "Drugs do not operate—or misfire—in a vacuum. You were one of sixty people participating in that trial. Of those sixty, you're the only one who has come forward experiencing these episodes." Clarice leans forward, slightly. "We've also spoken about your tendency to see our relationship as adversarial. Please remember that it isn't. You," and Clarice doesn't smile, exactly, so much as that the lines around her mouth become suffused with sympathy, "haven't even ever volunteered her name to me."

Madeleine begins to feel like a recalcitrant child instead of an adult standing her ground. This only adds to her resentment.

"Her name was Sylvie," she offers, finally. "She loved being in the kitchen. She loved making big fancy meals. But she hated having people over. My dad used to tease her about that."

Clarice nods, smiles her almost-smile encouragingly, makes further notes. "And did you do the technique we discussed to dismiss the memory?"

Madeleine looks away. "Yes."

"What did you choose this time?"

"Althusser." She feels ridiculous. "'In the battle that is philosophy all the techniques of war, including looting and camouflage, are permissible.'"

Clarice frowns as she writes, and Madeleine can't tell if it's because talk of war is adversarial or because she dislikes Althusser.

After she buried her mother, Madeleine looked for ways to bury herself.

She read non-fiction, as dense and theoretical as she could find, on any subject she felt she had a chance of understanding: economics, postmodernism, settler-colonialism. While reading Patrick Wolfe she found the phrase *invasion is a structure, not an event*, and wondered if one could say the same of grief. *Grief is an invasion and a structure and an event*, she wrote, then struck it out, because it seemed meaningless.

Grief, thinks Madeleine now, is an invasion that climbs inside you and makes you grow a wool blanket from your skin, itchy and insulating, heavy and gray. It wraps and wraps and wraps around, putting layers of scratchy heat between you and the world, until no one wants to approach for fear of the prickle, and people stop asking how you are doing in the blanket, which is a relief, because all you want is to be hidden, out of sight. You can't think of a time when you won't be wrapped in the blanket, when you'll be ready to face the people outside it—but one day, perhaps, you push through. And even though you've struggled against the belief that you're a worthless colony of contagion that must be shunned at all costs, it still comes as a shock, when you emerge, that there's no one left waiting for you.

Worse still is the shock that you haven't emerged at all.

"The thing is," says Madeleine, slowly, "I didn't use the sentence right away."

"Oh?"

"I—wanted to see how long it could last, on its own." Heat in her cheeks, knowing how this will sound, wanting both to resist and embrace it. "To ride it out. It kept going just as I remembered it—she brought me a little pink plastic bowl with yellow flowers on it, poured just a tiny bit of soup in, blew on it, gave it to me with a plastic spoon. There were little star-shaped noodles in it. I—" she feels tears in her eyes, hates this, hates crying in front of Clarice, "—I could have eaten it. It smelled so good, and I could feel I was hungry. But I got superstitious. You know." She shrugs. "Like if I ate it, I'd have to stay for good."

"Did you want to stay for good?"

Madeleine says nothing. This is what she hates about Clarice, this demand that her feelings be spelled out into one thing or another: isn't it obvious that she both wanted and didn't want to? From what she said?

"I feel like the episodes are lasting longer," says Madeleine, finally, trying to keep the urgency from consuming her voice. "It used to be just a snap, there and back—I'd blink, I'd be in the memory, I'd realize what happened and it would be like a dream; I'd wake up, I'd come back. I didn't need sentences to pull me back. But now . . ." She looks to Clarice to say something, to fill the silence, but Clarice waits, as usual, for Madeleine herself to make the connection, to articulate the fear.

". . . Now I wonder if this is how it started for her. My mother. What it was like for her." The tissue in her hands is damp, not from tears, but from the sweat of her palms. "If I just sped up the process."

"You don't have Alzheimer's," says Clarice, matter-of-fact. "You aren't forgetting anything. In fact it appears to be the opposite: you're remembering so intensely and completely that your memories have the vividness and immediacy of hallucination." She jots something down. "We'll keep on working on dismantling the triggers as they arise. If the episodes seem to be lasting longer, it could be partly because they're growing fewer and farther between. This is not necessarily a bad thing."

Madeleine nods, chewing her lip, not meeting Clarice's eyes.

So far as Madeleine is concerned, her mother began dying five years earlier, when the fullness of her life began to fall away from her like chunks of wet cake: names; events; her child. Madeleine watched her mother weep, and this was the worst, because with every storm of grief over her confusion, Madeleine couldn't help but imagine the memories sloughing from her, as if the memories themselves were the source of her pain, and if she could just forget them and live a barer life, a life before the disease, before her husband's death, before Madeleine, she could be happy again. If she could only shed the burden of the expectation of memory, she could be happy again.

Madeleine reads Walter Benjamin on time as image, time as accumulation, and thinks of layers and pearls. She thinks of her mother as a pearl dissolving in wine until only a grain of sand is left drowning at the bottom of the glass.

As her mother's life fell away from her, so did Madeleine's. She took a leave of absence from her job, and kept extending it; she stopped seeing her friends; her friends stopped seeing her. Madeleine is certain her friends expected her to be relieved when her mother died, and were surprised by the depth of her mourning. She didn't know how to address that. She didn't know how to say to those friends, *you are relieved to no longer feel embarrassed around the subject, and expect me to sympathize with your relief, and to be normal again for your sake.* So she said nothing.

It wasn't that Madeleine's friends were bad people; they had their own lives, their own concerns, their own comfort to nourish and nurture and keep safe, and dealing with a woman who was dealing with her mother who was dealing with early-onset Alzheimer's was just a little too much, especially when her father had only died of bowel cancer a year earlier, especially when she had no other family. It was indecent, so much pain at once, it was unreasonable, and her friends were reasonable people. They had children, families, jobs, and Madeleine had none of these; she understood. She did not make demands.

She joined the clinical trial the way some people join fund-raising walks, and thinks now that that was her first mistake. People walk, run, bicycle to raise money for cures—that's the way she ought to have done it, surely, not actually volunteered herself to be experimented on. No one sponsors people to stand still.

The episodes happen like this.

A song on the radio like an itch in her skull, a pebble rattling around inside until it finds the groove in which it fits, perfectly, and suddenly she's—

—in California, dislocated, confused, a passenger herself now in her own head's seat, watching the traffic crawl past in the opposite direction, the sun blazing above. On I-5, en route to Anaheim: she is listening, for the first time, to the album that song is from, and feels the beautiful self-sufficiency of having wanted a thing and purchased it, the bewildering freedom of going somewhere utterly new. And she remembers this moment of mellow thrill shrinking into abject terror at the sight of five lanes between her and the exit, and will she make it, won't she, she doesn't want to get lost on such enormous highways—

—and then she's back, in a wholly different car, her body nine years older, the mountain, the farmland all where they should be, slamming hard on the brakes at an unexpected stop sign, breathing hard and counting all the ways in which she could have been killed.

Or she is walking and the world is perched on the lip of spring, the Ottawa snow melting to release the sidewalks in fits and starts, peninsulas of gritty concrete wet and crunching beneath her boots, and that solidity of snowless ground intersects with the smell of water and the warmth of the sun and the sound of dripping and the world tilts—

—and she's ten years old on the playground of her second primary school, kicking aside the pebbly grit to make a space for shooting marbles, getting down on her knees to use her hands to do a better job of smoothing the surface, then wiping her hands on the corduroy of her trousers, then reaching into her bag of marbles for the speckled dinosaur-egg that is her lucky one, her favorite—

—and then she's back, and someone's asking her if she's okay, because she looked like she might be about to walk into traffic, was she drunk, was she high?

She has read about flashbacks, about PTSD, about reliving events, and has wondered if this is the same. It is not as she imagined those things would be. She has tried explaining this to Clarice, who very reasonably pointed out that she couldn't both claim to have never experienced trauma-induced flashbacks and say with perfect certainty that what she's experiencing now is categorically different. Clarice is certain, Madeleine realizes, that trauma is at the root of these episodes, that there's something Madeleine isn't telling her, that her mother, perhaps, abused her, that she had a terrible childhood.

None of these things are true.

Now: she is home, and leaning her head against her living room window at twilight, and something in the thrill of that blue and the cold of the glass against her scalp sends her tumbling—

—into her body at fourteen, looking into the blue deepening above the tree line near her home as if it were another country, longing for it, aware of the picture she makes as a young girl leaning her wondering head against a window while hungry for the future, for the distance, for the person she will grow to be—and starts to reach within her self, her future/present self, for a phrase that only her future/present self knows, to untangle herself from her past head. She has just about settled on Kristeva—*abjection is above all ambiguity*—when she feels, strangely, a tug on her field of vision, something at its periphery demanding attention. She looks away from the sky, looks down, at the street she grew up on, the street she knows like the inside of her mouth.

She sees a girl of about her own age, brown-skinned and dark-haired, grinning at her and waving.

She has never seen her before in her life.

Clarice, for once, looks excited—which is to say, slightly more intent than usual—which makes Madeleine uncomfortable. "Describe her as accurately as you can," says Clarice.

"She looked about fourteen, had dark skin—"

Clarice blinks. Madeleine continues.

"—and dark, thick hair, that was pulled up in two ponytails, and she was wearing a red dress and sandals."

"And you're certain you'd never seen her before?" Clarice adjusts her glasses.

"Positive." Madeleine hesitates, doubting herself. "I mean, she looked sort of familiar, but not in a way I could place? But I grew up in a really white small town in Quebec. There were maybe five non-white kids in my whole school, and she wasn't any of them. Also—" she hesitates, again, because, still, this feels so private, "—there has never once been any part of an episode that was unfamiliar."

"She could be a repressed memory, then," Clarice muses, "someone you've forgotten—or an avatar you're making up. Perhaps you should try speaking to her."

Clarice's suggested technique for managing the episodes was to corrupt the memory experience with something incompatible, something as of-the-moment as Madeleine could devise. Madeleine had settled on phrases from her recent reading: they were new enough to not be associated with any other memories, and incongruous enough to remind her of the reality of her bereavement even in her mother's presence. It seemed to work; she had never yet experienced the same memory twice after deploying her critics and philosophers.

To actively go in search of a memory was very strange.

She tries, again, with the window: waits until twilight, leans her head against the same place, but the temperature is wrong somehow, it doesn't come together. She tries making chicken soup; nothing. Finally, feeling her way towards it, she heats up a mug of milk in the microwave, stirs it to even out the heat, takes a sip—

—while holding the mug with both hands, sitting at the kitchen table, her legs dangling far above the ground. Her parents are in the kitchen, chatting—she knows she'll have to go to bed soon, as soon as she finishes her milk—but she can see the darkness just outside the living room windows, and she wants to know what's out there. Carefully, trying not to draw her parents' attention, she slips down from the chair and pads softly—her feet are bare, she is in her pajamas already—towards the window.

The girl isn't there.

"Madeleine," comes her mother's voice, cheerful, "as-tu fini ton lait?"

Before she can quite grasp what she is doing, Madeleine turns, smiles, nods vigorously up to her mother, and finishes the warm milk in a gulp. Then she lets herself be led downstairs to bed, tucked in, and kissed goodnight by both her parents, and if a still small part of herself struggles to remember something important to say or do, she is too comfortably nestled to pay it any attention as the lights go out and the door to her room shuts. She wonders what happens if you fall asleep in a dream—would you dream and then be able to fall asleep in that dream, and dream again, and—someone knocks, gently, at her bedroom window.

Madeleine's bedroom is in the basement; the window is level with the ground. The girl from the street is there, looking concerned. Madeleine blinks, sits up, rises, opens the window.

"What's your name?" asks the girl at the window.

"Madeleine." She tilts her head, surprised to find herself answering in English. "What's yours?"

"Zeinab." She grins. Madeleine notices she's wearing pajamas, too, turquoise ones with Princess Jasmine on them. "Can I come in? We could have a sleepover!"

"Shh," says Madeleine, pushing her window all the way open to let her in, whispering, "I can't have sleepovers without my parents knowing!"

Zeinab covers her mouth, eyes wide, and nods, then mouths *sorry* before clambering inside. Madeleine motions for her to come sit on the bed, then looks at her curiously.

"How do I know you?" she murmurs, half to herself. "We don't go to school together, do we?"

Zeinab shakes her head. "I don't know. I don't know this place at all. But I keep seeing you! Sometimes you're older and sometimes you're younger. Sometimes you're with your parents and sometimes you're not. I just thought I should say hello, because I keep seeing you, but you don't always see me, and it feels a little like spying, and I don't want to do that. I mean," she grins again, a wide dimpled thing that makes Madeline feel warm and happy, "I wouldn't mind *being* a spy but that's different, that's cool, that's like James Bond or Neil Burnside or Agent Carter—"

—and Madeleine snaps back, fingers gone numb around a mug of cold milk that falls to the ground and shatters as she jumps away, presses her back to a wall, and tries to stop shaking.

She cancels her appointment with Clarice that week. She looks through old yearbooks, class photos, and there is no one who looks like Zeinab, no Zeinabs to be found anywhere in her past. She googles "Zeinab" in various spellings and discovers it's the name of a journalist, a Syrian mosque, and the Prophet Muhammad's granddaughter. Perhaps she'll ask Zeinab for her surname, she thinks, a little wildly, dazed and frightened and exhilarated.

Over the course of the last several years Madeleine has grown very, very familiar with the inside of her head. The discovery of someone as new and inexplicable as Zeinab in it is thrilling in a way she can hardly begin to explain.

She finds she especially does not want to explain to Clarice.

Madeleine takes the bus—she has become wary of driving—to the town she grew up in, an hour's journey over a provincial border. She walks through her old neighborhood hunting triggers, but finds more changed than familiar; old houses with new additions, facades, front lawns gone to seed or kept far too tidy.

She walks up the steep cul-de-sac of her old street to the rocky hill beyond, where a freight line used to run. It's there, picking up a lump of pink granite from where the tracks used to be, that she flashes—

—back to the first time she saw a hummingbird, standing in her driveway by an ornamental pink granite boulder. She feels, again, her heart in her throat, flooded with the beauty of it, the certainty and immensity of the fact that she is seeing a fairy, that fairies are real, that here is a tiny mermaid moving her shining tail backwards and forwards in the air, before realizing the truth of what she's looking at, and feeling that it is somehow more precious still for being a bird that sounds like a bee and looks like an impossible jewel.

"Ohh," she hears, from behind her, and there is Zeinab, transfixed, looking at the hummingbird alongside Madeleine, and as it hovers before them for the eternity that Madeleine remembers, suspended in the air with a keen jet eye and a needle for a mouth, Madeleine reaches out and takes Zeinab's hand. She feels Zeinab squeeze hers in reply, and they stand together until the hummingbird zooms away.

"I don't understand what's happening," murmurs Zeinab, who is a young teen again, in torn jeans and an oversized sweater with Paula Abdul's face on it, "but I really like it."

Madeleine leads Zeinab through her memories as best she can, one sip, smell, sound, taste at a time. Stepping out of the shower one morning tips her back into a school trip to the Montreal Botanical Garden, where she slips away from the group to walk around the grounds with Zeinab and talk. Doing this is, in some ways, like maintaining the image in a Magic Eye puzzle, remaining focused on each other with the awareness that they can't mention the world outside the memory or it will end too soon, before they've had their fill of talk, of marveling at the strangeness of their meeting, of enjoying each other's company.

Their conversations are careful and buoyant, as if they're sculpting something together, chipping away at a mystery shape trapped in marble. It's easy, so easy to talk to Zeinab, to listen to her—they talk about the books they read as children, the music they listened to, the cartoons they watched. Madeleine wonders why Zeinab's mere existence doesn't corrupt or end the memories the way her sentences do, why she's able to walk around inside those memories more freely in Zeinab's company, but doesn't dare ask. She suspects she knows why, after all; she doesn't need Clarice to tell her how lonely, how isolated, how miserable she is, miserable enough to invent a friend who is bubbly where she is quiet, kind and friendly where she is mistrustful and reserved, even dark-skinned where she's white.

She can hear Clarice explaining, in her reasonable voice, that Madeleine—bereaved twice over, made vulnerable by an experimental drug—has invented a shadow-self to love, and perhaps they should unpack the racism of its manifestation, and didn't Madeleine have any black friends in real life?

"I wish we could see each other all the time," says Madeleine, sixteen, on her back in the sunny field, long hair spread like so many corn snakes through the grass. "Whenever we wanted."

"Yeah," murmurs Zeinab, looking up at the sky. "Too bad I made you up inside my head."

Madeleine steels herself against the careening tug of Sylvia Plath before remembering that she started reading her in high school. Instead, she turns to Zeinab, blinks.

"What? No. You're inside my head."

Zeinab raises an eyebrow—pierced, now—and when she smiles her teeth look all the brighter against her black lipstick. "I guess that's one possibility, but if I made you up inside *my* head and did a really good job of it, I'd probably want you to say something like that. To make you be more real."

"But—so could—"

"Although I guess it is weird that we're always doing stuff you remember. Maybe you should come over to my place sometime!"

Madeleine feels her stomach seizing up.

"Or maybe it's time travel," says Zeinab, thoughtfully. "Maybe it's one of those weird things where I'm actually from your future and am meeting you in your past, and then when you meet me in your future, I haven't met you yet, but you know all about me—"

"Zeinab—I don't think—"

Madeline feels wakefulness press a knife's edge against the memory's skin, and she backs away from that, shakes her head, clings to the smell of crushed grass and coming summer, with its long days of reading and swimming and cycling and her father talking to her about math and her mother teaching her to knit and the imminent prospect of seeing R-rated films in the cinema—

—but she can't, quite, and she is shivering, naked, in her bathroom, with the last of the shower's steam vanishing off the mirror as she starts to cry.

"I must say," says Clarice, rather quietly, "that this is distressing news."

It's been a month since Madeleine last saw Clarice, and where before she felt resistant to her probing, wanting only to solve a very specific problem, she now feels like a mess, a bowl's worth of over-cooked spaghetti. If before Clarice made her feel like a stubborn child, now Madeleine feels like a child who knows she's about to be punished.

"I had hoped," says Clarice, adjusting her glasses, "that encouraging you to talk to this avatar would help you understand the mechanisms of your grief, but from what you've told me, it sounds more like you've been indulging in a damaging fantasy world."

"It's not a fantasy world," says Madeleine, with less snap than she'd like—she sounds, to her own ears, sullen, defensive. "It's my *memory.*"

"The experience of which puts you at risk and makes you lose time. And Zeinab isn't part of your memories."

"No, but—" she bites her lip.

"But what?"

"But—couldn't Zeinab be real? I mean," hastily, before Clarice's look sharpens too hard, "couldn't she be a repressed memory, like you said?"

"A repressed memory with whom you talk about recent television, and who suddenly features in all your memories?" Clarice shakes her head.

"But—talking to her helps, it makes it so much easier to control—"

"Madeleine, tell me if I'm missing anything here. You're seeking triggers in order to relive your memories for their own sake—not as exposure therapy, not to dismantle those triggers, not to understand Zeinab's origins, but to have a . . . companion? Dalliance?"

Clarice is so kind and sympathetic that Madeleine wants simultaneously to cry and to punch her in the face.

She wants to say, *what you're missing is that I've been happy. What you're missing is that for the first time in years I don't feel like a disease waiting to happen or a problem to be solved until I'm back in the now, until she and I are apart.*

But there is sand in her throat and it hurts too much to speak.

"I think," says Clarice, with a gentleness that beggars Madeleine's belief, "that it's time we discussed admitting you into more comprehensive care."

She sees Zeinab again when, on the cusp of sleep in a hospital bed, she experiences the sensation of falling from a great height, and plunges into—

—the week after her mother's death, when Madeleine couldn't sleep without waking in a panic, convinced her mother had walked out of the house and into the street, or fallen down the stairs, or taken the wrong pills at the wrong time, only to recall she'd already died and there was nothing left for her to remember.

She is in bed, and Zeinab is there next to her, and Zeinab is a woman in her thirties, staring at her strangely, as if she is only now seeing her for the first time, and Madeleine starts to cry and Zeinab holds her tightly while Madeleine buries her face in Zeinab's shoulder, and says she loves her and doesn't want to lose her but she has to go, they won't let her stay, she's insane and she can't keep living in the past but there is no one left here for her, no one.

"I love you too," says Zeinab, and there is something fierce in it, and wondering, and desperate. "I love you too. I'm here. I promise you, I'm here."

Madeleine is not sure she's awake when she hears people arguing outside her door.

She hears "serious bodily harm" and "what evidence" and "rights adviser," then "very irregular" and "I assure you," traded back and forth in low voices. She drifts in and out of wakefulness, wonders muzzily if she consented to being drugged or if she only dreamt that she did, turns over, falls back asleep.

When she wakes again, Zeinab is sitting at the foot of her bed.

Madeleine stares at her.

"I figured out how we know each other," says Zeinab, whose hair is waist-length now, straightened, who is wearing a white silk blouse and a sharp black jacket, high heels, and looks like she belongs in an action film. "How I know you, I guess. I mean," she smiles, looks down, shy—Zeinab has never been shy, but there is the dimple where Madeleine expects it—"where I know you from. The clinical trial, for the Alzheimer's drug—we were in the same group. I didn't recognize you until I saw you as an adult. I remembered because of all the people there, I thought—you looked—" her voice drops a bit, as if remembering, suddenly, that she isn't talking to herself, "lost. I wanted to talk to you, but it felt weird, like, hi, I guess we have family histories in common, want to get coffee?"

She runs her hand through her hair, exhales, not quite able to look at Madeleine while Madeleine stares at her as if she's a fairy turning into a hummingbird that could, any second, fly away.

"So not long after the trial I start having these hallucinations, and there's always this girl in them, and it freaks me out. But I keep it to myself, because—I don't know, because I want to see what happens. Because it's not more debilitating than a daydream, really, and I start to get the hang of it—feeling it come on, walking myself to a seat, letting it happen. Sometimes I can stop it, too, though that's harder. I take time off work, I read about, I don't know, mystic visions, shit like that, the kind of things I used to wish were real in high school. I figure even if you're not real—"

Zeinab looks at her now, and there are tears streaking Madeleine's cheeks, and Zeinab's smile is small and sad and hopeful, too, "—even if you're not real, well, I'll take an imaginary friend who's pretty great over work friends who are mostly acquaintances, you know? Because you were always real to me."

Zeinab reaches out to take Madeleine's hand. Madeleine squeezes it, swallows, shakes her head.

"I—even if I'm not—if this isn't a dream," Madeleine half-chuckles through tears, wipes at her cheek, "I think I probably have to stay here for a while."

Zeinab grins, now, a twist of mischief in it. "Not at all. You're being discharged today. Your rights adviser was very persuasive."

Madeleine blinks. Zeinab leans in closer, conspiratorial.

"That's me. I'm your rights adviser. Just don't tell anyone I'm doing pro bono stuff: I'll never hear the end of it at the office."

Madeleine feels something in her unclench and melt, and she

hugs Zeinab to her and holds her and is held by her.

"Whatever's happening to us," Zeinab says, quietly, "we'll figure it out together, okay?"

"Okay," says Madeleine, and as she does Zeinab pulls back to kiss her forehead, and the scent of her is clear and clean, like grapefruit and salt, and as Zeinab's lips brush her skin she—

—is in precisely the same place, but someone's with her in her head, remembering Zeinab's kiss and her smell and for the first time in a very long time, Madeleine feels—knows, with irrevocable certainty—that she has a future.

OUR LADY OF THE OPEN ROAD

SARAH PINSKER

Sarah Pinsker's fiction has been published in magazines including *Asimov's, Strange Horizons, Fantasy & Science Fiction, Lightspeed, Daily Science Fiction, Fireside*, and *Uncanny* and in anthologies including *Long Hidden, Fierce Family, Accessing the Future*, and numerous *Year's Bests*. Her stories have been translated into Chinese, Spanish, French, and Italian, among other languages. In 2019, Sarah also published her first collection, *Sooner or Later Everything Falls into the Sea: Stories*, and her first novel, *A Song for a New Day*.

"Our Lady of the Open Road" is a love song to live shows and life as a traveling musician. It won the Nebula Award in 2016.

The needle on the veggie oil tank read flat empty by the time we came to China Grove. A giant pink and purple fiberglass dragon loomed over the entrance, refugee from some shuttered local amusement park, no doubt; it looked more medieval than Chinese. The parking lot held a mix of Chauffeurs and manual farm trucks, but I didn't spot any other greasers, so I pulled in.

"Cutting it close, Luce?" Silva put down his book and leaned over to peer at the gauge.

"There hasn't been anything but farms for the last fifty miles. Serves me right for trying a road we haven't been down before."

"Where are we?" asked Jacky from the bed in the back of the van. I glanced in the rearview. He caught my eye and gave an enthusiastic wave. His microbraids spilled forward from whatever he'd been using to tether them, and he gathered them back into a thick ponytail.

Silva answered before I could. "Nowhere, Indiana. Go back to sleep."

"Will do." Without music or engine to drown him out, Jacky's snores filled the van again a second later. He'd been touring with us for a year now, so we'd gotten used to the snores. To be honest, I envied him his ability to fall asleep that fast.

I glanced at Silva. "You want to do the asking for once?"

He grinned and held up both forearms, tattooed every inch. "You know it's not me."

"There's such a thing as sleeves, you know." I pulled my windbreaker off the back of my seat and flapped it at him, even though I knew he was right. In the Midwest, approaching a new restaurant for the first time, it was never him, between the tattoos and the spiky blue hair. Never Jacky for the pox scars on his cheeks, even though they were clearly long healed. That left me.

My bad knee buckled as I swung from the driver's seat. I bent to clutch it and my lower back spasmed just to the right of my spine, that momentary pain that told me to rethink all my life's choices.

"What are you doing?" Silva asked through the open door.

"Tying my shoe." There was no need to lie, but I did it anyway. Pride or vanity or something akin. He was only two years younger than me, and neither of us jumped off our amps much anymore. If I ached from the drive, he probably ached, too.

The backs of my thighs were all pins and needles, and my shirt was damp with sweat. I took a moment to lean against Daisy the Diesel and stretch in the hot air. I smelled myself: not great after four days with no shower, but not unbearable.

The doors opened into a foyer, red and gold and black. I didn't even notice the blond hostess in her red qipao until she stepped away from the wallpaper.

"Dining alone?" she asked. Beyond her, a roomful of faces turned in my direction. This wasn't really the kind of place that attracted tourists, especially not these days, this far off the interstate.

"No, um, actually, I was wondering if I could speak to the chef or the owner? It'll only take a minute." I was pretty sure I had timed our stop for after their dinner rush. Most of the diners looked to be eating or pushing their plates aside.

The owner and chef were the same person. I'd been expecting another blond Midwesterner, but he was legit Chinese. He had never heard of a van that ran on grease. I did the not-quite-pleading thing. On stage I aimed for fierce, but in jeans and runners and a ponytail, I could fake a down-on-her-luck Midwest momma. The trick was not to push it.

He looked a little confused by my request, but at least he was willing to consider it. "Come to the kitchen door after we close and show me. Ten, ten thirty."

It was nine; not too bad. I walked back to the van. Silva was still in the passenger seat, but reading a trifold menu. He must have ducked in behind me to grab it. "They serve a bread basket with lo mein. And spaghetti and meatballs. Where are we?"

"Nowhere, Indiana." I echoed back at him.

We sat in the dark van and watched the customers trickle out. I could mostly guess from their looks which ones would be getting into the trucks and which into the Chauffeurs. Every once in a while, a big guy in work boots and a trucker cap surprised me by squeezing himself into some little self-driving thing. The game passed the time, in any case.

A middle-aged cowboy wandered over to stare at our van. I pegged him for a legit rancher from a distance, but as he came closer I noticed a clerical collar beneath the embroidered shirt. His boots shone and he had a paunch falling over an old rodeo belt; the incongruous image of a bull-riding minister made me laugh. He startled when he realized I was watching him.

He made a motion for me to lower my window.

"Maryland plates!" he said. "I used to live in Hagerstown."

I smiled, though I'd only ever passed through Hagerstown.

"Used to drive a church van that looked kinda like yours, too, just out of high school. Less duct tape, though. Whatcha doing out here?"

"Touring. Band."

"No kidding! You look familiar. Have I heard of you?"

"Cassis Fire," I said, taking the question as a prompt for a name. "We had it painted on the side for a while, but then we figured out we got pulled over less when we were incognito."

"Don't think I know the name. I used to have a band, back before . . ." His voice trailed off, and neither of us needed him to finish his sentence. There were several "back befores" he could be referring to, but they all amounted to the same thing. Back before StageHolo and SportsHolo made it easier to stay home. Back before most people got scared out of congregating anywhere they didn't know everybody.

"You're not playing around here, are you?"

I shook my head. "Columbus, Ohio. Tomorrow night."

"I figured. Couldn't think of a place you'd play nearby."

"Not our kind of music, anyway," I agreed. I didn't know what music he liked, but this was a safe bet.

"Not any kind. Oh well. Nice chatting with you. I'll look you up on StageHolo."

He turned away.

"We're not on StageHolo," I called to his back, though maybe not loud enough for him to hear. He waved as his Chauffeur drove him off the lot.

"Luce, you're a terrible salesperson," Silva said to me.

"What?" I hadn't realized he'd been paying attention.

"You know he recognized you. All you had to do was say your name instead of the band's. Or 'Blood and Diamonds.' He'd have paid for dinner for all of us, then bought every T-shirt and download code we have."

"And then he'd listen to them and realize the music we make now is nothing like the music we made then. And even if he liked it, he'd never go to a show. At best he'd send a message saying how much he wished we were on StageHolo."

"Which we could be . . ."

"Which we won't be." Silva knew better than to argue with me on that one. It was our only real source of disagreement.

The neon "open" sign in the restaurant's window blinked out, and I took the cue to put the key back in the ignition. The glowplug light came on, and I started the van back up.

My movement roused Jacky again. "Where are we now?"

I didn't bother answering.

As I had guessed, the owner hadn't quite understood what I was asking for. I gave him the engine tour, showing him the custom oil filter and the dual tanks. "We still need regular diesel to start, then switch to the veggie oil tank. Not too much more to it than that."

"It's legal?"

Legal enough. There was a gray area wherein perhaps technically we were skirting the fuel tax. By our reasoning, though, we were also skirting the reasons for the fuel tax. We'd be the ones who got in trouble, anyway. Not him.

"Of course," I said, then changed the subject. "And the best part is that it makes the van smell like egg rolls."

He smiled. We got a whole tankful out of him, and a bag full of food he'd have otherwise chucked out, as well.

The guys were over the moon about the food. Dumpster diving

behind a restaurant or Superwally would have been our next order of business, so anything that hadn't made a stop in a garbage can on its way to us was haute cuisine as far as we were concerned. Silva took the lo mein—no complimentary bread—screwed together his travel chopsticks, and handed mine to me from the glove compartment. I grabbed some kind of moo shu without the pancakes, and Jacky woke again to snag the third container.

"Can we go someplace?" Silva asked, waving chopsticks at the window.

"Got anything in mind on a Tuesday night in the boonies?"

Jacky was up for something, too. "Laser tag? Laser bowling?"

Sometimes the age gap was a chasm. I turned in my seat to side-eye the kid. "One vote for lasers."

"I dunno," said Silva. "Just a bar? If I have to spend another hour in this van I'm going to scream."

I took a few bites while I considered. We wouldn't be too welcome anywhere around here, between our odor and our look, not to mention the simple fact that we were strangers. On the other hand, the more outlets I gave these guys for legit fun, the less likely they were to come up with something that would get us in trouble. "If we see a bar or a bowling joint before someplace to sleep, sure."

"I can look it up," said Jacky.

"Nope," I said. "Leave it to fate."

After two-thirds of the moo shu, I gave up and closed the container. I hated wasting food, but it was too big for me to finish. I wiped my chopsticks on my jeans and put them back in their case.

Two miles down the road from the restaurant, we came to Starker's, which I hoped from the apostrophe was only a bar, not a strip club. Their expansive parking lot was empty except for eight Chauffeurs, all lined up like pigs at a trough. At least that meant we didn't have to worry about some drunk crashing into our van on his way out.

I backed into the closest spot to the door. It was the best lit, so I could worry less about our gear getting lifted. Close was also good if the locals decided they didn't like our looks.

We got the long stare as we walked in, the one from old Westerns, where all the heads swivel our way and the piano player stops playing. Except, of course, these days the piano player didn't stop, because the piano player had no idea we'd arrived. The part of the pianist in this scenario was played by Roy Bittan, alongside the whole E Street Band, loud as a stadium and projected in StageHolo 3D.

"Do you want to leave?" Jacky whispered to me.

"No, it's okay. We're here now. Might as well have a drink."

"At least it's Bruce. I can get behind Bruce." Silva edged past me toward the bar.

A few at leasts: at least it was Bruce, not some cut-rate imitation. Bruce breathed punk as far as I was concerned, insisting on recording new music and legit live shows all the way into his eighties. At least it was StageHolo and not StageHoloLive, in which case there'd be a cover charge. I was willing to stand in the same room as the technology that was trying to make me obsolete, but I'd be damned if I paid them for the privilege. Of course, it wouldn't be Bruce on StageHoloLive, either; he'd been gone a couple of years now, and this Bruce looked to be only in his sixties, anyway. A little flat, too, which suggested this was a retrofitted older show, not one recorded using StageHolo's tech.

Silva pressed a cold can into my hand, and I took a sip, not even bothering to look at what I was drinking. Knowing him, knowing us, he'd snagged whatever had been cheapest. Pisswater, but cold pisswater. Perfect for washing down the greasy takeout food aftertaste.

I slipped into a booth, hoping the guys had followed me. Jacky did, carrying an identical can to mine in one hand, and something the color of windshield wiper fluid in a plastic shot glass in the other.

"You want one?" he asked me, nudging the windshield wiper fluid. "Bartender said it was the house special."

I pushed it back in his direction. "I don't drink anything blue. It never ends well."

"Suit yourself." He tossed it back, then grinned.

"Your teeth are blue now. You look like you ate a Smurf."

"What's a Smurf?"

Sometimes I forgot how young he was. Half my age. A lifetime in this business. "Little blue characters? A village with one chick, one old man, and a bunch of young guys?"

"Like our band?" He shook his head. "Sorry. Bad joke. Anyway, I have no idea what was in that food, but it might have been Smurf, if they're blue and taste like pork butt. How's your dinner sitting?"

I swatted him lightly, backhand. "Fine, as long as I don't drink anything blue."

He downed his beer in one long chug, then got up to get another. He looked at mine and raised his eyebrows.

"No thanks," I said. "I'll stick with one. I get the feeling this is a zero-tolerance town."

If twenty-odd years of this had taught me one thing, it was to stay clear of local police. Every car in the parking lot was self-driving, which suggested there was somebody out on the roads ready to come down hard on us. Having spent a lot of time in my youth leaving clubs at closing time and dodging drunk drivers, I approved this effort. One of the few aspects of our brave new world I could fully endorse.

I looked around. Silva sat on a stool at the bar. Jacky stood behind him, a hand on Silva's shoulder, tapping his foot to the Bo Diddley beat of "She's the One." The rest of the barstools were filled with people who looked too comfortable to be anything but regulars. A couple of them had the cocked-head posture of cheap neural overlays. The others played games on the slick touchscreen bar, or tapped on the Bracertabs strapped to their arms, the latest tech fad. Nobody talking to anybody.

Down at the other end, two blond women stood facing the Bruce holo, singing along and swaying. He pointed in their general direction, and one giggled and clutched her friend's arm as if he had singled her out personally. Two guys sat on stools near the stage, one playing air drums, the other watching the women. The women only had eyes for Bruce.

I got where they were coming from. I knew people who didn't like his voice or his songs, but I didn't know anybody, especially any musician, who couldn't appreciate his stage presence. Even here, even now, knowing decades separated me from the night this had been recorded, and decades separated the young man who had first written the song from the older man who sang it, even from across a scuzzy too-bright barroom, drinking pisswater beer with strangers and my own smelly band, I believed him when he sang that she was the one. I hated the StageHolo company even more for the fact I was enjoying it.

Somebody slid into the booth next to me. I turned, expecting one of my bandmates, but a stranger had sat down, closer than I cared for.

"Passing through?" he asked, looking at me with intense, bloodshot eyes. He brushed a thick sweep of hair from his forehead, a style I could only assume he had stuck with through the decades since it had been popular. He had dimples and a smile that had clearly been his greatest asset in his youth. He probably hadn't quite realized drinking had caught up with him, that he was puffy and red-nosed. Or that he slurred a bit, even on those two words.

"Passing through." I gave him a brief "not interested" smile and turned my whole body back toward the stage.

"Kind of unusual for somebody to pass through here, let alone bother to stop. What attracted you?" His use of the word "attracted" was pointed.

If he put an arm around me, I'd have to slug him. I shifted a few inches, trying to put distance between us, and emphasized my next word. "We wanted a drink. We've been driving a while."

His disappointment was evident. "Boyfriend? Husband?"

I nodded at the bar, letting him pick whichever he thought looked more like he might be with me, and whichever label he wanted to apply. It amused me either way, since I couldn't imagine being with either of them. Not at the beginning, and especially not after having spent all this time in the van with them.

Then I wondered why I was playing games at all. I turned to look at him. "We're a band."

"No kidding! I used to have a band."A reassessment of the situation flashed across his face. A new smile, more collegial. The change in his whole demeanor prompted me to give him a little more attention.

"No kidding?"

"Yeah. Mostly we played here. Before the insurance rates rose and StageHolo convinced Maggie she'd save money with holos of famous bands."

"Did she? Save money?"

He sighed. "Probably. Holos don't drink, and holos don't dent the mics or spill beers into the PA. And people will stay and imbibe for hours if the right bands are playing."

"Do you still play for fun? Your band?"

He shrugged. "We did for a while. We even got a spot at the very last State Fair. And after that, every once in a while we'd play a barbecue in somebody's backyard. But it's hard to keep it up when you've got nothing to aim for. Playing here once a week was a decent enough goal, but who would want to hear me sing covers when you can have the real thing?"

He pointed his beer at one of the women by the stage. "That's my ex-wife, by the way."

"I'm sorry?"

"It's okay." He took a swig of beer. "That's when Polly left me. Said it wasn't 'cause the band was done, but I think it was related. She said I didn't seem interested in anything at all after that."

He had turned his attention down to his drink, but now he looked at me again. "How about you? I guess there are still places out there to play?"

"A few," I said. "Mostly in the cities. There's a lot of turnover, too. So we can have a great relationship with a place and then we'll call back and they'll be gone without a trace."

"And there's enough money in it to live on?"

There are people who ask that question in an obnoxious, disbelieving way, and I tend to tell them, "We're here, aren't we?" but this guy was nostalgic enough that I answered him honestly. Maybe I could help him see there was no glamour left for people like us.

"I used to get some royalty checks from an old song, which covered insurance and repairs for the van, but they've gotten smaller and smaller since *BMI v. StageHolo*. We make enough to stay on the road, eat really terribly, have a beer now and again. Not enough to save. Not enough to stop, ever. Not that we want to stop, so it's okay."

"You never come off the road? Do you live somewhere?"

"The van's registered at my parents' place in Maryland, and I crash there when I need a break. But that isn't often."

"And your band?"

"My bassist and I have been playing together for a long time, and he's got places he stays. We replace a drummer occasionally. This one's been with us for a year, and the two of them are into each other, so if they don't fall out it might last a while."

He nodded. The wolfishness was gone, replaced by something more wistful. He held out his beer. "To music."

"To live music." My can clinked his.

Somebody shouted over by the bar, and we both twisted round to see what had happened. The air-drum player had wandered over—Max Weinberg was on break, too—and he and Jacky were squaring off over something. Jacky's blue lips glowed from twenty feet away.

"Nothing good ever comes of blue drinks," I said to my new friend.

He nodded. "You're gonna want to get your friend out of here. That's the owner behind the bar. If your guy breaks anything, she'll have the cops here in two seconds flat."

"Crap. Thanks."

Blue liquid pooled around and on Jacky, a tray of overturned plastic shot glasses behind him. At least they weren't glass, and at least he hadn't damaged the fancy bar top. I dug a twenty from the thin wad in my pocket, hoping it was enough.

"You're fake-drumming to a fake band," Jacky was saying. "And you're not even good at it. If you went to your crash cymbal that much with the real Bruce, he'd fire you in two seconds."

"Who the hell cares? Did I ask you to critique my drumming?"

"No, but if you did, I'd tell you you're behind on the kick, too. My two-year-old niece keeps a better beat than you do."

The other guy's face reddened, and I saw him clench a fist. Silva had an arm across Jacky's chest by then, propelling him toward the door. We made eye contact, and he nodded.

I tossed my twenty on a dry spot on the bar, still hoping for a quick getaway.

"We don't take cash," said the owner, holding my bill by the corner like it was a dead rat.

Dammit. I squared my shoulders. "You're legally required to accept U.S. currency."

"Maybe true in the U.S. of A, but this is the U.S. of Starker's, and I only accept Superwally credit. And your blue buddy there owes a lot more than this anyway for those spilled drinks." She had her hand below the bar. I had no clue whether she was going for a phone or a baseball bat or a gun; nothing good could come of any of those options.

I snatched the bill back, mind racing. Silva kept a credit transfer account; that wouldn't be any help, since he was already out the door. I avoided credit and devices in general, which usually held me in good stead, but I didn't think the label "Non-comm" would win me any friends here. Jacky rarely paid for anything, so I had no clue whether he had been paying cash or credit up until then.

"I've got them, Maggie." My new friend from the booth stepped up beside me, waving his phone.

He turned to me. "Go on. I've got this."

Maggie's hand came out from under the bar. She pulled a phone from behind the cash register to do the credit transfer, which meant whatever she had reached for down below probably wouldn't have been good for my health.

"Keep playing," he called after me.

Jacky was unremorseful. "He started it. Called us disease vectors. I told him to stay right where he was and the whole world would go on turning 'cause it doesn't even know he exists. Besides, if he can't air drum, he should just air guitar like everybody else."

Silva laughed. "You should have pretended to cough. He probably would have pissed himself."

He and Silva sprawled in the back together as I peeled out of the parking lot.

"Not funny. I don't care who started it. No fights. I mean it. Do you think I can afford to bail you out? How are we supposed to play tomorrow if our drummer's in jail? And what if they skip the jail part and shoot you? It's happened before."

"Sorry, Mom," Jacky said.

"Not funny," I repeated. "If you ever call me 'Mom' again I'm leaving you on the side of the road. And I'm not a Chauffeur. Somebody come up here to keep me company."

Silva climbed across the bed and bags and up to the passenger seat. He flipped on the police scanner, then turned it off after a few minutes of silence; nobody had put out any APBs on a van full of bill-ducking freaks. I drove speed limit plus five, same as the occasional Chauffeurs we passed ferrying their passengers home. Shortcutting onto the highway to leave the area entirely would've been my preference, but Daisy would have triggered the ramp sensors in two seconds flat; we hadn't been allowed on an interstate in five years.

After about twenty miles, my fear that we were going to get chased down finally dissipated and my heartbeat returned to acceptable rhythms. We pulled into an office park that didn't look patrolled.

"Your turn for the bed, Luce?" Jacky asked. Trying to make amends, maybe.

"You guys can have it if I can find my sleeping bag. It's actually pretty nice out, and then I don't have to smell whatever that blue crap is on your clothes."

"You have a sleeping bag?"

"Of course I do. I just used it in . . ." Actually, I couldn't think of when I had used it last. It took a few minutes of rummaging to find it in the storage space under the bed, behind Silva's garage sale box of pulp novels. I spread it on the ground just in front of the van. The temperature was perfect and the sky was full of stars. Hopefully there weren't any coyotes around.

I slept three or four hours before my body started to remind me why I didn't sleep outside more often. I got up to pee and stretch. When I opened the door, I was hit by an even deeper grease smell than usual. It almost drowned out the funk of two guys farting, four days unwashed. Also the chemical-alcohol-blue scent Jacky wore all over his clothes.

Leaning over the driver's seat, I dug in the center console for my silver pen and the bound atlas I used as a road bible. The stars were bright enough to let me see the pages without a flashlight. The atlas was about fifteen years out of date, but my notes kept it useable. The town we had called Nowhere was actually named Rackwood, which sounded more like a tree disease than a town to me. A glittery asterisk went next to Rackwood, and in the margin "China Grove—Mike Sun—grease AND food." I drew an X over the location of Starker's, which wouldn't get our repeat business.

I crawled inside around dawn, feeling every bone in my body, and reclined the passenger seat. Nobody knocked on the van to tell us to move on, so we slept until the sun started baking us. Jacky reached forward to offer up his last leftovers from the night before. I sniffed the container and handed it back to him. He shrugged and dove in with his fingers, chopsticks having disappeared into the detritus surrounding him. After a little fishing around, I found my dinner and sent that his way as well.

Silva climbed into the driver's seat. I didn't usually relinquish the wheel; I genuinely loved doing all the driving myself. I liked the control, liked to listen to Daisy's steady engine and the thrum of the road. He knew that, and didn't ask except when he really felt the urge, which meant that when he did ask, I moved over. Jacky had never offered once, content to read and listen to music in his back seat cocoon. Another reason he fit in well.

Silva driving meant I got a chance to look around; it wasn't often that we took a road I hadn't been down before. I couldn't even remember how we had wound up choosing this route the previous day. We passed shuttered diners and liquor stores, the ghost town that might have been a main street at one time.

"Where is everybody?" Jacky asked.

I twisted around to see if he was joking. "Have you looked out the window once this whole year? Is this the first time you're noticing?"

"I usually sleep through this part of the country. It's boring."

"There is no everybody," Silva said. "A few farmers, a Superwally that employs everyone else within an hour's drive."

I peered at my atlas. "I've got a distribution center drawn in about forty miles back and ten miles north, on the road we usually take. That probably employs anybody not working for the company store." There wasn't really any reason for me to draw that kind of place onto my maps, but I liked making them more complete. They had layers in some places, stores and factories that had come and gone and come and gone again.

Most backroad towns looked like this, these days. At best a fast food place, a feed store, maybe a run-down-looking grocery or a health clinic, and not much else. There'd be a Superwally somewhere between towns, as Silva had said, luring everyone even farther from center or anything resembling community. Town after town, we saw the same thing. And of course most people didn't see anything at all, puttering along on the self-driving highways, watching movies instead of looking out the windows, getting from point A to point B without stopping in between.

We weren't exactly doing our part either. It wasn't like we had contributed to the local economy. We took free dinner, free fuel. We contributed in other ways, but not in this town or the others we'd passed through the night before. Maybe someday someone here would book us and we'd come back, but until then we were passing through. Goodbye, Rackwood, Indiana.

"Next town has the World's Largest Salt Shaker." I could hear the capital letters in Jacky's voice. He liked to download tourist brochures. I approved of that hobby, the way I approved of supporting anything to make a place less generic. Sometimes we even got to stop at a few of the sights, when we could afford it and we weren't in a hurry. Neither of which was the case today.

"Another time," Silva said. "We slept later than we should have."

"I think we're missing out."

I twisted around to look at Jacky. He flopped across the bed, waving his phone like a look at the world's largest salt shaker might make us change our minds. "It's a choice between showers and salt shaker. You decide."

He stuffed his phone into his pocket with a sigh. Showers trumped.

About an hour outside Columbus, we stopped at a by-the-hour motel already starred in my atlas, and rented an hour for the glory of running water. The clerk took my cash without comment.

I let the guys go first, so I wouldn't have to smell them again after I was clean. The shower itself was nothing to write home about. The metal booth kind, no tub, nonexistent water pressure, seven-minute shutoff; better than nothing. Afterward, I pulled a white towel from the previous hotel from my backpack to leave in the room, and stuffed one of the near-identical clean ones in my bag. The one I took might have been one I had left the last time through. Nobody ever got shorted a towel, and it saved me a lot of time in laundromats. I couldn't even remember who had taught me that trick, but I'd been doing it for decades.

We still had to get back in our giant grease trap, of course, now in our cleanish gig clothes. I opened all the windows and turned on the fan full blast, hoping to keep the shower scent for as long as possible. I could vaguely hear Jacky calling out visitor highlights for Columbus from the back, but the noise stole the meat of whatever he was saying. I stuck my arm outside and planed my hand against the wind.

I didn't intend to fall asleep, but I woke to Silva shouting "Whoa!

Happy birthday, Daisy!" and hooting the horn. I leaned over to see the numbers clicking over from 99,999.

Jacky threw himself forward to snap a picture of the odometer as it hit all zeroes. "Whoa! What birthday is this?" I considered. Daisy only had a five-digit odometer, so she got a fresh start every hundred thousand miles. "Eight, I think?"

Silva grinned. "Try again. My count says nine."

"Nine? I thought we passed seven on the way out of Seattle two years ago."

"That was five years ago. Eight in Asheville. I don't remember when."

"Huh. You're probably right. We should throw her a party at a million." I gave her dashboard a hard pat, like the flank of a horse."Good job, old girl. That's amazing."

"Totally," said Jacky. "And can we play 'Our Lady of the Open Road' tonight? In Daisy's honor? I love that song. I don't know why we don't play it more often." He started playing the opening with his hands on the back of my seat.

"I'm on board," Silva agreed. "Maybe instead of 'Manifest Independence'? That one could use a rest."

"'Manifest Independence' stays," I said. "Try again."

"'Outbreak'?"

"Deal."

Jacky retreated to make the changes to the set list.

Our destination was deep in the heart of the city. Highways would have gotten us there in no time, not that we had that option. We drove along the river, then east past the decaying convention center.

We hadn't played this particular space before, but we'd played others, mostly in this same neighborhood of abandoned warehouses. Most closed up pretty quickly, or moved when they got shut down, so even if we played for the same crowd, we rarely played the same building twice.

This one, The Chain, sounded like it had a chance at longevity. It was a bike co-op by day, venue by night. Cities liked bike co-ops. With the right people running the place, maybe somebody who knew how to write grants and dress in business drag and shake a hand or two, a bike co-op could be part of the city plan. Not that I had any business telling anyone to sell themselves out for a few months of forced legitimacy.

Our timing was perfect. The afternoon bike repair class had just finished, so the little stage area was more or less clear. Better yet, they'd ordered pizza. Jacky had braved the Chinese leftovers, but Silva and I hadn't eaten yet. It took every ounce of my self-restraint to help haul in the instruments before partaking. I sent a silent prayer up to the pizza gods there'd still be some left for us once all our gear was inside.

I made three trips—guitars and gear, amp, swag to sell—then loaded up a paper plate with three pizza slices. I was entirely capable of eating all three, but I'd share with the guys if they didn't get their gear in before the food was gone. Not ideal dinner before singing, anyway; maybe the grease would trump the dairy as a throat coating. I sat on my amp and ate the first piece, watching Jacky and Silva bring in the drums, feeling only a little guilty. I had done my share, even if I hadn't helped anyone else.

The bike class stuck around. We chatted with a few. Emma, Rudy, Dijuan, Carter, Marin—there were more but I lost track of names after that. I gave those five the most attention in any case, since Rudy had been the one to book us, and Emma ran the programming for the bike co-op. We were there because of them. We talked politics and music and bikes. I was grateful not to have to explain myself again. These were our people. They treated us like we were coming home, not passing through.

More audience gradually trickled in, a good crowd for a Wednesday night. A mix of young and old, in varying degrees of punk trappings, according to their generation and inclination. Here and there, some more strait-laced, though they were as punk as anyone, in the truest spirit of the word, for having shown up at this space at all. Punk as a genre didn't look or sound like it used to, in any case; it had scattered to the wind, leaving a loose grouping of bands whose main commonality was a desire to create live music for live audiences.

The first band began to play, an all-woman four-piece called Moby K. Dick. They were young enough to be my kids, which meant young enough they had never known any scene but this one. The bassist played from a sporty little wheelchair, her back to the audience, like she was having a one-on-one conversation with the drummer's high hat. At first, I thought she was shy, but I gradually realized she was just really into the music. The drummer doubled as singer, hiding behind a curtain of dreadlocks that lifted and dropped back onto her face with every beat. They played something that sounded like sea chanties done double time and double volume, but the lyrics were all about whales and dolphins taking revenge on people. It was pretty fantastic.

I gave all the bands we played with a chance to win me over. They were the only live music we ever got to hear, being on the road full time. The few friends we still had doing the same circuit were playing the same nights as us in other towns, rotating through; the others were doing StageHolo and we didn't talk much anymore. It used to be we'd sometimes even wind up in the same cities on the same night, so we'd miss each other and split the audience. That didn't happen much anymore with so few places to play.

Moby K. Dick earned my full attention, but the second band lost me pretty quickly. They all played adapted console-game instruments except the drummer. No strings, all buttons, all programmed to trigger samples. I'd seen bands like that before that were decent;

this one was not my thing.

The women from the first band were hanging out by the drink cooler, so I made my way back there. I thrust my hand into the ice and came out with a water bottle. Most venues like this one were alcohol-free and all ages. There was probably a secret beer cooler hidden somewhere, but I wasn't in the mood to find it.

"I liked your stuff," I said to the bassist. Up close, she looked slightly older than she had on stage. Mid-twenties, probably. "My name's Luce."

She grinned. "I know! I mean, I'm Truly. And yes, that's really my name. Nice to meet you. And really? You liked it? That's so cool! We begged to be on this bill with you. I've been listening to Cassis Fire my whole life. I've got 'Manifest Independence' written on my wall at home. It's my mantra."

I winced but held steady under the barrage and the age implication. She continued. "My parents have all your music. They like the stuff with Marcia Januarie on drums best, when you had the second guitarist, but I think your current lineup is more streamlined."

"Thanks." I waited for her to point her parents out in the room, and for them to be younger than me. When she thankfully didn't volunteer that information, I asked, "Do you guys have anything recorded?"

"We've been recording our shows, but mostly we just want to play. You could take us on the road with you, if you wanted. Opening act."

She said the last bit jokingly, but I was pretty sure the request was real, so I treated it that way. "We used to be able to, but not these days. It's hard enough to keep ourselves fed and moving to the next gig. I'm happy to give you advice, though. Have you seen our van?"

Her eyes widened. She was kind of adorable in her enthusiasm. Part of me considered making a pass at her, but we only had a few minutes before I had to be onstage, and I didn't want to confuse things. Sometimes I hated being the responsible one.

"It's right outside. They'll find me when it's our turn to play. Come on."

The crowd parted for her wheelchair as we made our way through. I held the door for her and she navigated the tiny rise in the doorframe with practiced ease.

"We call her Daisy," I said, introducing Truly to the van. I searched my pockets for the keys and realized Silva had them. So much for that idea. "She's a fifteen seater, but we took out the middle seats for a bed and the back to make a cage for the drums and stuff so they don't kill us if we stop short."

"What's the mpg?" she asked. I saw her gears spinning as she tried to figure out logistics. I liked her focus. She was starting to remind me of me, though, which was the turnoff I needed.

I beckoned her to the hood, which popped by latch, no keys necessary. "That's the best part of all." She locked her chair and pushed herself up to lean against Daisy's frame. At my look, she explained, "I don't need it all the time, but playing usually makes me pretty tired. And I don't like getting pushed around in crowds."

"Oh, that's cool," I said. "And if you buy a van of your own, that's one less conversion you'll have to make, if you can climb in without a lift. I had been trying to figure out if you'd have room for four people and gear and a chair lift."

"Nah, you can go back to the part where we wonder how I'm going to afford a van, straight up. Right now we just borrow my sister's family Chauffeur. It's just barely big enough for all our gear, but the mileage is crap and there's no room for clothes or swag or anything."

"Well, if you can find a way to pay for an old van like Daisy, the beauty of running on fry oil is the money you'll save on fuel. As long as you like takeout food, you get used to the smell . . ."

Silva stuck his head out the door, then came over to us. I made introductions. He unlocked the van; I saw Truly wince when the smell hit her. He reached under the bed, back toward the wheel well, and emerged with a bottle of whiskey in hand. Took a long swig, and passed it to me. I had a smaller sip, just enough to feel the burn in my throat, the lazy singer's warm-up.

Truly followed my lead. "Promise you'll give me pointers if I manage to get a van?"

I promised. The kid wasn't just like me; she practically was me, with the misfortune to have been born twenty years too late to possibly make it work.

I made Silva tap phones with her. "I would do it myself, but . . ."

"I know," she said. "I'd be Non-comm if I could, but my parents won't let me. Emergencies and all that."

Did we play extra well, or did it just feel like it? Moby K. Dick had helped; it was always nice to be reminded that what you did mattered. I had a mental buzz even with only a sip of whiskey, the combination of music and possibilities and an enthusiastic crowd eager to take whatever we gave them.

On a good night like this, when we locked in with each other, it was like I was a time traveler for an hour. Every night we'd ever played a song overlapped with every night we'd ever play it again, even though I was fully in the moment. My fingers made shapes, ran steel strings over magnets, ran signals through wires to the amplifier behind me, which blasted those shapes back over me in waves. Glorious, cathartic, bone-deep noise.

On stage, I forgot how long I'd been doing this. I could still be the kid playing in her parents' basement, or the young woman with the hit single and the major label, the one called the next Joan Jett, the second coming of riot grrl, not that I wanted to be the young version of me anymore. I had to work to remember that if I slid on my knees I might not get up again. I was a better guitar player now, a better singer, a better songwriter. I had years of righteous rage to channel. When I talked, I sometimes felt like a pissed-off grump, stuck in the past. Given time to express it all in music, I came across better.

Moby K. Dick pushed through to the front when we played "Manifest Independence," singing along at the top of their lungs. They must have been babies when I released that song, but it might as well have been written for them. It was as true for them as it had been for me.

That was what the young punks and the old punks all responded to; they knew I believed what I was singing. We all shared the same indignation that we were losing everything that made us distinct, that nothing special happened anymore, that the new world replacing the old one wasn't nearly as good, that everyone was hungry and everything was broken and that we'd fix it if we could find the right tools. My job was to give it all a voice. Add to that the sweet old-school crunch of my Les Paul played through Marshall tubes, Silva's sinuous bass lines, Jacky's tricky beats, and we could be the best live band you ever heard. Made sweeter by the fact that you had to be there to get the full effect.

We didn't have rehearsed moves or light shows or spotlights to hit like the StageHolos, but we knew how to play it up for the crowd. To make it seem like we were playing for one person, and playing for all of them, and playing just for them, because this night was different and would only ever happen once. People danced and pogoed and leaned into the music. A few of the dancers had ultraviolet tattoos, which always looked pretty awesome from my vantage point, a secret performance for the performers. I nudged Silva to look at one of them, a glowing phoenix spread wingtip to wingtip across a dancer's bare shoulders and arms.

A couple of tiny screens also lit the audience: people recording us with Bracertabs, arms held aloft. I was fine with that. Everyone at the show knew how it felt to be there; they'd come back, as long as there were places for us to play. The only market for a non-holo recording was other people like this audience, and it would only inspire them to come out again the next time.

Toward the end of the set, I dedicated "Our Lady of the Open Road" to Daisy. At the tail of the last chorus, Jacky rolled through his toms in a way he never had before, cracking the song open wide, making it clear he wasn't coming in for a landing where he was supposed to. Silva and I exchanged glances, a wordless "this is going to be interesting," then followed Jacky's lead. The only way to do that was to make it bigger than usual, keep it going, make it a monster. I punched my gain pedal and turned to my amp to ride the feedback. Our lady of the open road, get me through another night.

Through some miracle of communication we managed to end the song together, clean enough that it sounded planned. I'd kill Jacky later, but at that moment I loved him. The crowd screamed.

I wiped the sweat out of my eyes with my shoulder. "We've got one more for you. Thanks so much for being here tonight." I hoped "Better to Laugh" wouldn't sound like an afterthought.

That was when the power went out.

"Police!" somebody shouted. The crowd began to push toward the door.

"Not the police!" someone else yelled. "Just a blackout."

"Just a blackout!" I repeated into the mic as if it were still on, then louder into the front row, hoping they were still listening to me. "Pass it on."

The message rippled through the audience. A tense moment passed with everyone listening for sirens, ready to scatter. Then they began to debate whether the blackout was the city or the building, whether the power bill had been paid, whether it was a plot to shut the place down.

Emma pushed her way through the crowd to talk to us. "They

shut this neighborhood's power down whenever the circuits overload uptown. We're trying to get somebody to bring it up in city council. I'm so sorry."

I leaned in to give her a sweaty hug. "Don't worry about it. It happens."

We waited, hoping for the rock gods to smile upon us. The room started to heat up, and somebody propped the outside doors, which cooled things down slightly. After twenty minutes, we put our instruments down. At least we had made it through most of our set. I had no doubt the collective would pay us, and no concern people would say they hadn't gotten their money's worth. I dug the hotel towel out of my backpack to wipe my dripping face.

A few people made their way over to talk to us and buy T-shirts and patches and even LPs and download codes, even though you could find most of our songs free online. That was part of the beauty of these kids. They were all broke as hell, but they still wanted to support us, even if it was just a patch or a pin or a password most of them were capable of hacking in two seconds flat. And they all believed in cash, bless them. We used the light of their phone screens to make change.

The girls from Moby K. Dick all bought T-shirts. Truly bought an LP as well—it figured she was into vinyl—and I signed it "To my favorite new band, good luck." She wheeled out with her band, no parents in sight. I wondered if they'd decided they were too old for live music, then chided myself. I couldn't have it both ways, mad that they were probably my age and mad that they weren't there. Besides, they might have just left separately from their kid. I knew I must be tired if I was getting hung up on something like that.

"You look like you need some water," somebody said to me in the darkness. A bottle pressed into my hand, damp with condensation.

"Thanks," I said. "Though I don't know how you can say I look like anything with the lights out."

At that moment, the overheads hummed on again. I had left my guitar leaning face down on my amp, and it started to build up a squeal of feedback. I passed the bottle back, wiped my hands on my pants, and slammed the standby switch. The squeal trailed away.

"Sorry, you were saying?" I asked, returning to the stranger, who still stood with water in hand. I took it from her again. I thought maybe I'd know her in the light, but she didn't look familiar. Mid-thirties, maybe, tall and tan, with a blandly friendly face, toned arms, Bracertab strapped to one forearm. She wore a Magnificent Beefeaters T-shirt with the sleeves cut off. We used to play shows with them before they got big.

"I was saying you looked like you were thirsty, by which I mean you looked like that before the lights went out, so I guessed you probably still looked like that after."

"Oh."

"Anyway, I wanted to say good show. One of your best I've seen."

"Have you seen a lot?" It was a bit of a rude question, with an implication I didn't recognize her. Bad for business. Everybody should believe they were an integral part of the experience. But really, I didn't think I'd seen her before, and it wasn't the worst question, unless the answer was she'd been following us for the last six months.

"I've been following you for the last six months," she said. "But mostly live audience uploads. I was at your last Columbus show, though, and up in Rochester."

Rochester had been a huge warehouse. I didn't feel as bad.

"Thanks for coming. And, uh, for the water." I tried to redeem myself.

"My pleasure," she said. "I really like your sound. Nikki Keller-man."

She held her arm out in the universal "tap to exchange virtual business cards" gesture.

"Sorry, I'm Non-comm," I said.

She looked surprised, but I couldn't tell if it was surprise that I was Non-comm, or that she didn't know the term. The latter didn't seem likely. I'd have said a third of the audience at our shows these days were people who had given up their devices and all the corporate tracking that went along with them.

She unstrapped the tablet, peeled a thin wallet off her damp arm, and drew a paper business card from inside it.

I read it out loud. "Nikki Kellerman, A & R, StageHolo Productions." I handed it back to her.

"Hear me out," she said.

"Okay, Artists & Repertoire. You can talk at me while I pack up."

I opened the swag tub and started piling the T-shirts back into it. Usually we took the time to separate them by size so they'd be right the next time, but now I tossed them in, hoping to get away as soon as possible.

"As you probably know, we've been doing very well with getting StageHolo into venues across the country. Bringing live music into places that previously didn't have it."

"There are about seven things wrong with that statement," I said without looking up.

She continued as if I hadn't spoken. "Our biggest-selling acts are arena rock, pop, rap, and Spanish pop. We now reach nine in ten bars and clubs. One in four with StageHoloAtHome."

"You can stop the presentation there. Don't you dare talk to me about StageHoloAtHome." My voice rose. Silva stood in the corner chatting with some bike kids, but I saw him throw a worried look my way. "'All the excitement of live entertainment without leaving your living room.' 'StayAtHome with John Legend tonight.'"

I clapped the lid onto the swag box and carried it to the door. When I went to pack up my stage gear, she followed.

"I think you're not understanding the potential, Luce. We're looking to diversify, to reach new audiences: punk, folk, metal, musical theater." She listed a few more genres they hadn't completely destroyed yet.

I would punch her soon. I was not a violent person, but I knew for a fact I would punch her soon. "You're standing in front of me, asking me to help ruin my livelihood."

"No! Not ruin it. I'm inviting you to a better life. You'd still play shows. You'd still have audiences."

"Audiences of extras paid to be there? Audiences in your studios?" I asked through clenched teeth.

"Yes and no. We can set up at your shows, but that's harder. Not a problem in an arena setting, but I think you'd find the 3D array distracting in a place like this. We'd book you some theaters, arenas. Fill in the crowds if we needed to. You could still do this in between if you wanted, but . . ." She shrugged to indicate she couldn't see why I would want.

"Hey, Luce. A little help over here?" I looked down to see my hands throttling my mic instead of putting it back in its box. Looked up at Silva struggling to get his bass amp on the dolly, like he didn't do it on his own every night of the week. Clearly an offer of rescue.

"Gotta go," I said to the devil's A&R person. "Have your people call my people."

Turning the bass rig into a two-person job took all of our acting skills. We walked to the door in exaggerated slow motion. Lifting it into the van genuinely did take two, but usually my back and knee ruled me out. I gritted my teeth and hoisted.

"What was that about?" Silva asked, shutting Daisy's back hatch and leaning against it. "You looked like you were going to tear that woman's throat out with your teeth."

"StageHolo! Can you believe the nerve? Coming here, trying to lure us to the dark side?"

"The nerve," he echoed, shaking his head, but giving me a funny look. He swiped an arm across his sweaty forehead, then pushed off from the van.

I followed him back inside. Nikki Kellerman was still there.

"Luce, I think you're not seeing everything I have to offer."

"Haven't you left yet? That was a pretty broad hint."

"Look around." She gestured at the near-empty room.

I stared straight at her. I wasn't dignifying her with any response.

"Luce, I know you had a good crowd tonight, but are there people who aren't showing up these days? Look where you are. Public transit doesn't run into this neighborhood anymore. You're playing for people who squat in warehouses within a few blocks, and then people who can afford bikes or Chauffeurs."

"Most people can scrounge a bicycle," I said. "I've never heard a complaint about that."

"You're playing for the people who can bike, then. That bassist from the first band, could she have gotten here without a car?"

For the first time, I felt like she was saying something worth hearing. I sat down on my amp.

"You're playing for this little subset of city punks for whom this is a calling. And after that you're playing for the handful of people who can afford a night out and still think of themselves as revolutionary. And that's fine. That's a noble thing. But what about everybody else? Parents who can't afford a sitter? Teens who are too young to make it here on their own, or who don't have a way into the city? There are plenty of people who love music and deserve to hear your message. They just aren't fortunate enough to live where you're playing. Wouldn't you like to reach them too?"

Dammit, dammit, dammit, she had a decent point. I thought about the guy who had paid for our drinks the night before, and the church van guy from outside the Chinese restaurant, and Truly if she didn't have a sister with a car.

She touched her own back. "I've seen you after a few shows now, too. You're amazing when you play, but when you step off, I can see what it takes. You're tired. What happens if you get sick, or if your back goes out completely?"

"I've always gotten by," I said, but not with the same vehemence as a minute before.

"I'm just saying you don't have to get by. You can still do these shows, but you won't have to do as many. Let us help you out. I can get you a massage therapist or a chiropractor or a self-driving van."

I started to protest, but she held up her hands in a placating gesture. "Sorry—I know you've said you love your van. No offense meant. I'm not chasing you because my boss wants me to. I'm chasing you because I've seen you play. You make great music. You reach people. That's what we want."

She put her card on the amp next to me, and walked out the front of the club. I watched her go.

"Hey Luce," Jacky called to me. I headed his way, slowly. My back had renewed its protest.

"What's up?" I asked.

He gestured at the bike kids surrounding him, Emma and Rudy and some more whose names I had forgotten. Marina? Marin. I smiled. I should have spent more time with them, since they were the ones who had brought us in.

"Our generous hosts have offered us a place to stay nearby. I said I thought it was a good idea, but you're the boss."

They all looked at me, waiting. I hadn't seen the money from the night yet. It would probably be pretty good, since this kind of place didn't take a cut for themselves. They were in it for the music. And for the chance to spend some time with us, which I was in a position to provide.

"That sounds great," I said. "Anything is better than another night in the van." We might be able to afford a hotel, or save the hotel splurge for the next night, in—I mentally checked the road-map—Pittsburgh.

With the bike kids' help, we made quick work of the remaining gear. Waited a little longer while Rudy counted money and handed it over to me with no small amount of pride.

"Thank you," I said, and meant it. It had been a really good show, and the money was actually better than expected. "We'll come back here anytime."

Just to prove it, I pulled my date book from my backpack. He called Emma over, and together we penned in a return engagement in three months. I was glad to work with people so competent; there was a good chance they'd still be there in three months.

We ended up at a diner, van parked in front, bikes chained to the fence behind it, an unruly herd.

I was so tired the menu didn't look like English; then I realized I was looking at the Spanish side.

"Is there a fridge at the place we're staying?" Silva asked.

Smart guy. Emma nodded. Silva and Jacky and I immediately ordered variations on an omelet theme, without looking further at either side of the menu. The beauty of omelets: you ate all the toast and potatoes, wrapped the rest, and the eggs would still taste fine the next day. Two meals in one, maybe three, and we hadn't had to hit a dumpster in two full days.

Our hosts were a riot. I barely kept my eyes open—at least twice I realized they weren't—but Emma talked about Columbus politics and bikes and greenspaces with a combination of humor and enthusiasm that made me glad for the millionth time for the kind of places we played, even if I didn't quite keep up my end of the conversation. Nikki Kellerman could flush herself down the toilet. I wouldn't trade these kids for anything.

Until we saw the place on offer. After the lovely meal, after following their bikes at bike speed through unknown and un-knowable dark neighborhoods, Silva pulled the van up. The last portion had involved turning off the road along two long ruts in grass grown over a paved drive. I had tried to follow in my atlas on the city inset, but gave up when the streets didn't match.

"Dude," I said, opening my eyes. "What is that?"

We all stared upward. At first glance it looked like an enormous brick plantation house, with peeling white pillars supporting the upper floors. At second, maybe some kind of factory.

"Old barracks," said Jacky, king of local tourist sites. "Those kids got themselves an abandoned fort."

"I wonder if it came with contents included." Silva mimed loading a rifle. "Bike or die."

I laughed.

Jacky leaned in to the front seat. "If you tell me I have to haul in my entire kit, I swear to god I'm quitting this band. I'll join the bike militia. Swear to god."

I peered out the windows, but had no sense of location. "Silva?"

"I can sleep in the van if you think I should."

It was a generous offer, given that actual beds were in the cards.

"You don't have to do that," I decided. "We'll take our chances."

I stopped at the back gate for my guitar, in the hopes of hav-ing a few minutes to play in the morning. Silva did the same. We shouldered instruments and backpacks, and Jacky took the three Styrofoam boxes with our omelets. The bike kids waited in a cluster by an enormous door. We staggered their way.

"So who has the keys?" Silva asked.

Emma grinned. "Walk this way."

The big door was only for dramatic effect. We went in through a small, unlocked door on the side. It looked haphazardly placed, a late addition to the architecture. A generator hummed just out-side the door, powering a refrigerator, where we left our leftovers.

I hoped it also powered overhead lights, but the bike kids all drew out halogen flashlights as soon as we had stored the food.

The shadows made everything look ominous and decrepit; I wasn't sure it wouldn't look the same in daylight. Up a crumbling staircase, then a second, to a smaller third floor. Walls on one side, railing on the other, looking down over a central core, all black. Our footsteps echoed through the emptiness. In my tired state, I imagined being told to bed down in the hallway, sleeping with my head pressed to the floor. If they didn't stop soon, I might.

We didn't have to go farther. Emma swung open an unmarked door and handed me her flashlight. I panned it over the room. A breeze wafted through broken glass. An open futon took up most of the space, a threadbare couch sagging beneath the window. How those things had made it up to this room without the stairs falling away entirely was a mystery, but I had never been so happy to see furniture in my entire life.

I dropped my shoulder and lowered my guitar to the floor. The bike kids stared at us and we stared back. Oh god, I thought. If they want to hang out more, I'm going to cry.

"This is fantastic," said Silva, the diplomat. "Thank you so much. This is so much better than sleeping in the van."

"Sweet. *Hasta mañana!*" said Rudy, his spiky head bobbing. They backed out the door, closing it behind them, and creaked off down the hallway.

I sank into the couch. "I'm not moving again," I said.

"Did they say whether they're renting or squatting? Is anybody else getting a jail vibe?" Jacky asked, flopping back onto the futon.

Silva opened the door. "We're not locked in." He looked out into the hallway and then turned back to us. "But, uh, they're gone without a trace. Did either of you catch where the bathroom was?"

I shook my head, or I think I did. They were on their own.

The night wasn't a pleasant one. I woke once to the sound of

Silva pissing in a bottle, once to a sound like animals scratching at the door, once to realize there was a spring sticking through the couch and into my thigh. The fourth time, near eight in the morning, I found myself staring at the ceiling at a crack that looked like a rabbit. I turned my head and noticed a cat pan under the futon. Maybe it explained the scratching I had heard earlier.

I rolled over and stood up one vertebra at a time. Other than the spring, it hadn't been a bad couch. My back felt better than the night before. I grabbed my guitar and slipped out the door.

I tried to keep my steps from echoing. With the first daylight streaming in through the jagged windows, I saw exactly how dilapidated the place was, like it had been left to go feral. I crept down to the first floor, past a mural that looked like a battle plan for world domination, all circles and arrows, and another of two bikes in carnal embrace. Three locked doors, then I spotted the fridge and the door out. Beyond this huge building there were several others of similar size, spread across a green campus. Were they all filled with bike kids? It was a pleasant thought. I'd never seen any place like this. I sat down on the ground, my back against the building, in the morning sunshine.

It was nice to be alone with my guitar. The problem with touring constantly was we were always driving, always with people, always playing the same songs we already knew. And when we did have down time, we'd spend it tracking down new gigs, or following up to make sure the next places still existed. The important things like writing new songs fell to last on the list.

This guitar and I, we were old friends. The varnish above her pick guard had worn away where I hit it on the downstroke. Tiny grooves marked where my fingers had indented the frets. She fit my hands perfectly. We never talked anymore.

She was an old Les Paul knockoff, silver cloudburst except where the bare wood showed through. Heavy as anything, the reason why my back hurt so constantly. The hunch of my shoulder as I bent over her was permanent. And of course with no amp she didn't make any sound beyond string jangle. Still, she felt good.

I didn't need to play the songs we played every night, but my fingers have always insisted on playing through the familiar before they can find new patterns. I played some old stuff, songs I loved when I was teaching myself to play, Frightwig and the Kathleen Battle School and disappear fear, just to play something I could really feel.

Then a couple of bars of "She's the One," then what I remembered of a Moby K. Dick whale song. I liked those kids.

When I finally hit my brain's unlock code, it latched onto a twisty little minor descent. The same rhythm as the whale song, but a different progression, a different riff. A tiny theft, the kind all musicians make. There was only so much original to do within twelve notes. Hell, most classic punk was built on a couple of chords. What did Lou Reed say? One chord is fine, two chords is pushing it, three chords you're into jazz?

I knew what I was singing about before I even sang it. That StageHolo offer, and the idea of playing for a paid audience night after night, the good and the bad parts. The funny thing about bargains with the devil was you so rarely heard about people turning him down; maybe sometimes it was worth your soul. I scrambled in my gig bag pocket for a pen and paper. When I came up with only a Sharpie, I wrote the lyrics on my arm. The chords would keep. I'd remember them. Would probably remember the lyrics too, but I wasn't chancing it.

Silva stepped out a little while later, wearing only a ratty towel around his waist. "There's a bucket shower out the back!"

"Show me in a sec, but first, check it out." I played him what I had.

His eyes widened. "Be right back."

He returned a moment later wearing jeans, bass in hand. We

SARAH PINSKER

both had to play hard, and I had to whisper-sing to hear the un-plugged electric instruments, but we had something we both liked before long.

"Tonight?" he asked me.

"Maybe . . . depends on how early we get there, I guess. And whether there's an actual soundcheck. Do you remember?"

He shook his head. "Four-band lineup, at a warehouse. That's all I remember. But maybe if we leave pretty soon, we can set up early? It's only about three hours, I think."

He showed me where the shower was, and I took advantage of the opportunity. The bike kids appeared with a bag of lumpy apples, and we ate the apples with our omelets, sitting on the floor. Best breakfast in ages. They explained the barracks—the story involved an arts grant and an old school and abandoned buildings and a cat sanctuary and I got lost somewhere along the way, working on my new song in my head.

After breakfast, we made our excuse that we had to get on the road. They walked us back the way we came, around the front.

My smile lasted as long as it took us to round the corner. As long as it took to see Daisy was gone.

"Did you move her, Jacky?" Silva asked.

"You've got the keys, man."

Silva patted his pockets, and came up with the key. We walked closer. Glass.

I stared at the spot, trying to will Daisy back into place. Blink and she'd be back. How had we let this happen? I went through the night in my head. Had I heard glass breaking, or the engine turn-ing over? I didn't think so. How many times had we left her outside while we played or ate or showered or slept? I lay down on the path, away from the glass, and looked up at the morning sky.

The bike kids looked distraught, all talking at once. "This kind of thing never happens." "We were only trying to help."

"It wasn't your fault," I said, after a minute. Then louder, when they didn't stop. "It wasn't your fault." They closed their mouths and looked at me.

I sat up and continued, leaning back on my hands, trying to be the calm one, the adult. "The bad news is we're going to need to call the police. The good news is, you're not squatting, so we don't have to work too hard to explain what we were doing here. The bad news is whoever stole the van can go really far on that tank. The good news is they're probably local and aren't trying to drive to Florida. Probably just kids who've never gotten to drive something that didn't drive itself. They'll abandon her nearby when she runs out of gas." I was trying to make myself feel better as much as them.

"And maybe they hate Chinese food," Jacky said. "Or maybe the smell'll make them so hungry they have to stop for Chinese food. We should try all the local Chinese food places first."

Silva had stepped away from the group, already on the phone with the police. I heard snippets, even though his back was turned. License plate. Yes, a van. Yes, out-of-state plates. No, he didn't own it, but the owner was with him. Yes, we'd wait. Where else did we have to go? Well, Pittsburgh, but it didn't look like we'd be getting there any time soon.

He hung up and dug his hands into his pockets. He didn't turn around or come back to the group. I should probably have gone over to him, but he didn't look like he wanted to talk.

The kids scattered before the police arrived, all but Emma disappearing into the building. Jacky walked off somewhere as well. It occurred to me I didn't really know much of his history for all the time we'd been riding together.

The young policewoman who arrived to take our report was standoffish at first, like we were the criminals. Emma explained the situation. No officer, not squatting, here are the permits. I kept the van registration and insurance in a folder in my backpack, which helped on that end too, so that she came over to our side a little. Just a little.

"Insurance?"

"Of course." I rustled in the same folder, presented the card to her. She looked surprised, and I realized she had expected something electronic. "But only liability and human driver."

Surprised her again. "So the van isn't self-driving?"

"No, ma'am. I've had her—it—for twenty-three years."

"But you didn't convert when the government rebates were offered?"

"No, ma'am. I love driving."

She gave me a funny look.

"Was anything in the van?" she asked.

I sighed and started the list, moving from back to front.

"One drum kit, kind of a hodgepodge of different makes, Ampeg bass rig, Marshall guitar amp, suitcase full of gig clothes. A sleeping bag. A box of novels, maybe fifty of them. Um, all the merchandise: records and T-shirts and stuff to sell . . ." I kept going through all the detritus in my head, discarding the small things: collapsible chopsticks, restaurant menus, pillows, jackets. Those were all replaceable. My thoughts snagged on one thing.

"A road atlas. Rand McNally."

The officer raised her eyebrows."A what?"

"A road atlas. A book of maps."

"You want me to list that?"

"Well, it's in there. And it's important, to me anyway. It's annotated. All the places we've played, all the places we like to stop and we don't." I tried to hide the hitch in my voice. Don't cry, I told myself. Cry over the van, if you need to. Not over the atlas. You'll make another. It might take years, but it could be done.

It wasn't just the atlas, obviously. Everything we had hadn't been much, and it was suddenly much less. I was down to the cash in my pocket, the date book, the single change of clothes in my backpack, my guitar. How could we possibly rebuild from there? How do you finish a tour without a van? Or amps, or drums?

The officer held out her phone to tap a copy of her report over to me.

"Non-comm," I said. "I'm so sorry."

Silva stepped in for the first time. He hadn't even opened his mouth to help me list stuff, but now he held up his phone. "Send it to me, officer."

She did, with a promise to follow up as soon as she had any leads. Got in her squad car. She had to actually use the wheel and drive herself back down the rutted path; I guessed places like this were why police cars had a manual option. She had probably written us off already, either way.

I turned to Silva, but he had walked off. I followed him down the path toward an old warehouse.

"Stop!" I said, when it was clear he wasn't going to. He turned toward me. I expected him to be as sad as me, but he looked angrier than I had ever seen him, fists clenched and jaw tight.

"Whoa," I said. "Calm down. It'll be okay. We'll figure something out."

"How? How, Luce?"

"They'll find Daisy. Or we'll figure something out."

"Daisy's just the start of it. It's amps and records and T-shirts and everything we own. I don't even have another pair of underwear. Do you?"

I shook my head. "We can buy . . ."

"We can buy underwear at the Superwally. But not all that other stuff. We can't afford it. This is it. We're done. Unless."

"Unless?"

He unclenched his left fist and held out a scrap of paper. I took it from him and flattened it. Nikki Kellerman's business card, which had been on my amp when I last saw it.

"No," I said.

"Hear me out. We have nothing left. Nothing. You know she'd hook us up if we called now and said we'd sign. We'd get it all back. New amps, new merch, new stage clothes. And we wouldn't need a new van if we were doing holo shows. We could take a break for a while."

"Are you serious? You'd stay in one place and do holo shows?" I waited for an answer. He stomped at a piece of glass in the dirt, grinding it with his boot heel. "We've been playing together for twenty years and I wouldn't have guessed you'd ever say yes to that."

"Come off it, Luce. You know I don't object the way you do. You know that, or you'd have run it past me before turning her down. I know we're not a democracy, but you used to give me at least the illusion I had a choice."

I bit my lip. "You're right. I didn't run it past you. And actually, I didn't turn her down in the end. I didn't say yes, but she said some stuff that confused me."

That stopped him short. Neither of us said anything for a minute. I looked around. What a weird place to be having this fight; I always figured it would come, but in the van. I waited for a response, and when none came, I prodded. "So you're saying that's what you want?"

"No! Maybe. I don't know. It doesn't always seem like the worst idea. But now I don't think we have another option. I think I could have kept going the way we were for a while longer, but rebuilding from scratch?" He shook his head, then turned and walked away again. I didn't follow this time.

Back at the building where we had stayed, the bike kids had reappeared, murmuring amongst themselves. Jacky leaned against the front stoop, a few feet from them. I sat down in the grass opposite my drummer.

"What do you think of StageHolo? I mean really?"

He spit on the ground.

"Me too," I agreed. "But given the choice between starting over with nothing, and letting them rebuild us, what would you do? If there weren't any other options."

He ran a hand over his braids. "If there weren't any other options?"

I nodded.

"There are always other options, Luce. I didn't sign up with you to do fake shows in some fake warehouse for fake audiences. I wouldn't stay. And you wouldn't last."

I pulled a handful of grass and tossed it at him.

He repeated himself. "Really. I don't know what you'd do. You wouldn't be you anymore. You'd probably still come across to some people, but you'd have the wrong kind of anger. Anger for yourself, instead of for everybody. You'd be some hologram version of yourself. No substance."

I stared at him.

"People always underestimate the drummer, but I get to sit behind you and watch you every night. Trust me." He laughed, then looked over my shoulder. "I watch you, too, Silva. It goes for you, too."

I didn't know how long Silva had been behind me, but he sat down between us now, grunting as he lowered himself to the ground. He leaned against Jacky and put his grimy glassdust boots in my lap.

I shoved them off. "That was an old-man grunt."

"I'm getting there, old lady, but you'll get there first. Do you have a plan?"

I looked over where the bike kids had congregated. "Hey, guys!

Do any of you have a car? Or, you know, know anybody who has a car?"

The bike kids looked horrified, then one—Dijuan?—nodded. "My sister has a Chauffeur."

"Family sized?"

Dijuan's face fell.

Back to the drawing board. Leaning back on my elbows, I thought about all the other bands we could maybe call on, if I knew anybody who had come off the road, who might have a van to sell if Daisy didn't reappear. Maybe, but nobody close enough to loan one tonight. Except . . .

"You're not saying you're out, right?" I asked Silva. "You're not saying StageHolo or nothing? 'Cause I really can't do it. Maybe some-day, on our terms, but I can't do it yet."

He closed his eyes. "I know you can't. But I don't know what else to do."

"I do. At least for tonight."

I told him who to call.

Truly arrived with her sister's family-sized Chauffeur an hour later. We had to meet her up on the road.

"It'll be a tight squeeze, but we'll get there," she said. The third row and all the foot space was packed tight with the Moby K. Dick amps and drums and cables.

"Thank you so much," I said, climbing into what would be the driver's seat if it had a wheel or pedals. It felt strange, but oddly freeing as the car navigated its way from wherever we were toward where we were going.

I was supposed to be upset. But we had a ride to the gig, and gear to play. We'd survive without merch for the time being. Somebody in Pittsburgh would help us find a way to Baltimore if Daisy hadn't been found by then, or back to Columbus to reclaim her.

With enough time to arrange it, the other bands would let us use their drums and amps at most of the shows we had coming up, and in the meantime we still had our guitars and a little bit of cash. We'd roll on, in Daisy or a Chauffeur, or on bikes with guitars strapped to our backs. No StageHolo gig could end this badly; this was the epic, terrible, relentlessness of life on the road. We made music. We were music. We'd roll on. We'd roll on. We'd roll on.

A STUDY IN OILS

KELLY ROBSON

Kelly Robson's short fiction has been published in *Asimov's*, Tor.com, *Clarkesworld*, and *Uncanny*. She has been a wine and spirits writer for *Chatelaine Magazine* and has contributed several essays on writing to *Clarkesworld*'s "Another Word" column. Her novella "Gods, Monsters, and the Lucky Peach" was a finalist for the 2019 Nebula, Hugo, Theodore Sturgeon, Locus, and Aurora Awards.

"A Study in Oils" is a gentle story about rehabilitation, remorse, and redemption through art.

Halfway up the winding cliff-side guideway, Zhang Lei turned his bike around. He was exhausted from three days of travel and nauseated, too, but that wasn't the problem. He could always power through physical discomfort. But the trees, the rocks, the open sky above, and the mountains closing in—it was all too strange. He kept expecting something to drop on his head.

He pinged Marta, the social worker in Beijing Hive who'd orchestrated his escape from Luna seventy-two hours earlier.

Forget Paizuo, he whispered as his bike coasted the guideway's downslope. *This is too weird.*

Turn that bike back around or I'll hit your disable button, Marta whispered back.

You wouldn't.

He turned the bike's acceleration to maximum.

I would. You can spend the next two weeks lying at the bottom of a gully while the tribunal decides what to do with you. Turn around.

No, I'm going back to the Danzhai roadhouse.

When she scowled, her whole face crumpled into a mass of wrinkles. She didn't even look like a person anymore.

I'd do anything to keep you alive, kid, and I don't even like you. She jabbed at him with an age-spotted finger, as if she could reach across the continent and poke him in the chest. *Turn back around or I'll do it.*

He believed her. Nobody had hit his disable button since he'd left Luna, but Marta was an old ex-Lunite and that meant she was both tough and mean. Zhang Lei slowed his bike, rotated back to the guideway's uphill track, and gave the acceleration dial a vicious twist.

You don't like me? he asked.

Maybe a little. Marta flipped through the graphs of his biom. She had full access to that, too, and could check everything from his hormone levels to his sleep cycle. *You're getting dehydrated. Drink some water. And slow your bike. You're going to make yourself puke.*

I feel fine, he lied.

Marta rolled her eyes. *Relax. You'll love Paizuo. Nobody wants to kill you there.*

She slapped the connection down, and the image of her elderly face was replaced by steep, verdant mountainside. Danzhai County was thick with an impossible greenness, in layers of bushes, trees, grasses, and herbs he had no name for.

Everything was unfamiliar here. He knew he was deep in southwestern China, but that was about all. He knew he was surrounded by mountains, with Danzhai's transit hub behind him. It was a two-pad skip station, the smallest he'd ever seen, next to a narrow lake surrounded by hills, everything green but the sky—which actually was blue, like everyone always said about Earth—and the buildings. Those were large, brown, and open to the air as if atmospheric weather was nothing.

An atmosphere people could breathe. That was Earth's one unique claim. Unlike Luna, or Venus, or Mars, or any of the built environments in the solar system, here in Danzhai and a few other places on Earth, humans lived every day exposed to weather. It was traditional, or something.

Weather was overrated, Zhang Lei decided. The afternoon was so humid, he'd sweated through his shirt. And the air wasn't clean. Bits of fluff floated in it, and it smelled weird, too. Birds zipped through the air like hovertoys launched from tree limbs—were they even birds? He'd seen so few on Luna.

At least he was alone. A year ago, he would have hated not having anyone to goof around with or show off for. No coach, no team, no fans. Now he was grateful. Marta was watching out for him, always on the other end of a ping if anything went wrong. It was a relief not having to stay ultra-alert.

He pinged Marta.

How long do I have to stay in Paizuo?

Her face appeared again. She was shoveling noodles into her mouth with a pair of chopsticks. The sight of the food made his stomach heave.

At least two weeks. More if I can wrangle an extension. Ideally, I'd like you to stay until the tribunal decides your case.

Okay.

Two weeks. Fine. He'd keep doing what she said, within reason. Drinking water, yes. Slowing the bike down, no. He wasn't going to toil up the mountain like some slack-ass oldster.

Wasn't long before he regretted that decision. The nausea wouldn't be denied any longer. He shifted on the bike's saddle and hung his head over the edge of the guideway. His mouth prickled with saliva until his guts heaved, forcing what was left of his luxurious, hand-cooked Danzhai lunch—black fungus, eggplant, cucumbers, and garlic with pepper, pepper, and more pepper—up, out, and over into the green gulch below. The nausea eased.

When he got to the Paizuo landing stage, the guideway came to a dead end. He couldn't believe it. Just a ground-level platform with a bike rack on one side and a battery of cargo floats on the other. Zhang Lei had never even seen a landing stage with only one connection, not even in the bowels of Luna's smallest hab. Everywhere was interconnected. Not Paizuo, apparently.

He hooked his bike on the rack, shouldered his duffle bag, and wiped his mouth on his sleeve, flicking away a few stray pepper seeds. His lips burned.

I said you'd puke, Marta whispered. No visual this time, only a disembodied voice. *Bet you feel like shit.*

Yeah, but you look like shit.

It was the traditional Lunar reply. Marta laughed.

Don't pull that lip here, okay? You're a guest. Be polite.

He shifted his bag from one shoulder to the other. Nobody seemed to be watching, aside from Marta. Behind the trees, a few brown houses climbed the side of the mountain. Where was the village? A few people were visible through the trees, but otherwise, Paizuo was a wilderness—a noisy wilderness. Wind in the leaves, birds chirping, and buzzing—something coming up behind him.

Zhang Lei spun, fists raised. A cargo conveyor zipped up the guideway. It slid its payload onto a float and slotted itself into place on the underside of the landing stage. The float slowly meandered up a leafy path.

A hospitality fake showed him the way to the guest house, where he stumbled to his room, fell on top of the bed, and slept fourteen hours straight. If someone had wanted to kill him then, they easily could have. He wouldn't have cared.

_____

The other three artists in the guest house were pampered oldsters from high-status habs. They made a big show of acting casual, but Zhang Lei caught each of them exchanging meaningful looks. They were probably pinging his ID to ogle his disable button, marveling at the label under it that said KILLER—FAIR GAME, and discussing him in whispers.

During lunch, Zhang Lei ignored them. Instead of joining their conversation, he watched a hygiene bot polish the floor.

"The wood bothered me at first," said Prajapati, gesturing with a beringed hand at the guest house's wooden walls, floor, and ceiling. She looked soft, her dark skin plush with fat and burnished with moisturizers. Her metadata identified her as a sculptor from Bangladesh Hell. "But organic materials are actually quite hygienic, if treated properly."

"I don't like the dirt," said Paul, an ancient watercolorist from Mars. "It's everywhere outside."

"It's not dirt, it's soil," said the sculptor. She picked a morsel of flesh out of the bubbling pot of fish soup in the middle of the table.

"People from the outplanet diaspora forget that soil is life," said Han Song, a 2D photographer from Beijing Hive.

"Yes, we've all been told that a thousand times," replied the watercolorist with a smile. "Earth thinks very well of itself. But I have to say, I like Paizuo. The Miao traditional lifestyle is extremely appealing."

A woman shuffled into the dining room, bearing plates of egg dumplings and sweet millet cake. The oldsters smiled and thanked her profusely. The woman wore a wide silver torque around her neck, hung with tiny bells and charms. They tinkled as she arranged the dishes. She was slender, but the profile of her abdomen showed a huge tumor under her colorful tunic.

"What a waste of billable hours," the watercolorist said once the chef was gone. "Couldn't they task a bot with the kitchen-to-table supply chain? I know tradition is important to the Miao, but the human ability to carry plates is hardly going to die out."

The chef had tagged the food with detailed nutritional notes, and it said millet was good for digestive upset. After vomiting his Danzhai lunch yesterday, he couldn't face more peppers. But the millet cake was good—honey-sweet and crunchy. The egg dumplings were delicious, too. He could eat the whole plate.

Marta pinged him.

I thought you'd never wake up. Listen, don't worry about the other guests, okay? We've had them investigated. They're all nice, quiet, trustworthy people. They agreed not ask too many questions.

He shoved another dumpling in his mouth. Zhang Lei knew he ought to be grateful but he wasn't. The three oldsters were getting something out of the deal, too. They would be able to tell stories about him for the rest of their lives. *I once shared accommodations with a murderer. Well, not a murderer, I suppose, not exactly, my dear, but a killer. No, I never asked him what happened but you should have seen the disable button on his ID. It said KILLER right under it. I couldn't help but stare.*

Zhang Lei finished the dumplings and claimed the rest of the millet cake. He left the table, still chewing, and slammed the front door behind him.

What did you tell them about me? he asked Marta.

Not much. I said you weren't responsible for what happened and we're working to have the disable button removed.

I was responsible, though.

Zhang Lei, we've discussed this. Do you want to ping a peer counselor? Talk therapy is effective.

No. I hate talking.

The guest house was part of a trio of houses, fronted by a cabbage patch. Large birds—domestic poultry he guessed—pecked at the gravel walkway that led to the guest house's kitchen door. Nearby, a huge horned mammal was tethered in the shade, along with a large caged bird that stalked back and forth and shrieked.

Zhang Lei trudged toward a peak-roofed pavilion. The midday sun stood high over the valley, veiled by humid haze. Not at all hot, but in the unfamiliar atmosphere, sweat beaded on his scarred forearms.

The pavilion overlooked the terraced fields descending the valley and the hazy fleet of mountains on the horizon. No blue sky today. He might as well be in a near-Sun-orbit greenhouse hab, deep in the eye of its dome, every sprout, bud, and bloom indexed and graphed. The locals probably used the same agricultural tech here. Each of the green-and-yellow plants in the terraces below was probably monitored by an agronomist up the mountain, watching microsensors buried in the soil and deploying mineral nutrition with pinpoint accuracy.

Zhang Lei pinged one of the plants. Nothing came back, not even an access denial. He tried pinging one of the farmers working far below, then a nearby tree. Still nothing. Frantic, he flung pings across the valley.

All of the Paizuo guest houses answered immediately. A map highlighted various routes up and down the valley. The guideway landing stage sent him the past two days of traffic history and offered average travel times to various down-slope destinations. A lazy stream of ID information flowed from the guest artists, thirty in total.

Several hazard warnings floated over their targets: *Watch for snakes. Beware of dog. Dangerous cliff.* But no pings from the locals, or any of the crops, equipment, or businesses. Not even from the wooden hand truck upended over a pile of dirt at the side of the path. But no way this village ran everything data-free.

His pings summoned the hospitality fake. It hovered at his elbow, head inclined with a gently inquiring look.

"Why can't I get a pingback from anything here?" he demanded.

It gave Zhang Lei a generic smile. "Paizuo data streams are restricted to members of the Miao indigenous community."

"So I can't find out anything?" His face grew hot with anger. Stuck here for weeks or more, totally ignorant, unable to learn anything or find out how the village worked.

The fake nodded. "I'll be pleased to answer your questions if I'm able."

Zhang Lei wasn't in the mood for crèche-level games. He slapped it down, hard. The fake misted away, immediately replaced by Marta in full length. She had her fists on her hips and didn't look pleased.

Feeling a little aggressive, Zhang Lei? You didn't say two words to your fellow guests, and now you're getting testy with a fake.

I'm sorry, okay? Embarrassing. He should have controlled himself. *I hate this place.*

No, you don't. You're out of your element. Nothing here is any threat to you. She grinned. *Not unless you have a phobia of domestic animals.*

Hah, he grumbled.

Go for a walk. Do a little sketching. Get familiar with the village. There's lots to see, and it's all gorgeous. There's a reason why artists love Paizuo.

Okay. He booted up his viewcatcher. Marta gave him an approving nod and dissolved.

True, Paizuo was beautiful. From the pavilion, mountains thick with trees stretched sharp and steep over the valley, where green and yellow terraced fields stepped up and down the lower slopes, punctuated by small groups of wooden houses under tall trees. He framed the composition in his viewcatcher. It was perfect, pre-chewed—the whole reason the pavilion had been built there in the first place. The fang-like form of the tallest mountain clutched in the spiral fist of the golden mean. Nice.

Even though the view was pre-packaged, framing it in his view-catcher was satisfying. And what a relief to be able to do it openly. Back on Luna, he had to be careful not to get caught using the view-catcher, or he'd get smacked by one of his teammates or screamed at by his coach. Zhang Lei was allowed to draw cartoons and cari-catures, but everything else was a distraction from training and a waste of time and focus.

Total commitment to the game, that's what all coaches demanded.

"What do you love better, hockey or scribbling on little bits of paper?" Coach had demanded, and then smacked him on the back of the head when he hesitated.

"Hockey," he answered.

"Right. Don't forget it."

So he drew cartoons of his teammates, their rival teams, and stars from the premier leagues they all wanted to get drafted into. He got good. Fast. Accurate. In thirty seconds, he could toss off a sketch that got the whole team hooting. Coach liked it, said it was good for morale. But quick, sketchy work didn't satisfy. Neither did the digital-canvas painting he snuck past Coach on occasion, but both were better than nothing.

He padded down a trail to the first terrace, flipping his view-catcher through its modes—thirds to notan to golden mean to phi grid—as he strode along the edge. The earthen berm bounding the terrace was less than a meter wide, and seemed to be made entirely of dirt. The next terrace was ten meters below on his left.

He blacked out edges of the view, widened the margins until noth-ing was visible outside his constantly expanding and contracting search for a composition. He swept back and forth across the landscape. Then he slipped and fell. The viewcatcher framed a close-up of green plants in brown water.

Zhang Lei lurched sideways, regaining his footing, the right leg of his pants wet to the knee and slimy with mud. He dismissed the viewcatcher and stared incredulously around him.

The matrix of the terraces was liquid, not soil. Water and mud. He'd seen it glinting between the greenery, but he hadn't realized it was water. And now he was covered in it.

A fleeting thought—*I'm going to die here*—easily dismissed. All he had to do was watch where he put his feet as he explored.

Paizuo wasn't what Zhang Lei expected. The village wasn't all one piece like ancient towns in crèche storybooks. It was spread thin, covering the whole valley, the houses clustered in groups under the trees and separated by fields and paddies. The Miao didn't build on flat or even sloping land—those areas seemed dedicated to crops. Instead, they chose the precipitous and rocky landscape for their multi-level wooden homes. Each house stood on stilts over the canted landscape, the weight of the structures leaning back on the mountainside. Livestock sheltered in the shade beneath, some tethered or penned, some roaming free.

Actual live animals, like the ones behind the guest house, and a lot of them. With humans living literally on top of them.

A deep voice knocked Zhang Lei out of his thoughts. Unfamiliar syllables. When he turned to look, the translation word balloon hung over the man's head:

"Hello, can I help you?"

No ID accessible, but the balloon was tagged with his name: Jen Dang. Not tall, but broad-shouldered and athletic, with skin deeply burnished by the sun and a wide, strong face. Old, but not an oldster.

Zhang Lei switched on his translation app.

"I arrived yesterday," Zhang Lei said. "Trying to get used to everything."

Jen Dang scanned the balloon overhead.

"Are the insects troubling you?"

"Insects?" Zhang Lei frowned and scanned the ground. "I haven't seen any yet."

"Right there." Jen Dang pointed at one of the fluttering creatures he had no name for.

"Oh, I thought insects lived on the ground. I'm from—" He almost said Luna but caught himself in time. "I've never been on Earth before. It's different."

"Most of our guests use seers to help them identify plants and animals. Paizuo is a biodiversity preserve, with thousands of different species."

"I'll do that, thanks."

Jen Dang fell silent. Zhang Lei could feel himself warming to the stranger. Lots of charisma and natural authority. He'd do well on Luna.

"The food is really good here," he said.

A shadow of a smile crossed Jen Dang's face.

"Jen Dla is my daughter. She's an experienced chef."

"I'm sorry," Zhang Lei said, and the other man squinted at him. "I couldn't help but notice she's sick." He gestured vaguely in the region of his stomach.

Jen Dang shook his head. "You're a guest. There are lots of things guests can't understand. Would you like to see another?"

Two large baskets lay under a tree. Jen Dang plucked them from the ground and led Zhang Lei down a tree-lined path, the slope so extreme the route soon turned into uneven stairs, cut into the dirt and haphazardly incised with slabs of rock. Mammals grazed on either side, standing nearly on their hind legs while cropping the ground cover.

They descended five terrace levels before Zhang Lei's thighs started getting hot. Stairs were a good workout, mostly cardio but some leg strength, and uneven steps were good balance training, too. For a moment he lost himself in the rhythm of their rapid descent. It was enjoyable. He could run the stairs in morning and evening before doing his squats and lunges—but then he remembered. He wasn't an athlete anymore. And with the disable button on his ID labeling him a killer, nobody in Danzhai, Miao or guest, needed to wonder what he was training for, or if he was chasing someone.

He slowed, letting the distance widen between himself and the farmer. If someone got worried and hit the button, he'd roll right down the mountain.

Jen Dang shucked his shoes and rolled up his trouser legs as he waited for Zhang Lei at one of the lower terraces.

"Many guests are squeamish of the rice paddies, but it's only water and mud," he said when Zhang Lei joined him. "And worms. Bugs of course. A few snakes. And fish." He hefted the large basket. It was bottomless—an open, woven cylinder.

"Not a problem." Zhang Lei pulled off his shoes, but didn't roll up his pant legs. One was still damp. The other might as well get wet, too.

Jen Dang handed him the smaller basket and waded into the sodden paddy, bottomless basket clutched in both hands.

"Step between the rice plants, never on them. Try not to stir up too much mud, or you can't see the fish."

Jen Dang demonstrated, moving slowly and looking at the water through the basket. Zhang Lei followed. The mud was cool. It squelched through his toes.

"Use the basket to shade the water's surface," the farmer said. "Look for movement. A flash of scales or the flick of a tail."

As Zhang Lei followed the farmer through the paddy, he took care to keep his feet away from the knee-high rice plants. Each one was topped by knobby spikes—the grain portion of the crop, he assumed. Some of the grain was coated with a milky substance, and some was turning yellow.

Jen Dang plunged the bottomless basket in the water and said, "Come look."

A fish was trapped inside. Jen Dang reached into the water and flipped it into Zhang Lei's basket. It struggled, thrashing.

"That's one, we need six. You catch the rest."

Zhang Lei made several tries before he trapped a fish large enough to meet Jen Dang's standards. Catching the rest took a full hour. The sky cleared and turned Earth-blue. The older man betrayed no trace of impatience, even though it was a ridiculous expenditure of effort to procure basic foodstuffs when a nutritional extruder could feed hundreds of people an hour, with personalized flavor and texture profiles and optimal nutrition.

When they finished, Zhang Lei's eyes ached from squinting against the flare of sun on water. He wiped his fish-slick hands on his pants and followed the farmer up the stairs.

"Why do you do this?" he asked.

Jen Dang stopped and eyed the word balloon over Zhang Lei's head.

"Stubbornness. That's what my wife says. She's an orthopedic surgeon, takes care of all the Miao in Danzhai county. She won't farm. Says her hands are meant for higher things. She loves to cook, though. She taught all our daughters."

"But why do manual labor when you could use bots?"

"We use some, but we're not dependent on them. If we don't do the work, who will?"

"Nobody."

"Then nobody will know how to do it. All traditional skills and knowledge will be lost, along with our language, stories, songs—everything that makes us Miao. We do it to survive."

"You could write it down."

Jen Dang laughed. He lifted the fish basket to his shoulder and ran up the stairs two at a time. His word balloon blossomed behind him.

"Some things can only be mastered with constant practice."

That was true. Nobody could learn to play hockey by watching a doc. Or learn to draw or paint without actually doing it.

An insect landed on a nearby plant. Its wide, delicate wings had eye-like patterns in shades of gold and copper. Zhang Lei framed it in his viewcatcher, then panned up to include the mountains in the composition. Gold wings and green slopes, copper eyes and blue sky. Perfect.

Another insect hung in the sky, hovering motionless, shaped like a half circle and very faint. Zhang Lei stared for a whole minute before realizing what he was looking at.

The moon. Luna itself. The home of everything he knew, and everyone who wanted to hurt him. Watching.

Over the next week, the moon turned its back on him, retreating through its last quarter to a thinning sickle. In the morning, when he ventured onto the guest house's porch for a stretch, there it was, lurking behind the boughs of a fir tree, half-hidden behind mountain peaks, or veiled in humid haze to the east. Sometimes it hid on the other side of the globe. Then the next time he looked, it was right overhead, staring at him.

Night was the worst. The lights of the habs glared from the dark lunar surface aside the waning crescent—the curved sickle of Purovsk, the oval of Olenyok, the diamond pinpoint of Bratsk, the five-pointed star of Harbin.

A few years back, an investment group had tried to float a proposal to build a new hab on Mare Insularum, its lights outlining a back-turned fist with an extended middle finger. Zhang Lei and his teammates had worn the proposed hab pattern on their gym shirts for a few months, the finger mocked up extra large on a dark moon, telling Earth and all its inhabitants what Lunites thought of them.

He could stay inside at night, but he couldn't hide from the moon during the day. It watched him with a sideways smile. *We see you—we're coming to get you.*

He tried not to think about it, and concentrated on finding compositions with his viewcatcher. He made sketches and studies, and looked up plants and animals with his seer, and tried to learn their names. When he ran into artists from the other guest houses, they were friendly enough, but all much older than him.

At night, he worked on studies and small canvases in his room, door closed and windows dark. They were disasters: muddy greens, lifeless brushwork, flat compositions. He tried all the tricks he'd learned in the crèche—glazing, underpainting, overpainting, scraping with a palette knife, dry brush, but nothing worked.

Why don't you try some familiar subjects? Marta suggested. *Limber up first, then branch out into new things.*

If you say so.

He was so frustrated, he'd try anything. He lugged his easel and kit up to the guest house's communal studio and set up in his own corner of the work space.

"I was beginning to think we'd never see you up here," said Paul. "Welcome."

"The light's especially good in the afternoon," said Prajapati.

Han Song paused his hands over his work surface for a moment and nodded.

Nothing motivated Zhang Lei like competition. He would destroy the watercolorist with his superior command of light and shadow, teach the sculptor about form, show the photographer how to compose a scene.

His old viewcatcher compositions and stealthily-made reference sketches were gone forever, so he worked from memory. He attacked the canvas with his entire arsenal, blocking out a low-angle view of Mons Hadley and the shining towers of Sklad, with the hab's vast hockey arena in the foreground under a gleaming crystal dome. The view might be three hundred eighty thousand kilometers away, but it lay at his fingertips, and he created it anew every time he closed his eyes.

The paint leapt to Zhang Lei's brush, clung to the canvas, spread thin and lean and true exactly where it should, the way it should, creating the effects he intended. After a week of flailing with sappy greens and sloppy, organic shapes, he finally had a canvas under control. He worked late, muttering good night to the other artists without raising his eyes from his work. When dawn stretched its fingers through the studio's high windows, the painting was done—complete with a livid crimson stain spreading under the arena's crystal dome.

He didn't remember deciding to paint blood on the ice, or putting crimson on his palette. But the color belonged there. It was the truth. It showed what he did.

Zhang Lei lowered himself to the floor, leaned his back against the wall with his elbows on his knees, and rested his head in his hands. He pinged Marta. She blinked blearily at him for a few seconds, her eyes swollen with sleep. He pointed at the canvas.

Have any of the other artists seen this? she whispered.

I don't know. I don't think so.

It's important they don't. Okay? Do you understand why?

Because people are looking for me.

Not only that. She scrubbed her eyes with the heels of her hands. *The Lunite ambassador is trying to block your immigration application. If the media gets interested, we'll have to move you, fast. And yes, people are searching. Three teams of Lunite brawlers have been skipping all over the planet, asking questions. They found someone in Sudbury Hell who remembers you getting on a skip bound for Chongqing Hive. That's too close for comfort.*

I can destroy the canvas, he said, voice flat and scraped clean of emotion. It was the first real painting he'd done since he left the crèche. But he couldn't look at it. When he did, his flesh crawled.

No. Don't do that. Hide it.

He nodded. *It's a decent painting.*

Yeah. Not bad. You worked out the kinks.

He knocked his head against the wall behind him. Wood was harder than it looked. He swung his head harder.

Stop that.

There's no point, Marta. Those brawlers are going to find me.

No, they won't. And chances are good the tribunal will rule in your favor. We have to be patient.

Even if I get to live in Beijing, people will still find out what I did.

They'll assume you had no choice. Everyone knows Luna is the most dangerous place in the solar system.

I did have a choice—

Marta interrupted. *It was a mistake. An accident. It could happen to any hockey player.*

I aimed for Dorgon's neck.

You did what you were taught, and so did Dorgon. Playing hockey isn't the only way to die on Luna. If you live in a place where getting killed is accepted as a possible outcome, then you also accept that you might become a killer.

But we don't understand what it means.

No. Marta looked sad. *No, we don't.*

The day after he'd killed Dorgon, Zhang Lei's team hauled him to a surgeon. Twenty minutes was all it took to install the noose around his carotid artery, then two minutes to connect the disable button and process the change to his ID. His teammates were as gentle as they could be. When it was all done, the team's enforcer clasped Zhang Lei's shoulder in a meaty hand.

"We test it now," Korchenko said, and Zhang Lei had gone down like a slab of meat.

When he woke, his friends looked concerned, sympathetic, even a little regretful.

That attitude didn't last long. After the surgery, the team traveled to a game in Surgut. Zhang Lei's disable button was line-of-sight. Anyone who could see it could trigger it. He passed out five times along the way, and spent most of the game slumped on the bench, head lolling, his biom working hard to keep him from brain damage. His teammates had to carry him home.

For a few weeks, they treated him like a mascot, hauling him from residence to practice rink to arena and back again. They soon tired of it and began leaving him behind. The first time he went out alone, he came back on a cargo float, with a shattered jaw and bootprint-shaped bruises on his gut. That was okay. He figured he deserved it.

Then one night after an embarrassing loss, the team began hitting the button for fun. First Korchenko, as a joke. Then the others. Didn't take long for Zhang Lei to become their new punching bag. So he ran. Hid out in Sklad's lower levels, pulling temporary privacy veils over his ID every fifteen minutes to keep the team from tracking him. When they were busy at the arena warming up for a game, he bolted for Harbin.

He passed out once on the way to the nearest intra-hab connector, but the brawler who hit his disable button was old and drunk. Zhang Lei collected a few kicks to the ribs and one to the balls before the drunk staggered off. Nobody else took the opportunity to get their licks in, but nobody helped him, either.

Boarding the connector, he got lucky. A crèche manager was transferring four squalling newborns, and the crib's noise-dampening tech was broken. The pod emptied out—just him and the crèche manager. She ignored him all the way to Harbin. He kept his distance, but when they got to their destination, he followed her into the bowels of the hab. She was busy with the babies and didn't notice at first. But when he joined her in an elevator, she got scared.

"What do you want?" she demanded, her voice high with tension.

He tried to explain, but she was terrified. That big red label on his button—KILLER—FAIR GAME—didn't fill people with confidence in his character. She hit the button hard, several times. He spent an hour on the floor of the elevator, riding from level to level, and came to with internal bleeding, a cracked ocular orbit, three broken ribs, and a vicious bite mark on his left buttock.

He limped down to the lowest level, where they put the crèches, and found his old crèche manager. She was gray, stooped, and much more frail than he remembered.

"Zhang Lei." She put a gentle palm on his head—the only place that didn't hurt. "I was your first cuddler. I decanted you myself. I won't let anyone hurt you."

If he cried then, he never admitted it.

Zhang Lei watched Jen Dla carry a pot of soup into the dining room. She moved awkwardly, shifting her balance around that bulbous gut. He couldn't understand it. Why hadn't she had an operation to remove the tumor? Her mother was even a surgeon.

Terminal, he guessed, and then realized he'd been staring.

Jen Dla nestled the pot on the stove in the middle of the table, and lit the flame. He caught the chef's eye as she adjusted the temperature of the burner.

"Your father must be an important man here in Paizuo," he said. Jen Dla laughed.

"He certainly thinks so." She laid her hand on the embroidered blouse draped over her bulging abdomen. "Fathers get more self-important with every new grandchild."

She tapped her finger on her stomach. Zhang Lei sat back in his chair, abruptly. She wasn't sick, but pregnant—actually bearing a child.

"Are all Miao children body-birthed?" he asked.

She looked a little offended. "Miao who choose to live in Paizuo generally like to follow tradition."

Abrupt questions leapt behind his teeth—*does it hurt, are you frightened*—but her expression was forbidding.

"Congratulations," he said. She smiled and returned to her kitchen.

After talking to Marta, he'd taken the painting down to his room and hidden it under the bed, then collapsed into dream-clouded sleep. The arena at Sklad, deserted, the vast spread of ice all his own. The blades of his skates cut the surface as he built speed, gathered himself, and launched into a quad, spinning through the air so fast the flesh of his face pulled away and snapped back into place on landing. He jumped, spun, jumped again.

Dreams of power and joy, ruined on waking. He'd pulled the painting from under his bed and hid it behind the sofa in the guest house lounge.

Jen Dla's soup began to bubble. Tomatoes bobbed in the sour rice broth. Zhang Lei watched the fish turn opaque as it cooked, then pinged one word at the three artists upstairs—*lunch*. They clattered down.

"Looked like you were having a productive session yesterday," Prajapati said. "Good to see."

"Don't stop the flow," Han Song added.

Paul grinned. "Nothing artists love more than giving unwanted advice."

"It's called encouragement," said Prajapati. "And it's especially important for young artists."

"Young competitors, you mean."

"I don't see it that way." She turned to Zhang Lei. "Do you?"

All three artists watched him expectantly. Zhang Lei stared at his hands resting on the wooden tabletop. He'd forgotten to roll down his sleeves. His forearms were exposed, the scarred skin dotted with pigment. He put his hands in his lap.

"I think the fish is ready," he said.

After lunch, while exploring for new compositions, he found Jen Dang behind the guest house. The water buffalo—one of the first creatures he'd looked up on his seer—was tethered to a post by a loop of rope through its nose. It was huge, lavishly muscled, and heavy, with ridged, back-curving horns, but it stood placidly as Jen Dang examined its hooves.

"Stay back," Jen Dang said. "Water buffalo aren't as friendly as they look. He's not a pet."

"Yeah, I know," said Zhang Lei. When he'd sketched the water buffalo, a stern warning had popped into his eye: *Do not approach. Will trample, gouge, and kick.*

He lifted his viewcatcher and captured a composition: Jen Dang stooping with his back turned to the water buffalo, drawing its massive hindquarter between his own legs and trapping the hoof between his knees.

"All he has to do is back up, and you'll get squashed," said Zhang Lei.

"He knows me." Jen Dang dropped the hoof and patted the animal's rump. "And he knows the best part of his day is about to begin."

The farmer untied the rope from the post and led the animal up the narrow trail behind the houses. Zhang Lei followed. A bird stalked from between the trees, its red, gold, and blue body trailing long, spotted brown tail feathers. His seer tagged it: *Golden Pheasant*, followed by a symbol that meant *major symbolic and cultural importance to the indigenous people at this geographical location*. Which was no different from most of the plants and animals the seer had identified.

"So, I've been using a seer," he said, as if his rice paddy conversation with Jen Dang had happened that morning instead of days before. "It doesn't explain anything. Why is every butterfly important to Miao but not the flies? Why one species of bee but not the other?"

"The butterfly is our mother," Jen Dang said.

"No, it's not. That's ridiculous."

"I might ask you who your mother is, if I were young and rude, and didn't know better."

"I don't have a mother. I was detanked."

"That means you're the product of genetic advection, from a tightly edited stream of genetic material subscribed to by your crèche. How is that less strange than having a butterfly mother?"

"Is the butterfly thing a metaphor?"

Jen Dang glanced over his shoulder, his gaze cold. "If you like."

The water buffalo lipped the tail of Jen Dang's shirt. He tapped its nose with the palm of his hand to warn it off. The trail widened as it began to climb a high ridge. The water buffalo was heavy but strong. It heaved itself up the slope, like a boulder rolling uphill. Jen Dang ran alongside to keep pace, so Zhang Lei ran after. The exertion felt good, scrambling uphill against the full one-point-zero, with two workout partners. So what if one of them was an animal? Zhang Lei would take what he could get.

When the trail widened, he took the chance to sprint ahead. He made it to the top of the ridge a full ten seconds before the water buffalo. Jen Dang looked him up and down.

"Not bad. Most guests are slow."

Zhang Lei grinned. "I train in the dubs."

"Dubs?"

"Double Earth-normal gravity. You know. For strength."

"I never would have guessed."

"I know," Zhang Lei said eagerly. "I look bottom-heavy, right? Narrow above a wide butt and thick legs. That's what makes me a good skater."

Shut up, Marta hissed in his ear. But he couldn't stop. Finally, a real conversation.

"I train for optimal upper-body flexibility, like all center forward play—"

One twinge in his throat, that was all it took to send Zhang Lei plummeting to the ground. He twisted and rolled when he hit the dirt—away from the edge of the hill, and then the world faded to mist.

Zhang Lei clawed his way to consciousness.

You're fine, you're fine, nobody's touched you.

Okay, he mumbled.

You've only been down five minutes, Marta added. *Tell him you have a seizure disorder and your neurologist is fine-tuning your treatment protocol. Say it.*

Zhang Lei struggled to focus. His eyelids fluttered as he tried to form the words.

"I get seizures." He licked his lips. "Doc's working on it."

Jen Dang said something. Zhang Lei forced his eyes to stay open. He was collapsed on his side, cheek pressed to the dirt. Three ants crawled not ten centimeters from his eye. He flopped onto his back to read the farmer's word balloon.

"Your medical advisory said it wasn't an emergency, and I

shouldn't touch you." Behind Jen Dang, the water buffalo cast a lazy brown eye over him and shook its head.

Tell him you'll be fine, Marta demanded. *Ask him not to mention it to anyone.*

"I'm fine." Zhang Lei pushed himself onto his elbows, then to his knees. "Don't talk about this, okay?"

The farmer looked dubious. He gathered the water buffalo's lead rope.

"I'll walk you back to the studio."

"No." Zhang Lei jumped to his feet. "There's nothing wrong with me. It won't happen again."

Better not, Marta grumbled.

Zhang Lei led the way up the trail. Jen Dang followed. The water buffalo wasn't dawdling anymore, it was moving fast, nearly trotting. The track converged on a single-lane paved road, which snaked up the valley in a series of switchbacks. They were higher now, the guest houses far below, and everywhere, rice terraces brimmed with ripening grain yellow as the sun. He could paint those terraces with slabs of cadmium yellow. Maybe he would.

"Which way?"

Zhang Lei needn't have asked. The water buffalo turned onto the road and trundled uphill. Before long, the slope gentled. Houses lined the road, with gardens and rice paddies behind. The road ended at a circular courtyard patterned with dark and light stones and half-bounded by a stream. At the far end, a footbridge arched over the water, leading to more houses beyond.

The animal's tail switched back and forth. It trotted toward the water, splayed hooves clopping on the courtyard's patterned surface. A hygiene sweeper darted out of its path. At the stream's edge, where the courtyard's stone patterns gave way to large, dark slabs, the water buffalo paused, lowered its head, and stepped into the water.

A man called out from one of the houses across the bridge. Jen Dang shouted a reply. No word balloon appeared.

Jen Dang offered the lead rope to Zhang Lei.

"He'll stay in the water. I'll only be a few minutes."

Zhang Lei leaned on the bridge railings, flipping the rope to keep it from tangling in the animal's horns as it luxuriated in the water below. The stream wasn't deep, only a meter or so, but the beast lay on its side and rolled, keeping its white beard, eyes, and horns above water.

When Jen Dang returned, the water buffalo was scratching its long, drooping ear on a half-submerged rock. Zhang Lei kept the rope.

"It's fun," he said. "Best part of my day, too."

The farmer sauntered across the courtyard and joined a pair of friends working in the shade of a mulberry tree.

Zhang Lei composed a series of canvases. The water buffalo with its eyelids lowered in pleasure, lips parted to reveal a gleaming row of bottom teeth. Three women in bright blue blouses weaving in an open workshop, their silver torques flashing. A man in deep indigo embroidered with pink and silver diamonds, sorting through a table piled with feathers. Jen Dang leaning on a low stone wall, deep in conversation with two friends using gleaming axes to chop lengths of bamboo. A white-haired woman in an apron stirring a barrel of viscous liquid with a wooden paddle. A battery of pink-cheeked, scrubbed children racing across the courtyard as a golden pheasant stalked in the opposite direction. A row of cabbages beside the road. Herbs clinging to a slate outcropping. A dragonfly skipping over the water. The tallest peak puncturing the western horizon like a fang on the underjaw of a huge beast.

Aesthetically pleasing, peaceful, picturesque. But all communities had tensions and contradictions. Only a Miao could identify the deeper meaning in these scenes. Only a great artist could paint the picturesque and make it important. He wasn't Miao and he was no great artist. Could he capture the water buffalo's expression of ecstasy as it pawed the water? Not likely. But he could paint the mountain. Nothing more banal than another mountain view. But he loved that unnamed peak. He'd loved Mons Hadley, too.

Jen Dang waved. A word balloon blossomed over his head: *Let's go.*

He jiggled the rope. The water buffalo ignored him. He flapped it, then gave the gentlest of tugs. The buffalo snorted and heaved itself out of the water. It stood there dripping for a moment, then its skin shivered. It lowered its head, shaking its great bulk and coating Zhang Lei in a local rainstorm.

Zhang Lei wiped his face on his sleeve. The men were still laughing when he joined them. Nothing more fun than watching a rookie fall on his ass.

Jen Dang was still chatting. Zhang Lei waited nearby, in the shade of a house. Along the wall was a metal cage much like the one behind the guest house. A rooster stalked back and forth, its face, comb, and wattle bright red, its bare breast and scraggly back caked with clean, healing sores. It stared at Zhang Lei with a malevolent orange eye, lifted one fiercely taloned yellow leg, and flipped its water dish.

"Stupid bird," Zhang Lei muttered.

Around the corner was another cage, another rooster in similar condition, its comb sliced in dangling pieces. When it screamed—raucous, belligerent—the other bird answered. Zhang Lei knew an exchange of challenges when he heard it.

"Are these fighting cocks?" he asked when Jen Dang joined him.

"You don't have them on Luna?" he answered.

Shit, whispered Marta. *Tell him you're from the Sol Belt. You've never been to Luna.*

Why don't you hit my disable button again? Load me on a cargo float and stick me in a hole somewhere? Or better yet—a cage. Evict one of the birds and get me my own dish of water.

I might have to do that. Listen kid, it's never been more important for you to be discreet.

Why? Are they coming for me?

Silence.

They are, aren't they? Answer me.

A Lunite team tracked you to the Danzhai roadhouse, but don't worry. We've got people on the ground, planting rumors to lure them to Guiyang. Even if they don't take the bait, Danzhai County has lots of towns and villages. You're still safe.

"I'm from the Sol Belt," he told Jen Dang. "I've never been to Luna."

The farmer didn't look convinced.

Zhang Lei's hand stole up to his throat. Under his jaw, where his pulse pounded, the hard mass of the noose waited to choke off his life.

When Zhang Lei got back to the studio, the other three artists were upstairs. He shoved the sofa aside. The painting leaned against the wall, facing out, a layer of breathable sealant protecting the drying oil paint. He was sure he'd turned it to face the wall, but apparently not. It didn't really matter. He wanted it gone.

He sprayed the canvas with another layer of sealant, trying not to look at the thick wet bloody gleam on the arena's ice. He wrapped it in two layers of black polymer sheeting, and requested a cargo wrap to meet him at the guideway landing stage.

When he got there, the area was packed with Miao arriving on sliders and bikes, whole families crowded onto multi-seat units, laughing and talking. He edged his way to the cargo drop, slid the cargo wrap around it, addressed it to Marta, and shoved the painting inside the conveyor. Done. He'd never have to think about it again.

The Miao were on holiday. Women wore their blue blouses with short skirts trailing with long, flapping ribbons, or ankle-length red and blue dresses. All the women's clothing was dense with colorful embroidery and tinkling with silver, and all wore their silver torques. The younger women pierced their top-knots with flowers. Mothers and grandmothers layered their torques with necklaces, and wore tall silver headdresses crowned with slender, curving horns. Silver everywhere—charms in the shape of flowers, bells, fish, and butterflies dangled from their jewelry, sleeves, sashes, and hems.

They were, in a word, gorgeous. Happy, laughing, leading children, carrying babies, holding hands with their friends, and among them, men of all ages in embroidered black, blue, and indigo. The men were also happy, also laughing, also embracing their friends, helping their children and elders. But the young women—ah. They caught his eye.

Zhang Lei retreated to the side of a corn patch, capturing compositions while watching the steady flow of arrivals. Some pinged for mobility assistance, and rode float chairs up the road, but most walked. Some eschewed the road, and ran uphill toward the guest house, making for the steep shortcut up the ridge. Zhang Lei followed.

Paul, Prajapati, and Han Song watched from the studio porch. Zhang Lei joined them.

"Jen Dla told me we can go watch the festival after supper," Prajapati said. "It's called Setting Free Your Daughter, or something like that."

"Setting them free from what?" asked Han Song.

Six young women ran toward them, through Jen Dla's cabbage patch.

"Family control, I would imagine," Paul answered.

The girls didn't even glance up. At home, he never had work to get a girl's attention—nobody on the team did. Unless Coach called a ban for training reasons, sex was on offer everywhere he looked. Here, he might as well be invisible. But then, he hadn't exactly been making himself available. If the girls were being set free, and he was in the right place at the right time, maybe one of them would land in his lap. All he had to do was get them to notice him.

"I'm going to the festival," Zhang Lei said.

"I'll go too," said Han Song. "I haven't done enough exploring."

"We'll all go," said Prajapati. Paul nodded.

After Jen Dla served them an early supper, Zhang Lei led the oldsters up the winding road to the village center. They admired the views from every switchback as if they hadn't already had a week to explore, and examined every clump of flowers as if Paizuo wasn't one big flower garden. Guests from the other studios joined them, which made the whole group even slower.

Zhang Lei was tempted to leave them all behind, run to the village center, and see if the girls had been set free yet. He jogged up a few switchbacks, and then thought the better of it. Even the most adventurous girl would flee from a lone man bearing a disable button labeled KILLER. If he wanted someone to take a chance on trusting him, he'd better stick with the group.

Zhang Lei sat on a boulder at the side of the road and waited for the oldsters to catch up. They weren't bad people. All three were kind and clever in their own ways. And patient. He'd been unfriendly but they hadn't taken offence.

"We should really walk faster," Prajapati told the other two when they caught up. "We don't want Zhang Lei to miss his chance with the girls."

Zhang Lei grinned. "I could ping you a cargo float."

She laughed and took his arm.

The roadside floating lights winked on, turning their route into a tunnel of light snaking up the mountainside. When they got to the village center, night had fallen. The courtyard was lit with flaming torches and in the middle of the crowd, a bonfire blazed, sending up a column of sparks to search the sky. Faces flickered with shadows. Silver glinted and gleamed. Laughter pealed. A singer wailed.

"I don't know when I last smelled something burning," said Han Song.

"Is that what the stench is?" asked Paul.

"Wood smoke is the most beautiful scent," said Prajapati. "Primal."

Most of the guests stayed on the courtyard's edge. They joined a group under the mulberry tree, a gender-free triad of performance artists from Cusco Hab. Zhang Lei had seen them around the village. They always looked like they were in a meeting—heads down, conferring, arguing, making notes.

"Have the daughters been set free yet?" Han Song quipped. "Asking for a friend."

The triad laughed.

"Apparently it's only one daughter, and no, the ceremony hasn't begun yet," said Aiko, the tallest of the three.

"Just one girl?" Zhang Lei said. "Then what's the point?"

"Shakespeare! One performer, one night only. The complete works." Aiko was obviously joking but their face was perfectly sober.

Prajapati grinned. "Don't tease the boy."

Another pair of artists joined them, a cellist from Zurich and an opera singer from Hokkaido. They seemed to know more about the festival than anyone else.

"We won't catch much of the performance unless the girl throws the switch on her translation balloon," the cellist said in a low voice. "The one last year didn't."

"Someone told me they translate in Kala, for the tourists visiting from Danzhai Wanda Village," said Aiko.

"Paizuo is more traditional than Kala. Which is why we come here." The cellist shaded her eyes against the torches' flare and scanned the crowd.

"It's better they don't translate," the opera singer said. "What the girl says won't make sense if you don't know the context. It's more meaningful to watch the reactions of the Miao."

With so many people in the square, Zhang Lei could only catch glimpses of the action. He put his viewcatcher on full extension, sent it a meter overhead and switched its mode to low lux. Much better. The musicians were at the far end of the courtyard, near the bridge, playing drums and tall, upright bamboo flutes. The singer stood with them, wearing her silver headdress like a crown. Jen Dang and his family didn't seem to be around. But he spotted the girl—the one who was being set free. She was alone. No friends, no fussing parents, no little siblings hanging on her arms.

She wore hoops of silver chain around her torque, a blue blouse and short black skirt embroidered with butterflies, and a woven sash around her waist. A deep red flower pierced her top-knot. Her hands rested at her sides. She didn't pick at her nails or play with her jewelry like Lunite girls. She looked prepared, like a goalie in a crease, waiting for the game to begin.

He zoomed in on her face. His age or a little younger. Pretty, like all the Miao girls. Tough, too. What would a girl like her think of him?

Not much, he suspected.

The music stopped, the crowd hushed. The girl's lips thinned in concentration. She stepped toward the bonfire and the circle of elders welcomed her into their arms. No drums this time, no bamboo flutes, no practiced wail from a powerful throat. The elders sang softly, their song a hum in the night, drowning under the buzz of the cicadas and crickets.

Near the artists at the back of the crowd stood a mother with a baby clutched to her chest. She wore little silver, and looked upset.

"Poor thing," said Prajapati.

The woman scowled at her and made a hushing motion.

Zhang Lei waited for something to happen, some reason why the Miao were paying such close attention. The girl wasn't doing anything, just standing in the circle of softly singing elders, eyes closed, face tight with concentration. Maybe nothing would happen—that was the point? Perhaps it was a test of her patience. It certainly was a test of his.

As he was considering sneaking away, the girl began singing along. Her voice was high, with an eerie overtone that the pierced the sky. She sang higher and higher, drowning out the elders' voices. The Miao were rapt, breathless. When she spoke—loud as if amplified—the crowd exhaled a collective sigh of wonder.

"No translation balloon," Aiko breathed. "Damn."

Zhang Lei expected the crying mother to turn and scold them again, but she was pushing through the crowd, sobbing and holding her baby out like an offering.

"Must be her dead husband," said the cellist, quietly. "You see? They set the girl's soul free to visit the spirits, and now she's bringing messages back."

"Messages?" said Zhang Lei. "What kind of messages?"

"Every kind. Instructions. Admonitions. Warnings. Blessings. What kind of messages would you send from beyond if you could?"

"I don't know, maybe something the girl could easily guess?" said Han Song.

"Hush," said Prajapati. "This is serious."

It was serious. Zhang Lei didn't even have to look up to know the new moon was watching him, the lights of its habs inscribed like a curse on the sunless black disc punched through the middle of the Milky Way.

On Luna, hockey was a blood sport. Lunar hockey was played at one-sixth gravity on a curved surface, with a Stefoff field to keep the puck low and snap players back to the ice. One of the major defensive moves was to disable the other team's players. Clubbing with weighted carbon fiber hockey sticks resulted in a penalty, though all referees were selectively blind. Slashing with skate blades, however, was a power move. An over-dominant team could cut their way through their opponents' starting lineup, into the benched players and fourth-rates, and by the end of the fourth quarter stage an assault on an undefended goalie.

Deaths were rare. Heads, legs, torsos, and groins were armored. Arms and throats were not. Medical bots hovered over the ice, ready to swoop in for first response, but rookies from the crèches quickly picked up scars, even playing in the recreational leagues. Anyone who remained unscarred was either a goalie or a coward.

Zhang Lei's crèche manager had tried to do right by him, direct his talents so he'd have choices when he left the crèche. She nurtured his talent for drawing and painting as much as possible. But she was practical, too. Luna had far more professional hockey teams than artist collectives. All her children were on skates as soon as they could walk.

With powerful legs and a low center of gravity, Zhang Lei could take a hit and keep his speed. He could jump, spin, and kick. He could slice an opposing defenseman's brachial artery, drag his stick through the spurting blood, and spray the goalie as he slid the puck into the net. The fans loved him for it. His teammates too.

It made him a target, though. He spent more time on the bench than anyone else on the team, healing wounds on his forearms. No matter. The down time gave him the opportunity to perfect the rarest of plays—jump and spin high enough to slice a blade through an opponent's throat. He practiced it, talked about it, drew cartoons of it. He gave up goals attempting it, which got him a faceful of spittle whenever Coach chewed him out.

Then finally he did it.

Dorgon wasn't even Zhang Lei's favorite proposed target. He was just a young, heavy-duty defenseman with a loud mouth who wasn't scared of Zhang Lei's flying blades.

He should have been.

Dorgon bled out in ten seconds. The med bot wrapped him in a life support bubble and attempted a transfusion right there on the ice, but stumbled over the thick scars on the defenseman's arms. When it searched for alternate access, Dorgon's coach was too busy screaming at Zhang Lei to flip the master toggle on his player's armor.

Whose fault was it, then, that Dorgon died?

"Your fault, Zhang Lei," the Miao girl said. "You opened a mouth in my throat and my whole life came pouring out."

She pointed to him, standing under the mulberry tree with the other guests. Heads turned. He should have run but he was frozen, breathless as if in a vacuum. He might have collapsed without the tree trunk behind him.

Marta? he whispered. *Help.*

No answer. Prajapati grabbed his arm.

"Ignore her, it's a trick," she said. And then louder: "That's not funny."

The crowd parted to allow the girl a clear sight of him.

"There's nowhere you can go that I won't follow. I'm inside your mattress when you sleep. Behind the door of your room, inside the closet. When you painted the Sklad arena, who do you think put the blood on the canvas? It was me."

She raised her fists and swung them toward him, as if shooting a puck with a phantom hockey stick.

"You're fair game."

The girl's head snapped back. She coughed once, and began speaking her native language again. The crowd turned away.

Marta? Answer me.

Prajapati tugged on his sleeve. "It's late. Walk me home. We'll take the shortcut."

She took his arm again, pretending to need it for balance on the rocky path, but in truth she was holding him up. Han Song and Paul trailed behind, talking in low voices.

Marta? Marta!

She answered before they got to top of the ridge.

Sorry, kid. I was in a closed-session meeting. Total privacy veil.

Are they coming for me?

What? No. Is there a problem in Paizuo?

Zhang Lei groaned. Prajapati looked at him sharply. Worry lines creased her plump face.

They know who I am. What I did.

Who knows?

Everyone. And all their relatives. From all over. Dorgon told them.

That's impossible.

He grabbed his viewcatcher, pinched off the last ten minutes of data, and fired it to her.

Watch this.

The path descending the ridge was treacherous, lit by nothing but stars. If he'd been alone, Zhang Lei would have run down the ridge. If he fell and broke his neck, he deserved it. But the oldsters needed his help.

He took Prajapati's hand—warm, dry, strong—and used the fill flash on his viewcatcher to light each step while Han Song shone the brighter light from his camera down the trail. The two oldster men helped steady each other, Paul's hand on the photographer's shoulder. When Han Song slipped, Paul caught him by the elbow.

Yeah, okay, Marta whispered. *Someone figured out who you are and told the girl. I'll talk to the security team. Don't do anything stupid, okay? We're on this.*

When they got to the studio, Paul fetched a bottle of whiskey from his room. He poured four glasses and handed the largest one to Zhang Lei.

"I found the news feed from Luna a couple days ago," Paul said. "But I didn't tell anyone."

"I found the painting," said Prajapati. "I wasn't looking for it, but the sofa was in the wrong place. I showed it to Paul and Han Song. It's effective work, Zhang Lei. Palpable anguish."

"If you want to keep something private," said Han Song, "don't put it in the common areas."

"None of us told anyone," Prajapati added.

"So, how did the story get to the Miao girl?" Paul asked. The other two oldsters shook their heads.

"Jen Dla?" Han Song ventured.

"I'll ask her in the morning." Prajapati patted Zhang Lei's knee. "Try to get some sleep."

The whiskey burned Zhang Lei's throat and filled his sinuses with the scent of bonfire. *What kind of messages would you send from beyond if you could?* Vengeance. Dorgon had watched and waited for his opportunity. The news would travel fast. Brawler teams were searching the county for him.

Zhang Lei poured the rest of the whiskey down his throat.

"When they come for me, keep hitting my disable button," he said.

The three oldsters exchanged confused looks. A whirring sweeper bot bumped Zhang Lei's foot. He nudged it away with his toe and headed for the stairs.

Don't be so dramatic, Marta whispered.

"When who comes for you?" Prajapati asked.

"Let them do whatever they want to me," he said. "Don't put yourself in danger. But if you can, keep knocking me out. Please."

Marta sighed. *Honestly.*

You, too. Keep hitting the button. Whatever they do to me, I don't want to know about it.

He climbed the stairs two at a time. If his life was about to crushed under the boots of a Lunite brawler gang, there was only one thing he wanted to do.

The scarred face of the new moon glared through the high windows of the communal studio. Zhang Lei chose the largest of his prepared canvases and flipped through his viewcatcher compositions. The water buffalo lying in the stream. Jen Dang catching a fish. Ripening rice terraces under golden mist. Jen Dla carrying a pot of sour fish soup, a lock of hair stuck to the sweat of her brow.

The fighting cocks in their cages, separated by the corner of a house, their torn flesh healing only to be sliced open another day.

He flipped the canvas to rest on the long side and projected the composition on its surface. How to make the three-dimensionality of the scene clear in two dimensions—that was the main problem. Each cock each knew the other was just out of sight. If they could get free, they would fight to the death.

It's in their nature, he whispered.

What nature? Marta asked. *Oh, I see. Are you going to paint all night?*

I'll paint for the rest of my life.

Okay, ping me if there's a problem.

First, he drafted with a light pencil, adjusting the composition. The corner of the house dividing the canvas into thirds, with one caged brawler directly in front of the viewer and the other around the corner. It was a difficult compositional problem—he had to rub out the draft several times and start again. Then he began a base layer in grays, very lean and thin. What the old masters called *en grisaille*. Solve the painting problems in monochrome before even thinking about color. The texture of the wooden walls of the house, the figures of the birds filling the canvas with belligerence. It took all night.

A few hours before dawn, Han Song brought him a cup of tea.

"That's good," he said, squinting at the canvas. "I've got some pictures of those birds, too." He settled at his workstation and sipped his own tea as he ruffled through his files. "You can use them for reference if you want."

A package hit Zhang Lei's message queue—the only communication he'd received since leaving Luna that didn't relate to his immigration status. The photos were good. Details of the cocks' livid faces and dinosaurian legs, the pinfeathers sprouting from their bald backs, the iridescent sheen of their ruffs.

He added crimson and madder to his palette and used Han Song's photo of the cock's flayed wattle to get that detail exactly right, then moved on to the next problem. He thinned the paint with solvent to make a glaze. No time to wait for fat oils to oxidize, for thick paint layers to cure. In places, the paint was so thin the texture of the canvas showed through. That was fine. He would never be a master painter, but this would be the best painting he could make.

His friend's photos helped. Gradually, color and detail began to bring the painting to life.

"Thank you," Zhang Lei said, hours later. Han Song didn't hear him. Prajapati smiled from across the studio, her hands caked with clay to the elbow.

"Don't skip lunch," she said. "Even painters need to eat."

"And sleep," Paul added.

Sleep. He had no time for it. And Dorgon was in his mattress, behind his door, in his closet. He would join Dorgon soon enough, and next year, when Paizuo's rice crop had turned yellow, they could scream public challenges at each other through a Miao girl.

Until then, there was only the work. Work like he'd never known before. As an athlete, he practiced until instinct overtook his mind. On the ice, he didn't think, he just performed. In the studio, he used his whole body—crouching, stretching, sweeping his arms—continuing the action of his brush far off the canvas like a fighter following a punch past his opponent's jaw. And then small, precise movements—careful, considered, even loving. But his intellect never disengaged. He made choices, second-guessed himself, took leaps of faith.

It was the most exhausting, engrossing work he'd ever done.

The eye of the cock flared on the canvas, trapped in the pointlessness of its drive to fight and fight and die. Zhang Lei hovered his brush over that eye. One more glaze of color, and another, and another, over and over until nobody looking at the painting could misunderstand the meaning of that vicious and brainless stare.

Paul put his arm around Zhang Lei's shoulders.

"Come on down to lunch. The painting is done. If you keep poking, you'll ruin it."

"Ruin yourself, too," said Han Song.

"He's young, he can take it," said Prajapati.

They fed him rice and egg, bitter green tea, and millet cake. No fish soup. No Jen Dla.

"She's giving birth," Prajapati explained. "Went into labor last night. Brave woman."

"We should break out Paul's whiskey again," said Han Song. "Drink a toast to her."

Paul laughed. "Maybe. We have something else to celebrate, too."

They all looked at Zhang Lei. His mouth was crammed with millet cake.

"I don't know. What?" he said though the cake.

"Your button is gone, dear," Prajapati said gently.

He swallowed, pinged his ID. Zhang Lei, Beijing resident. No caveats, no equivocations. And no button.

Marta, he whispered. *Is it done?*

The notice has been sitting in your queue for half an hour. I pinged you when it came through. Looked like you were too busy painting birds to notice.

Are the brawlers gone? he whispered.

They're on their way home. They can't touch you now and they know it. I don't recommend going to Luna anytime soon, but if you did and there was a problem, at least you could fight back.

Zhang Lei excused himself from the table and stumbled out of the guest house. He skirted the cabbage patch and followed the trail to the pavilion, with its perfectly composed view. Up and down the valley, farmers walked the terraces, examining the ripening rice.

How? You said it would be weeks, at least. Maybe never.

I took your painting directly to the tribunal.

That made no sense. His painting was upstairs in the studio, on his easel.

They were impressed, Marta added. *So was I.*

I don't understand.

The wet blood. Smart move. Visceral. The tribunal got the message.

Blood?

On the ice. They brought in a forensic expert to examine and sequence it. That gave me a scare because I had assumed the blood was yours. Didn't even occur to me it might be somebody else's. If it had been, things wouldn't have turned out so well.

My blood?

I guess the tribunal wanted to be convinced you regretted killing Dorgon.

Zhang Lei leaned on the pavilion railing. A fresh breeze ruffled his hair.

I do regret it.

They know that now. I'll keep the painting for you until you get a place of your own. So keep in touch, okay?

I will, he whispered.

On the terrace below, Jen Dang walked along the rice paddy with four of his grandchildren. The farmer waved. Zhang Lei waved back.

The author acknowledges the generous support of the Future Affairs Administration and Danzhai SF Camp.

ABOUT THE EDITORS

Hannu Rajaniemi is the author of *The Quantum Thief*, *The Fractal Prince*, *The Causal Angel*, and a stand-alone novel, *Summerland*. Rajaniemi was born in Finland and completed his doctorate in Mathematical Physics at the University of Edinburgh. His works have received Finland's top science-fiction honor, the Tähtivaeltaja Award, and *The Quantum Thief* was nominated for the John W. Campbell Award for Best Science-Fiction Novel. He is the CTO of HelixNano, a synthetic biology startup based in the Bay Area, where he currently lives.

Jacob Weisman is the publisher at Tachyon Publications, which he founded in 1995. He is a World Fantasy Award winner for *The New Voices of Fantasy* (co-edited with Peter S. Beagle) and is the series editor of Tachyon's critically acclaimed novella line, including the Hugo Award–winning *The Emperor's Soul*, by Brandon Sanderson, and the Nebula and Shirley Jackson Award–winning *We Are All Completely Fine*, by Daryl Gregory. Weisman has edited the anthologies *Invaders: 22 Tales from the Outer Limits of Literature*, *The Sword & Sorcery Anthology* (with David G. Hartwell), and *The Treasury of the Fantastic* (with David M. Sandner). He lives in San Francisco.